The Reichsbank Robbery

The Reichsbank Robbery

Colin Fulton

First published in Great Britain in 2012 by
CLAYMORE PRESS
An imprint of
Pen & Sword Books Ltd
47 Church Street
Barnsley
South Yorkshire
S70 2AS

Copyright © Colin Fulton, 2012

978-1-78159-078-2

A CIP catalogue record for this book is
available from the British Library

Printed and bound in England
By CPI Group (UK) Ltd, Croydon, CRO 4YY

Pen & Sword Books Ltd incorporates the Imprints of Claymore Press, Pen
& Sword Aviation, Pen & Sword Family History, Pen & Sword Maritime,
Pen & Sword Military, Wharncliffe Local History, Pen & Sword Select,
Pen & Sword Military Classics, Leo Cooper, Remember When, Seaforth
Publishing and Frontline Publishing

For a complete list of Pen & Sword titles please contact
PEN & SWORD BOOKS LIMITED
47 Church Street, Barnsley, South Yorkshire, S70 2AS, England
E-mail: enquiries@pen-and-sword.co.uk
Website: www.pen-and-sword.co.uk

Historical Background

In February 1945 the US Air Force launched the largest daytime bombing offensive against Berlin, dropping over 2,250 tons of bombs on the German capital.

The Reichsbank, Germany's state bank, received twenty-one direct hits. This left the building badly damaged, its vaults unsafe and meant that most of its contents were at risk. The German authorities decided to take most of the Reichsbank's treasure away and hide it for safekeeping. Some US $200 million (1945-worth) in gold bars, weighing around 100 tons, plus much of the paper currency reserves, as well as a great deal of foreign currency (approximately $4 million in US currency alone) was sent in trains from Berlin. All this loot was placed in a salt mine at a place called Merkers. This was captured intact by the US Army. After this disaster, the Germans spent the next six weeks transferring their remaining bullion and currency reserves around what remained of the Reich in armoured trains, an area that included parts of northern Italy, Czechoslovakia, Austria and Germany, looking for somewhere safe.

Much of the treasure ended up back in Berlin, was stolen, disappeared or captured, mainly by American troops and the SS.

For example, one consignment of 730 gold bars, sacks of gold coin and currency worth US $10 million (in 1945 figures or $250 million in today's figures) earmarked for shipment to Bavaria went missing and was never found. In another incident, a group of SS Troopers under the command of a thirty-nine-year-old SS Brigadier General Josef Spacil, robbed the new Reichsbank headquarters in Berlin at gunpoint. They stole jewels, securities and foreign exchange valued at US $9 million.

There were many other robberies, smaller and larger, during this time. In fact, after the war, US Army officers in league with former SS officers stole a major proportion of the remaining Reichsbank's reserves. It was never recovered and is listed in *The*

Guinness Book of Records as the largest robbery ever. In 2010 terms the figure would be in the region of US $4.5 billion.

Note

In order to retain a sense of authenticity, German spellings have been used on several occasions throughout the book.

18 January 1944

The radar operator's voice was tense over the intercom. The pilot could hear the man's sharp breath as he strove to keep the excitement from his voice.

"We should be able to pick up the coast very soon, Major. That is if the navigator has done his job correctly."

The pilot smiled to himself. He turned to the co-pilot who lifted his eyes upwards and gently shook his head. It was no secret that the navigator and radar operator did not see eye-to-eye. Professional jealousy, or just different people with an inability to get on, the pilot did not know nor at that particular moment did he care. Their constant bickering, which at first had been amusing, was now beginning to get on his nerves.

"If that electrician can get his fancy," said the navigator.

"Cut the shit or I'll have you both cleaning the latrines for a week," the pilot's voice cut across the querulous reply.

The toilets at Mont de Marsan were not known for their cleanliness, a situation not helped by Luftwaffe regulations that no French civilians were allowed onto the base to clean them or do any other menial duties.

"I am almost certain that we are on course, Major." The navigator's voice contained a hint of contrition. "The cloud is continuing to make accurate reading almost impossible, but ..."

As if in answer the big plane was suddenly bathed in glaring sunlight as it emerged from the cloud.

The co-pilot put up his right hand to shield his eyes from the glare while at the same time search for his sunglasses with the other. With an exclamation he hurriedly placed them on his nose cutting the glare instantly.

The Ray-Bans were much prized for they were the best sunglasses available. These had been liberated from a B17 captain and the co-pilot made sure that they never left his person. There were greedy hands everywhere. However, no sooner had he put them on his nose and tried to re-focus his eyes when the plane was enveloped in greyness once again. But, as the plane droned westwards the sky began to lighten and gradually the clouds dissipated from almost ten-tenths to half that. This made the navigator's job easier and he was able to confirm (with a hint of superiority for the benefit of the radar operator), that yes, they were on course.

"That's fine," said the pilot. "Now I want everyone to keep their eyes wide open. The coast cannot be far away even if radar has not picked it up yet."

A few minutes later the radar operator, sweating over his instruments, informed the pilot that the FuG 200 Hohentwiel search radar had indeed done its job. This time he made no attempt to hide his glee.

"It's the coast, Major, about fifty kilometres away, maybe a few kilometres less."

There was a moment's silence while the news sunk in. After just over thirteen hours in the air they had reached the coast of America.

The pilot's voice cut into the intercom. For once even he was excited. In an effort to keep this excitement from his voice he became very terse, sounding clipped and officious.

"Now keep your wits about you. All of you, keep a careful watch for any other aircraft. We are unlikely to be expected, but you never know."

The cloud was dispersing rapidly until the aircraft, alone in a blue sky, was bathed in brilliant sunshine. As the heat permeated through the Perspex the two men at the controls began to perspire, the moisture running down their faces soaking their shirt collars.

The pilot removed his microphone headpiece so that he could take off his battered peaked cap. He replaced the headpiece and peered out over the nose of the aircraft.

Both he and the co-pilot saw the coast at the same time, though the pilot with years of experience was the first to react. He dipped the nose of the aircraft slightly so that he could see the distant coast better, at the same time speaking into the intercom.

"There you are comrades … the promised land." He spoke

neither in jest nor in irony. To many in Europe it seemed, even at this time, to be the land of peace and opportunity.

The pilot glanced at his altimeter. It read just under 2,000 metres. I wonder if I should climb any higher, he thought.

"My God," the co-pilot exclaimed softly.

The pilot had seen it too. There in the distance was a greyish brown haze and at its base the unmistakable outlines of tall, tall buildings.

"New York?" queried the co-pilot, although he knew the answer.

"New York."

"Oh what I would not give for one small 250-kilogram bomb to drop on the Empire State building. That would give those bastards a taste of what the Reich has been receiving … just one little 250-kilogram bomb."

"Save your breath, Klaus," snapped the pilot. "We have done what we set out to do. It is possible. Now, if Speer and his lot can build us enough of these beauties we can do what you would like to do. Flatten New York." He called up the radar operator. "Sigi! What distance are we from New York?"

"About twenty kilometres, Herr Major, maybe a little less. Please, Herr Major, can I come up and see?" The radar operator was always the most formal in addressing the pilot.

The pilot answered in the affirmative and a few moments later the radar operator was standing, half crouching between the two pilots. The pilot let him gaze for less than ten seconds and then began to turn the huge six-engined plane away. A few seconds later it was back on an easterly course, returning the way it had come.

"Gunners give me a quick report. Do you see anything?"

One by one they answered in the negative. The pilot ordered them to keep their eyes open and not to relax as they still had a long way to go. He then ordered the flight engineer to make a report on the fuel situation and the state of the engines. Everything was reported to be in order. The Junkers JU 390 was as perfect as when it had taken off from its French airfield in the dark early hours of the morning.

Germany's most advanced long-range aircraft and its crew had been sent on a special mission: to see whether it was feasible for the Luftwaffe to bomb America, particularly New York, and return safely. Already the crew of the big bomber had proved such a raid was possible. Now, all that was left was to return to Europe safely.

Ten minutes later the clouds closed in around the Junkers once again and the crew began to relax. As far as they could tell the Americans were none the wiser and now they were safe from prying eyes.

So far it had been almost too easy.

The pilot handed over to his co-pilot and began to review the flight in his mind, searching once again for any hidden problem that might hinder such a mission occurring again. Easy, though this flight may have been, it was another matter entirely to return with a load of high explosives with the aim of actually crossing the coast to bomb America's most iconic and largest city. Yet, he knew it could be done. The question was when? Germany was already bleeding heavily and time was not on her side.

To have any effect, a raid on New York would have to be mounted within the next six months. America was sending vast amounts of men and material to Great Britain and its bombers were flying in ever-imposing numbers over the Reich. A serious raid on New York would force the Americans to divert valuable fighter planes to protect their homeland and this would leave the American B17s with fewer escort fighters as they flew across Europe. It would also be a huge morale boost for the German people.

He turned to his co-pilot. "Well, Klaus. What do you think? Will the High Command give us some of these beauties and allow us to bomb the shit out of New York, or will it all be too hard?"

The co-pilot shrugged his shoulders and lifted his eyebrows. He did not reply, but the gestures said it all.

In his heart the pilot hoped he was wrong. He badly wanted to fly the North Atlantic again. Strangely, his wish was to be answered, but not because of any decision by the Luftwaffe High Command. He would make that return flight, but in a completely different guise and for a completely different reason.

Chapter One
20 October 1944

Sturmbannführer Friedrich Schonewille was one of those people whose looks and demeanour are improved by a uniform. And when that uniform bore the jagged runes of the dreaded SS then its occupant became truly imposing.

In civilian life Schonewille looked to be what he once was: an inoffensive, moderately successful accountant. His limited success was not because he lacked brains or the ability to use them, but rather because he was cautious by nature. This was heightened by the times in which he lived. The Depression had instilled in the German people a sober caution about anything to do with money, especially their own money.

With neither the backing of a rich family nor the necessary contacts to help his career, he had soberly and carefully built on his clients to further his small practice. One of those clients had been a local Nazi Party official who, in the winter of 1931, had attempted to recruit Schonewille. At first the accountant had not wanted to commit himself, although he was careful to make his hesitation appear like a minor matter caused by an excess of work and other commitments, rather than a lack of interest in the party.

The truth was that he was not easily swayed by oratory and Hitler's speeches left him un-moved. Although not interested in politics, he was aware that the Nazis were not yet regarded as quite legitimate in Germany even though their political power was growing rapidly. At any rate, he did not want to alienate his more conservative clients.

But, all this changed in January 1933 when Hitler was made Chancellor. Even though Hitler only headed a coalition government and President Hindenburg was still alive, Schonewille recognised that now was perhaps the time to join the National Socialist Party. This had an instant and positive effect on his practice, which translated itself very quickly to his bank account.

The party had plenty of brown shirt toughs. What it needed was organisers, technocrats and planners. Schonewille's financial ability was quickly recognised and he became very valuable in organising the finances of the party in the surrounding districts. Although he gave his time freely, local businessmen soon learnt of his growing importance and switched their allegiance to his practice, which began to prosper.

By 1936 he was an official of some importance and his growing recognition and authority within the Nazi Party began to manifest itself in his character. It also gave him the impetus to join the SS and thus be part of Germany's elite.

Friedrich Schonewille was a driven man and the political party to which he belonged enabled him to release those insecurities and personal hatreds that had bedevilled him for so long. At another time, in another place, he would have remained a normal person, albeit one who nursed a deep-seated grudge. Now, eight years later he had become a truly twisted and evil man.

None of this showed in his person. Stripped of his uniform he would have looked almost nondescript. He was of average height with bland looks, brown eyes, brown hair and a rather slight physique. His smile, when he used it, was rather engaging and his voice, though quiet, with little presence and penetration, was well modulated.

On entering the SS in 1938 he had quickly adopted a military bearing and affected attitude that fed his growing feelings of self importance and superiority over many of his fellow countrymen, especially if they were civilians. Yet he still carried the shibboleths that had plagued much of his life and with many people his feelings of superiority were only skin deep. To his superiors he was deferential and largely acquiescent, although he became adept at making sure they were well aware of his work and successes. Partly because of this he had earned a reputation of self effacing, ruthless efficiency.

One thing he did keep well-hidden, though, was the size of his ambition. He knew only too well the forces that existed in the SS and the people who controlled the organisation. It was not wise to tread on too many toes. Despite this he was not above subterfuge and subtle bribery to gain advancement.

To an observer the only thing that made him appear different from the rest of his ilk was a little leather pouch attached to his gleaming belt. This pouch contained a silencer, something that was not standard issue to officers in the SS or in any section of the Wehrmacht. Schonewille had a gunsmith modify his army issue 9mm Walther so the silencer could be screwed onto the barrel of the automatic. The SS officer had originally wanted the silencer fitted to a smaller Walther PP, but the gunsmith had advised him it would have an adverse effect on the stopping power of the 7.65mm bullet and, therefore, he should have a weapon of heavier calibre and with a greater muzzle velocity. He recommended the larger, heavier Walther, known throughout the German Army as the P-38 and which had acquired a good reputation for reliability and accuracy.

It was this weapon, together with his quiet manner, that had earned Schonewille the nickname Stille Maus, or quiet mouse. To those special inmates of the camps, those who were political prisoners, or of the old political order, the appearance of the quiet mouse meant instant death, the executions carried out almost without sound for the silencer reduced the gunshots to a strangled cough.

But, on that October morning Schonewille was not thinking about what went on in the camps. Rather, how maybe he should have used his staff car to take him to his destination instead of walking in the late autumn sunshine.

As he strode briskly down one of the streets radiating out from the Victory Monument on the East West Axis, the boulevard that divided the Berlin's beautiful park, the Tiergarten, he could hear the mournful wail of the air-raid sirens.

For a moment he hesitated, undecided as to what to do. Stay in the open spaces of the park, or try to reach an air-raid shelter before the bombs started falling? However much he hated the shelters he knew that this was his best chance of survival, for the openness of the Tiergarten was no shelter at all. So he continued towards the Tiergartenstrasse, the avenue that ran around the southern boundary of the park. As he hurried along he was joined by other Berliners, all heading for the safety of the shelters. Then he heard the sound of an engine, very faint, almost indistinct from the noise of the city. A few minutes later it had vanished and almost immediately the all-clear siren was sounded. Must have been a reconnaissance aircraft, he thought. Relieved, he slowed his gait back to a brisk walk. The further he got into the city the worse the bomb damage became. He was appalled at the level of devastation.

For months, ever since the allies had broken out of the Normandy beach-head, destroying the Vll Army and the V Panzer Army in the Falaise gap, as well as killing 10,000 and capturing 50,000 battle-hardened front-line troops, Schonewille had begun to have serious doubts as to the long term future of the Third Reich. During the latter part of 1941 he had spent a few weeks on the Eastern Front and had not regarded the Russians as a tough enemy, not even after the debacle of Stalingrad and the failure of the Kursk offensive. But now, with the Russian steamroller sweeping westwards he began to fear the Red Army also.

The bomb damage in the German capital reinforced his growing apprehension. He had not visited the German capital since early in August and in the intervening ten weeks the destruction had been awesome.

The constant raids of the British heavy bombers by night and the Americans by day had destroyed almost one quarter of Berlin's one-and-a-half million dwellings. For every one destroyed there was another badly damaged. The casualty figure was horrendous with some 40,000 people officially regarded as dead or missing. The wounded and injured numbered tens of thousands more.

As Schonewille skirted piles of debris and walked past the blackened shells of buildings, some still smouldering, he was amazed to see how people were apparently still going about their daily lives. In fact, almost three quarters of the city's factories were still functioning, albeit with some difficulty. Many industries were being decentralised or being put underground, so German industry in Berlin was able to keep up a high rate of production.

Services were also still being maintained: postmen delivered letters and telegrams, the garbage was being collected, the police were still on duty and the shops still standing were offering a large selection of goods. Some department stores were even running sales.

When the bombing had started two years before, Schonewille, ever prudent, had moved his own residence to the western outskirts of Spandau in the sub-district of Staaken. This was a pastoral area, although Spandau itself was the centre of the huge Berlin armaments industry. Nevertheless, this area had missed most of the saturation bombing that had laid waste to half the other suburbs. Consequently, though he had been able to see the fires and hear the explosions from his window, it was damage being inflicted on others.

Schonewille's destination that morning was the Berlin headquarters of the Reichsbank, the National Bank of Germany. The bank was like most of its kind, a solid imposing structure built a decade or so before the First World War. So far it had escaped any damage, its 5,000 employees busily running the finances of the Third Reich while much of the world burned around them.

It was almost a relief to Schonewille when he stepped through the main entrance of the Reichsbank. The quiet atmosphere and orderly queues of people waiting to be served helped steady his thoughts.

The walk had taken him longer than expected so he was late for his appointment with the senior vice president of the Reichsbank, Emil Puhl. The banker was of the old school. He believed in his country, good order and the importance of the banking establishment. He was one of the thousands of senior bureaucrats and functionaries who turned a blind eye to what was happening both within and outside the Reich.

Despite his background and basic decency this former pillar of the Weimer establishment had helped turn the Reichsbank into the biggest clearing house of stolen funds in the world. It was the biggest money laundering operation in history. Money from the looted countries of Europe and the inmates of the concentration camps was all collected and placed in the vaults of the bank to become the reserves of the German government.

The bank also had another important client, the most powerful and feared organisation in the Reich, the SS.

It was for this reason that Schonewille was visiting Emil Puhl.

16

The SS major's boss was Obergruppenführer Dr Oswald Pohl, Head of the Economic and Administrative Department of the SS. This department was charged with the responsibility of administering the concentration camps.

Early in the war Vice-President Puhl concluded an agreement with SS General Pohl, which enabled the Reichsbank to receive and act as a clearing house for the huge amounts of loot stolen from the hapless Jews of Europe and the inmates of the concentration camps. This money was credited to the bank accounts of the SS.

Schonewille was the accountant who controlled much of this vast ill-gotten treasure. It was he who itemised the currency, gold coins, jewellery, personal affects and clothing stripped from the camps' inmates. It was on these trips to itemise the monthly tallies that he visited many of the charnel houses of eastern Germany and Poland, and it was here that he regularly seized the opportunity to exorcise his hatreds by executing a dozen or so victims with his silenced automatic.

He waited in a small ante-room for ten minutes and just as he began to grow impatient a door opened and a tall thin man in his mid thirties beckoned.

"Good Morning Herr Major, it is a pleasure to see you again. It has been what … nine, ten weeks?"

Schonewille smiled and nodded his head. "That is correct Klaus. Almost ten weeks and by the looks of what has been happening outside it has been a long ten weeks, nicht war?"

"Unbelievable," replied the other man.

Klaus Heger was the closest friend that Schonewille had ever had: the closest he had allowed another person of the same sex to become. This friendship was part of the key to Schonewille's character for Heger owed his position to the major and his background was much the same.

Both men were products of broken marriages. In Schonewille's case his parents' divorce had made him into a victim, partially through circumstances beyond his control and partially through his own innate feelings of inferiority. Schonewille's real name was Wenck. He had it changed in deference to his mother who had reverted to her maiden name after the divorce and because of the hatred he felt for his father.

Helmuth Wenck had been a diplomat for most of his adult life. A much decorated pilot during the First World War he had married Inger Schonewille in 1908 when the Fatherland's future was assured. He was only twenty-one and had as yet not decided what to do with his life. His father was dead, the victim of a riding accident, and his doting mother had no control over him. To a large extent he did what he liked.

It was felt by Wenck's mother and many of his relations that the young man had married beneath him. Inger was a vivacious, beautiful brunette but her intellect lagged far behind that of her husband. His attraction to her was, to a large extent, physical and she was smart enough to trade her sexuality for marriage to an attractive man with an important pedigree. Wenck also appreciated her ability to make him look on the bright side, for he had a pessimistic view to life. That he loved her there was no doubt, but when he entered the Diplomatic Corps and began to forge a successful career he found her limited knowledge of world events a hindrance. Worse still was her refusal to try and improve her basic knowledge and she thus became a source of constant embarrassment to him.

The war intervened and when he realised the fighting would not end quickly, Wenck joined the air force. Any differences that had become apparent early on in their marriage disappeared during the hostilities. This was partly because their enforced separation lessened those differences and a soldier home on leave does not worry about his wife's intellect.

But when the war ended the old problems re-surfaced. Worse, Inger became a clinging wife consumed by fears of imagined infidelities. Yet, knowing her own shortcomings she still made no attempt to change.

Like many German officers the defeat and humiliation of the Versailles Treaty rankled, but for the pilot it was made even more difficult because the nation was allowed no air force. Neither could he return to his old profession since the Diplomatic Corps was almost non existent. The war had ruined his family fortune and, although he and his mother were not destitute, money was in short supply.

The family had good connections in Holland and it was through these connections that he was able to find employment.

The aircraft designer Anthony Fokker, denied the right to continue building and designing in Germany, smuggled much of his equipment and plans as well as several aircraft to Holland where he set up another manufacturing base. Wenck's Dutch connections put up some much needed funds and, in return, he was offered a job with the fledgling organisation as a test pilot and office clerk.

A week after arriving in Holland he attended a diplomatic reception where he met a tall blonde Icelander, the daughter of a Reykjavik fishing tycoon. Two days later he initiated divorce proceedings.

He married Vigdis Hermannsson the morning after his divorce became absolute. The haste was necessary for scarcely one month later she presented Wenck with a son who was christened Peter.

Meanwhile, for Friedrich and his mother life became a series of snubs and humiliations, or so it seemed to the embittered woman. True, divorce still contained a social stigma and the Wenck family did not exactly crowd around with offers of support, but neither did they abandon them. After all, young Friedrich was still a Wenck.

The divorce settlement was sufficient so Inger never had to work, although it would have been easier on them both if she had tried to obtain some sort of employment to augment their income. She never bothered and always complained loud and long about the injustices that had been perpetrated on them both. Nevertheless, young Friedrich was enrolled in a good school, the fees paid for by his father. Although a good student he never fitted in. Indifferent at sport and with no father to guide him he felt an outsider, especially when parents were invited to school functions. Helmuth Wenck made many attempts to show an interest in his son and often came to the school, but the meetings were not a success.

Though the boy craved his father's attention, perversely he gave little in return. Attempts at affection were met with indifference and any questions that Friedrich deemed to be interference in his mother's life or privacy he refused to answer. At his son's sullen refusal to co-operate, Helmuth Wenck usually became exasperated. Their meetings, therefore, became fewer and further apart.

Eventually, they ended all together. Wenck rejoined the Diplomatic Corps in 1924 and was immediately posted to Iceland, a natural turn of events considering his wife's nationality.

In Vigdis the diplomat had the perfect companion and partner, consequently the marriage prospered. She was everything that Inger was not. Sure of herself, well-educated and intelligent, she fitted in well with her husband's career. In their young son Peter, the father found a kindred spirit who looked like a Wenck but had inherited his mother's sunny nature. It was natural then that his feelings for his first born should wane and emotionally he left the lad to fend for himself.

Klaus Heger had been a fellow student at Friedrich's school. Partly because of their similar backgrounds and partly because they were both good at mathematics and figures, they became friends. Friedrich was always the dominant partner in the friendship; for some reason young Klaus was the only boy of his own age group to whom he felt superior.

On leaving school both trained to be accountants, though Heger opted to join the Reichsbank while Friedrich went out on his own. The reason was that he always felt uncomfortable with the establishment, whether it be represented by his father, the Wenck family, senior bureaucrats, or the other students at his school.

It was this discomfort that eventually turned to a dislike of the establishment so strong that it verged on a pathological hatred, which enabled him to fit in so well with the other misfits within the Nazi Party.

Heger had none of those feelings. He had joined the Nazi Party only after Schonewille had pressed him to do so. Similarly, his rise in the bank's hierarchy was due in no small measure to the SS major's patronage.

"Well Klaus, where is the esteemed vice president?"

"He was unable to wait any longer, Sturmbannführer." Heger always started any meeting by being very formal, being careful to address Schonewille by his SS military rank. "He had an important meeting at the Reichs Ministry with Doctor Funk. At any rate, you know I have been increasingly taking over control of these matters so I am aware of all the details."

Schonewille nodded his head and reached down for his briefcase. "This is the latest tally from the camps." He placed a sheaf of papers on Heger's desk. "And these contain details of what was gathered from those renegades in the Warsaw ghetto after the uprising."

Heger quickly perused the second sheaf of papers, his accountant's mind quickly adding up the columns of figures.

"One-hundred-and-seventy-thousand reichsmarks. I would have expected more. Also, there's very little gold listed here."

"No, you are wrong. In fact I was surprised it was so large," countered Schonewille. "Those bastards in the Warsaw ghetto had spent most of their money on obtaining arms on the black market."

Heger shook his head and swore softly. "Verdammte Jews. I hear they caused us more than twenty thousand dead, both civilian and army?"

"More I understand, although how did you come by that figure. I understand it is classified?"

Heger's long face broke into a smile. He tapped his nose conspiratorially. "Oh, I have my contacts, Friedrich," he answered with a smirk. Schonewille noted the change in his address. It had come quicker than usual. But he said nothing. He extracted another sheaf of papers from his briefcase, glanced quickly at the last page to refresh his memory and handed them to the banker.

"Study these my friend," he said, fitting in with the change in formality. "I think you will find these figures more to your liking."

Heger picked up the papers and immediately turned to the last page. He lifted his eyebrows and nodded his head in appreciation.

Turning to the first page he asked, "Where does this lot come from? Not from the camps, surely?"

"No, from Hungary. Eichman has been busy fleecing the Jews of Budapest. And very successful he was too, as you can see. Quite apart from the paper money, which is significant, is the gold total, don't you think?"

The other nodded his head and looked directly at the SS officer.

"What camps did you visit this time?"

"Two Polish camps, Chelmno and Treblinka and, of course I went to Warsaw and Budapest. Why do you ask?"

"I just wondered."

There was a moment's silence and then Heger asked what it was like in the concentration camps. What the hell is the reason for these questions, thought Schonewille. He answered carefully.

"It is certainly not how the newsreels or Doktor Goebbels tells us, I assure you ..." He let the rest of the sentence hang.

"Oh well, they are only Jews," said the other.

Schonewille did not answer. In truth he was not anti-Semitic.

In the past, before he had joined the party, the Jews had been among his best customers. At any rate, his link with the Jews was stronger than anybody could have possibly imagined. His cold blooded executions were not perpetrated against the hapless Jews, but rather against the former elite of the German community, political prisoners and those who had fallen foul of the New Order. He always gained a great deal of pleasure in seeing the look of terror on their faces just before he pressed the bulbous snout of the silencer on their temples and blew their brains out.

The discussion returned to financial matters for a few minutes and then Heger abruptly got his feet. He crossed over to a cupboard, unlocked the door and reached inside. On finding what he wanted he closed the door and returned to his seat. He reached forward and placed a round tin on the edge of the desk in front of Schonewille. He motioned for him to pick it up.

"What is it?"

"Open it, take a whiff." And then as Schonewille complied, "Wonderful smell is it not?"

The tin's content was a brown powder. The aroma was heady.

"Groβer Gott, it smells like coffee."

"That's correct, coffee. But wait until you taste it." He pressed a lever on his intercom. "Frau Metz, bring in the kettle with boiling water and two cups on the black tray if you please."

When these arrived Heger motioned the woman away and then proceeded to spoon a quantity of the powder into each cup. After pouring in a measure of boiling water, he stirred the drink and handed it over.

"Milk? No, what about some saccharine, although I advise you not to spoil the taste with that shit? No, good," he said as Schonewille again shook his head.

Schonewille blew into his cup and then carefully sipped. As an SS major who travelled a great deal he had access to all sorts of contraband and luxury goods, yet it had been almost three years since he had tasted coffee as good as this. He smacked his lips in appreciation and asked how this had come into Heger's possession.

"One of my clients is an old family friend, a paratrooper. He was stationed in France when the Allies landed in Normandy. A few days after the main landing he was out on patrol with his men when they came across a parachute container hanging in a tree. It had obviously been destined for the American paratroops who had been dropped during the initial landings. They opened the container expecting to find arms and instead found it to be crammed with food stuffs. Not iron rations, mind you, but delicacies like ham, chocolate, jam and of course this powdered coffee. Now I ask you, how can we hope to win the war if our enemies can afford to send supplies like this to their front-line troops by aeroplane?"

As if realising what he had said Heger abruptly got up from his desk, crossed the room and quickly opened the door. When he was satisfied that the corridor was empty he went back to his desk.

"Well, before I answer that Klaus, you realise this is defeatist talk, don't you?" He asked the question with a trace of menace in his voice.

The other nodded his head soberly, but said nothing. Schonewille chose his words carefully, for he had no intention of revealing his thoughts.

"I think we still have a chance. I know things are looking increasingly difficult, but the Führer is not a stupid man and he has promised us another secret weapon."

Heger looked like he wanted to yell, but he kept his voice low. Nevertheless, there was vehemence in his words. "For God's sake, Friedrich. The Allies are at this moment at the Siegfried Line, the Ruskies are less than one hundred kilometres from Konigsberg.

Army Group North has just been wiped out, and now I learn that we are evacuating Belgrade." He stopped for breath and then went on. "What about the bombing? You've seen what it is like out there. Soon there will be nothing left."

Schonewille again chose his words carefully, not committing himself to any line of thought. He asked what Heger was trying to say. The banker changed his tone slightly, but went on.

"Two months ago a group of leading financiers and industrialists met at the Hotel Maison Rouge in Strasbourg. I can't tell you their names, it is more than my life's worth. But what I will say is that they met to discuss plans on what to do with all this," (he waved his arm at the sheaf of papers) "and the rest of the Reich's monetary assets in the event of a defeat."

He paused for a moment and then went on.

"For the past few weeks large amounts of funds have been taken out of the Reich and re-invested in neutral and non-belligerent countries, both here in Europe and in South America. These funds are for the use of the party if we are ever defeated. At least that is the official line agreed to at the meeting, but I would bet a thousand Reichsmarks to a Pfennig that some of those bastards are lining their own pockets as well."

Schonewille sat in stunned silence. He had always regarded himself as more intelligent than Heger and prided himself on knowing more about what was going on. But now things were obviously different.

"What has this got to do with me?" he asked carefully.

"Friedrich you are a very influential man within the SS. You are involved in what is going on in the camps. What do you think will happen if either the Russians or the Allies win? What do you think will happen to you, or me for that matter?" He went on quickly, pointing his finger. "I'll tell you what will happen. We will be shot!"

Even though Schonewille was growing angry at being put on the defensive like this, he did not know what to say. The conversation had taken him into territory in which he had not yet dared enter. In truth, Schonewille like many others in the Reich was beginning to fear for his future. Again he spoke carefully.

"But what is it that you want of me. Why are you saying this?"

Heger gave a small sigh. He smiled slightly. "Come to my house tonight. I have a proposition to make. I need you. In fact we might need each other. Will you come?"

Major Friedrich Schonewille nodded his head.

It was past two o'clock when Schonewille got back to his small two storey house in Spandau.

He used a key to let himself in by the front door and, as he usually did, remained standing silently in the hallway for a moment or two, listening. There were sounds from the ceiling and he realised she was upstairs having a bath.

Good, he thought to himself. He liked her when she smelt clean and the knowledge that she was naked sent a tremor through his groin. It would be a pleasant afternoon, he mused.

However, he made no attempt to go upstairs. Quietly, he turned and walked into the sitting room, took off his belts and holster, his jacket and undid the top button of his shirt.

Sitting down, he opened his briefcase and extracted a manila folder. There were about six sheets of paper inside, the top one containing a photograph of Klaus Heger. It was the banker's official SS file.

After leaving the Reichsbank he had stood in the street for a few moments, undecided at what to do. The recent conversation had both disturbed and intrigued him and his natural caution was now working overtime. He knew that what was happening could be the key to his survival and this brought about a realisation that he was woefully short of any accurate information of what the military situation was really like. He also needed to gain some added information about his friend. This resolved he had made his way to the SS and Gestapo headquarters.

He had taken a tramcar part of the way and walked the rest. All the time his mind had been racing. The result was that he arrived at the H-shaped building knowing exactly what he wanted and how he could get it without raising any awkward questions. Suspicion was always on duty in the SS. As usual security was tight, but with his credentials it was a mere formality to gain access.

He had asked for an audience with several people in the economic section of the SS and this was duly given. It seemed nobody was too busy even in these parlous times.

He requested up-to-date information on the military situation and the likelihood of the Third Reich's armies being able to stem the flood of foreign armies. His excuse on needing this sensitive information was the need to obtain as much loot from the east as quickly as possible if there was the likelihood of the Red Army breaking through any further westward.

The information coming his way both surprised and appalled him. All the main extermination camps in the east of Poland were now within striking range of the Russians. In fact Treblinka was in the process of being de-commissioned as was another camp, Sobibor. The Treblinka closure had been known to him, but the full reason had never been explained. In April, a revolt by Jewish prisoner-workers had led to a mass escape and the death of a dozen or more camp guards. Following this and, with the knowledge that the approaching Russian Army might cause the inmates to become even more bold, the SS decided to hasten the execution of the remaining prisoners and the removal of those who could still be of some use as slave labour.

The huge complex of Auschwitz-Birkenau though, which now covered an area some eight miles round (and at any one time housed upwards of 70,000 prisoners, of which 50,000 were slave labourers feeding the labour demands of the special war plants of such industrial giants as Krupp, Siemens and IG Farben), was still some distance away from the advancing Russian hordes. Nevertheless, the Red Army was still very close.

Schonewille was also able to gain knowledge of some hard-to-obtain intelligence, namely the size of the approaching Russian Armies. On reading this information he quickly realised Germany had no hope. Others around him seemed to be in no doubt as to Germany's ability to survive, but to the SS major it seemed as though they were unwilling to face the truth, or at best were too fanatical to even contemplate defeat.

Obtaining Heger's file had been much easier. The filing clerk had owed him a favour and Schonewille, with a promise of replacing the file the next day, had been allowed to take it away with him after signing the required book. On an impulse he had made one more information gathering sortie. At the time he was not sure why, but a germ of an idea had begun to form in his mind. It was disjointed, a fragment of a puzzle which, in effect, had not even been created yet.

His second destination was the Air Ministry, situated almost exactly opposite the Gestapo headquarters, although the main entrance was around the corner in Wilhelmstrasse. On entering, he asked to be taken to the records section where, after some preliminaries, he was able to obtain the file of a certain Major Peter Wenck. Since his direct authority was not as strong in the Luftwaffe's headquarters he was not able to borrow the file, but he was given as much time as he wanted to read it. It proved to be very enlightening.

Back in his house, Schonewille spent fifteen minutes perusing Heger's file. It did not tell him anything he did not already know.

He sat back, his shiny boots outstretched in front of him, one heel resting on his ankle. He folded his arms and leant his head back on the sofa and tried to martial his thoughts. It was in this position that the woman found him few moments later.

She had sensed his presence as soon as she had got to the bottom of the stairs. As she always did in such circumstances, she waited a moment to prepare herself before entering the sitting room.

Schonewille stood up as she entered and smiled. Those few who had met them together noted how his smile for her was particularly warm. It was a smile he reserved for no one else, except perhaps his mother and she was now dead, a victim of an air-raid while visiting friends in Hamburg a year before.

"Sophia, how nice you look. As always you are a vision of loveliness," he said gallantly and moved to take her in his arms.

She smiled thinly and allowed herself to be held, even answering his kiss with a degree of warmth. She knew by his embrace that he wanted her, so it was not unexpected when he asked her to come upstairs to the bedroom. Once there she helped him undress, something he always liked, and allowed herself to be undressed in turn. This took only a few seconds because under her dressing-gown she was entirely naked, her body still pink and warm from the effects of the bath.

Schonewille stepped back and looked at her for a moment. She was so beautiful. Tall, almost as tall as he, with long black hair, dark brown eyes atop a small straight nose and a full generous mouth. The perfection was heightened by the only blemish on her skin, a small beauty mark on the left of her chin. Her breasts were full and un-marked by any child-bearing, the nipples round, large and hardening as they sniffed the cold air.

Schonewille had never been fully at ease with women of his own strata. He found the intelligent or worldly wise ones too intimidating and the simple ones too silly. He had always needed somebody of intelligence, yet somebody over whom he could exercise his power. The combination was not easy to find. With Sophia, that power was his.

Despite his lack of experience with women he was not a bad lover and his caresses, if not fully arousing the woman, were at least pleasant. For this she was always thankful. She was aware that he loved her and had proved this by risking much for her, but the unpalatable fact was she hated him and all he stood for. Paradoxically, within this hate there was also a degree of gratefulness, combined with the knowledge that without him she would now be dead.

He climaxed with a groan, murmuring endearments as he collapsed on her body. She answered by entwining her legs around him, though saying nothing in return. But, when he raised his head to look at her, she gave him a small smile.

Schonewille rolled over and sat up, reaching over to pull the blankets over them. As he did so he caught sight of the numbers on her arm. As always, he decided they would have to be destroyed. Removal was impossible, but a burn would hide their incriminating evidence. Yet, he knew that unless this was done forcibly she would not permit the numbers to be obliterated. Why, he could not fathom, because if they were seen by someone there was a strong chance she would end up from where he had rescued her, Auschwitz.

Chapter Two

Time with Sophia always had a calming effect on Schonewille. Love-making extended this a few degrees so that the man who began to dress three hours later was less driven and a more inner-satisfied individual. It even showed in the way he dressed. He was usually very careful to wear his service uniform when he left the confines of his home, complete with belts, holster, breeches, black boots and dour demeanour. Quite simply he needed the authority it gave him. There was also, of course, the fear and respect accorded to anyone wearing the Totenkopf, the skull-and-crossbones motif on their peaked cap that so aptly described the Waffen SS and all it stood for.

But now, with this feeling of well-being, he decided it was better to tone down his official image for his next meeting with Heger and wear Ausgehanzug, or walking out dress. This was a much more casual affair. The front and rear belt supports of his tunic were replaced by clips and he wore no holster. A white shirt and black tie (for the tunic was now open at the neck) softened the image still further and instead of breeches and riding boots he now wore long trousers and soft leather shoes. They were Italian, purchased in Milan on his last visit and, as he laced them up, he hoped it would not rain.

Whatever Schonewille wore, he was always very careful to include two items: his iron cross (second class) and his combat medal. Both had been earned, in a fashion, and were another clue in the complex make-up of his character. They were also another example of the lengths to which he went to create a new image for himself.

Schonewille was a member of the SS-HA, or the SS-Hauptamt, to give its full title. This was the main office that controlled all branches of the SS.

As an accountant he also belonged to the SS-WYVH, or the SS-Wirtschafts-und-Verwaltungshauptamt, which was the

Economic and Administrative Main Office of the SS and controlled all its finances. It also administered the use, sale and acquisition of SS property, supply and installations, plus the concentration camps.

Originally he had been part of Amtsgruppe A1V, the Prüfungsamt or auditing office for the troops. He was then seconded to Amtsgruppe B1V, which controlled raw materials, bulk purchases of equipment and all foreign currency looted from the occupied countries and camps. It was his work in these two sections that brought him to the attention of his superiors and ultimately saw him promoted in August 1942 to major and transferred to Amtsgruppe D, the branch that administered the concentration camps.

Schonewille was to become a man of status within this section. In official terms he was a SS-Fachführer. These were men with specialist qualifications earned in civilian life. It was they who performed all the necessary administrative, legal and technical services within the Waffen SS. To all intents and purposes they were the bureaucracy, and like all bureaucrats they largely controlled the inner workings of this huge, multi-faceted organisation.

Although an administrator, Schonewille was also an officer and, therefore, before he had been allowed to attain officer rank, he had to attend Junkerschule, or officer cadet school. This was not a perfunctory course either. To be an SS officer required three qualifications: be of good German character, be a good National Socialist or SS member and have leadership potential.

In Schonewille's case the latter was open to question, but membership of the party at such an early date had given him a degree of influence and power that had translated itself into the ability to give orders and put forward ideas. In other words, he had found a measure of leadership.

At any rate, the course lasted six intensive months and when it finished he was perfectly able to handle himself in a fight if he so desired.

Schonewille was not a physical coward, he just regarded himself as superior to the everyday soldier and had little regard for the aims, ambitions and dedication of the front-line officer. However, in a perverse way he admired the status and glory that went with being a successful fighting man. At the same time he was well aware of the contempt that soldiers or officers felt for those who only acted as administrators and had never seen action.

The SS had given him a greater self-confidence in his abilities outside his chosen profession. It also helped him feel more at ease in the company of those that in the past he had regarded as his social superiors. He realised that front-line experience, no matter how small, would enhance his social status still further. Therefore, he set out to gain some of this experience. He had not sought combat, but as it transpired, this is what he actually got. As usual, he used the experience to his best advantage.

In September 1941, as the German Army headed eastwards across the Ukraine, Schonewille attached himself to one of the most famous of the SS fighting divisions, the Leibstandarte SS Adolf Hitler. While at divisional headquarters, some forty kilometres behind the front, he was informed of a mission being mounted against some dissidents. These, he was told, were either a newly-formed guerilla band or the remnants of some Red Army force that had been decimated when the Wehrmacht had fought its way through the area some three weeks before.

A colonel had told him blandly, "It will be no more than a policing or mopping up operation, Captain. It will be very easy. Go along and enjoy the experience."

Four hours later he found himself in a pine forest with a force of some forty soldiers fighting for his life. There was only one other German officer left alive, a young second-lieutenant just out of officer school. High on patriotism but low on experience, the twenty-year-old lieutenant was very much under the sway of a thirty-year-old sergeant, a veteran of the French, Yugoslav and Greek campaigns as well as having served on the Russian front since the start of Operation Barbarossa.

With the original commanding officer dead, Captain Schonewille was now the senior rank and out of necessity took charge, although he was wise enough to also heed the advice of the sergeant.

The Germans were cut off and nearly surrounded by a

well-armed band of Red Army regulars numbering at least 300, the remnants of an infantry regiment that had been destroyed in the fierce fighting of almost a month before. They had lain doggo after the main battles had past and in the ensuing three weeks had rested and recuperated, waiting to attack the soft rear echelons of the German forces.

Schonewille had taken a dozen men (including the sergeant) and held one wing of their defensive position for a period of nearly ten hours until reinforcements arrived.

The fighting had been bloody with much close combat. At one stage he had defended himself against three Russians whom he cut down with a machine pistol at a range of no more than ten metres. Slightly wounded by a shell splinter from a mortar round, he had nevertheless continued fighting and even went back several times to check on the status of the lieutenant and his troops guarding the other wing of their redoubt. By any estimate he had acquitted himself well.

At the end of it all, he had a quiet discussion with the sergeant. The gist of the conversation was quite simple. If the sergeant would make a report saying how gallant he had been, Schonewille in turn would make a recommendation that the other be given a battlefield commission. With the lieutenant, there was no such bargain needed. The young soldier had been very impressed with Schonewille's efforts and he spoke in glowing terms of his role in the action.

Schonewille was duly awarded an Iron Cross second class and given the right to wear the Wehrmacht's combat badge on his tunic. But from then on, Schonewille always made perfectly sure he never again put himself in such a hazardous position. At any rate the opportunity was never to eventuate as on 1 February 1942 he was transferred to the newly-formed SS Economic and Administrative Main Office where he always made certain he was recognised as an officer who had risked life and limb for the Fatherland. With this in mind he sometimes wore his uniform in the manner of a fighting soldier. One of these affectations was in the way he wore his service cap. To be fair, though, in this he was not alone.

The SS officer's headgear was a distinctive peaked cap with a field grey cover, black cap band bearing the Totenkopf and black leather visor. This was festooned with two silver cap-cords fastened with matt silver buttons. In standard issue the cap was fitted with a spring that made the top of the cap more rigid and gave it its distinctive upward sloping profile. Many front-line officers removed the spring so as to give the cap a softer, more jaunty shape. It also made it easier to wear. Of course, this was against regulations, but so many senior officers followed the practice that use of the cap spring was never enforced, except perhaps at SS headquarters or official functions. For his meeting with Heger that night, the SS major decided on the more official cap with its spring inside.

It was dark when he left the house. Sophia did not see him off. He had not seen her since his bath following their love-making. There seemed nothing unusual in this for unless they were sleeping in the same bed, she always kept to herself for several hours after they had been intimate. To Schonewille, inexperienced with women, it was perfectly natural. To any other man it would have been cause for concern.

For Sophia it was a time when she felt unclean, a time when she always took a bath and tried to erase the smell of sex from her body. In an effort to excuse what had happened she always told herself that she had given her body in order to survive. Yet she was never quite able to divorce herself from the feeling of safety and security when in the company of the SS officer. She knew what lengths he had gone to in his efforts to save her from the gas chambers and the risks he still ran in harbouring her despite her new identity and the papers to back it up. Yet equally she knew who and what he was. As a defensive mechanism she usually shut her mind to the essential evil behind the man. She also never planned ahead. She existed from day-to-day, tomorrow was too far off and too full of danger to be contemplated. Only when she was sure he had left did she venture down to the ground floor and have something to eat.

Heger lived near Potsdam and it took Schonewille a good thirty minutes to reach the banker's apartment, an undistinguished two-storey edifice set back a little way from the street. The ground floor apartment was quite large and comfortable, especially now when any accommodation was at a premium with much of Berlin's residents without proper shelter, or living in sub-standard quarters.

Heger greeted him at the door and effusively ushered him inside. He was still wearing the drab suit he had worn at their meeting earlier in the day. After a few minutes he took his jacket off revealing a threadbare cardigan and a white shirt with an old-fashioned detachable collar.

They had just sat down when Frau Heger walked into the sitting room, necessitating Schonewille to rise and giver her a formal, stiff bow in greeting. As usual, she was nervous in his presence and to get over her awkwardness she busied herself with picking up his overcoat, which he had draped over a sofa, and taking it to the hallway where she hung it up. Returning, she gave Schonewille a small smile and offered him a drink. On inquiring what they had, Heger rather boastfully answered that they were well-stocked.

"My dear Friedrich, I have some important friends in the Reich and in return for a few favours they have been able to supply me with all manners of luxury, even in these hard times. Remember the coffee?"

The major nodded his head, but said nothing. I wonder how he is being used, he thought. He turned to Frau Heger.

"Really, Alice, I would be perfectly happy with a beer. Do you have any? I am a little thirsty after my walk" His voice was warm and friendly.

"Of course, Herr Sturmbannführer. Please sit down again and I will get it for you."

As usual she addressed him by his SS rank even though they had known one another for years and he always addressed her by her first name. She was a relatively tall woman with pretty though sharp features. In England her demeanour would be described as prim.

Originally she had maintained a condescending attitude towards him, but as his power and influence increased so her manner softened and she managed to mask her dislike. This was not only because she feared him, but also because her husband owed much to Schonewille's good graces and patronage.

In turn, the Nazi was ambivalent about Alice Heger. She was everything he disliked in a female: shrewd rather than intelligent, with a truncated simplistic view of the world. She was a product of her class, a bourgeois housekeeper who looked down on everything and everyone who was different from her and her ilk.

A sudden malicious thought crossed Schonewille's mind and he wondered how she would react to being an inmate in a concentration camp. He smiled to himself.

Heger saw the smirk and looked at his friend speculatively but, before he could speak his wife returned with two steins of beer on an ornate silver platter.

Such pretensions, thought Schonewille and then turned to the other man. "Well now, Klaus, what is this mysterious matter you want to discuss with me?"

Heger paused for a moment before answering and looked across to his wife. She nodded her head and rose from her seat with a frown. She was clearly not happy at the unspoken message contained in the look, but she obviously knew what he wanted. With an irritated "Ja, ja," she left the sitting room without a backward glance.

Whether this meant she knew the subject matter to be discussed and was just being left out of the detailed conversation or was completely in the dark he was not sure yet. Knowing the woman and her nature he surmised that she had at least some idea about the topic at hand. As it later transpired, he had guessed correctly.

Heger had ruled out having her present when the initial approach was being made because of her strong antipathy towards the SS officer. He hesitated for a moment or two after his wife left the room and took a long pull of his stein before carefully setting it down on a small glass-topped table at his elbow. He lifted his eyes to look at the SS man and found him returning the gaze, the eyes intense and the eyebrows raised speculatively.

"You remember the gist of our conversation this morning?" he finally asked.

Schonewille played hard to get. "We spoke of many things, Klaus. The war, money from the camps, Warsaw, Hungary, coffee."

A look of annoyance spread over the banker's features. He pursed his lips and shook his head slightly with frustration. "Friedrich, please do not play games. What I am about to discuss with you could get us both shot. But …" He paused for breath and then went on vehemently. "It could guarantee our future in the event of the Reich being defeated." Schonewille still gave nothing away, though he nodded his head. The gesture could have been one of understanding or acquiescence. Heger did not know which, but he went on.

"This morning I told you about a meeting at the Hotel Maison Rouge in Strasbourg and the scheme to take money out of the country … and, as I said, those who took part are probably lining their own pockets as well, in order to safeguard their future. Well, what I have in mind is that we also guarantee our financial future and our personal well-being. I said a moment ago that what I was about to propose could get us shot. However, this could only happen if one of us, or a third party who I will talk about later, reveals what we plan to do. Otherwise, the plan is very safe."

While Heger was speaking Schonewille wondered whether the room was bugged, or there was anybody listening. He chose his words carefully. "Klaus, at the moment I have no idea what you are talking about. Nevertheless, I will listen further. You must be frank though and get to the point. Otherwise I will not be able to make up my mind about anything. Do you understand?"

Heger was no fool. He understood perfectly well that what he had already said was enough to put him in the hands of the Gestapo. At the same time he understood that the SS major sitting opposite him was playing a cagey game. He was asking for more information before committing himself and without running the risk of implication if the conversation was being recorded. If transcripts of their talk so far were ever placed in the hands of the Gestapo then Schonewille could legitimately say that he had never agreed to be part of anything illegal and was just gaining information on behalf of the authorities.

Nevertheless, he felt he knew enough about the man to feel relatively certain that if the safeguards were sufficient enough, then the ever careful Sturmbannführer would join him in what he was about to propose.

There was also one very simple fact. Without Schonewille there was no hope of the plan ever getting off the ground, let alone succeeding.

Heger smiled conspiratorially. "My dear friend, what we have in mind is quite simple. You are the person who audits and checks the money and valuables that come from the Polish and some of the German camps. With the Russians moving towards our borders, the Polish camps are being closed down and destroyed. Yet there is still much booty to be gained from these camps and the other eastern territories, namely Hungary and Czechoslovakia.

"What is of equal importance for this plan is that there is now much confusion in the camps with no precise auditing of what is being collected and where its destination. Therefore, what we plan to do is create a special account in the Reichsbank. From now on and in the time that remains, some of the profits from the camps will be placed in this account.

"If there comes a time when the Reich is faced with collapse then this money can be withdrawn by us in either gold or foreign currency. For example, US dollars. These can be used for our escape, or to provide for our continued health and prosperity."

Heger paused for a moment still smiling, his voice rising as he enthused. "You see, Friedrich. It is foolproof. Until such time as we withdraw the money we cannot be accused of anything. And, when we do, if we do, it will only be because the Third Reich is finished and there will be no one left in authority to be a threat to us."

"Who will control this account?" asked Schonewille.

"You and this third person. As a banker I will administer it and keep its existence hidden but it would be strange if my signature was on any withdrawal authorisation. Do you understand?"

Schonewille nodded his head. He was becoming more and more intrigued. "Who is this mysterious third person? Before I commit myself any further, I must know his name?"

Heger shook his head. "I'm sorry Friedrich. I am not at liberty to reveal his identity at present. I must first know whether you are with us. But, this I can say. He is a senior officer with considerable influence … verstehst?"

Schonewille again nodded his head. He did understand. He reasoned that Heger's words must be true. His old friend had neither the courage nor the creativity to think up such a scheme. Or so he thought. He was later to find out that much of the plan had indeed been initiated by the banker.

"The key to this whole affair is the rank and importance of your mysterious third person. I cannot throw in my lot with you unless I know his name," persisted Schonewille.

Heger smiled wryly and shook his head. "No Friedrich. For the last time, I cannot do that. You will learn the name when I know you are committed, not before."

Schonewille was surprised at his friend's strength of purpose. It made him feel uneasy and he wanted time to think. He asked several more questions but got nowhere. Heger refused point blank to give away any more information.

It was the banker who abruptly ended the conversation by standing up and opening a door, through which he called his wife. "Alice, Liebling, können wir zwei Bier haben, bitte?"

Schonewille hurriedly got to his feet. "Nein. Thank you Klaus, but I must be going. I have some important work to do tonight and I also want to think about our conversation."

Frau Heger stood at the opposite doorway and watched him leave. She made no attempt to get his coat and it was left to her husband to help him on with the garment and see him to the door. He said a curt goodbye and without a backward glance walked to the gate, opened it and headed off down the street.

When he had walked about a hundred metres he stopped and stood in a doorway uncertain what to do, trying to martial his thoughts. With his uncertainty came anger.

More than anything Schonewille did not like to be in a situation over which he had no control or understanding. It reminded him of his lonely boyhood. He swore under his breath and looked back in the direction from whence he had come. The street was empty. Anyway, with the blackout in force it was difficult to see more than thirty or forty meters.

He walked back in the direction of the Heger's apartment. The street was still deserted. In the distance he could hear a radio blaring, but otherwise the night was quiet. He checked for cars parked in the street. Nothing.

He waited for fifteen minutes, standing in the shadows, waiting to see if anybody entered or left the apartment ... Still nothing. Then an elderly man walked up the street towards where he was lurking. He peered inquisitively at Schonewille, but when he recognised the SS uniform turned his head and quickly hurried away. I cannot stand here all night, he thought.

There was another problem. With four apartments in the block several people could come and go and he would not be able to ascertain if they were associated with the Hegers. Still, he had to try, but how?

The answer came in the form of a thirteen-year-old boy. He was a Hitlerjunge, the youth corps through which the creed of the Third Reich was instilled in almost every German child.

Schonewille hailed the youth, who came over obediently. The SS major asked the lad's name and his Hitler Youth rank. The answer was given without hesitation.

"Well, Emil, can you tell me how many of your section live close by?"

"Vier, Herr Sturmbannführer."

Schonewille thought quickly. Four, five including the lad standing in front of him. It should be enough.

"Well boy, I want you to collect your kameraden now, and quickly. Then report back here to me immediately and tell no one except your parents. Verstanden?"

"Jawohl, Herr Sturmbannführer, ich verstehe." The lad gave a snappy salute and with a firm "Heil Hitler" ran back up the street. He was back in less than fifteen minutes with four other Hitler Youth in tow; their ages ranging from about eleven to fourteen years. They stood to attention in front of him, excited and expectant.

Schonewille smiled in spite of himself.

"Kameraden, listen carefully. I want you to do something for me, something that is important for the Reich."

The youths took in every word. He pointed in the direction of the Heger's apartment block.

"That apartment block, number thirty-eight. I want you to make a list of all the people who enter or leave between now and seven o'clock in the morning. Now, how many of you are familiar with who lives there?"

The first lad, Emil, and one of the others, indicated how they knew at least by sight those who lived in the block.

"That is good, Emil and ..." He paused and motioned towards the other boy who immediately volunteered his name ... "And Wolfgang will point out if anybody is not a resident of number thirty-eight. Those that are not and are leaving I want followed. I will give you some money to cover any fares. You must tell me where they go and attempt to find out who they are. But, and this is vital, be discreet."

Schonewille spent the next few minutes answering questions from the brighter of the boys. No, they were not to approach any of the residents. No, they could not tell any other member of the forces. Further questions could only be directed to him. Yes, they should as far as possible keep hidden and yes, they were to stay where they were unless there was a bad air-raid.

Finally Schonewille told Emil and Wolfgang to report to his home at eight o'clock in the morning. The two puffed themselves up with pride. Schonewille dismissed them and they all saluted. This time their Heil Hitlers were much more muted although still very enthusiastic.

He then went home. Sophia was already in bed and he made no attempt to wake her. He went to his study and thought about the day's events. The information learned that evening had not given him much to go on. In truth he had been smart enough to guess the gist of the plan before he had gone to Heger's apartment. In one or two vital areas he was already one step ahead of the banker, but heading on a slightly different tack. In effect he had been playing dumb while he learned more details of what Heger was up to. In this respect though, his subterfuge had only been partly successful.

All that the evening's meeting had really brought about was the realisation that he was now in a very difficult position. If he did not report what had transpired by the morning, he was implicated whether he liked it or not. Schonewille could not have cared less whether Heger and his wife were picked up by the Gestapo. Yet by the same token he now fully understood the military situation and what this held in store for Hitler's Reich. Therefore, he had to plan ahead if he was to save his own skin.

The question was, whether to say yes or no to Heger. There was one other problem. He did not know the rank or identity of the mysterious third member and it was quite likely that if he attempted to report on what was being planned he might find himself being arrested on the orders of that third party. At eleven o'clock the air-raid siren started its mournful wailing.

"Teufelnoch a mal," he swore. He remembered the lone reconnaissance plane in the sky above Berlin. He should have understood then that there was a good chance the capital would receive yet another visit from the Terrorflieger, as Goebbels' propaganda unit called them. Schonewille smiled to himself. The Gauleiter was conveniently forgetting Warsaw, Rotterdam, London, Coventry, Moscow and the dozens of other cities visited by the Luftwaffe.

His annoyance and frustration increased when he realised the residents at Heger's apartment block were likely to leave and go to the air-raid shelters providing an almost impossible task for the watching Hitler Youth.

He swore again and wondered whether he should go to the shelter himself. He hated the claustrophobic feeling of the shelters and their sweaty, fearful inhabitants. He decided against it. If the bombing got too close he would go down to his own cellar. It was not as deep as a proper shelter, but it would protect him against anything except a direct hit.

At any rate, Sophia would not leave the house. She was paranoid about going out in the streets at night when security and identity checks were at their peak. Although her identity papers were legitimate and therefore foolproof, she was still afraid that somehow she would be arrested. The only incriminating evidence against her was the number tattooed on her arm, yet she still resolutely refused to have it removed. To Schonewille's logical mind this was sheer stupidity as it also put him in danger. He kept telling himself he should force her to remove the tattoo, but lately

42

he had not been able to make himself confront her over the issue. When he had first done so the look of loathing she gave so unnerved him that he let the matter drop.

The Jewish woman was the one chink in his armour. He loved her and the more time he spent with her the more emotionally attached he became. That she did not reciprocate the feeling never entered his head. After all, had he not rescued her from a holding station prior to her deportation to a concentration camp, risking his career and maybe even his life?

To his relief the bombing was distant, still loud and frightening but not close enough to cause him to leave the house or even go to the cellar. It was obviously a raid on a particular strategic target, probably a factory or industrial complex rather than an indiscriminate attack on the city and its population. In less than an hour it was over and the all-clear sounded.

When he finally went to bed he first opened Sophia's door to see how she was. She answered his solicitous questions, assuring him she was not afraid of the bombing, although it had kept her awake. She wished him a good night and as an afterthought added, "I hope your meeting was successful?"

He gave her a curt non-committal answer and went to his own room. Sleep eluded him and he was hollow-eyed and irritable when he arose just after six in the morning. He went to the kitchen and made himself some Ersatzkaffee. God it tasted foul after the wonderful brew served to him by Heger. The thought irritated him still further. He made Sophia breakfast in bed and then settled down to wait for his spies.

The two Hitlerjungen arrived on the dot at eight o'clock. He let them in and made them some coffee. They had done a thorough job and Schonewille was most impressed. Emil did most of the talking.

"We were very worried when the air-raid siren sounded, but we were lucky, Sturmbannführer. Everyone left the building and went to the one shelter. Just to make sure there was nobody left inside we went into the building and knocked on every door yelling 'air-raid, everybody into the shelter', but nobody answered," he smiled smugly. "When the all-clear sounded all the people went back to their apartments. There were no visitors and nobody left the

43

building until just before five o'clock. Then two men and one woman left and, as you ordered, we followed them. It was simple. The two men worked at the same factory and clocked on for the morning shift. The woman went to the station where she met her husband, an artillery major home on sick leave. We guessed that because his arm was all bandaged up and he used a stick, he limped very badly."

"Were there any visitors to the block, people you did not know?" questioned Schonewille.

"Nein, Herr Sturmbannführer. Nobody came to the apartments at all."

As far as he could be Schonewille was satisfied, though he realised that this did not preclude his fear of being set up. But, if this was happening why ... what would be the reason? He was not aware of any enemies within the SS.

The two youths were looking at him questioningly. Finally Wolfgang spoke. "Did we do right, Herr Sturmbannführer?"

To the boys' delight he was profuse in his thanks. He went to his study and returned with three blocks of chocolate that had been filched from some prisoner-of-war Red Cross parcels.

On being handed these prize delicacies they stammered their thanks. He saw them to the door and answered their salutes. His final order was that they tell no one what had happened.

At nine in the morning he rang Heger at the bank and told him he would join them. To his annoyance Heger did not seem surprised. As he put the receiver back in its cradle he wondered when he would meet the third man.

Chapter Three
6 November 1944

The Seafire was moving to cut off their retreat to safety, turning its white spinner up to meet them.

Major Peter Wenck swore to himself. If he got back to Tromso he would have a word to say to the intelligence officer for he had not warned them that the convoy had contained an aircraft carrier. True it was only an escort carrier, a converted freighter of some 13,000 tons and only able to carry eighteen aircraft. But if some of those eighteen aircraft were Seafires, the naval version of the Spitfire, then any German bomber meeting them was in for trouble.

The distance to the safety of the clouds was perhaps ten kilometres and the Seafire was between them and it. The British aircraft would be able to make at least two passes before they could reach its woolly confines, more than enough time for the Junkers to suffer a mortal blow.

Although the Seafire was a Mark III version, a derivative of the Spitfire Mk Vc and therefore not the most advanced of the famous aircraft, it was still at least forty miles an hour faster than the Junkers 188 and infinitely more nimble.

Wenck's first decision was to jettison the bomb load. There was absolutely no chance of evading the Seafire with the bombs still on board and it would not help the German war effort if he was killed. He told the bomb aimer to jettison and moments later four 1,000-kilogram anti-shipping bombs left their wing racks and tumbled towards the Barents Sea.

He spoke to his radar operator and the gunner who manned the power-operated turret immediately behind and above him. "Sigi, forget the radar, there's no chance of going for the convoy. Get on the radio and tell headquarters the convoy has a carrier and then get to the belly gun. Manfred, you had better look lively now. If you don't know already, that little bit of nasty out there can turn on a Pfennig and he won't stay in your sights for long. Heaven help us if he gets on our tail."

He then addressed the navigator. "Rolf, leave your pencils and charts and man your gun. What I just said to Manfred is the same for you. Now, I want you all to talk to one another just like we've done before, but only more so. I want to know everything that's happening." His mind raced as he thought to escape the British fighter. "I'm going to try and take a shot at him as we head for the clouds. I don't think he will be expecting this and it might give us the breather we need."

The Junkers armament included a single twenty millimetre cannon firing forward, controlled by the pilot. He flicked off the safety catch of the firing button on the spade control and took a quick look around the sky to make sure there were no other enemy fighters about. The Seafire was about three kilometres away, 1,000 metres below and closing rapidly. I hope you don't expect this, thought Wenck as he manipulated the pedal controls and turned the control column to his right.

The big German bomber dived at a shallow angle towards the British naval fighter, picking up speed as the pilot activated the boost switch feeding a volatile mixture of water and methanol into the Jumo engines. With both engines giving out their maximum overload horsepower the distance between the two closed in seconds.

Wenck squinted into his gun-sight, turned his aircraft slightly and, as the Seafire approached the outer ring, pressed the gun button. The Junkers shuddered as the MG 151 cannon spewed forth its armour-piercing and tracer shells, but in less than three seconds the Seafire was out of danger with not a shot having landed.

Surprised the British flier might have been, but he was a good pilot and quickly evaded Wenck's shells by dipping his nose and heading under the Junkers. Unless Wenck wanted to make his dive even steeper so he could continue to bring his gun to bear on the Seafire, there was no way he could continue to be a threat to the fighter. To do so would reduce his chance of reaching the clouds and safety. So he kept on going, for he had gained the breather.

The Seafire was now a little to the German's left about 500 metres below and as the Junkers sped past it lifted its nose to start a loop and at the same time fired thirty twenty-millimetre cannon shells and over one hundred .303 bullets in a quick deflection shot. This manoeuvre meant that as he reached the top of his climb he would be able to drop his nose and dive after the fleeing Junkers.

Wenck turned the aircraft slightly to port so the Seafire would have to turn even tighter, and then banged the throttles to the end of their gates. It would be a near thing.

Two shells and half-a dozen bullets had already struck the rear of their plane, a testimony of the accuracy of the British pilot.

"Skipper, he's above us and closing rapidly," yelled the gunner, turning his turret to meet the threat.

"Fine, fine Manfred. Tell me when you think he's within range, and start firing the moment you think you can reach him. Try to put him off his aim." Little chance of that, he thought.

Suddenly he heard the twenty millimetre gun in the turret start to yammer and could hear the cartridge cases spilling into the collection sack.

"He's shooting, he's shooting," yelled the gunner and navigator in unison. The latter also started firing his smaller calibre weapon from the rear of the cockpit, though in reality it was a wasted gesture since the Seafire was still out of range of the thirteen millimetre machine-gun bullets.

Wenck jinked the aircraft slightly, but to no avail. The Junkers staggered from repeated cannon shell strikes and then suddenly the light was cut as they entered the cloud.

Lieber Gott, I hope there are no breaks in the cloud, he prayed as he checked the Junker's mad dive. The prayer was not answered.

Again the cockpit was bathed in light as they emerged from the cloud, but immediately in front there was another column of white and he turned slightly towards it. Ten seconds later they were again enveloped in its woolly mass.

This happened several times and by the time they emerged into clear air five minutes later they had no idea where they were. More importantly, there was no sign of the Seafire.

Checking his instruments he noted that the starboard engine was running hot and spied a thin stream of grey smoke emitting from under the engine's cowling flaps.

"Oh shit," he said. He had already turned the boost off, for the engines were not designed to give an over-boost of power for very long, and now he throttled them back still further.

He monitored the oil and cylinder head temperatures of both Jumos for a few minutes and was relieved to see the gauges hold and not climb any higher. Still, it was a long way home and a flight on only one engine was not something to look forward to.

The altimeter registered 1,000 metres and for a moment he contemplated trying to climb higher. Height was all important at a time like this, but he quickly reasoned against it.

The Junkers 188 was painted with a mirror wave camouflage, wavy pale blue lines over a dark green base. This made the aircraft almost impossible to see from above. If he stayed at this height he would be safe from any fighter overhead.

"Rolf can you give me a course for home yet?"

The navigator answered in the affirmative and gave some instructions. Wenck swung the bomber round by nineteen degrees and headed back almost due south towards the coast of Norway.

They were approximately half-way between Bear Island and their base at Tromso situated in the extreme north of Norway. That meant they were about 240 kilometres from the airfield. Wenck asked the navigator to also work out an alternative course for a closer base, Banak, only about one hundred kilometres from North Cape, the northern most tip of Norway. He wanted an alternative route in case the engine started to give up.

The sky through which the Germans were flying was among the most desolate in the world. Although winter was officially three weeks away the air was just a few degrees above freezing and the sea below was vicious even though the day was relatively calm. A crash-landing and their survival could therefore be measured in minutes. This was compounded because in these northern November climes the light was already very low, creating a hazard for fliers, especially those nursing a crippled plane.

Wenck had been leading a pack of eight bombers to attack an Allied convoy that was skirting the Arctic pack ice just south of Bear Island on its way to the Russian port of Murmansk. He had lost sight of the rest of his squadron because of cloud shortly before the Seafire had stumbled upon them.

Now, free of any immediate danger he wondered how they had faired. He decided against using his radio to find out. Whatever had happened had happened. There was nothing he could do now. If he got back to base he would find out soon enough.

As it transpired the plane gave no further trouble, although by the time he sighted his airfield the starboard engine was running very hot. Still, he landed safely enough and avoiding the mud puddles carefully taxied to the dispersals area. His ground crew were there to greet him and quickly began to make a thorough examination of the damage.

It was with some relief he noticed some of his charges were already back, but it changed to apprehension when he counted two missing. After two hours they still had not returned and he knew there would be eight empty chairs in the mess that night. The telegrams back to the Fatherland would be brief. Missing in action. The reality was there was little chance of them surviving.

The other five crews all had a similar tales to tell. Only one crew had sighted the convoy, but before they could attempt an attack they had been bounced by Seafires. They were lucky to have made it back. Despite their search radar the others had been unable to find the main body of the convoy and had turned away on sighting the enemy fighters. With nightfall just an hour away there was little use in trying another sortie. Weather permitting they would have to wait until tomorrow.

Following the de-briefing Wenck made his way to his hut. His corporal had stoked up the pot belly stove. making the hut warm and inviting. He sat hunched on the edge of his bed for a few minutes rubbing his eyes before turning up the wick on his hurricane lamp and turning to a pile of papers in a wire tray.

After reading the first official missive he tossed it away with a groan and turned instead to two letters on the edge of the small table. The first was from his father who was a Luftwaffe area commander in southern Norway. His parent had little to say, except the usual banalities about health and survival. But, as usual, there was warmth in the letter and Peter Wenck was grateful to have received news about his father. Of his mother he had not heard for more than a year. Vigdis was back in Iceland and had

49

been so since her husband had sent her there early in 1940. Letters through the Red Cross were unreliable to say the least.

The second letter was much more interesting; intriguing in fact. It was a short note from his half-brother. It inquired after his health, apologised for not having written for four years and suggested that when he next came to Germany on leave they should get together.

Hardly likely, he thought. He had more important things to do than visit a man he hardly knew and did not much care for, even if he was his brother.

He then turned back to his papers and after working his way through half the pile came across something that took him totally by surprise. It was an official document stating that he was being flown back to Germany for seven days leave. He returned again to his brother's letter and wondered whether the two were linked.

It was too much of a coincidence.

Chapter Four

At four in the morning Wenck crawled out of his bed. The wind was shrieking outside and he could hear the rain banging against the tin roof and the single window with its four opaque panes of glass. A stream of ice cold air rushed in under the door, lifting the dust in little whirling eddies and moving the papers on his desk.

Mouthing obscenities he knelt down and folded a newspaper that was lying on the floor and wedged it under the door. The pot-belly was almost out and he used another newspaper and some kindling to re-start the embers before loading it up with timber.

Satisfied that the room would be warm again in half-an-hour he went back to bed, grateful that he did not have stay up and prepare himself for a dawn take-off whenever the light finally appeared in this northern clime. At any rate, if this weather kept up there would be no flying today.

Three hours later his adjutant opened the door and let the full force of the cold air in as he stumbled on the step and came inside.

"Shit, it's cold. God, I hate this weather," he said setting down a thermos on the table and taking off his overcoat and balaclava.

Wenck did not stir. The thought of getting out of his snug cocoon did not excite him at all, even though the room was now quite warm courtesy of the pot-belly. The other man put his hands on the form under the mountain of blankets and shook it vigorously. It immediately changed shape and a muffled voice ordered him to go away. The intruder persisted.

"Come on Peter, rise and shine. It's a lovely day outside. It's already three degrees above freezing and the met boys have promised that the temperature will soar upwards by another two degrees at least. Großer Gott, we might even be able to take our shirts off and get brown."

"More likely windburn and frostbite," retorted Wenck cautiously, poking has head out from under the blankets like a seal surveying the terrain from the safety of an ice hole.

The other man stepped back and laughed. "Come on Peter, I have brought some coffee for you and I have some good news."

"What is it?"

"No, I won't tell you until you get up ... So come on, shake a leg."

"All right, all right. But, I tell you what Leo, it had better be good," grumbled Wenck, throwing back the bedclothes and gingerly placing his be-socked feet onto the floor.

Captain Leo Swabisch busied himself with pouring steaming black coffee into a mug and adding a generous measure of sugar from a paper bag, which he returned to his pocket.

Wenck had made him his adjutant chiefly because of his ability to scrounge. The coffee and sugar were perfect examples. The former was real coffee and almost impossible to obtain and the latter also real and strictly rationed. Yet Swabisch had managed to obtain both in some quantity through the black market the last time he had visited Oslo. His scrounging prowess was not only limited to foodstuffs and other perishables. He also had a winning way with women.

The mechanics were equally impressed with his ability to barter, swap, procure and even steal hard to obtain parts for their much abused aircraft.

He was a popular officer, his rank partially a reward for this popularity and his scrounging abilities. But, a captain was as far up the ladder as he would go. Though brave, his flying abilities were barely average and his leadership qualities were severely stretched at his current rank. Nevertheless, his attributes made him an ideal adjutant and with Wenck making all the hard decisions Swabisch was proving to be an admirable helper. After getting partially dressed and with both hands clasped around a warm mug, Wenck was at last willing to face the day

"Now Leo, what is this news? Has the Führer decided he is not infallible and we are going to give in or has he promised yet another terror weapon with which to win the war?"

Swabisch grinned at this sacrilege. "Now, now Major," he said with mock severity. "You mustn't say those things. It could reach the ears of Burgdoff."

Wenck sighed and grunted in derision. Hans Burgdoff was one of their senior pilots, an able zealot who regarded Hitler as God. "There has to be one in every squadron doesn't there Leo?" said Wenck with a sigh. "Now for God's sake, tell me the good news."

"Young Hans Ulrich and his crew are safe. They crash-landed on a small island just off the coast. He was trying to make Banak but the engines gave up the ghost. It also seems that the plane is salvageable."

"This is good news, Leo. Check up on his Junkers, although I doubt we have either the resources or the time to try and get it back. Any news of the other crew?" Swabisch shook his head. "Oh well, getting Ulrich and his lot back is a bonus. What's the weather forecast like?" Swabisch took out a torn piece of paper from his pocket and read from the scrawled notes.

"Gale force winds, forty to fifty knots, raining and ten-tenths cloud. But, and it is a big but, the met boys predict that it might weaken sufficiently to allow us another crack at the convoy later this afternoon."

Wenck was not impressed. He told his friend to get a status report ready by 0900 hours and to schedule a squadron meeting that should include all flight leaders, the head mechanic, chief armourer, the meteorological officer and a naval representative from the nearby base.

"You know Leo, it is amazing how much more co-operative the navy is these days now that they depend on us even more to protect that useless fat bitch out there." He was referring to the battleship Tirpitz, which was moored gravely wounded only a few kilometres away.

Swabisch nodded his head, his face losing its sunny disposition for a moment. "Do you think the Engländer are going to have another go at the old girl again?" He was a romantic at heart and it hurt him to see the once proud and beautiful capital ship in such dire straits.

"Teufel, Leo. Use what the devil gave you. They have tried so many times now and you know what they're like. They're a bloody tenacious race. It takes them a while to become angry, but when they do they're more stubborn than us. You can bet a million

Reichsmarks to Göring's medals they'll be back to finish the job." His adjutant sighed and nodded his head.

Both knew the Tirpitz's days were numbered. The British had feared the battleship almost as much as her sister ship the Bismark and had dubbed her the Lone Queen of the North.

The Tirpitz had spent most of the war based in northern Norway and although she had rarely left her anchorage, her very presence was a threat to the Allied convoys heading for Murmansk and Archangel. Put simply, the Allies (mainly the British) had to guard most of the Russian convoys with battleships and cruisers or at least ensure a task force containing these ships was nearby just to make sure the Tirpitz never tried anything nasty.

By her very presence the German ship was tying down many of the Royal Navy's heavy units, ships that were sorely needed elsewhere. Consequently, through the auspices of the Fleet Air Arm they made repeated attempts to sink or at least cripple the Lone Queen. In this they were only partially successful. It was not until the RAF stepped into the act and sent a force of Lancasters from No.9 and the 617 Dambuster squadrons to Russia that they accomplished their task.

The Tirpitz had been based at Altenfjord, out of the reach of land-based British bombers. So the Lancasters were sent to Yagodnik near Archangel in northern Russia to await good weather. On 15 September 1944, twenty-eight Lancasters left Yagodnik for their first strike. Each was armed with the monster 12,000 pound armour piercing bomb known as the Tallboy. They reached her just as the smokescreen hid her from view. The Tirpitz survived, but only just. Wenck described her condition.

"I have been told, not officially of course, she is now no longer seaworthy and with her top speed down to a mere eight knots any strike against an allied convoy in the wild Barents Sea is out of the question. At any rate High Command still believes the Allies could make a seaborne landing in northern Norway and with the Russian forces now close by, that's why they decided to move her further southward and use her as a floating fortress."

Consequently, the Tirpitz limped 320 kilometres south and was anchored just off Haakoy Island, five kilometres from Tromso. This was a Godsend to the British for the ship was now just within range of its Lancaster bases in Scotland. On 29 October the Lancasters once again tried to sink the Tirpitz, but bad visibility spoiled their attack and only one near miss was recorded. Immediately, the Germans moved two squadrons of fighters to the nearby airfield of Bardufoss where Wenck was stationed.

At precisely 0900 hours Wenck met with his flight leaders and the other personnel he had requested. The naval representative arrived late, but at least he was there.

The first questions were directed to the meteorological officer. He was a small man with a receding hairline above a high sloping forehead. He was out of his depth in such rambunctious company and had the annoying habit of always hedging his bets whenever he was asked to predict the weather. This earned him the nickname of Vielleicht, or Maybe.

When asked what the forecast for the next twenty-four hours was, he prevaricated. "The weather is being affected by a big cold front and we can expect forty-five-to-fifty-knot gale force winds for most of today. Cloud cover should be up to ten-tenths at altitude and dropping to 1,000 metres or less when the winds abate. There will also be some rain. Flying is out of the question." He paused for a moment and everybody waited expectantly.

"Maybe the cloud will lift a little and the rain will stop about ..."

The rest was drowned out by a roar, followed by much hilarity.

"Good old Vielleicht ...", "Make us guess why don't you ...", "In other words you don't know..."

The naval officer, on the other hand, was more precise and certain in what he had to say. He warned that unless another attack was made on the convoy before nightfall it would be too late as the ships were already within range of Russian fighters and would reach the Kola Inlet by nightfall. From there it was just a short distance to Murmansk.

Wenck was not impressed. "I tell you this, comrade, you can wish as much as you like. If the weather does not improve significantly there is no way I'm taking my men up in this muck. We probably would not be able to take off anyway, and as for finding the convoy ... well you can forget it." Wenck shook his head with finality.

At any rate, the report on the serviceability of the aircraft was giving him cause for concern and there was some doubt whether they could actually field a strikeforce of sufficient strength. With the loss of two Junkers the day before and Wenck's damaged plane not yet repaired, the squadron was down to five operational aircraft. There were a similar number of Heinkel He 111s available, but nobody wanted to fly these outmoded and superseded models.

The rest of the morning was spent with paperwork or resting in the mess reading dog-eared copies of *Signal*.

Late into the afternoon the wind abated sufficiently for Wenck to take off and make a short flight to gauge the weather conditions. It was useless. The cloud cover was absolute with rain squalls and visibility down to nothing. After half-an-hour he called it off and returned to Bardufoss.

In the evening, the missing crew arrived making it a good excuse for a party, a drunken affair livened by the arrival of half-a-dozen female members of the Kriegsmarine. Outnumbered at least five-to-one the ladies received an overwhelming degree of attention.

The next morning the weather had abated somewhat and the squadron was ordered to start flying standing patrols to the east and out to sea just in case there were any more air attacks on the Tirpitz. This move was necessary since the storm had damaged the radar station. However, Wenck did not take part.

A coded message was received in the early hours of the morning ordering him to immediately fly to Narvik where he would be picked up by another plane and flown to Oslo. From there he would be transferred to a third aircraft and flown to Germany.

Perplexed, he did what he had been ordered, though a sense of foreboding began to gnaw away at his thoughts. Similar coded messages had been a feature of his career in the past and each one had brought about difficult missions coupled with extremes of danger. He reasoned that any such mission, at this stage of the war would be suicidal and he was now too war-weary and tired to contemplate such an effort. It was a dour and irritable man who left for Narvik at 0800 hours.

From there he boarded a Heinkel He 111, which had been converted to a military transport. They re-fuelled at Trondheim and reached the Norwegian capital after a six-and-a-half hour journey. He was due to board the other plane almost immediately but it had developed engine trouble, so he was told to report back at seven o'clock the following morning.

Unsure of where to go and with no accommodation arranged, he stood uncertainly for a moment to collect himself. A thought struck him and almost on a whim he went to an administration block and enquired as to the whereabouts of his father. He was in luck. Wenck Senior was now stationed at a military airbase some fifteen kilometres away. A phone call followed and his father promised to dispatch a staff car, which could pick him up within the hour. As it transpired it was almost two hours, but the thought of seeing his parent again after almost a year nullified his annoyance at the extra wait.

"My boy, it is wonderful to see you," said the general when they met, placing his hands on the younger man's shoulders and then hugging him in a most un-military way. They stepped apart and looked at one another with affection. No strict Prussian reserve and formality here. The affectionate Vigdis had banished such stiffness long since. At any rate, father and son were very close and it showed.

"Hello Father, you look well. Keeping out of trouble?"

"I try Peter, God knows I try. But, you know how it is. To get ahead and stay out of trouble these days one needs to be a real arschlecker and I still refuse to say yes when I know it should be no, or vice versa."

His father led him through a series of corridors returning the salutes of half-a-dozen-or-so flunkies as he strode to his destination. At the door of his office he ordered his secretary to make sure they were not disturbed and then ushered his son inside. Motioning him to sit down he crossed to a large and very ornate oak sideboard and poured a generous helping of a clear liquid into two large crystal tumblers.

"Vodka my boy. I now know why the Russians fight so well. I'm told their troops are given liberal quantities of this rocket fuel before they're sent against our boys. Quite a kick eh?"

He downed a large measure, breathed deeply and rubbed his stomach. Looking at his son, he paused for a moment and then said soberly, "You look tired Peter. What's it been like up north?"

Wenck Junior described the conditions in half-a-dozen earthy and pithy sentences and then downed another mouthful from the tumbler. He studied his father.

Generalmajor Helmuth Wenck had just turned fifty-seven, but the years had been more than kind. Peter scrutinised his father's face and for the first time realised that if he looked after his health he would weather the years just as well and become a mirror image of his parent. The older man could have passed for forty-five. His hair was still thick and blonde with only a hint of silver. The eyes were clear, the skin tanned and healthy, the bearing straight and the movements firm and decisive.

"Well, Father, as for you though, you don't look at all tired."

"No, not now, but I was in Finland until they capitulated early in September and this was a very rough period. I was buggered when it was over." He paused for a moment's reflection and then went on. "When I got back they gave me three weeks leave and instead of going back to Germany I went up to Bergen and stayed with a German woman who has a house on the coast there ... No, no it wasn't like that at all," he said hurriedly at his son's raised eyebrows. "She is elderly, about sixty or so (Peter thought this funny considering his father's age, but he did not say anything). Ugly as sin, though a lovely person. She was a friend of the family and married a Norwegian businessman just before the last war. Anyway, she has a house right on the sea and I stayed there and slept and fished and slept."

He laughed. "Did me a world of good. And as to your dirty thoughts a few seconds ago, the answer is no. I have been faithful to your mother since I last saw her four years ago. I cannot believe it myself, but there it is. I have been like a Jesuit." He paused, closed his eyes and then spoke wistfully. "By Jesus, I miss her." He raised his voice an octave or two and went on vehemently. "I tell you, Peter, when this stupid war is over I am going to leave Europe.

58

I am going to take your mother and go somewhere warm and far away. Maybe back to America, I do not know. But, I tell you this, I am not living in Germany again unless there is no alternative." His son said nothing. He was not surprised, though his father's bitterness was more pronounced than usual.

"Well my boy, what brings you here?"

Peter Wenck spoke briefly of his orders and then added, "I'm worried, Father. The orders were in code and marked secret. That can only mean trouble, something big and I have not the faintest idea what it's all about. There is something else that is strange. It may be a coincidence, but I also received a short letter from Friedrich suggesting we meet when I next returned to Germany."

Helmuth Wenck looked shocked. "You might be right, it certainly smells to me ... and from what I know of your brother anything to do with him is schlecht ... schlecht, schlecht, schlecht." He shook his head, more in sorrow than annoyance. "When did you see him last?" The younger man thought for a moment.

"Around late 1940. Yes, December 1940, when I was home on leave. We had a short meeting. It was at my instigation, but it was not a success. You know what he is like," he went on. "What about you?"

"Oh some time in late 1942. His mother was killed during the first of the big raids, on Hamburg. You remember, I wrote to you? I thought it right to see him. After all, she was my first wife even though she was a silly, shrewish bitch. Strangely, though, he was quite reasonable. I think he was touched by my coming to see him. At any rate for the first time I was quite impressed with him. He had won an Iron Cross second class for his part in some skirmish in Russia and by all accounts thoroughly deserved the medal. And I told him so.

"Still, he is in the SS and you know how I feel about those psychopaths. When I was in Germany again last ... oh, late in August last year, I tried to see him again. He was then with the administrative arm of the SS. Economic section I seem to recall, something to do with the concentration camps. On learning that I tried no further. I had been hearing some pretty ghastly things about those camps and God help us Germans if they're true." Peter asked what he had meant. "I'm not sure, but I've been told that we are slaughtering thousands of people, Jews mainly."

"Oh come now, Father. I grant you these camps are probably not nice, but ..." He got no further.

His father broke in angrily. "Teufel, Peter. You cannot be that naïve. You were in Russia. Surely you heard about what went on there?" He paused for a moment and then continued vehemently. "We are led by a madman, a common little guttersnipe, surrounded by common little guttersnipes. Have you met Himmler or Goebbels, eh? No? Let me tell you, in the old days they would not have been allowed in a decent club let alone been given the sort of power that we've let them amass. Even Göring, my old comrade Göring, is now, to use a British expression, as mad as a March hare!

"When I asked him to tell me about the camps he told me in no uncertain terms not to stick my nose into things which did not concern me. He did not deny anything. Just told me to mind my own business."

He lapsed into silence and his son looked around the room nervously. The older man caught the look and told him not to worry. The room was almost sound proof and the door very thick. He suggested that if Schonewille was implicated in this recall to Germany then he should try and refuse becoming a part of whatever his half-brother was involved in.

As they left the office, a very pretty uniformed secretary stopped them and handed his father some papers that needed to be signed. While his parent read them she looked up at Peter and, after studying his face intently for a few seconds, gave him a stunning smile. The major general noted the smile and introduced them.

"Gretchen, this is my brave son, Major Peter Wenck." The woman looked up, gave another stunning smile and then walked away without saying a word. The two men looked at one another and grinned.

They left the base shortly after and spent a convivial evening in each other's company, drinking in several bars before enjoying a first class meal in a top restaurant. A little worse for wear, Peter spent the night sprawled on a sofa in his father's tiny apartment.

Despite the amount of liquor he had consumed the previous

night, Peter Wenck awoke in the morning fairly clear-headed. More importantly, the man who caught the plane south two hours later was in a much better frame of mind than when he had arrived in Oslo.

Chapter Five
8 November 1944

Five o'clock in the morning is not the best time to alight from a train into the cold blackness of a late autumn morning, especially when it is raining and a numbing wind is blowing from the north-east.

Schonewille was glad he had finally reached Berlin, but he would have preferred to be on the other side of the city and on his way home. His head ached and he felt dirty. The rank smell of stale sweat, cigarette smoke and over-cooked cabbage had permeated his clothing till he thought he would vomit. He shook his head in frustration and immediately regretted the action. The migraine sent flashing messages of pain through his temples and he was forced to climb back into the train's compartment and sit down until the throbbing had subsided somewhat.

He knew there would be no car to meet him. He was almost five hours late from his already overdue schedule. The train trip back from Auschwitz had been a nightmare.

Germany's railroad system was in such chaos that to get anywhere was a hit-and-miss affair. One of the main targets of the allied bombing was the Third Reich's transport and communications systems and the railways were slowly being pulverised under the incessant depredations of the giant bombers that roamed the skies over occupied Europe and Germany almost without pause. Time and again on his trip back from Poland the train was shunted onto sidings to make way for supply and munitions trains heading eastwards, or was re-routed onto another track to bypass damaged sections of line.

To make matters worse, he had picked up a stomach bug and had spent much of his time in the carriage's smelly toilet. His anus stung from the constant use and inadequate cleansing abilities of the coarse paper provided by the Reichsbahn. The desire for a bath was all-encompassing, but he knew that he first had to deliver his papers to Heger at the Reichsbank. A spasm grabbed at his bowels and he swore. He called over a porter, an elderly man with only one arm, and ordered him to carry his overnight bag. The briefcase he kept hold of himself.

The man followed him to the station's toilets and stood outside the cubicle, respectfully waiting. Here at least the paper was softer, but the pain was still irritating and sharp.

With three hours to kill until he could gain entry to the bank. He ordered the porter to take him to the station master's office. There he brusquely told the man in charge that he intended using his office for a few hours. The man was only the night station master and since he was clocking off in half-an-hour saw no reason to argue the point. At any rate nobody but a fool would say no to an SS lieutenant-colonel, especially one who was obviously in such a bad temper.

Schonewille had been promoted to Obersturmbannführer the previous week and the method of promotion had taken away much of the joy this advancement should have engendered. The fact was that his new rank was a gift from the mysterious third man.

On 4 November Schonewille had been contacted by Heger who informed him that a meeting with this mysterious third party had been arranged for the following day. For Schonewille this was none too soon. He had already placed the first sums of money in the spurious account, the proceeds of his visit to the Mauthausen concentration camp in southern Germany.

The meeting was arranged to be at the Reichsbank, a factor Schonewille at first found very strange. But, after a moment's thought, he realised that at the bank there would be much more chance of keeping the meeting free of prying eyes and official records. Such an encounter at an SS establishment would mean at best the recognition and memory of personnel and at worst official entries in some duty book.

However, before this meeting actually took place he was ordered to visit another camp. So, on the fifth he boarded a train heading for the south-east, a 500-kilometre journey that normally would have taken no more than ten or eleven hours. It took almost twice that time. He was forced to switch trains at Breslau and then two hours later his train was switched onto a siding to let a munitions train through. They remained stationary for three hours while military traffic passed by, including a goods train hauling fifteen flatcars with their valuable load of King Tiger tanks.

On his trips to Auschwitz, Schonewille never went directly to either of the two main camps that made up part of the vast complex. At any rate, passenger and goods trains seldom stopped at one of the sidings directly outside. Those were generally only for the cattle trucks carrying their human cargo of misery.

The main rail line carrying Schonewille came from Katowice via Breslau and Berlin. A few miles north of the camps this line was joined by two other routes, one from the north-east, originating from Warsaw and passing through Lubin and Radom, and one from the east which came from Cracow.

As soon as his train crossed the Vistula River, Schonewille began to pack the papers he had been perusing away into his briefcase and put on his leather overcoat. A few minutes later he stepped out onto the platform of Auschwitz station.

As he suspected, there was no one there to meet him, but he managed to cadge a lift with another passenger, an industrial chemist working at the nearby IG Faben plant who dropped him off at a small inn just outside Auschwitz town. He was known here and the owner, a German World War One veteran who had been badly gassed at the Somme, greeted him effusively. The man had migrated to Poland in 1940 as part of the German lebensraum, or living space policy, which had been part of Hitler's basic tenet ever since he penned *Mein Kampf* while in prison in 1923.

Schonewille returned the greeting curtly. He was tired and bad tempered. He asked to use the phone and rang the camp. His temper did not improve when he learned that Kommandant Rudolf Höss was not available, nor was his aide.

The functionary at the other end of the line apologetically explained that they were both attending to some problems and would be back later. He did not elaborate. Since it was past five o'clock, he suggested Schonewille freshen up and have an early dinner and then wait for the kommandant's call. He took the advice and then checked with the railway station on when the next train would leave for Berlin. The one he had originally planned to use had long since gone. To his annoyance he learned there was none scheduled until 1.15pm the next day. Therefore, there was no need to visit the camp before morning, although he would have preferred to get the visit over and done with. He also contacted his office to tell them of the delay.

The phone eventually rang just after nine o'clock. The same functionary relayed a message that Kommandant Höss was very weary and would see him at 1000 hours the next morning.

By this time Schonewille did not mind in the least. He had partaken of a reasonable meal and had found a pleasant enough drinking companion, a Waffen SS captain who, after being severely wounded in the battle for the Kursk salient, had volunteered for work with one of the SS commando units that roamed the east slaughtering any ethnic group the Reich deemed to be inferior.

After much swapping of stories and much vodka and schnapps they had parted as friends, the way drunks usually do, with laughter, elaborate gestures and solicitous comments, each bidding the other "Schlafen sie gut". Surprisingly, his hangover in the morning was slight, but he did feel exceedingly seedy. Consequently, breakfast was light, with once slice of bread and three cups of coffee. By the time his VW Kübelwagen arrived   his hangover had gone, though the seediness remained.

It was raining, a slight drizzle emanating from a grey leaden sky. The water drops were mixed with a light soot and the air had the pungent odour of burning. The ovens were working full blast as usual.

They crossed over the River Sala and turned left and then almost immediately turned right but, to his surprise instead of turning left again down the road that would have taken him to the Auschwitz main camp, or Auschwitz 1 as it was officially known, the Volkswagen continued straight on towards the huge Birkenau camp, or Auschwitz 2.

Schonewille disliked this complex. Strangely, he did not have any feelings one way or another about camp one or the many other camps he visited on his rounds. Here, Birkenau's main function was death. It was in this place that the gas chambers and ovens were situated and it was here that Sophia would have ended if she had boarded one of the notorious cattle-trains that carried those Jews to the camp. It had been relatively easy to create papers to take her from the holding centre, but from here it would have been impossible.

In a strange unfathomable way this incredibly evil charnel house touched at something buried deep in a corner of his soul and he always left it feeling depressed and slightly nauseous. Maybe it was the smell, though all the camps had an odour and he always made sure that he put on plenty of cologne before entering their confines. Or maybe it was the constant falling soot and ash that one SS officer had called the black winter of death. He did not know, nor did he try to analyse the feeling. To do so would have lifted the lid, ever so slightly, on his conscience.

They drove between the huts of the main SS barracks and turned left down a short, narrow, well-maintained road. On either side were more huts. These were the administration buildings and the office of the camp commandant. The Kübelwagen slowed down and finally halted in front of a path leading to one of the buildings. Although it had stopped raining Schonewille hurried to the front door and let himself in. The room was well-lit with three empty desks and their accompanying chairs arranged in an L formation. A shortish, thick-set sergeant with the pock-marked residue of a long-gone acne scaring his face was in the act of putting on an overcoat. He straightened at Schonewille's entrance and immediately saluted, at the same time offering a lukewarm smile whose brilliance was dimmed further by the NCO's lack of front teeth.

"Wo ist der Kommandant?" Schonewille demanded curtly, deigning himself to return the salute.

The man shook his head. "Ich weiss nicht, Herr Obersturmbannführer."

Just then a door on the far side of the room opened and an SS captain walked in, calling a greeting, before stopping and saluting.

"My dear Obersturmbannführer, let me congratulate you on your new rank. A well-deserved promotion, no doubt."

Schonewille had met the other man at a previous visit to the camp though he had no feeling about him one way or another. His greeting therefore was curt.

"Thank you, Hauptsturmführer Eicke. Now, where is the Kommandant? I want to get my business completed and be back on my way to Berlin as soon as possible. I have an important meeting there," he added to reinforce his wish to leave as soon as possible.

The younger man shook his head. "I am sorry, Herr Obersturmbannführer. The Kommandant had to go to the Farben plant again early this morning. A problem with the standard of prisoners they have recently received. He just rang through to give his apologies. He has been delayed and it may be several hours before he returns." Eicke shook his head apologetically and went on. "But, no matter. I have full authority to attend to the matter at hand and rest assured you will find all the paperwork in order."

In reality Schonewille did not care who handed him the paperwork. He had little regard for Kommandant Höss and found his ponderous enthusiasm and constant acclamations of what a fine job he was doing both unnecessary and boring.

He nodded his head in agreement and the SS captain ushered him into another room before motioning him to sit in a chair in front of a large ornate desk. On the far wall underneath a portrait of Hitler was a large free-standing safe, and it was to this that Eicke crossed.

He chatted on while opening the safe and marshalling the required documents. Schonewille hardly responded. In reality he hardly heard what the man was saying, his thoughts were far away. Irritably he snapped, "Das ist unglaublich. I expected the papers to be ready and waiting."

Eicke stopped talking and looked over enquiringly. He was a good-looking man with soft, boyish features and blue eyes. His close-cropped blonde hair heightened rather than detracted from his rather effeminate looks while his gestures and hand movements were those of an artist rather than a soldier.

He shrugged his shoulders and lifted both palms upwards in a gesture of supplication. He was unsure of Schonewille and did not know how to pander to the older man's obvious irritation.

He spoke softly, but with an aggrieved tone. "Mein Freund. The papers are in order. Here they are. I have not kept you waiting and

67

there is really no hurry. The next train for Berlin does not leave for almost three hours. At any rate I have a treat for you. No, it is a surprise that will keep," he went on hurriedly as Schonewille raised his eyebrows and opened his mouth to speak.

Schonewille did not apologise, but nodded his head in agreement and held out his hands for the papers. There was silence for a few minutes as he studied the figures. The total was impressive and included four kilograms of gold. It amounted to a lot of teeth. Schonewille commented on the haul.

Eicke explained proudly that everybody had been working overtime and for the month of October just over 33,000 people had been exterminated. Schonewille asked where the dead had originated from.

"Theresienstadt, Herr Obersturmbannführer."

Schonewille nodded his head. He had only been to the camp once. He smiled in memory. Theresienstadt had been formed as part of an elaborate hoax. It was designed as a holding camp for Jews and was used as a showpiece for observers from the neutral countries and the Red Cross. In fact a propaganda film was even made about the supposedly wonderful conditions at the camp and used to counteract the growing claims around the world that the concentration camps were being used to exterminate the Jews. Now with the Reich's frontiers crumbling, this Czech camp was being denuded of all its inhabitants, who were being railed to Auschwitz and herded straight into the gas chambers.

After checking the figures and signing the appropriate forms, Schonewille approved the transportation of the loot and placed the papers in his attaché case.

"Gut, gut, alles in ordnung," he nodded his head, giving the captain a thin smile.

Eicke returned the smile a trifle nervously, paused for a moment and then as if making up his mind about something slid open a drawer from the desk and extracted a thick folded piece of paper. He paused again and then pushed it across the desk. The other took the package with a questioning look.

It was actually pale green blotting paper folded to create a small oblong parcel some twelve centimetres by eight centimetres. He unfolded the paper to reveal five cut diamonds. Not one was smaller than two carats and one, a superb stone which, despite the poor backdrop and indifferent light, sparkled with a brilliant intensity, was probably just over three carats.

Schonewille looked up questioningly and Eicke with no expression on his face explained how they had been found in the anus of a dead Jewess and the Kommandant had left them for the SS colonel. The word gift was not mentioned.

Schonewille cursed inwardly. There was no doubt it was a bribe, but for what? With Höss not present, no such request could be forthcoming, so he decided to accept the gift. Nevertheless, he protected himself.

"Wonderful. They will help the Reich's war effort. Better than on some fat Jewess, eh? I will see they are passed onto the Reichsbank. Thank the Kommandant for his diligence." He placed the package in his tunic pocket and stood up. To change the subject he said, "Now, what about this surprise?"

Eicke nodded his head and motioned for Schonewille to follow. They left the building and passed through a number of electrified fences into the main part of the camp. They were joined by two guards armed with machine pistols. As they walked down a road between the various camps and their wooden huts he suddenly heard a muffled sound, a moaning wail heightening in intensity. He felt the hairs on his neck start to rise and after a moment asked what the noise was. Eicke answered disinterestedly. One of the guards even went so far as to give a smirk.

"Oh, that must be a gassing at crematorium five. As you know number four was put out of action by some Sonderkommando Jews during the mass escape attempt on the seventh of October. Now we're too far away to hear anything from the other gas chambers, so it must be number five."

As they continued to walk towards the source of the noise Schonewille began to sweat. Eicke turned and they were let through a gate into one of the men's camps. The smell that wafted through the buildings was rank. A combination of sweat, disease and excrement, which had combined to give a powerful all pervading odour that hung about the camp like a poisonous cloud.

Schonewille knew he would have to have his uniform carefully washed to get rid of the smell, which was already permeating the fabric.

They passed between two huts to a cleared area. There were five men standing to attention. Two guards, one holding a leashed Alsatian and three emaciated skeletons dressed in the striped remnants of the prisoner's uniform. Eicke turned his head with an indulgent smile.

"There you are, Herr Obersturmbannführer. I know how you like to use your automatic on certain prisoners. Well, I have personally selected three political prisoners for you." He surveyed the three wrecks in disgust and said vehemently. "Useless bourgeois pigs."

Schonewille stood for a moment uncertain what to do. He was not in the mood for any killing. The noise of those choking in the nearby gas chamber had unnerved him and although it had now ended, he wanted to leave as quickly as possible. He turned away, shaking his head. Then one of the prisoners spoke in a thin quavering voice. "Friedrich. Mein Gott, is that you Friedrich?"

Schonewille swung round and peered at the man. He looked searchingly into his face, but did not recognise him, something which in the circumstances was not surprising. The man was thin and stooped with eyes sunk deep into his skull. The skin was yellow and blotchy with two festering sores under his left eye. His age was indeterminate.

"Friedrich, Friedrich Schonewille, is it you?" the prisoner repeated. His uncertainty caused his voice to drop to a whisper and a dribble of yellow saliva appeared on his lips. In the background Eicke laughed.

"He seems to know you, Herr Obersturmbannführer."

Schonewille ignored him, but the prisoner heard Eicke's words and said pleadingly, "Danke Gott. It is you Friedrich. It's your old friend, Carl Wilmersdorf."

With those words the prisoner sealed his own death warrant. Wilmersdorf had been a friend of the family, or rather a friend of Schonewille's mother. He had been a prominent banker and had even served for four years in the Reichstag in the days of the old

Weimer Republic. Though married with five children, he had a reputation as a ladies man. He had taken it upon himself to act as Inger Schonewille's financial adviser and confidant after her divorce, and she soon repaid him by becoming his mistress.

Young Friedrich had found them one afternoon in his mother's bedroom. The sight and sounds of his mother moaning under the thrusting form of the banker was too much for the boy and he had nursed an abiding hatred of the man ever since. Over the years Wilmersdorf had tried to ingratiate himself into the lad's affections, but to no avail. Finally, to ease the situation, his mother refused to allow Wilmersdorf in the house if young Friedrich was home or expected for a visit.

Schonewille did not answer the man. He extracted the Walther and quickly screwed the silencer onto the barrel. Cocking the weapon, he held it at arm's length until the snout of the silencer was only inches away from the man's left temple. A moment's fear and panic showed in the banker's eyes and then with a sigh he said, "Danke Friedrich, you are going to help me escape from hell, you..."

The words were cut short as Schonewille pulled the trigger. There was a small cough from the Walther and the right side of Wilmersdorf's head erupted as the heavy-calibre nine-millimetre bullet blew his brains out. The man standing next to him was spattered with blood, brain tissue and bits of bone, though he hardly flinched. The body fell to the ground, twitched for a second and then was still.

Still holding the smoking automatic, Schonewille swung around and snapped to Eicke, "Let us leave. You can have the rest to yourself."

As he strode away Eicke motioned to one of the guards who nonchalantly lifted the barrel of his machine pistol and emptied the entire thirty-two-round clip into the two remaining prisoners. Eicke hurried after Schonewille. He caught up and was about to say something, but the look on the older man's face made him stop.

They walked in silence back to the office of the camp Kommandant and it was only when they were inside that Schonewille busied himself with unscrewing the silencer and putting it and the weapon away in their respective holsters.

With a curt Dankeschön, Schonewille gathered up his briefcase and left the office, ignoring the salute of the sergeant with the pock-marked face.

Once back in the hotel Schonewille stripped, had a bath and washed his hair. As usual he had brought a spare uniform with him and he put it on, thankful of its clean smell. Unfortunately his cap still carried the odour of the camp and since he did not carry a spare there was nothing he could do about it.

The car that had delivered him back to the hotel was still waiting and after checking out he was driven to the station. Surprisingly, the train was on time. It took exactly sixteen hours before the exhausted and irritable SS leutnant-colonel alighted onto the Berlin platform.

The station master's office was warm and the leather armchair in the corner of the room though old and cracked was supple and comfortable. He was left alone. The day shift station master did not enter the office and although the phone rang several times no one came to answer it. Schonewille let it ring. In a perverse way he was determined that as many people as possible were inconvenienced that morning.

Just after seven he roused himself from the seat and opened the office door. The corridor was deserted. Obviously everybody was keeping as wide a berth as possible to the irritable SS officer. Nobody wanted to end up on the Eastern Front.

He walked out onto the platform and looked around. It was still crowded with people and for a moment he looked in vain for a porter. Reluctantly he picked up his overnight bag and with his briefcase hanging from his other arm walked from the station. Here his luck changed. An ex-British army Humber staff car with SS number plates was just pulling away from the curb. Schonewille hailed the driver and on questioning him was told he had just dropped a General Somebody-or-Other off and was now on his way back to the underground garages behind Hitler's bunker near the Reichskanzlei. Seizing the opportunity, he ordered the driver to take him to the Reichsbank.

On entering the bank he was shown into Heger's office. His old friend looked tired and was obviously nervous. He scarcely returned the SS officer's greeting and looked askance at his appearance.

"Himmel Friedrich. You look like you have slept in your uniform and you could have shaved. Our meeting is most ..."

Schonewille waved his arm in irritation and cut him off. "Shut up Klaus. That is just what I have done. I've spent God knows how many hours in a stinking train. I'm tired, bad-tempered and I want a bath. So let us get this meeting with your mysterious man over and done with." Heger opened his mouth, but then decided to say nothing other than a curt "Come with me, please."

Schonewille followed him wordlessly down a number of corridors. Finally, they stopped in front of a large ornate oak door, the wood dark with age. He presumed it was the office of the bank's senior vice-president, Emil Puhl. Heger paused for a moment and then gave a hesitant knock.

"Bitte," a voice answered.

They stepped inside.

It was a large office, well-furnished, though with the black-out curtains still closed, a trifle dark and gloomy. The central room light was on but its glow was not sufficient to open up the whole room and the corners and walls were left in shadows. At the far end of the room, facing them, was a tall man dressed in an SS uniform. Heger edged further into the room and addressed the stranger.

"Herr Brigadeführer, let me introduce Obersturmbannführer Schonewille."

The man stepped forward and extended his hand. Schonewille first clicked his heels and saluted before taking the proffered hand.

The grip was strong and the hand full of calluses. Schonewille's brain, which was working overtime, found this strange since the Brigadier General's Waffenfarbe on his shoulder straps was coloured red, which meant he was in the legal division. Therefore, he was either an SS Fachführer or Sonderführer and not a front-line soldier. With his rank it was unlikely he engaged in any manual work, so why the calluses? His uniform was immaculate and he wore the Iron Cross first class plus a number of other decorations. Schonewille put his age at about fifty and a fit, strong fifty at that.

What worried him was that he did not recognise the general.

"Brigadeführer Emil Grauwitz," the man said formally. He looked at the lieutenant-colonel carefully, noting his rather unkempt appearance. Schonewille, interpreting the look explained the reason, while at the same time desperately searching his memory for any details of the man standing in front of him.

Grauwitz was an imposing figure. His height was backed up by a solid frame and there seemed not an inch of surplus flesh on him. He had a high forehead, accentuated by a severely receding hairline and a fine Patrician nose. The eyes in the half-light appeared black, the same colour as his hair. Schonewille mentally told himself to beware. He still could not place the officer and this fact bothered him. It put him at a grave disadvantage. He was irritated, but like the man in front did not let a trace of expression cross his face. In contrast, Heger's face showed nervous concern as he looked from one man to the other.

Grauwitz motioned Schonewille to a high-backed lounge chair and took a seat on a similar piece of furniture opposite. After a moment's hesitation Heger filled a third such chair, though he strategically positioned himself mid-way between the two.

Grauwitz folded his arms and lifted his chin arrogantly as he stared at Schonewille. The room went quiet as the stare continued for four or five seconds. Heger started to speak, but the general raised one wrist without unfolding his arms. Finally he spoke.

"Well, Herr Obersturmbannführer, what do you think of our little ploy?" It was a leading question and it left Schonewille with little room to manoeuvre. So, he answered just as directly.

"I think it is an interesting situation, Herr Gruppenführer. We are like a trio of mice salting away some cheese before the cat gets us. The trouble is this cheese does not belong to us and in reality we are all thieves."

Grauwitz raised his eyebrows and gave a hint of a smile. "And how will we get our cheese out of the Reich?"

Schonewille hesitated. He was about to lie, but he had a vague feeling of being played with. He took a calculated risk and looked directly at the other man.

"I think we will have to fly the cheese out. In fact, I have already put something in motion to that effect," he said quietly. Then he took a stab in the dark. "But of course, Herr Brigadeführer, you would be aware of that." His intonation made it a statement of fact, not a question and it had an immediate effect on Grauwitz. For a moment he looked slightly surprised, though he attempted to hide the emotion under a thin smile. He nodded his head.

"You are much wiser than I gave you credit for, Obersturmbannführer. I was intrigued at your moves to contact your brother and now I wonder how you knew I was checking up on you. You might have guessed, but either way I now realise I will have to be very careful in my dealings with you. I'm not sure whether your intelligence is a good or bad thing." He paused for a moment. "At any rate only time will tell."

Heger sat in bemused silence. He again opened his mouth to speak and again Grauwitz cut him short. "In a moment, Klaus. Now, Obersturmbannführer, tell me ... Where would you like to fly to?"

Schonewille shook his head. "I am not sure; at least, not yet," he lied.

He already had a good idea of where he wanted to go, but there were three reasons why he did not want to reveal the possible destination. Firstly, he was not sure of the feasibility of his plan. Secondly, he was certain the general had his own ideas of where the plane should fly to and thirdly, he wanted to keep something up his sleeve. He did not trust Brigadeführer Emil Grauwitz.

Chapter Six

Schonewille sat across the chair so that he could rest against the brick wall of the restaurant. It had once been the wine cellar of the establishment, which had been forced to move its tables underground by the bombing.

In this position he could see the entrance and spot his brother when he arrived. Not only would it give him a few more moments in which to decide on how to greet the flier but, more importantly, how to bring him in on the plan, something he had not yet decided. He glanced at his watch, irritated by the delay. Wenck was already fifteen minutes late.

He let his mind wander back to the morning's meeting with Grauwitz. The man worried him. He now knew that what transpired with his half brother would be vital. What was cause for concern was that his own plan was still only partly formulated. There were too many loose ends and it would depend to a large degree on the coming discussion on whether the plan would actually be feasible. Instinctively he knew he would have to be completely open with Wenck if he was to obtain his help, and this was against both his nature and experience.

On reading the flier's record he realised just how little he knew of the man. Not for the first time he wished they had been closer. Perversely, he had always wanted to be friends, but as with his relationship with their father, he had turned them both away with his attitude and rudeness.

There was a stir at the steps that led down from the surface. He felt rather than saw his brother so it was not until he actually sighted Wenck being led to his table by an elderly waiter that he knew for certain it was him.

Most of the patrons were senior officers and party members with their wives and mistresses. There was only a sprinkling of younger fighting men. In reality, though, it was not Wenck's youth, but the Knight's Cross at his throat which caused much of the murmured comment. Although he was aware of the decoration and the reason for it being awarded, Schonewille still felt a moment's twinge of jealousy. He realised that against its aura of bravery his Iron Cross was a mere bauble, yet he was grateful nevertheless that it was pinned to his tunic.

He rose to greet his brother, extending his hand with a smile. Schonewille outranked Wenck, yet he was surprised when the flier saluted him before grasping the proffered palm. Schonewille smiled again. This time it was less forced.

He motioned to the chair and wordlessly they sat down. For a moment the silence continued as they searched each other's face. Schonewille was aware that many of the people seated nearby were staring at them. He began to wish they had chosen a less conspicuous place. The pilot was the first to speak.

"Well, older brother. What's this all about then?"

His directness caught Schonewille off guard. For a moment he did not know how to answer. He attempted to say something, but to his annoyance began to stutter.

To his relief Wenck saved him from further embarrassment. "I'm sorry, Friedrich. I did not mean to be quite so direct. It's just that I'm not used to playing around and I've had a long day. I only landed late this morning and I discovered they've lost part of my kit. Then I found there was nowhere for me to stay." He laughed, a harsh sound that contained little mirth. "Shit, Berlin is a mess. Haven't been here for more than a year. I knew it was bad but I cannot believe the devastation." He shook his head and fell silent and looked around before continuing. This time, though, he dropped his voice. "The Allies are certainly giving it back in spades, aren't they?" He looked directly at his brother.

This was just the tack Schonewille wanted the conversation to take, so he answered without hesitation. "That is right, Peter. We are being hit very hard, grievously I think, and that is why you are here. There is something I want to discuss with you, but let us wait for a little while. We have much to catch up on first."

He motioned over the waiter and went on. "For Berlin, the menu is quite good. I have even been able to procure a bottle of champagne. A thirty-four, though only of average quality I'm afraid, but beggars cannot be choosers as the saying goes."

After ordering, Schonewille made another move to try and cement their relationship. "I must congratulate you Peter on your Knight's Cross. And with Oak Leaves as well. The Fatherland is proud of you." He spoke without rancour.

Wenck congratulated him in return. "Oh, I don't know. I think it is easier to get a decoration in the air. There is much more chance for glory. Father told me you got your bit of metal in some brawl on the Eastern Front. Well done."

Schonewille warmed to the words. Maybe they could get on, he thought. While they exchanged pleasantries, he ran his mind back over what he had read of his brother's service record and what he himself knew of the man.

Wenck had actually learned to fly in America. He had been taught by their father who had spent six months attached to the German embassy in Washington during 1937. It was natural, therefore, that eventually he would be drafted into the Luftwaffe. During much of 1938 the elder Wenck was despatched to a number of European countries, including England, in order to gain as much intelligence as possible about their air defences. Peter Wenck had stayed with his parents because he liked travelling and although he loved flying and intended to be an airman, he was not yet sure the German Air Force was the sort of career he wanted. Pylon racing and record breaking were more his line.

On returning to Germany in May 1939 the decision was made for him, though he went willingly enough. Since he did not actually start flight training immediately it was not until a year later that he joined his first operational squadron in France, just in time for the Battle of Britain.

Although his flying had been rated as extraordinary, his gunnery was barely average and this, coupled with his rather free spirit, had meant his instructors had earmarked him for bombers. They reasoned that the discipline of looking after a crew and the necessary tactics of flying a twin-engined bomber would curb his impetuousness and be the best way to make him a useful member of the Luftwaffe. In effect it was a stupid move for he had just the right skill and temperament to be a fighter pilot (not withstanding his shooting ability).

Nevertheless, despite themselves, the authorities gained a highly effective weapon for the Fatherland.

Effective he might ultimately have become, but his career almost ended before it began. In early August 1940 he was part of a raiding force of Heinkel He 111s, which was attacked by fighters shortly after crossing the English coast near Ipswich. The escorting Messerschmitt Me 110s were engaged by a squadron of Spitfires and had consequently been too busy defending themselves to pay heed to their charges. This left the way open for two squadrons of Hurricanes to attack the loaded, lumbering bombers. Warned by radar and with the sun on their backs, the British fighters dived on the Heinkels with a cold ferocity that split their tight defensive formation.

Two Hurricanes latched onto Wenck and proceeded to use their combined firepower of sixteen Brownings to cut him to pieces. Their first pass killed his mid-upper-gunner and the wireless operator. Their second killed the navigator, destroyed half the instrument panel and put a piece of 303 bullet into his left thigh.

In desperation he had flung the Heinkel downward, twisting and turning in a vain effort to elude his tormentors. It was to no avail, yet somehow, for the next seven or eight minutes he managed to keep the big bomber out of their reach. He yelled for the belly gunner to take over the mid-upper defensive position and then, using every ounce of his prodigious skill proceeded to manoeuvre his aircraft around every obstacle he could find. Tall trees and buildings, electricity pylons and hills were all aimed for and dodged by the barest margin.

The British pilots were faced with a difficult proposition. If they stayed above the Heinkel and tried to dive down on him, there was a chance that they might lose him when they pulled back into a climb, or turned away. If they followed him they could only do so line astern since at that height it was impossible to conduct a co-ordinated attack from two directions. The line astern route also meant only one aircraft at a time could bring its guns to bear. This was made even worse because, for much of the time, they had to fly defensively in case they ran into one of the obstructions that Wenck cleverly placed in their path.

The upshot was that both Hurricanes finally ran out of ammunition. With their fuel also running low, much to their chagrin, they had to disengage and leave the battered German bomber to head back out across the English Channel.

Exhausted, weak from loss of blood and with no navigator to guide him, Wenck nursed his sick aircraft back to his base in Northern France. Just before he reached the coast one engine gave up and he was forced to struggle the remaining eighty kilometres back to the aerodrome.

Despite this added handicap he landed without further incident and managed to taxi to the dispersals area. Later, while in hospital, the squadron adjutant informed him that his ground crew had counted 143 bullet holes in his plane.

That sortie saw an end to his part in the Battle of Britain.

The Hurricanes had decimated his squadron, destroying eight aircraft and damaging to varying degrees the remainder. On being repaired the aircraft were attached to another squadron, which shared the airfield and were sent back into the fray. By the end of the week only two of the original crews were left. The rest were either dead or prisoners-of-war.

At any rate, the squadron had virtually ceased to exist, so the survivors were sent back to Germany to form the nucleus of a new Kampfgeschwader.

In the meantime Wenck was flat on his back. The loss of blood had so weakened his system that he contracted pneumonia and was forced to stay in hospital for just over two weeks. He was then sent back to Germany for a month's rest and recuperation. This was followed by six weeks attached to an operational training unit helping new pilots gain experience on more advanced aircraft.

The second day of 1941 saw him once again in the cockpit of an operational Heinkel He 111. This time he was bound for an airfield just outside Vienna. The first half of the year meant the Yugoslav and Greek campaigns, which gave him the necessary combat experience and sharp edge to enable him to survive when the Luftwaffe took on the might of Russia.

The following eighteen months were a kaleidoscope of events

that were the everyday life for a bomber pilot on the Russian Front. He lost count of the number of airfields he flew from and the number of sorties he engaged in. Only the terse, truncated reports in his log book and odd photograph or two helped him recall the events that had taken place. That was until Stalingrad.

The winter of 1942/43, the second their forces had spent in Russia, became a nightmare. The Germans, after their success of 1942, were now so deep inside Russia that the Wehrmacht and the Luftwaffe were severely stretched to hold what they had gained, let alone keep going on the offensive. Yet, this is what they were forced to do. The Red Army, despite the terrible battering it had suffered, was far from defeated and was quickly building its strength. The sheer size of the country meant the Russian forces could retreat and retreat until the exhausted Axis forces outran their supply lines and were too stretched to continue.

Like most bomber squadrons, Wenck's was forced to alternate between flying operational bombing missions against the Russian forces that had surrounded General von Paulus's troops in Stalingrad, and supplying the beleaguered garrison from the air. More than 330,000 men from two German and two Rumanian armies were trapped and Reichsmarschall Göring ordered the Luftwaffe to keep them supplied from the air. It was an impossible task.

By the time von Paulus's V1 Army finally capitulated on 2 February 1943, Wenck and what remained of his squadron were exhausted. Short of equipment, tired beyond reason and with their morale beginning to suffer, they were temporarily withdrawn from the front.

It was at this time when Wenck's star began to ascend. Up to that point he was regarded as a brilliant pilot with a great deal of luck. His record, though, was laced with incidents of insubordination and a history of doing things his own way. The former, although minor in nature had hindered his promotion, but the latter had undoubtedly saved his life.

Wenck's rest lasted all of five days. He had spent the entire time sleeping, so when he was ordered to join a new squadron there was at least a veneer of calm and strength over the previous week's exhaustion.

His new squadron was Fern-Kampfgeschwader 50, which had been operating the new Heinkel He 177 Greif bomber from Zaporozhe on transport missions to Stalingrad.

Though very advanced and with a good performance, the Greif was a major disappointment to the German Air Force. Conceived as a long-range bomber it suffered a protracted gestation period and an unenviable reputation for unreliability and for catching fire. Its propensity to ignite was so bad that it gained the nickname Luftwaffenfeuerzeug, or the Luftwaffe's petrol lighter. The reason for this was its complicated power units. In order to save drag and increase manoeuvrability, the German designer gave the aircraft coupled engines – two liquid-cooled engines mounted side-by-side on each wing with a single gear case connecting the two crank cases and the two crankshaft pinions driving a single airscrew shaft. This arrangement had a propensity to overheat and boil its oil. The engine's connecting rod bearings would then disintegrate with a fire the subsequent result.

Despite these problems the Greif was fast, heavily armed and with a very long range, and it was the latter that gave him the vast experience that would be so valuable in the flight to America and later, in his plans with Schonewille.

On joining FKG 50 Wenck discovered that some of the giant bombers, as well as having been used as transport aircraft, had been modified in the field with a fifty-millimetre BK 5 anti tank gun mounted in the ventral gondola. Thus armed, they had been used as a ground attack aircraft in between transport duties.

To Wenck it was a waste of a fine aircraft. Although he had never flown the Greif, or any other multi-engined plane of similar size, the conversion took less than a week and his squadron commander quickly realised Kapitän Wenck was undoubtedly a natural.

Never reticent about putting his ideas forward, the new recruit suggested the plane was being wasted and why was it not being used for what it had been intended. The answer was if Wenck could come up with a proper strategy and a suitable target then he could have the honour of leading the first raid.

Wenck's squadron commander, a dour man, obviously recognised some peculiar qualities in this newest recruit and his comments were not meant to be as sardonic as they appeared.

Wenck spent two days with German intelligence choosing suitable targets deep inside Russia, but his first mission almost never went ahead. With the spring thaw approaching and the German's reeling from their losses at Stalingrad, the Red Army went on the offensive, pushing the Axis forces back towards the Dniepr River. By the middle of February they had recovered Kharkov and had moved as far east as Novomoskovsk. The Luftwaffe High Command faced with the Russian steamroller was forced to think tactically rather than strategically. All aircraft were needed to attack the build-up of Russian troops rather than hit targets far behind the lines.

Nevertheless Wenck, backed up by his squadron commander and several key intelligence experts, gave a very detailed written submission explaining how even a series of small raids deep inside Russia would, quite apart from damaging important factories and halting their production, cause vital fighter aircraft to be pulled back from the front. Reluctantly and a little dubiously, the High Command gave him permission to assemble a raiding force of no more than six aircraft and ordered him to succeed, or else.

On 20 February 1943, the Wehrmacht under General von Manstein began a major counter attack to not only stabilise the front but to also throw the Red Army off guard and re-capture territory. That same night Wenck took off with three other Heinkel He 177s from an airfield just north of Orel, which in turn was some 200 kilometres north of Kursk. His destination was a factory complex at Ufa, deep in the Ural Mountains.

At the time Ufa was almost 1,500 kilometres from the front and had never seen a German aircraft let alone a force of four German heavy bombers. The Junkers JU 86P high altitude reconnaissance plane that had made two photographic missions over the complex late in January had never even been heard, let alone seen.

Wenck and his raiders reached the town in the soft dawn of the winter's early morning light and found their target quite easily. Between them they dropped 9,000 kilograms of bombs on the factories from a low height, completely destroying one and severely damaging a second. They returned to base without incident.

The following night, again with four aircraft. Wenck returned to Ufa, but this time the target was covered with fog forcing them to drop their bombs blind. On the return journey one of the Greifs suffered engine failure and caught fire. After a short struggle to stay in the air, it turned, lost height and cart-wheeled into the ground near the town of Penza. There were no parachutes.

The third raid was aborted when another two Greifs caught fire, one crashing with the loss of its entire crew and the second just managing to stagger back to base.

Two days later Wenck tried something even more ambitious. Just after three in the morning his heavily loaded bomber staggered into the air heading for the town of Sverdlovsk in the northern Urals, a distance of almost 1,700 kilometres. His target was a ball-bearing factory. Although this time his offensive load was small because of the need to carry as much petrol as possible, his bomb aimer managed to land two 500 kilogram projectiles right in the middle of the complex.

The return, however, was not as easy. Some 300 kilometres from the front the starboard engine broke. Luckily, this time the fire extinguishers worked and there were no flames. With engine temperatures rising on the two port engines Wenck had to throttle back to stop them also failing. The crew were forced to jettison as much loose equipment they could lay their hands on in order to save weight. Oxygen bottles, ammunition, some of the guns and some fittings were all thrown overboard. It was in this weakened state that the Russian fighters found them. The three Loavochkinn 5 fighters managed two passes and were setting themselves up for the kill when some FW 190s arrived. Before being rescued half of Wenck's crew were either killed or wounded. Despite this, he managed to bring the badly damaged plane back to its home base.

It was the last long-range Russian raid undertaken by him. Although it had been a strategic success and the German propaganda machine played it up for all it was worth, the Luftwaffe High Command didn't have the resources, the technical expertise or the will to mount further raids of this type in Russia.

All their energies were taken up by providing their hard pressed army with effective ground support on the front-line.

At any rate, Wenck was vindicated and lionised for his skill and bravery. The subsequent Knight's Cross of the Iron Cross was presented personally by Hermann Göring. At the same time his far-sighted attitude was also noticed and on March 11 he was transferred back to Germany to begin testing some of Germany's secret aircraft including the big Junkers 390.

While Schonewille ruminated on his brother's service record the airman lit a cigarette, pushed his cap back on his head, swivelled around in his chair and insolently surveyed the other guests.

Catching the eye of a pretty girl, he winked and then smiled as her middle-aged escort scowled in return. The exchange made the SS officer uncomfortable and again he wondered whether he had chosen the right place for their meeting. His brother's decoration and haughty manner were like a magnet and they were the centre of attention. For a moment he felt like telling his younger brother to behave, but wisely thought better of it.

The first course was a potato and leek soup served with some half-decent bread. Faced with a cure for his appetite, Peter Wenck gave up ogling the girls and after a while the surrounding people lost interest in them, although a few women glanced their way every so often. Schonewille began to relax.

When the soup was finished, Wenck once more began to question Schonewille.

"You were saying something about why I am back in dear old Berlin?"

Schonewille glanced around before speaking, his voice low.

Wenck noticed the look and also lowered his voice. "Well, what's it about then?"

Schonewille hesitated. Now that it had come to the crunch he was not sure how to start the conversation. He was saved for a moment by the waiter who appeared at their table and refilled their glasses. He had scarcely walked away when the main course arrived. Schonewille could never remember having been served so quickly and guessed the Knight's Cross was the cause for this solicitous and rapid service.

The urge to eat was stronger than his curiosity and Wenck let the matter drop while he tackled his plate. In the meantime, Schonewille gathered his thoughts. When the food was consumed, Schonewille motioned over the waiter and told them they would wait for a while before having their dessert and that they wished to be left in peace. The waiter nodded in understanding and left them alone.

"Before I start I want to ask you one question," began Schonewille. "Then I will tell you what I am engaged in, or rather what I am planning." There was a movement at the next table as its occupants got up to leave. Good, thought Schonewille, now there was no chance of them being overheard. He returned his gaze to his brother, cocked his head to one side and lifted his eyebrows in an unspoken question. Wenck nodded his head in return.

"Now then Peter, tell me truthfully. How do you think the war is going?"

Wenck hesitated for a moment, gave a quick furtive look around him and then, speaking quietly, said, "Shit Friedrich, you don't have to be von Rundstedt to work that out. Unless the Führer pulls something out of his hat, or the Allies and the Russians fall out, I give us six months at the most."

"If that is the case, brother, what do you intend to do?"

Wenck moodily shrugged his shoulders and shook his head. "I don't know, never given it much thought. Just surviving has been my main priority."

Schonewille chose his words carefully. He explained how he was part of a group of three men who were setting up a false bank account with a view to withdrawing the money when and if it looked like Germany was about to be defeated. He covered the plan in some detail, leaving out only two factors: where the money was coming from and his role in the running of the concentration camps.

For a moment Wenck was silent. Although he tried not to show it he was genuinely surprised. Finally, he enquired as to what his role would be.

"It is simple. I need somebody I can trust to fly the money out of the country and help me plan a suitable destination."

While he was speaking, Schonewille was carefully surveying the surrounding guests. To his horror he recognised the tall figure of Brigadeführer Emil Grauwitz appear at the bottom of the steps accompanied by another SS officer. The shock must have registered on his face, because his brother immediately asked him what was wrong.

Schonewille shook his head. "I'm not sure, but I want you to leave, now! No, please don't ask any questions. Just go. And if you can, meet me at my apartment in an hour."

He hurriedly scribbled down his address on a piece of paper and passed it to Wenck. The air force officer nodded his head, pocketed the address and nonchalantly stood up. He then strode to the stairs. In ten seconds he had disappeared.

His brother took a deep breath and then motioned the waiter over; at the same time glancing over to where Grauwitz and his companion were now seated. The SS brigadier was looking over in his direction, but when Schonewille caught his eye there was no flicker of recognition. After a moment, Grauwitz went back to perusing the menu.

The waiter arrived and Schonewille asked for the bill. Dropping the required number of bank notes on the table, he stood up. As he walked towards the stairs he had to pass quite close to the two men. Obviously, he could not ignore them; that would be suspicious. So he saluted and greeted the general.

Grauwitz nodded, returned Schonewille's salute and wished him a pleasant evening. Then he turned his attention to his dinner companion. Schonewille escaped up the stairs.

. Once he was out in the street, he paused. He half expected to find a car outside and would not have been surprised if he had been arrested. But, there was no car and no arrest. He strode away and as he hurried through the pitch black streets he wondered whether the appearance of Grauwitz had been premeditated or just chance. Whichever, he realised from now on he would have to be very careful, for as well as not trusting Grauwitz, Schonewille had his own ideas about how the Reichsbank's money was to be transported out of Germany and he doubted whether the general would agree.

Now that he had calmed down, he realised his decision to leave the restaurant was rather hasty. After all, Grauwitz obviously knew about his brother, he had virtually said as much when they had met at the Reichsbank. Yet, he still wondered why Grauwitz had turned up. If it had been pre-meditated, the question was why. There was no need to show how suspicious and devious he was. He had already shown this side of the character. So why the appearance? Maybe it was just a coincidence.

Troubled, he hurried on.

Chapter Seven

The following afternoon Wenck boarded a FW200 transport at Tempelhof airport and flew back to Norway. It was raining and as the plane headed north through the clouds he ruminated on what had occurred over the past twenty-four hours. It had left him disturbed, worried but also very excited. Disturbed, since he was about to undertake something that was treasonable and worried because the outcome, if they were caught, was a firing squad. The excitement was simple. It gave him a way out of an increasingly hopeless situation: either death in the Barents Sea or a soldier of a defeated nation.

He had taken more than the requested hour to reach Schonewille's apartment. In fact it had taken more than twice that time and he could see how relieved his brother was to see him when he opened the door and hurriedly ushered him inside. There was no heating in the apartment and the room was quite cold. Nevertheless it was much warmer than outside and both men took off their jackets. Schonewille dragged out a bottle of schnapps and when they had both taken the prescribed mouthful they began to talk.

Schonewille explained why he had aborted their dinner. He had decided to take his brother even more fully into his confidence and reveal several other aspects of the, as yet, unfinished plan. The only things he did not discuss were the camps and Sophia. He judged, quite rightly, that the flier, like the majority of the population, did not fully realise the extent or the scope of the camps and what they really were. That all Germans knew there were places such as concentration camps was obvious, but their true purpose was beyond the average person's ability to comprehend. As far as his mistress was concerned, the reason was much more complex. He did not want to lose her, whether back to the camps or to the possible affections of another man.

Sophia was lying in bed upstairs. He had told her not to come down because he had a male visitor. He had not explained who his visitor was, nor why he was visiting the apartment. With her aversion to anything in uniform he knew she would not interrupt them.

Unbeknown to the SS man, however, was that the pilot had guessed there was a woman in the house, or at least that there had been a woman in the apartment recently. He could smell something feminine on the furnishings and could sense a woman's hand in the way the furniture was laid out and the neatness of the kitchen. Most probably a cleaning woman he mused, but not thinking it important, he kept his thoughts to himself.

At any rate, Wenck was a little unsure of himself and shocked at the turn of events. While he was not used to the Machiavellian ways of the SS like his brother, he was still aware of the deceit and cunning which, as always, was their stock in trade. Therefore, he was now beginning to be very cautious of what he said. At the same time, he already reasoned that his brother needed him not only because he was a pilot, but also because the SS officer had few friends. Therefore family, however distant, were perhaps the only people he could trust.

They had talked for almost three hours, the conversation so intense that it had left him with a mild headache.

At first his questions had mainly centred on what sort of money or valuables would be taken out of the Reichsbank. Schonewille said he favoured a mixture of American dollars, Swiss francs and, if possible, some gold bullion.

In turn his brother questioned him about aircraft, their range and accessibility. The more they talked, the more both realised how they were faced with a number of very difficult problems, any one of which could spell the end of the operation. There was also the omnipresent spectre of Grauwitz, who obviously had his own plans, most of which had not been passed onto Schonewille.

"Grauwitz told me he wanted to fly to Spain," said Schonewille. "And although he gave no other details of where he wanted to go from there, I believe his ultimate destination will probably be South America. There are many Nazi Party sympathisers in Argentina and Paraguay, so they are the logical choice. The question is, what will happen when we get there? I want this money for myself … I mean us," he corrected himself quickly and went on. "Quite bluntly, Peter, I do not trust him."

Out of curiosity Wenck asked who had actually ordered him from Norway. Schonewille told him how he had been owed a favour by a very senior Luftwaffe officer whose son, a junior SS officer, he had managed to get transferred from the Eastern Front to France. It had been a simple matter to have the order transmitted to Norway. Similarly, there was no problem as long as he returned to his squadron.

However, there was now the problem of how Wenck could be utilised any further. It was no simple matter to arrange long-term leave of absence for such an important air force major. Finally, they made a list of the problems they would have to overcome: How was Wenck to gain the freedom to help plan the operation? How could they obtain a suitable aircraft? Where could it be based, especially now that the Allies virtually controlled most of the air space over Germany? Who would actually withdraw the money from the Reichsbank? How would it be transported to their aircraft? Where and how could they obtain sufficient fuel for an aircraft with the range they needed? How far would Grauwitz actually take them into his confidence? What should their own destination be?

The more they discussed the issues the more they realised that they needed another ally. Someone who was senior enough to pull strings and open doors yet could be trusted to remain on their side. They both reached the same conclusion at the same time. Their father.

When the Condor landed at Oslo, Peter Wenck immediately contacted the general and was duly picked up by his father's staff car. They had lunch and discussed what had transpired over the past thirty-six hours. The older man frowned a lot and shook his head.

"Verdammt, I do not like it … it smells so bad I can almost taste it, but …" he paused for a moment and rested his chin on his clasped hands. "It has promise and maybe, just maybe, if I can utilise my authority and contacts properly, we might just pull it off and do so without Herr Grauwitz."

They talked at some length until Helmuth Wenck suddenly interrupted the flow of conversation. "There's one thing I cannot understand. Why has your brother been brought in on this mad scheme? Surely Grauwitz and that banker could look after the bank account by themselves without Friedrich's help. It does not make sense."

He looked questioningly at his son who shook his head and remarked that he had no idea, had in fact never even thought of the angle.

"I tell you what, Peter, I'll start by asking a few questions. I used to have pretty good contacts with the Abwehr, all us diplomats did, although, I now have to be careful since they have been absorbed into the SS."

The Abwehr had been the German Army's intelligence branch and had, until February 1944, operated completely separately and without any control by either the SS or the Gestapo. Its chief, Admiral Wilhelm Canaris, was a mysterious and devious professional spy who had hedged his bets in his relationship with the German High Command, especially in regard to the Führer and the SS. At first he was a diligent supporter of the regime, although as its excesses increased his support waned. By the middle of 1943, he could see the writing on the wall and increased his contacts with the small German Resistance. This grew until he became if not a fully fledged member then at least a benevolent spectator for the attempt on Hitler's life in July 1944.

"I used to know Canaris and his deputy Hans Oster, but I know both of them have been arrested. So I cannot go there. Still, there are a few people I can go to who can give me some off-the-record knowledge of Grauwitz and what he is and does," he said, rubbing his jaw reflectively. "I will also try and obtain some up-to-date information on your brother."

"You know, Father. For the first time, I felt some kinship with Friedrich. I even admired him for trying to put this ... this ..." he paused for loss of words.

"This fraud, bank robbery, call it what you will," Helmuth

Wenck interrupted. Peter Wenck smiled wryly and nodded his head. "Be that as it may, Peter. Friedrich belongs to a nasty organisation and I want to know more. I'll make some enquires first thing in the morning."

A short time later Peter Wenck left his father and reported to the station commander of the main Oslo aerodrome. The man was bad-tempered and furiously informed him that they had been trying to locate him for almost two hours.

"I am sorry, Herr Oberst, but I had to see my father, General Wenck. I had to pass on some information from Luftwaffe High Command." He lied easily, at the same time lightly fingering his shirt collar where the Knight's Cross nestled at his throat.

The gesture was not lost on the station commander who lowered his voice and said testily, "We have a replacement aircraft and some crew members for your squadron. You were supposed to leave this afternoon," he accused.

Wenck, eager to be away before any more questions were asked, assured him that if they left within half-an-hour he could make Trondheim by nightfall. Moments later he was hurrying over to one of the hangars with a sheaf of papers in one hand and his luggage in the other.

The replacement crew were lounging in deckchairs trying to gain some warmth from the weak rays of the late autumn sun. Half asleep, bored and obviously far away with their thoughts, not one spied their new commanding officer's arrival. By this stage Wenck's usually benevolent demeanour was decidedly frayed around the edges. The happenings of the past forty-eight hours plus the just finished contretemps with the station commander had left him tired and irritable.

He waited quietly for about fifteen seconds until finally he was spotted by one of the recumbent forms. Before the startled airman could react, Wenck bawled at the top of his voice. "Get up, get up you lazy lot. Schnell, schnell ... I don't have time to waste."

As the startled men scrambled to their feet, he ordered them to stand to attention and wait to be inspected. Reading from a list, he called out their names. At the same time he gave a perfunctory glance at their records. Only one, the navigator, had any combat experience. The remainder, of which the eldest was barely nineteen, were all joining their first operational squadron.

The youngsters gazed at him in awe. Even the navigator, a tall, thin individual of twenty-one, stared nervously at the irate figure with the Knight's Cross.

"All right, stand easy. If you have not already guessed I am Major Wenck, your new commanding officer. We have a long flight ahead of us and our destination is as close to Santa Clause's domain as you are ever likely to get. Your new home, if you don't already know, is Bardufoss near Tromso and I want to get to Trondheim by nightfall. So look smart and get to your stations. You," he pointed at the navigator, at the same time looking down at his sheaf of papers to find the youngster's name ... "Krampnitz, kommen Sie herein."

He moved away and the navigator followed. "Do you know our destination, Herr Leutnant?"

Krampnitz shook his head and swallowed. He said half defiantly, "We have been told nothing, Herr Major. However, I managed to obtain the charts for most of western and northern Norway. I guessed by the paintwork on the Junkers that we would be on anti-shipping operations, so I took the liberty of asking for what I thought would be the relevant charts."

Wenck smiled and clapped the other on the shoulder, at the same time congratulating him on his foresight. Krampnitz coloured with pleasure and grinned.

Wenck then walked over to the ground crew who were standing just within earshot and spoke to the sergeant in charge. The man assured him the Junkers was in good condition, fully armed, fuelled and ready to go.

Five minutes later, they were airborne.

The flight to Trondheim was without incident, as was the one to Tromso the following morning. Surveying the bleak landscape he felt no pleasure at having returned to his command. All he, could think about was the plan to liberate some of the Reichsbank's money and escape.

Chapter Eight
14 November 1944

The Reichsmarschall rose ponderously to greet him as the aide softly closed the door. Wenck saluted his commanding officer and then took the extended hand. Hermann Göring gripped it warmly, placing his left hand over Wenck's right wrist.

"Helmuth, my old friend, how good to see you. You look very well. Norway must agree with you."

It was a statement, not a question, so Wenck said nothing and just smiled in return.

"I trust all is well with you and the family, Vigdis and your son, Peter. It is Peter who is in the Luftwaffe and to whom I awarded the Knight's Cross?"

"Ja, that is correct, Herr Reichsmarschall. They are all well, although if you remember Vigdis is back in Iceland and I have not seen her for over four years."

Göring nodded his head. "Ja, ja ... I remember." He motioned to a chair and, as Wenck sat down, lowered his bulk into a large ornate, high-backed affair behind a desk. He smiled again, and there was genuine warmth in the grin.

Wenck and Göring went back a long way. Although Wenck was six years older than the legendary head of the Luftwaffe, their paths had crossed continually since before the start of the First World War. They had first met in April 1912, at a function held at the headquarters of the Prinz Wihelm Infantry Regiment in whose august company Göring had just been commissioned. As a diplomat of some eight years standing, Wenck would probably not have engaged the nineteen-year-old infantry leutnant in anything other than a few words of greeting had not his wife, Inger, taken a shine to the bluff and exuberant soldier. Consequently, they had spent nearly an hour in each other's company.

After a spell in the trenches, where he suffered badly from rheumatism, Göring transferred to the Imperial Air Force in 1915. His squadron, Jagdstaffel 5, was mainly involved in reconnaissance work on the Western Front and he quickly gained a reputation as a skilful and brave flier. By the time he was seriously wounded in a dogfight in 1916, he had already been awarded the Zaehring Lion with Swords, the Karl Friedrich Order, the Hohenzollern Medal with Swords, and the Iron Cross first class. Wenck, on the other hand, had only been awarded the last two.

Eventually, Göring took over Jasta 11, the legendary squadron that had been commanded by von Richthofen. Up to this stage they both had the same number of victories, but from then Göring had surged ahead. By the war's end, he had twenty-two kills to his name and had been awarded the coveted Pour La Merite, the Knight's Cross. Wenck's final tally was fourteen victories.

They met again shortly after the war while Wenck had been working with Fokker in Holland, and again in 1921. By this stage Göring was virtually a vagrant, living hand-to-mouth as an aircraft agent and pilot.

In 1923, Göring's luck changed and he married Carin van Kantzow, a Swede whose mother was English. The gentle Carin and Wenck's second wife Vigdis became quite good friends, possibly because of their common Viking background.

The two men, while friendly enough, were really never close friends. There was too much rivalry between them and when Göring joined Hitler's entourage their association lapsed. Not only did Wenck not become a member of the party, but as a diplomat he moved in different circles, at least until Hitler came to power.

Strangely, on reaching his exalted rank, and when they did meet, Göring never lorded his power over Wenck even though their relationship was now quite distant. From 1933, Göring and Wenck had only really mixed on official business. This was partly because Vigdis did not care for Göring's second wife, the actress Emmy Sonnemann. Nevertheless, Göring made no move to stop Wenck from re-entering the Luftwaffe. In fact, quite the opposite.

As he waited for the Reichsmarschall to start the conversation again, Wenck went over the previous day's happenings and wondered whether the order to meet Göring was fortuitous or not.

After Peter left Oslo, Colonel General Wenck had begun to search for a Junkers 390. He reasoned that if they were going to escape Germany by air, then only a plane with a range in excess of 6,000 kilometres would be suitable. His telexes quickly bore fruit. One of the giant six-engined bombers was still in existence, hidden in an airfield in northern Germany on the Baltic coast. The remaining 390s had been destroyed by Allied aircraft.

The next problem was to try and gain control of the bomber, a difficult task since officially he had no need for such an aircraft. He knew that to gain control he would have to go through General Pelz, who was in charge of the Luftwaffe's bomber arm, or ask Göring himself. There was a problem though. He could not think of any legitimate reason why he needed such an aircraft.

His command was virtually a backwater in the war. He had only four operational squadrons and only one of these flew bombers. They consisted of two units flying coastal command flying boats, one bomber squadron flying elderly Heinkel 111s for mine laying duties and one fighter squadron equipped with outdated Messerschmitt ME 109Es. The remainder were training units.

Then fate took a hand.

On 11 November, orders came through that all area commanders and ranks above colonel in Denmark and Norway were to attend a special conference at the headquarters of the Reich Air Fleet at Wannsee on 13 November. On joining the assembled officers and hearing the reason for the conference he became both alarmed and exultant. Alarmed, because he realised that the cause of all the fuss, plans for a new offensive on the Western Front, could disrupt their own schemes, and exultant, because he had now thought up a legitimate excuse to ask for the all-important Junkers 390.

This was the second such conference of senior airmen to discuss the new strategy. The other had been held a few days earlier.

The assembled airmen were told by an excited Göring how almost the entire Luftwaffe's fighter arm was being brought together for an offensive in the west. The aircraft were to be the strike component for a blitzkrieg that would create air superiority for three German armies assembled on the western borders of the Reich.

Waving his arms Göring told them he was assembling 3,700

aircraft and pilots into eighteen fighter groups in readiness for the attack. Most would act as fighter-bombers. There were also various bomber squadrons being readied. Although there was much excitement and, for a while, even Wenck was caught up in the infectious optimism, a few officers were obviously not keen on the move, though they kept their criticism and doubts muted.

That evening, Wenck and one other officer had a drink with the Luftwaffe's General of Fighters, the ace Adolf Galland. The young general spoke in no uncertain terms when he said he thought the air offensive was a mistake.

"We are all certifiable. We need to protect our reserves and keep them to defend the Reich until we can strengthen our forces and build more of our terror weapons and jet aircraft. This campaign leaves us too weak, especially in the east." Even though he kept his voice relatively low there was no hiding the intensity and vehemence of his feelings.

Wenck was not sure what to think, although he had no doubt that in the end Germany would be defeated. There were just too many countries and too many armies ranged against the Reich. Whatever the result, he still wanted to escape.

The next morning, he requested an audience with his old friend. Wenck had carefully thought out what he was going to say to the Reichsmarschall but, before he could begin his spiel Göring asked what he thought of the planned offensive. Wenck said it looked good on paper and then remarked how the strategy did not seem to include much in the way of planning for an offensive by the bomber arm.

Göring's answer was both petulant and vehement. "Bombers, bombers, that's all I hear these days. I have lost count of the number of times I have appealed to the Führer to let us concentrate on our fighter arm so we can effectively handle those cursed raids by the allied bombers, and you know what I get?" His voice rose and he half yelled. "I get gratuitous advice on how we should fight terror with terror and mount our own raids on British cities. Of course the Führer gets egged on by that scum, Bormann, and the chicken farmer, Himmler!" He spat out the words.

Red-faced, he reached over to a small brown bottle on his desk, unscrewed the cap and shook out a small white tablet. This he put in his mouth and began to chew. There was silence for a few seconds and then he went on. "They are all fools. Not the Führer, of course," he added hurriedly. "But those fawning ingrates. We have new fighters, jets. We have this new Messerschmitt, the 262, which is almost 200 kilometres faster than any allied fighter and they want me to turn it into a bomber? Pah." He again paused for breath.

Wenck saw his chance. "Herr Reichsmarschall, I have an idea that might not only find favour with the Führer but also help in the planned offensive without using too many resources." He hurried on as Göring's eyes quickened with interest. "At present the Americans are mounting raids on the Reich with impunity. Yes we are shooting them down, but they come over Germany in the certain knowledge that their homeland is safe from attack. Why do we not mount an attack on America? New York to be precise?"

Göring cocked his head and said caustically, "With what?"

"Reichsmarschall, as you no doubt remember, my son Peter undertook a dummy run to New York early this year with Fernaufklärungsgruppe 5 flying the big Junkers 390. There is one still left and I am prepared to stake my reputation that it could be used to raid New York successfully."

Göring was sceptical. He had no doubt the Junkers could reach New York, but what could one aircraft achieve?

"Helmuth, they are raiding us almost without respite with hundreds, even thousands of bombers. Almost every night and we are still fighting. Our factories are still producing. Therefore, what is the use of one, or even half-a-dozen aircraft over America? We went all through this before we decided to abandon our plans." He shrugged his shoulders and reached over to the bottle and put another pill into his mouth.

Seizing his opportunity, Wenck went on the attack. "With respect, Hermann," he said using Göring's Christian name for the first time. "You don't understand Americans like I do. I have lived among them. They are a passionate, undisciplined race. Full of inferior races, Jews, blacks, Spaniards. They would panic. The press would scream for the country to be protected. The American government would be forced to bring back hundreds of their fighters to defend the mainland." He paused, noting Göring's growing interest and then pressed on. "Think what a propaganda victory it would be. What would the Führer say?"

The last sentence was a master stroke.

Göring slapped the table hard and grinned with enthusiasm. He pledged his support and agreed to Wenck's request for secrecy.

Wenck explained how he wanted the Junkers stationed near his headquarters in southern Norway where it would be relatively free from attack. They would move it to another airfield closer to the Atlantic just before the planned offensive. He also asked to be given written orders granting him, or the bearer, the right to requisition vital equipment. At first Göring hesitated at this request, but after some more discussion, he gave way.

Finally, Wenck received permission for his son to be transferred to his command.

Together they drafted the order giving him the authority to requisition the Junkers and any other material he might need. When it was finished, Göring had a secretary type it up on official paper. As they waited for the document to be printed Göring took a third pill, remarking almost apologetically how he was a sick man and all his old war wounds were playing up. The document was brought back and the Reichsmarschall signed it with a flourish.

Now that he had what he wanted, Wenck was able to pay closer attention to the Luftwaffe's commanding officer and what he saw alarmed him. Göring was grossly overweight. There was nothing new in this, but now his colour was pale and his skin blotchy. His eyes at times seemed vacant and his breathing short and a little laboured. What medicines he was taking Wenck could only guess at, but whatever they were, three in scarcely an hour could not be good. Although Göring obviously wanted him to stay and talk longer, all Wenck wanted to do was escape.

He excused himself, saying that obviously the Reichsmarschall had important things to attend to and that he would inform him of the progress of their little plan. An hour later he flew to Hamburg for an important meeting.

Before journeying back to Germany, he had made some discreet enquiries about Friedrich and Emil Grauwitz. As his father, and of senior rank, he was able to find out some information about the former, but of the latter almost nothing. Rather than raise some unnecessary suspicion about his questions, he took the matter no further. He had a contact in Hamburg, a former diplomat and member of the Abwehr, who might be able to shed some light on Gruppenführer Emil Grauwitz and Friedrich.

Chapter Nine
17 November 1944

The weather had closed right in again at Bardufoss and there was no flying. For this respite Wenck was exceedingly grateful. More than ever he had lost his taste for flying over the Arctic Ocean.

On arriving back at his command he had learned of the loss of yet another crew to inclement weather. The Junkers bomber had gone out on a reconnaissance mission and simply disappeared. There was no radio signal, nothing. The plane and its crew simply vanished into the grey blackness of the Barents Sea.

There was one good point, however. The missing aircraft had been flown by the obnoxious party man Hans Burgdorf.

"It's a pity that in order to get rid of that shit Burgdorf we had to lose the others," said Leo Swabisch, filling him in on what had happened with the squadron while he had been away. It was Swabisch who brought him the telex. He said matter-of-factly as he handed it over, "Strange message boss?"

Wenck glanced at the paper and said off-handedly, "Yes, I'll tell you about it sometime." He walked away and remarked casually over his shoulder. "I'll be away for a couple of hours. I'm going to Tromso."

Borrowing one of the airfield's smaller communications trucks, he drove to the local naval base and went to its communications section. He was well-known there and when he requested the use of a phone, exclaiming with a wicked grin how he wanted to ring a married lady in Bergen, they gave him the instrument without comment and left him alone.

The telex message had been short. It said simply: 'contact E' and was signed RB.

He chuckled to himself as he asked the operator to connect the number he had written down in his pocket diary.

E was short for Else, the elderly German woman his father had known for years and whom he had lodged with when he returned from Finland. The letters RB stood for Rupert Bear, the children's character so beloved by English youth, to whom young Peter had been introduced as a lad of seven by his mother. Before leaving Oslo his father had told him that in order to keep their activities secret any sensitive information would be sent to him with the signature RB and, if necessary, vital messages could be relayed through Else.

There was no delay in the connection. A female voice asked him what RB meant and when he gave the correct answer, said quickly, "RB says that he has made very good progress. Tomorrow morning you will receive orders transferring you to another base. You are to comply, but tell nobody anything. You are to pretend ignorance, understand?"

He answered in the affirmative and the woman hung up without further comment.

Back at the base Swabisch made several oblique comments about the message, but Wenck refused to be drawn.

At eight-thirty the next morning his orders arrived telling him to report to an airfield near Kragero in the Skagerrak. They were signed by the commander of the Luftwaffe's Norwegian bomber fleet, not his father. Perplexed, he nevertheless began to put in train the handover of his command.

Swabisch was most upset and asked if there was any way he could be included in whatever secret mission Wenck was to be engaged in. He was convinced his friend had been chosen for something especially secretive and heroic. Wenck asked him not to mention anything about the previous day's message and promised that if it could be arranged, he would see what he could do.

Shortly after noon he flew one of the older Heinkels to Trondheim where he connected with a military transport flying to Oslo. From there he went by train to Kragero.

The station commander, a major of about forty-five years of age, was eager to help. He volunteered that he had been ordered to give any assistance required, but obviously knew nothing about what was happening. Like a good officer he did as he was told. Wenck was directed to his quarters and handed two envelopes, one sealed with wax. The former contained news of his promotion forthwith to the rank of lieutenant-colonel. The latter, a handwritten note from his father, informed him that there was an FW 190 for his personal use at the Kragero base and he should fly immediately to another airfield at Halden on the other side of Oslo Fjord.

He found it pleasant to be flying a single-seater again and although his experience on fighters of this type was less than fifty hours, he found no difficulty in piloting it the hundred-odd kilometres to Halden.

His father was waiting and without further ado ushered him into a deserted office. Major General Wenck kept the door open and placed his chair so he could see down the deserted corridor. Opening a thermos flask, he poured some coffee into a mug and handed the black, aromatic liquid to Peter. After a perfunctory question as to his son's health, he got straight to the point.

"Well, Peter, I have a lot to tell you, some good, some bad, although I am happy to say that as far as you and I are concerned, it is mainly good."

He spoke of his meeting with Göring and the gaining of the vital document authorising the acquisition of the Junkers 390, Peter's transfer and whatever help he needed in organising the supposed raid on New York. He also revealed that he had located the big bomber, but had no idea as to its condition.

"I have also thought out a very detailed and complex plan to make it much harder for anybody to know what we are up to, and believe me, Peter, we have every reason to be careful. Your brother is a bastard and his boss, by all accounts, is the devil's first cousin."

He outlined his trip to Hamburg and his conversations with an old diplomatic contact. "Conrad Meunier served in the Diplomatic Corps with me and at one time we were both stationed in America together. You even met him on several occasions. Do you remember? Eh? No? Oh well. He also spent some time in Latin America, particularly the Caribbean, but I'll get into the importance of this later. Anyway, he was also a member of the Abwehr, like so many of us diplomats were," he said with a smile. "He was pretty close to Canaris at one stage, but found all the intrigue too much. Also, since he was not a party member, many doors were not open to him. To cut a long story short, he resigned from both the Diplomatic Corps and the Abwehr just after Stalingrad. His resignation was not questioned. His son was killed at Stalingrad, his wife was very ill and anyway, he was over sixty. Since he resigned so long ago and since he had every excuse to resign, he has been left alone and was not one of those questioned after the aborted attempt on our beloved Fuhrer," he said with irony.

He paused for a moment and took another mouthful of coffee.

"At any rate, Meunier has kept up his contacts and is a fount of information. He was able to give me some important background information on the shadowy Herr Brigadeführer Emil Grauwitz." He shook his head and said quietly, "Now there's a one."

He paused again, glanced down the still deserted corridor and went on. "Grauwitz is with the Waffen SS. He's a Sonderführer, you know, on the administrative side. He's actually in the Gerichtsdienste, their legal service, and is one of their top lawyers. Very secretive and very powerful. You know, hobnobs with Himmler and the like. He apparently had much to do with the setting up of the concentration camps and is involved with the forced transportation of Jews from Italy and Hungary."

He lowered his voice. He looked near tears. "Jesus, Peter, Meunier told me he had seen evidence showing how in many of the camps we're quite literally killing thousands of Jews and other prisoners. It's the same information I heard before. Meunier claims it is a set policy. He does not know anything specific about Friedrich, but is pretty certain that as an accountant he must be involved with the financial side of the running of the camps, especially if he's tied up with Grauwitz."

There was a silence as Peter Wenck stared at his father. "I do not want to believe all this. Father, he does not seem the type."

"Who does my boy, who does? I will give him the benefit of the doubt, but Meunier believes Friedrich must be involved in the actual transfer of money from the camps to the Reichsbank. It makes sense. Otherwise, why would Grauwitz need him? Remember, Grauwitz is with the legal section, not the financial section."

They talked further and his father explained why he had taken such elaborate precautions.

"If Grauwitz wants Friedrich to fly the money out of Germany, he will need an aircraft. Well, let them organise their own transport. I don't want Friedrich to know just yet about Göring's document and what we've done and, more importantly, I don't want Grauwitz to know anything at all. I want to be more than two steps ahead of that scum at all times." He gave a little chuckle. "Peter my boy, if we are careful, we might just get away with it and make ourselves very rich in the process."

"Ja, and we might also get ourselves shot," said his son soberly.

They continued to plot. Even though much was starting to fall into place there were still several large holes in their overall plan. Peter wanted to know how the money would be transferred to the aircraft, who would be expected to join them and what their ultimate destination would be.

His father explained that at this early stage the details of the Berlin end would have to be left up to Schonewille. Despite this, their ultimate destination was still something they could plan for.

"Where do you think we should go to, Peter?"

His son shrugged and shook his head. "Friedrich said Grauwitz had mentioned Spain as a first stop and from there he believed the ultimate destination would be South America, Argentina probably."

"Makes sense. It's also what I thought. We've always had good contacts in that country and there is a sizeable German population. Before the war we used them as intelligence gathering sources," said his father.

"I tell you what, Father. Friedrich suggested that we choose another destination because South America is too obvious and this is beginning to be my feeling also."

"I agree," nodded his father. "I am beginning to think your brother might be on the same thought pattern as myself and, maybe you?" He raised his eyebrows in a quizzical gesture.

Peter Wenck nodded his head and smiled. "America?"

"Ja ... well almost," answered the general. He gave a conspiratorial smile. For a moment he paused and then choosing his words carefully, went on. "I told you Meunier served in the Caribbean and this could be important in whatever decision we make on where we should ultimately end up. He's been making a few very discreet inquiries, via Switzerland, to see if his contacts are still about or are even contactable. We both think the Caribbean should be our ultimate destination. There are several reasons why, but we both have some more work to do before we are in a position to make a definite decision," he said, holding up his hand for silence as his son started to speak. "Look, you'll just have to leave this end to me. At any rate I'll need your input before we can make a final decision. First, we have to do something about the aircraft."

They argued and planned for another hour. There were still too many loose ends and their frustration level increased as the conversation continued. Eventually, they finished their deliberations and Peter flew back to the Kragero base.

Nobody bothered him, although the station commander stuck his head around the door of his sleeping quarters and enquired whether he wanted anything. The young pilot, deep in thought irritably waved him away. An almost sleepless night followed, but in the dead hours either side of four o'clock his jumbled thoughts began to find solutions. One idea was the key. If properly handled and with luck on their side, it would considerably reduce the risks of their dangerous venture.

In order to solidify his ideas and because his addled brain was beginning to find the strain of coherent thought too taxing, he got up and, wrapping his flying jacket around his shoulders to ward off the late autumn chill, began to put his thoughts down on paper.

Half-an-hour later, with the plan approved in his own mind and a logical strategy locked in his brain, he took the five sheets of roughly-scrawled paper and set them on fire. As he watched the flames in the waste paper tin consume the evidence he felt a growing sense of pride and excitement.

It was the same feeling he had experienced on the Russian Front almost two years before when he had planned the long-range bombing raids and again in September the same year when he was part of the team that schemed and organised the flight to New York.

Chapter Ten
3 December 1944

The Focke Wulf FW190 bounced twice over the uneven concrete and then, as its speed lessened, dropped its tail wheel onto the ground.

Swinging the fighter from side-to-side so he could see around the bulk of the huge BMW 801 radial engine, he cautiously swung off the runway. He taxied down a short perimeter track and was then guided across a strip of grass to a small blast pen constructed of sandbags reinforced with pine logs and rammed earth.

Two ground crew immediately began re-fuelling the fighter while a third helped him slide back the canopy and assisted him down the wing onto the ground. With a curt Dankeschön he returned their salute and began the 150-metre walk to the nearest buildings.

Nearby he could see some more revetments, though these were much larger than the one that now housed his fighter. Curious, he diverted his course slightly and strode over to the nearest pen, a massive affair similarly constructed, but with the added protection of camouflage netting to hide its contents from prying eyes in the air.

Fifteen metres away he stopped, his excitement mounting. Inside its protective walls was a large four-engined aircraft. This was what he had come for.

A corporal in the uniform of the Luftwaffe ground corps stepped out of the shadows and approached. Scarcely three metres away he halted. Wenck saw that he held the regulation Mauser Gewehr 98 across his chest and noticed his right forefinger was curled around the rifle's trigger.

The soldier eyed Wenck up and down for a moment, noting the airman's rank and the decoration at his throat. Then he said quietly, "I am sorry, Herr Oberleutnant. You cannot be here without a pass, es ist verboten."

Wenck nodded his head slowly and walked away. Security was

certainly tight. He was not sure whether this was a good or bad omen.

The nearest building was an unprepossessing concrete structure, built next to what had once been a large farmhouse. Surrounding both in a large semi-circle were several more buildings, some wood and some made of corrugated tin. On the far side were half-a-dozen more large revetments. All seemed quiet.

A figure appeared at the door of the concrete building and walked with a purposeful stride towards Wenck. On reaching him, the man saluted and said by way of introduction, "Raetzer, Sir. Kapitan Nils Raetzer. We were expecting you, Herr Oberleutnant."

He motioned Wenck inside the building and led him through what appeared to be an operations room. It was empty except for a dozen chairs and a number of map boards leaning on trestles. All were covered in black cloth. At the far end was an open door. Passing through, Wenck was confronted by a Luftwaffe major with the same Knight's Cross hanging from his throat.

"Oberleutnant Wenck, I presume? Welcome to Finow. I am Major Peter Stahl. I command this Staffel." He motioned to the captain. "You can go, Nils. Now, Oberleutnant, how can I help you?"

Wenck spoke succinctly and with authority. This would have to be handled very carefully. It also helped that he outranked Stahl. "What I am about to say is top secret, Stahl."

The other nodded with a gentle shake of his head. "Everything here is top secret, Sir. One more secret won't make the slightest difference to me."

Wenck smiled inwardly, but he kept his voice and demeanour cold. "I am requisitioning one of your aircraft ... at least I will be after I have familiarised myself with its handling characteristics."

Stahl shrugged his shoulders. He did not seem surprised. Nor did he seem to care. He held out his left hand. "Your orders."

Wenck took out an envelope from his breast pocket and carefully extracted the document. "They are not specific, Major. However, they are all I need and all you need to provide me with assistance."

Stahl looked at the signature at the bottom and then looked into

Wenck's eyes. "This is somewhat irregular, Sir." The voice was questioning, probing. "I may have to check this out with headquarters. The Reichsmarschall has never been involved in our operations before and these planes are very valuable."

Wenck narrowed his eyes and his voice took on a hard edge. "Major, you will obey my orders to the letter. If it is further authority you need, here is something I'm sure will convince you." He extracted a second document from another envelope and held it in front of Stahl's face.

The major noted the letter's origins and scanned its contents until his eyes came to the signature. His features stiffened and he swallowed. His whole demeanour changed and he stammered slightly. "Of course, Sir. I will do whatever you wish."

"Fine, fine," acknowledged Wenck, allowing a frosty smile to appear on his lips. "Now, listen and listen carefully. If there are any enquiries as to what we are doing, you are to say nothing. But you must inform me immediately as to who has been asking questions. I will give you a radio frequency and a call sign later. To your staff you can just say that the aircraft has been transferred to another squadron for a special operation."

Stahl nodded, said he understood and then asked what sort of aircraft he wanted. Wenck told him and without any hesitation the major led him out of the building to the revetment where he had stopped only ten minutes before.

This time the corporal stayed clear.

The two airmen walked over to the revetment and entered through a small gap at the rear of the structure. Once inside Wenck reached up and gripped the leading edge of one rear wing. He had never seen one up close, although he had once seen several dozen as they flew in a box formation across Belgium on their way to northern Germany.

It was a B17, Boeing's big four-engined bomber which, together with the B24 Liberator and the British four-engined heavy bombers, was laying waste to much of Germany.

"It is a Boeing B17F, one of the last of that model," said Stahl. "It is one of the best we have. It was captured in October last year. The pilot managed to land in a large field in Denmark after one of its engines was damaged and failed. The undercarriage was also damaged in the forced landing, but our engineers had enough spare parts on hand to repair it. Unfortunately, there were no immediate spares on hand for the damaged engine.

Wenck moved slowly around the American bomber as Stahl went on with its history.

"At any rate the biggest problem was getting it into the air again from such a small field on only three engines. So, it was completely stripped of its armour and armament and then successfully flown to Rechlin for flight testing. From there it was transferred to 2. Staffel of the Versuchsverband Oberbefehlshaber to help in training our fighter pilots on how to attack American bomber formations." He paused and then continued. "After a complete re-fit, it joined this Staffel only two weeks ago."

Wenck was now at the back of the pen staring up at the aircraft's nose. Underneath one of the navigator's windows in line with the wing root was a painting of a semi naked woman. Wenck laughed and pointed to the voluptuous figure. Stahl's lips barely moved. He had seen it often enough. The title in front of the painting was still in English. The B17 was called Miss Nonalee Two.

"What's she like, Major?"

"As I have already said, Sir, she is fine. In fact she is one of our best aircraft. Since the re-fit she's never been damaged and she has already served us well," he said.

"Right, Major. Then I'll take her."

After his sleepless night fifteen days earlier Wenck had again flown to Halden to talk to his father. It was an important conversation. When it ended five hours later they had, for the first time, set the groundwork for a coherent scheme on which they could build a strategy to escape from Germany.

Peter Wenck's plans were based on two premises. Firstly they had to keep the elder Wenck's role secret from Grauwitz and secondly, they had to find a suitable aircraft able to fly them unhindered over a long distance.

"Father, I do not think the Junkers is the right aircraft," said Peter.

Wenck senior listened silently as his son went on to explain his theory.

"We agree that the major ingredients are an aircraft with sufficient range and of a sufficient size to fly a long distance with at least three people, plus a reasonable pay load. There is no doubt the 390 fits the bill. However, I do not think it, or any other German aircraft for that matter, is suited for the task ..."

"What do we do then?" broke in his father with a perplexed frown and a wave of his hand. "Use a British aircraft?"

"Close, Father, close. We use an American one." General Wenck stared at his son incredulously. "That's right, we use an American plane. A B17."

"Ha ha ha. I suppose we just ask Eisenhower."

Peter Wenck was enjoying himself. He shook his head and grinned. "Nein, we already have B17s. In fact I believe the Luftwaffe has several of them, as well as most other Allied aircraft."

Peter explained how after the reconnaissance mission to New York he had flown the 390 to an airfield in northern Germany for some radar tests. The base was a top secret establishment and housed many of the Reich's latest aircraft.

"You would not believe what I saw there, Father. All manner of aircraft. Some of which still amazes me. Anyway, one day last year I saw a Boeing B17 land. I was intrigued because, although it was painted in German markings, it had no yellow paintwork on its under-surfaces. In other words, it was not being used for training or combat training purposes."

He went on to explain that on the same evening the American bomber took off shortly after dusk and returned eleven hours later. At all times security around the aircraft was very tight and its crew were housed in a separate billet away from the main body of the airfield.

"Later on, after I had been there for a week or so, I found out more about what was going on. One evening after a few schnapps, one of the senior officers let slip what the B17 and its crew were up to. Himmel, it's quite a story."

The young pilot dropped his voice conspiratorially.

"Apparently, there is a special squadron in existence called Kampfgeschwader 200. They have all manner of allied aircraft: several B17s, B24 Liberators, British bombers as well as a large range of fighters. In fact just about one of every type of combat aircraft flown by the Americans and British."

He explained how the B17s were mainly used for reconnaissance and intelligence work and operated far behind enemy lines, often wearing their original insignias and markings. Although he had not been told the precise nature of their missions, Peter Wenck told his father he believed that KG200 was mainly being used to drop or land agents in Russia and North Africa.

"Himmel, Father. The officer even told me how they had flown to West Africa and back."

Returning to the matter at hand, they discussed the relative merits of using the American aircraft as against the Junkers or another Luftwaffe machine.

Peter Wenck said he thought their biggest problem would come when they left the confines of German air space. Aircraft recognition was widespread and wherever they ultimately landed a German bomber would be immediately recognised. Then there was the problem of enemy fighters. There was more chance of being intercepted by Allied fighters than German ones.

The general commented, "This is all well and good, but how can we commandeer a B17?"

Wenck nodded his head and said smugly, waggling his finger at the same time, "Has your son inherited brains, or has your son inherited brains? Friedrich told me Grauwitz was expecting to fly the money out of Germany. Therefore, either he has an aircraft lined up, or at least has the authority to get one. I hope it is the latter."

"What I propose is this. We contact Friedrich and tell him to ask Herr Grauwitz for some sort of authority to allow me to get hold of a big plane. We don't let either Friedrich or Grauwitz know about Göring's letter, we just keep it up our sleeve. If they ask what type of plane, I'll tell them about the 390. I mean, that would be perfectly logical, wouldn't it?"

Intrigued, his father just nodded his head.

The younger man paused for a moment, collected his thoughts and then hurried on. "As planned we use Göring's letter to get hold of the Junkers 390. Whatever authorisation Grauwitz gains we use to get hold of one of KG200's B17s."

His father broke in. "Why do we need Grauwitz's letter or authorisation?"

"A number of reasons, Father. We want to keep your name out of Grauwitz's earshot if possible. Similarly, it was your idea for Göring's letter to be kept secret from both my brother and the SS Gruppenführer. You have made sure my transfer was to the Kragero base while you are stationed here at Halden. Also, my transfer was signed by the commander of the Norwegian bomber fleet. Therefore, if somebody digs very deeply you are not involved at all and this gives us an ace or two up our sleeve."

He gave a conspiratorial grin and went on. "My brother told me he did not trust Grauwitz and consequently he would not mention your being involved. I think he's telling the truth, but just to be sure, we tell him no more than is necessary. If he asks, we appear vague, or say that things are still being worked out."

He asked whether his father agreed. The other nodded.

"Now, back to the bases, and this is important. We station the Junkers at Kragero while the B17 can be stationed secretly here at Halden. There is even a hangar here and it is large enough to hide it from prying eyes." He paused and took a deep breath. "Finally, if we want to get our hands on a B17 we might need greater powers of persuasion than that provided by the Reichsmarschall's letter. Grauwitz might just be able to provide that. If not, we will have to chance it with Göring's letter."

He leant back in his chair and clasped his hands behind his head, grinning in satisfaction. "Well, Herr General, Father dear. What do you think, eh?"

Chapter Eleven
30 November 1944

Brigadeführer Emil Grauwitz paced up and down the small anteroom. After a few minutes of this aimless and restricted form of exercise, he clasped his hands behind his back and stared at the small portrait of the Führer hanging on the wall opposite. Sighing, he transferred his gaze to his feet and for the second time in as many minutes became irritated at the smudge of mud on his otherwise immaculate left boot.

Grauwitz was not normally nervous. The fact that he was made him even more irritable, especially since the occupant of the next room was beneath his contempt. Unfortunately, that person was undoubtedly the most powerful person in the Reich, bar none.

There came the sound of a door opening and Grauwitz looked up.

A voice said: "The Reichsführer will see you now."

He followed the underling down a short passageway and knocked on a solid oak panel door. A muffled voice said, " Kommen Sie herein." They entered into a largish room and the door was shut behind him. He stepped forward and willed himself to appear calm.

The figure behind the desk was neatly writing something at the bottom of a document. For a moment he did not look up and when he did so the light from his desk lamp glinted on his owl like glasses.

Heinrich Himmler did not smile. There was no expression on his face. There was a chair by the desk, but Himmler made no suggestion that he be seated. He just asked what he wanted.

Grauwitz started with a bang. "Reichsführer, your orders are not being followed and I ..."

"Orders, what orders?" interrupted Himmler, his voice rising slightly and his eyes squinting through his glasses in concentration.

Grauwitz's mind was racing. Now that he was committed he had to go on. Yet he knew he must be careful. The man in front of him might be small in stature, but he was powerful, utterly ruthless and he was no fool. Second man in the Reich he might be, but he had amassed an awesome degree of power.

After the abortive attempt on his life four months ago, Hitler had turned more and more to his loyal lieutenant. The Führer had nobody else to turn to. He did not trust the Wehrmacht generals any more, the navy had proved itself ineffective, while his faithful paladin Göring could not be relied upon to do anything properly.

With the army in disgrace, the Reichsführer's Waffen SS grew in size and importance as more and more equipment and men were diverted to its ranks. Now it numbered some thirty-eight divisions with three-quarters of these at full strength and numbering some of the most powerful fighting units left to the Reich.

Nor did it end there. Himmler was also in command of the Home Army, the rag-tag defence force made up of sub-teenagers and elderly civilians. He was also in charge of the police force, concentration camp labour and the industrial complex that it slaved in and was now the overall Chief of Intelligence.

To top it off, Hitler had recently conferred on him control of the V rocket production program, made him Minister of the Interior and Chief of Army Armaments. There were others as well. Himmler was collecting titles and power as Göring was collecting art.

Despite this, Himmler was also astute enough to realise things were going badly for Germany and was endeavouring to try and gain kudos with the Allies. Grauwitz knew some of Himmler's moves in this area and it was through this that he hoped to gain what he wanted: the authorisation to obtain the vital escape aircraft. He was not stupid enough to try blackmail. His moves were much more Machiavellian.

Even though the Reich had looted most of Europe, it was still desperately short of hard cash and Himmler had devised a scheme whereby Jews were being sold for foreign currency. As well as gaining the much needed dollars, these Jews who had not yet been in any of the concentration camps would be a living proof to the Americans that the ghastly rumours leaking from Europe about the extermination camps were not true. Most of these Jews were being transported directly from Hungary, but the chaotic state of Germany's rail system meant the flow of deportees was being halted.

At the same time, the American Jews were being tardy in paying and Adolf Eichmann was threatening the Jewish community in Budapest. Unless the matter of payments was straightened out another 75,000 Jews would be taken from Hungary and immediately transferred to the Reich.

This was the key to Grauwitz's argument.

He told Himmler how the flow of deportees had been halted yet again because senior officers from the Concentration Camp Inspectorate were being tardy in their job. Since it was Grauwitz's job to organise the legal transfer of funds in exchange for the Hungarian Jews, he could not fulfil his duty.

Himmler drew his lips into a thin line and glared up at him. His voice was low, almost a hiss. "I am aware of this lamentable state of affairs, Herr Brigadeführer. What I would like to know is, are you here to apportion blame, or do you have something constructive to say to me?"

"The latter, mein Reichsführer."

Himmler's eyes behind the horn-rimmed glasses opened a fraction and a shadow of a smile formed on his lips. He nodded his head and asked Grauwitz to continue. The officer shifted his feet and Himmler's smile widened somewhat. "Oh, I am forgetting my manners, please sit down."

Grateful of the opportunity to be able to break away from Himmler's steely stare, if for only a moment, he sat down and continued. "Herr Reichsführer, in order for us to get those accursed dollars and Swiss francs we need the Jews to arrive in Switzerland in good condition. Even when they finally get there, if they get there, they are in poor condition. Why do we not fly them there?"

Himmler said nothing, his eyes never leaving Grauwitz's face. For a moment there was silence. "Why indeed?" he answered, raising his eyebrows.

The SS brigadier went on, choosing his words carefully. He explained the problems in shifting the Jews by air. There was a lack of aircraft suitable for the task, plus, an acute shortage of petrol, as well as other logistic and bureaucratic difficulties.

"Despite this, Reichsführer, I believe that if I can lay my hands on two or three aircraft I can make this operation successful."

A hint of anger crept into Himmler's voice. "You may have a point there, but it galls me to think those Jewish swine will be able to travel in comfort while the Reich's fighting men have to use their feet to travel ... Pah," he finished in disgust. "Well, what is it you have in mind?"

"Reichsführer, my plan is simple. We should try to fly some of the Hungarian Jews to southern Germany and then truck them across the border. I also believe we should look at the possibility of using Sweden as another outlet." He paused for a moment to see if Himmler would take the bait. Himmler nodded his head in thought, so Grauwitz plunged on. "Sweden would be a good alternative since we could base at least one aircraft in southern Norway where there is not much allied air activity."

Grauwitz paused and Himmler motioned him to continue.

The SS officer explained how he believed the legal niceties would be easier when dealing with the Swedes. He also believed the much needed foreign currency would be forthcoming far more readily if the American Jews were dealing with Swedish officials rather than the cautious and conservative Swiss.

Himmler readily agreed and asked what he wanted.

The other replied how he needed some sort of authorisation that would allow him to gain the necessary aircraft, whether from the SS's own transport fleet or even from the Luftwaffe.

At the latter option Himmler smiled. "Good, good. Try to get them from the Luftwaffe, mein Herr. Göring does nothing with them anyway."

The Reichsführer lifted the handset of his phone and spoke to his secretary. He asked a question, paused and then dictated the contents of a letter to the man at the other end. Scarcely five minutes later there was a knock at the door and the secretary entered carrying a stiff leather document holder. Himmler opened it and extracted a single sheet of his official note paper. He perused it carefully, signed it and handed the document over to Grauwitz.

"Is this sufficient?"

"Ja, mein Reichsführer, das ist gut."

Himmler immediately returned to the pile of papers on his desk, at the same time bidding Grauwitz gute Nacht.

The latter rose to his feet, extended his hand with a guttural Heil Hitler, and walked to the door. Just as he had his hand on the handle, Himmler's voice cut in.

"Keep me informed, Herr Brigadeführer. Keep me informed and be successful."

Grauwitz took the lift to the underground car park and found his driver leaning against his vehicle's boot smoking. At his appearance, the man leapt to attention, flicked the half finished cigarette away, saluted and opened the rear near side passenger door.

As they drove out into the night air of Berlin he extracted the Reichsführer's letter and, ignoring the blackout, turned on the car's interior light. Holding it up so he could read it properly, he scanned the two paragraphs, checking virtually every word to see if there was anything missing. Short and to the point it might be, but it was sufficient. He leant back in his seat and switched out the light. He sighed with relief. It had been easier than he could have hoped.

When Schonewille had told him to gain authorisation in order to obtain a transport aircraft with a long range capability and had even suggested Himmler, Grauwitz had at first baulked at the idea. Nevertheless, he quickly realised that unless he could obtain an aircraft with sufficient range to transport them far from the borders of the Third Reich, there was no way of making their plan work.

When he and Heger first dreamed up the plan of the false bank account he had hoped to use the secret Odessa organisation to spirit himself and his loot to Spain. However, Grauwitz was by inclination and experience a secretive man and he did not fully trust the newly-formed SS escape organisation. They were too fanatical and too keen to continue the fight from South America. He had joined both the SS and the party, because it was the expedient thing to do. Quite simply, his prestige and power were dependent on them. If the German communists had won government instead of the Nazis, he would have joined the Communist Party. The thought of stealing money for the greater glory of some government in exile did not appeal to him in the least.

As a Brigadeführer in the SS's legal section he had access to aircraft and after dismissing the Odessa idea he had thought of bribing a pilot to fly him to Spain. From there he had planned to use his legal and banking contacts, plus his financial resources, to get to South America. While he had originally needed Schonewille to provide the vital concentration camp connection, the man's links with the pilot Wenck had been both unknown and fortuitous.

Nevertheless, he was troubled. He had initially not told Schonewille directly about Spain, but he knew from their conversations that the SS accountant had believed Spain to be the immediate answer. In their later conversations, Schonewille had hinted how it might be possible to fly further with the right type of aircraft and in return Grauwitz had told him to make plans in this direction and to report back to him when they were finalised. He wondered how these plans were progressing.

Now, the idea of a plane ultimately able to reach Argentina or even Paraguay was very appealing. How Wenck and Schonewille were planning this part of the operation he was not sure, nor at the present time did he care. He had checked up on the pilot and had been sufficiently impressed by his record to reason that Wenck could be left to plan this part of the operation by himself.

At any rate, he was now not sure whether he would need to activate the plan. Despite the intense secrecy, he knew of the planned offensive in the Ardennes. With any luck, the attack might succeed and there would be no need to leave Germany.

Yet, if the attack failed he now had the wherewithal to escape from the doomed Reich. Through the power of Himmler's letter he had permission to obtain at least two aircraft. If the plans by Schonewille and Wenck fell through, or if he decided he wanted to double-cross them, he now had the ability to fly to Spain on his own. From there he could activate his original plans.

I've been very smart, he told himself smugly. Then he remembered the look on Himmler's face as he ordered him to be successful. Maybe lucky is a better word, he thought to himself soberly.

Wearily, he placed his thumb and forefinger against his temple. The nervous tension had brought on a headache and he knew that over the next few weeks there would be many more. Crossing Himmler was almost as bad as crossing the Führer. Treachery, or what was perceived as treachery, resulted in a terrible fate. A mental picture crossed his mind as if in warning.

Like many others he had been forced to watch a film of the execution of the surviving eight bomb plotters after they had been sentenced to death by the president of the People's Court, Ronald Freisler. The condemned men had been herded into a room at Ploetzensee Prison and then hung with piano wire from meat hooks suspended from the ceiling. The sight of Field Marshal von Witzleben's contorted face as the wire bit deep into his neck and his feet pawed the air in a useless attempt to release the strain had been almost too much for him. By all accounts he had not been the only one. It had been whispered how even Goebbels had nearly fainted at the sight.

Back at his office he poured himself a schnapps and then called Schonewille on the telephone.

Half-an-hour later the accountant was ushered into his office. The conversation was short. Grauwitz believed in the maxim of walls having ears. He handed over Himmler's document. Schonewille was expecting some sort of authorisation, though not one actually signed by the Reichsführer. While he had suggested Himmler as a source to Grauwitz, he had not really believed such an authority would actually be forthcoming.

He raised his eyebrows and gave a questioning look to the SS Brigadier. The man ignored the hidden question and said curtly: "I think you will agree this is more than sufficient to get what you want." He explained the subterfuge he had used on Himmler to gain the authorisation.

"We may have to obtain a second aircraft to fly those Jews I told you about out of the country and I've now got both the written and verbal permission to do so. I've also convinced the Reichsführer that Sweden might be a better destination than Switzerland. Therefore, I have permission to base an aircraft in southern Norway where I believe your brother is stationed." Then as an afterthought in case the walls did have ears.: "The scheme has the complete approval of the Reichsführer, so we had better do a good job. Therefore, I hope your brother is the right man for this operation."

On the way back to his apartment Schonewille was a worried man. The letter from Himmler frightened him. Despite Grauwitz's explanation about the Jews he began to wonder whether the Reich's second most important man might also be part of the plot. After a moment's reflection he came to the correct conclusion that if Himmler wanted to escape from Germany, he could do so without this elaborate scheme.

Still, he was in an agitated frame of mind when he entered his home. This agitation was heightened by the scene that met his eyes.

Sophia was sitting on a sofa facing the door to the entrance hall, her face as white as a sheet and her dark eyes staring and strained. At his entrance she gave an audible sigh of relief. "Oh Friedrich, I'm so glad you are here."

Pleased as he would normally have been by such a greeting, the look on her face immediately told him neither love nor affection were the cause of her sentiments, rather relief and fright. He asked what was the matter.

In a quavering voice she explained how she had broken their rule about her venturing out at night alone. She had wanted to buy some bread and had gone out just as the shops were ready to close. Hurrying back in the early darkness, she had been stopped by a young and officious SS officer who had demanded to see her identity papers. Her agitation had caused him to be suspicious and it was only when she produced her papers and explained how she was staying with her cousin, Brigadeführer Schonewille, that his suspicions were allayed.

Schonewille shook his head. He knew her papers would stand up to all but the most thorough scrutiny, but the number on her arm would give her away instantly.

"Liebling," he said softly. "We have to get rid of those accursed numbers and we must do so immediately. I will not put it off any longer."

She nodded her head mutely and Schonewille went into the

kitchen. Reaching up he opened a cupboard door and extracted a small glass bottle with a rubber stopper. He carefully placed it on a sideboard and then went to another cupboard under the sink where he chose a number of clean rags. He took the bottle and rags back to the sitting room before returning to the kitchen where he filled a kettle with cold water. Taking some cord from a drawer he returned with the articles to where Sophie was sitting silent and unmoving. There was a wooden chair with thick arms in the corner. He dragged it over and motioned for Sophie to sit in it. Without a word, she did as she was bid.

Schonewille quickly undid the buttons of her linen blouse and helped her take it off. He then deftly tied her hands to the arms of the chair and wrapped the rags around both her wrist and upper arm, leaving the crude tattoo visible in between.

He left the room for a moment before returning with an old and thick woollen rug which he placed on her lap with one edge hanging down her right side onto the floor.

"Are you ready mein Liebling?" he asked.

She nodded her head and closed her eyes.

Schonewille knelt down on one knee and carefully withdrew the stopper from the flask. Holding the container a few centimetres from her arm, he carefully allowed a thin stream of sulphuric acid to pour onto the naked skin. Sophia jerked her arm involuntarily as the acid bit, but still Schonewille allowed the liquid to fall until the area of unprotected flesh was a congealed mess. At first she made no sound, but finally Sophia gave a cry of pain and then promptly fainted.

Putting down the flask, Schonewille waited a few moments more and then picking up the kettle began to pour the cool water onto the arm, diluting the acid and reducing its effect. He dabbed the wound, noting with a mixture of relief and distaste how the flesh had lifted away and how the tattoo seemed to have disappeared. He continued to pour more water on the wound until the rug and the floor around was soaked.

Undoing the cords he lifted her in his arms, carried her upstairs and tenderly bandaged her arm. She regained consciousness and moaned but said nothing. In soft words he assured her it was all over and that the acid had done its work. Schonewille did not see the look she gave him. If he had he would have been acutely distressed. It was as if the disappearance of those incriminating figures had released her from bondage, as though the pain had awakened her from her enforced slumber of fear. The Jewess was suddenly much stronger and even though he was her protector the complicated relationship that had bound them together was, for the first time, beginning to fracture.

Chapter Twelve
10 December 1944

"Zum Teufel, Leo. Sei nicht so langsam." Wenck swore at his friend because he was so slow.

Captain Swabisch remained unperturbed. He was still unused to the B17 and he was determined the pre-flight check was done fully and in sequence. He sat on Wenck's right, a clipboard balanced on his lap as he went through the start-up sequence.

"Master switch, on; generator and batteries, on; throttles, idle cut off; fuel, full rich." Swabisch's left hand moved to the mixture control levers set immediately in front of the throttle levers and then to the turbo and mixture control lock lever. Satisfied, he continued. "Fuel pumps, on; boosters, on; carburettor air, off; gyros, locked; tanks, cross feed; altimeter ..." he paused for a moment and then went on. "Altimeter, pressure altitude, set; supercharger, off; controls, free; automatic pilot, off and locked."

He looked up and grinned. The small fluorescent light in the centre panel above their heads gave off enough radiance so they could see each other's facial expressions. Wenck gave a half smile in return. He was nervous, partly through lack of sleep and partly because he was taking this still largely unknown aircraft off on their first night flight together.

Although the cockpit was well laid out, there were almost 200 dials, levers, knobs and other sundry gadgets to be memorised and their function understood. Experienced though he was, it was still a daunting task, especially since nearly all the instruments were still calibrated in their original imperial measurement. The only German instruments were add-ons designed to harmonise with German navigation and radio aids.

He remembered Major Peter Stahl's final words as they had clambered into the aircraft scarcely five minutes before.

"Hals- und Beinbruch," he said gravely, using the old German salutation to downhill skiers as they launched themselves down a slope. Break your neck and legs could be very apt, Wenck thought.

Finow had one runway and it was not very long at that.

Swabisch's left hand moved to the number one engine switch. He paused and looked at Wenck. The latter nodded.

"Energise number one," he said, using the American term written on the start-up check-list.

With those words the direct crank inertia system was energised and a low whine began to emit from the number one Wright Cyclone. It rose in crescendo until Wenck said crisply, "Start one."

The engine caught on the first try. Bluish-black smoke belched from the exhaust and then thinned as the engine settled down to a healthy resonant roar.

The same sequence continued successfully with the number two and three engines. Number four was a little hesitant. It belched. "Verdammtes Zeug," he swore and, as if in answer, the engine belched again before catching and joining in harmony with its sisters.

With all four now turning at 1,000 revolutions and the cowl flaps fully open, Wenck paused for a second to gather his thoughts. Satisfied that everything was correct he ran the engines up to 1,600 revolutions and checked the magnetos. The drop was minimal, so he taxied out onto the runway. Once aligned on the concrete strip he locked the tail wheel and set the directional gyro on zero.

Another pause.

"Flaps twenty degrees and coming down," intoned Swabisch.

The engine throttles were set in an H pattern, which enabled the pilot to easily control each engine separately, or all four at once through a central cross bar.

Wenck slowly advanced the throttles as both he and Swabisch kept pressure on the brake pedals. The B17 strained and trembled as the revolutions built up.

As Wenck's gloved hand continued to manipulate the throttles, Swabisch called out the manifold pressure. When it reached thirty-four inches (courtesy of the turbo superchargers), Wenck said, "Release brakes," and Miss Nonalee Two fairly leapt down the runway.

All B17s had a slight tendency to swing left on take-off so Wenck countered by opposite rudder. As the runway lights flashed under both wings, Swabisch counted out the plane's speed. Because the instrument still read in the imperial the co-pilot read out the figures in miles per hour. When he had first flown the American bomber Wenck had found the take-off speed to be very slow, that was until he transposed the figures to kilometres per hour. Fully loaded, a B17 would take off when the speed reached 115 miles an hour. Lightly loaded as she was and with the manifold pressure at forty inches, Miss Nonalee Two left terra firma at barely a hundred miles an hour and quickly climbed into the black, wintry, early morning sky.

Once the wheels were retracted he reduced the manifold pressure to thirty-nine inches and set the climb to a steady 150 miles an hour. It was necessary to re-set the turbo superchargers every 2,000 feet so, when the altimeter needle reached the figure, Swabisch adjusted the levers.

At 25,000 feet Wenck levelled off, reduced power to cruising speed and checked the compass to make sure they were on course for Halden. At this height, flak was not a huge problem especially since it was still night.

Wenck had timed the take-off so they would arrive at the Norwegian base at dawn. Now all he had to do was hope his identification, friend or foe was working so no prowling German night fighter misread the signals and tried to shoot them down. Similarly, there was also the danger of a British Mosquito or Beaufighter finding them. With only two turrets in operation and with both operators not fully cognisant of their workings the thought of a British night fighter finding them did not bear thinking about.

He handed over the controls to Swabisch and settled back into his seat. God he felt tired, it had been a long and hectic seven days since he had first set eyes on the Boeing.

Once he knew the American bomber was available, they had started looking for a Junkers 390 to cover themselves in case either Schonewille or Göring (for different reasons) checked on how things were progressing. Schonewille did not yet know about the plan to use the B17 and both Wencks decided they would keep it secret until the last possible moment.

Unfortunately, obtaining the vital Junkers proved impossible. After three days of searching, they eventually found one at an airfield near the Czechoslovak border. When Peter Wenck flew down to see it he quickly realised it was highly unlikely that it would ever fly again.

It was a wet Sunday morning and in the distance a church bell clanged mournfully under a leaden sky. The young lieutenant who had accompanied him from the dispersals area where he had parked his Focke Wulf looked at him anxiously as they surveyed the once proud bomber. "Zum Teufel, zum Teufel," he repeated in frustration.

He recognised the aircraft for he had flown her on two occasions. She was one of the prototypes and now she was a mess. Only two engines remained in situ, one undercarriage was minus half its retraction struts and wheels plus there were several very large holes in the wings and fuselage. One tail plane and the port aileron were missing. Skirting the gantry holding up one wing, he hoisted himself up through one of the crew hatches. At first the inside seemed intact until he surveyed the cockpit. Some key instruments had been removed as were the interior mechanisms of the two fuselage turrets.

With a sigh he sat down in the pilot's seat, idly playing with the control column. He looked back at the lieutenant and asked him where the missing engines were.

"Ich weiss nicht," the man answered with a shake of his head.

It would take a major operation to make the giant aircraft airworthy again. That and time. He did not have time and he could not afford to bring undue attention to their operation by trying to have the plane repaired and made airworthy.

Not that it mattered, but out of curiosity he asked why the aircraft had been reduced to such a state. The lieutenant again shook his head apologetically and said he'd heard the plane had been damaged in an air-raid and had subsequently been cannibalised for spare parts.

Since there was nothing left for him, he had his fighter re-fuelled and immediately set course back to Swinemunde where he re-fuelled once more before flying onto Norway. Most of the entire trip home was spent in thought as he tried to think of an alternative to the big Junkers. By the time he landed at his father's base at Halden he had the answer.

Helmuth Wenck was leaning back in his chair, a pair of old carpet slippers adorning his feet, which were precariously propped up on the edge of his large writing desk among a pile of papers. The general did not get up, but waved his hand towards the schnapps bottle and told his son to help himself. "Well Peter, how did it go? Did you find what we are looking for?"

The young pilot poured himself a good measure and gulped down a mouthful before turning to answer. "Yes, Father, I found the old girl, or what's left of her. She's a bloody mess and will probably never fly again." He took another swallow of the liquor as his father jerked upright, a move that sent several files crashing to the floor.

The general stared at him silently for a few moments trying to gauge whether his son was pulling his leg. "You're not joking, are you?" he said at last with a sigh. The other shook his head and emptied the tumbler.

They both knew how imperative it was for them to have another aircraft with which to complete the deception. Too many people expected it. Göring wanted an aircraft capable of reaching and bombing New York while Schonewille and perhaps Grauwitz expected a German bomber with sufficient range to fly them far from the borders of the Third Reich.

The general enquired whether there were any more Junkers 390s available. Peter Wenck shook his head, reminding the older man that less than half-a-dozen had ever been built and the one they had found was the last to survive virtually intact.

"However, I think I have an alternative. But first, can you get me something to eat? I'm starved." Helmuth Wenck called in one of his aides and when the man had left the room motioned his son to explain.

"Well, Father, it is not as difficult as one would first imagine. As we have discussed so often, range is the key. We have several aircraft with a range as long as the 390. The thing that made the 390 so special was its ability to also carry a useful bomb load, or cargo for that matter. At first I thought the only alternative would be a Condor, but then I remembered another aircraft that will be almost as good as the big 390."

He paused as there was a knock at the door and an orderly entered with a tray bearing sardines, cheese, butter, bread and a large mug of milk. The general thanked the man and then dismissed him with a curt wave of his hand. When he had gone, Peter Wenck continued.

He explained how the 390 had been a development of the four-engined Junkers 290 transport and long-range maritime patrol bomber. In order to make their New York bomber the Junkers design team had simply fitted an extra panel section in each wing to house the two extra BMW engines and had added a new fuselage centre section to increase the length. In almost every other aspect the two aircraft were identical.

"There's still the question of range, Father. If my knowledge is correct, the 290 has an insufficient range. With a full defensive armament it has a range of only 6,000 kilometres, although this can be increased substantially. The question is, by how much?"

The young pilot explained how he knew the whereabouts of at least two such aircraft. They were based at Narvik and as such would be relatively easy to gain control of.

They discussed the matter at length and by the time they went to bed had managed to tie up any loose ends the change in aircraft might bring to their plans. This included partially stripping the 290, fitting extra tanks, but leaving sufficient space in the bomb bay for an offensive load of 500 kilograms. That way any questions from the Reichsmarschall about the plan to bomb New York could be answered.

They had also agreed on the necessity of another pilot joining the team and Peter Wenck unhesitatingly suggested his old comrade Leo Swabisch. The following day arrangements were made through the commander of Bomber Fleet Norway and, duly, thirty-six hours later Swabisch presented himself at Kragero.

Peter Wenck was shocked at his former adjutant's appearance.

The pilot was clearly very sick. He had lost a considerable amount of weight and his skin was an unhealthy pallor. Pushing a lock of greasy black hair off his forehead, Swabisch gave Wenck a mocking salute and attempted what would normally have been his flashing, slightly sardonic smile. Now it gave the impression of a grimace from a scarecrow.

"Hell, Leo you look like death warmed up. In fact that's being kind. What the fuck's wrong with you? You got the clap or something?"

"Jesus, Peter, I don't know. I've been at Banak for the past two weeks and there's no proper doctor at the base. I've had this bloody cold for all of this time and it's been interspaced with bad bouts of diarrhoea on and off, for the past few days."

Wenck shook his head and led him to the infirmary. There was no doubt Swabisch needed medical treatment. He just hoped his friend's malaise was not serious. Whatever he was suffering from, Swabisch's sense of humour was intact.

"Speaking of the clap, boss, there any women around here? It's been a long time now. I've got my standards and you know how the Laplanders smell."

The doctor gave him a thorough examination, which lasted half-an-hour. His diagnosis was brutally frank. "Captain Swabisch is well on the way to getting influenza. He has also caught some sort of stomach bug and I believe he could be in the early stages of gaining a stomach ulcer. He needs a complete rest and under no circumstances should he fly again for at least two weeks. If he does so, I cannot be held responsible for his health."

Wenck sighed and pursed his lips before speaking. "Well doc, you've got five days, maybe even a week to get him right. Certainly, no more. There's a lot dependent on his health. So you get him right or I'll see you're transferred to a place where the air is cold and the natives very unfriendly."

The doctor sighed inwardly. He was wary of the Oberleutnant with the Knight's Cross and the determined manner. He had come across the type before and like many others on the base he wondered what the officer was up to. The secrecy surrounding Wenck worried everybody, so they all kept out of his way. Now the doctor had been drawn in and at fifty-eight years of age and with the war nearly over, all he wanted was a quiet life.

He saluted and immediately had Swabisch admitted to a small nearby clinic where he could give him his undivided attention. He felt sure that with rest, good food and whatever medicines and drugs he could lay his hands on, the pilot would recuperate quickly.

In the meantime, both the Wencks had other things on their mind than Swabisch's health.

While Peter flew north to pick up the Junkers, his father flew south to Hamburg to ostensibly meet with other high command personnel planning the forthcoming winter air offensive. In reality though, he was to make contact with the former diplomat Conrad Meunier.

Peter's trip was by far the easiest. The Junkers turned out to be in perfect condition and with the paperwork having been prepared beforehand it was a simple matter to collect the big bomber. With a commandeered crew he flew back to Kragero.

Helmuth on the other hand had a much more fraught time. He arrived at dusk and subsequently had to endure two uncomfortable hours in an air-raid shelter comforting a terrified child who had been separated from its parents while British bombers pounded the wrecked city and its port facilities. When he emerged, Hamburg was in chaos and on reaching his destination found the scheduled meeting had been cancelled and was now to be held at seven o'clock the next morning. Finally, with the phone lines down, he had been unable to contact Meunier.

After an uncomfortable night in a rundown third rate hotel and without the benefit of breakfast, the major general headed for his meeting.

Although sceptical about the chances of the forthcoming offensive in the west being successful and with little knowledge about the ground offensive, he was nevertheless very impressed with the planning and possible execution of the air campaign.

What if it was a success? Would Grauwitz and Friedrich abandon their plans? His thoughts just added another dimension to the growing complexity of this whole episode. Yet, whatever the result, there was no option but for he and Peter to continue with their plans. Reichsbank loot or not, he was still determined to leave if it looked like Germany was going to be defeated and despite the coming battle he did not believe that, long-term, the Third Reich would survive. Too much was against them.

There was also the matter of the concentration camps. If what he had been told was true, he wanted nothing more to do with a country guilty of perpetrating such crimes. The world would not let the Germans forget and he knew a defeated Germany would not be a nice place in which to live, especially if the Russians were in control.

Finally, there was the question of his wife. He missed Vigdis and as time went on their enforced separation was increasing his longing for the fair-haired Icelander. He knew she still loved him. Though the war meant their letters were infrequent, he was still averaging one from her every two months, courtesy of the Red Cross. She wrote with love and longing and still continued to ask whether he would give his permission and arrange for her to return to Germany, or Norway, to be with him. Such loyalty was rare in a woman, he thought.

The conference lasted throughout the day and well into the night, although the inclusion of a hearty lunch and even better dinner helped the officers stand the mental rigours of such a meeting. During a short break in proceedings early that afternoon he had managed to get through to the former diplomat and, on completion of the conference, headed for Meunier's house in the outer suburbs of Hamburg.

"Helmuth, my old friend. You are looking well." He greeted Wenck at the doorstep.

Meunier was a study in opposites. Everything about him was not quite what it seemed. Although of medium height, he seemed much shorter, courtesy of a rather corpulent figure. Yet, he was not fat. He carried his extra kilos well and was extremely fit. He resembled Oliver Hardy and like the famous comedian had spent a lifetime in pursuit of sporting activities, particularly golf. In his youth he had been a champion boxer and had even learned to play cricket while stationed in the Bahamas.

At sixty-two he was still in the prime of life. He looked his age, though his movements and purposeful stride belied his years. The death of his wife had both saddened and relieved him. They had been married thirty-three years and to watch her suffer the ravages of cancer had left him feeling helpless and distraught. Now, alone and free, he began to look at his own future.

Like his Luftwaffe friend, he did not intend to stay on in a defeated Germany, especially now that he had a good deal of information about what was occurring in the concentration camps. His feelings about Hitler had never been of the approving kind, but he was now beginning to have a strong aversion to the German people as well.

Over a strong brew of Ersatzkaffee, the imitation drink made from acorns, they discussed the future of the war. Although they were sitting outside, both men kept their voices low. Meunier was another strong believer in the axiom about walls having ears and he made sure that as far as possible, very little of what was discussed with Wenck was done so under the roof of his house.

As they talked, they could both smell and see the smoke of the fires still blanketing the city and the surrounding suburbs. It was a potent example of what was happening to the once great Third Reich.

Meunier spoke bluntly. He explained that since the death of his wife two months before he had begun to plan his own future and if there was a chance, he wanted to join Wenck on whatever escapade the Luftwaffe general was involved in.

Helmuth Wenck was only too happy to oblige and over an hour's conversation explained in the minutest detail what was being planned. He had no fear in telling his old friend, since in their previous conversations he had already revealed to him some of what they were planning and so far there had been no repercussions.

There was also another reason. While Helmuth and Peter were well advanced in their plan to escape Germany, their ultimate destination and how they actually got there was causing them some headaches. Quite simply, they needed Meunier. His contacts and intimate knowledge of what was happening politically in some of the likely countries of destination would be invaluable in helping formulate their escape plans. Although it had been two years since Meunier had served in either the Foreign Office or the Abwehr, he had kept up his contacts and through them a steady source of reliable information. On top of this he had a surprise for his friend.

"Three days ago I applied to re-join the Foreign Office," he said with a smug smile, clicking his tongue and raising his eyebrows. "I explained how with Helene now dead I could once more devote my energies towards the future of my country. It was quite simple." He clicked his tongue again and nodded his head at his own cleverness.

He recounted how he had even spoken to the head of the German Foreign Office, von Ribbentrop. "As usual the old fool fell for my flattery and welcomed me back with open arms. This means I can be of use to you my friend. My only fear is, they might transfer me somewhere outside Germany, although I told Ribbentrop that for the immediate and foreseeable future I would like to remain in Germany. Since most diplomats are trying to get out of this hell-hole, it was a smart move and as from tomorrow I am back on the payroll of the old firm."

He then explained how it was possible he could even obtain information from the RSHA, the main security department of the Reich which, as a branch of the SS, controlled the Gestapo and the other security services, including the old Abwehr organisation.

"As you probably know, after the Abwehr was disbanded nearly all the staff were transferred as a whole to the RSHA. But, and this is very important, offices two and three of Canaris's old organisation even remained under their old chiefs. You remember Freytag-Loringhoven and old Georg Hansen?" Wenck nodded. "They're still there and in charge of their men. The only difference is, they're now part of the military office of the RSHA's section six. Apart from a little more vetting by the SS, things apparently remain as when we were there. In other words, the group Canaris set up and that we worked with at one time or another is largely intact."

"What happened to the old boy?" asked the general.

Meunier shrugged his shoulders and raised his eyebrows. "Don't know," he said shaking his head to reinforce the words. "Rumours say he's dead, been executed like the rest. But, and it's a big but, there are conflicting rumours suggesting he is still alive in some prison or camp somewhere. Probably the latter. I didn't ask. It would not have helped me, or for that matter us."

Wenck was silent for a moment, then gave a small smile and clapped his portly friend on the knee. "At any rate now you can start to obtain the information we need, nicht war?"

Meunier nodded enthusiastically, explaining how it would only be a matter of days before he found out whether the old system of foreign agents remained and who there was in the Caribbean who could be of use to them in their attempt to flee Germany.

"Helmuth my old friend, I am positive I can be of help. I can certainly identify our agents in some of the countries we've discussed. I know it has been two-and-a-half years since I've been in the organisation and things could have changed, but if the ones we need are still in position we have a bloody good chance."

He passed a hand over his face and rubbed his chin with his thumb and forefinger, ruminating. "There are some big problems. For example, how can I talk to them in secret? I almost certainly will be able to contact them. Yet, how can I trust them and what can I tell them in safety?"

"Is the Himmler letter of any use?" asked Wenck.

The other shook his head and said maybe. But it would be a risk. At any rate the first thing to be done was to ascertain which agents were left in that part of the world and if they could use them.

They discussed their options for another hour and then the air force officer took his leave. It was agreed. Meunier would only contact him in an emergency. All other contact was to be initiated by Wenck and at a pre-arranged time. Most messages would be re-routed through friends in the Luftwaffe.

Chapter Thirteen
15 December 1944

Peter Wenck sat staring at the computations spread on the table in front of him. Here was a new problem to solve. Two days previously his father had contacted him to say he'd had a very short message from Meunier telling him to consider the Dominican Republic and this needed a new set of fuel and range figures. He was not bad at figures, but there were too many vagaries. It was becoming very difficult to work out just how much extra fuel they would need in order to fly the B17 to this new destination.

Opposite him Leo Swabisch shook his head. He was irritated and it showed.

"Himmel, Peter. How can I be of help when you won't let me know what's happening. All I know is we have two planes, both completely different and you are planning another one of your crazy, harebrained schemes. And what for? We're done for, and you know it. Or is this something that is going to win us the war?"

Swabisch had made a good recovery. He had put back some of his lost weight, his colour was almost back to normal and his black hair was sleek and shiny again. He was an invaluable member of the team, yet Peter Wenck purposefully kept him in the dark. It was not because he did not trust the pilot, but rather he believed there was too much at stake for more than two or three people to actually know what was going on.

His problem was accentuated since within the various groups nobody quite knew what the other was doing. With their own plans there were just he, his father and Meunier. Schonewille knew some of their plans while they knew almost nothing of his. Grauwitz, on the other hand, worried them the most for undoubtedly the SS general had his own nefarious ideas of what should be done and for that reason they were careful of what they told Schonewille.

They had no idea as to when Grauwitz and Schonewille planned to withdraw the money from the Reichsbank and what would be the procedure to transfer it to Norway. While Schonewille had said he expected their escape route to be through Spain, both Peter and his father were desperately searching for another route. Spain worried them.

Meunier had warned them that though Spain was nominally a neutral country, it was full of Allied agents and every German flight to and from General Franco's country was being logged by Germany's enemies. Therefore, if they were to simply disappear it was vital that nobody was able to trace any part of their escape route.

Meunier had already come up trumps and had put in place the rudiments of a plan that would ensure at least one place where they could land, the Dominican Republic.

Though they now had at least part of their destination, their ultimate home port was still in the planning stages. Meunier had picked the Dominican Republic for many reasons, but there were too many problems for them to make this Caribbean country their final destination.

Just thinking about the problems still to be surmounted increased his blood pressure and depressed him, so he left those to his father and the diplomat and concentrated on those aspects of the plan over which he could find a solution.

Still soliciting information, Swabisch tried another tack. "Well, Peter. At least let me know what sort of distance we'll be travelling, that way I can try to help."

"At least 10,000 kilometres," he said for he had worked out the distance from southern Norway to the Dominican Republic.

"Shit. It's not New York again is it? I mean does this mean the total range needed is 10,000 kilometres or is this only the radius?" Without waiting for an answer he went on. "At any rate, then it cannot be New York," he said answering his own question. "The distance from here must be oh, something like 12,000 kilometres at least," he said, shaking his head in bewilderment.

"Can't say yet, Leo. I'm sorry," answered Wenck lamely.

They both stared back at the mass of figures on the table. The B17 had a normal operating range with a 2,500-kilo bomb load of about 3,000 kilometres. Their aircraft already had some extra tankage and consequently its range was now just over 4,000 kilometres, which was less than half what they needed.

"What we have to work out is whether we can utilise the bomb bay for extra fuel tanks," Wenck suggested. "We should ..."

"You're right, it's the ideal place," broke in Swabisch and then quickly added, "So we're not carrying any bombs eh"?

Wenck shook his head with a rueful grin.

"Okay then, you're right. The bomb bay is perfect. It will not upset the centre of gravity, it is certainly large enough and the tanks will be easy to get inside."

Wenck nodded his head and asked Swabisch to see about getting the necessary tanks fabricated. Once they were constructed, they would run some tests and see how much additional fuel the Flying Fortress would now be able to carry and how this translated itself into the extra range they so desperately needed.

There was another problem worrying the life out of him. Earlier in the morning his father had received a radio message from Reichsmarschall Hermann Göring demanding to see him immediately. It could only mean one thing. The head of the Luftwaffe wanted to know what the status was with their supposed plans to bomb New York. His father had given him details of Hitler's planned winter offensive on the Western Front and it was due to start the next day, 16 December.

They had both hoped Göring would have been too busy to remember Helmuth Wenck's plan. Obviously, they had been wrong. The question now was what could be done? Even if they had wanted to bomb New York, they certainly did not now possess an aircraft with the range to get there and back.

Despite their best efforts, they had not been able to cram sufficient fuel into the Junkers for a two-way mission with a bomb load. They could certainly reach America on a one-way trip, but this was not how they wanted to reach the promised land. A parachute ride followed by the inevitable prison camp would be an inglorious end to all their conniving.

Chapter Fourteen
18 December 1944

The radar operator picked up the blips on the FuG 216 Neptun tail warning radar some five minutes previously. At first Peter Wenck hoped the blips represented aircraft that just happened to be in the area and nothing to do with their presence in this strategically important part of the North Atlantic.

Fat hope, he thought, as the radar operator informed him the spots on the screen were closing rapidly. He knew automatically what they represented. Allied fighters were being vectored onto them by ground-controlled radar. I wonder what they will be, he thought. It was not idle inquisitiveness but rather professional curiosity born of logic.

What the aircraft actually were could determine their survival in the next few minutes. He was not afraid, for he had flown operationally for too long to worry about the likelihood of death in any potential confrontation. As well, his aircraft was heavily armed and, properly handled, could give a very good account of itself.

His thoughts were cut off by a garbled exclamation from the crewman in the forward mid-upper turret. His compatriot in the aft mid-upper turret was much clearer in his comments.

"Der Gabelschwantz Teufel," he shouted excitedly, giving the sobriquet of the Lockheed Lightning, the fork-tailed devil.

Wenck's blood pressure rose several degrees. The American fighters would be tough opponents. They had a long range, which meant any fight could be protracted for he knew they would have sufficient fuel to stay in the air for a considerable time. They were also heavily armed.

There was now no chance of reaching their target even if he had really wanted to.

"Jettison the bomb load," he told the bomb aimer.

They had been right to worry about Göring's reason for waiting to see Helmuth Wenck.

The Reichsmarschall had been in a testy frame of mind. The pressures of helping plan the massive and complex air campaign for the Ardennes offensive had obviously played havoc with his nerves. Gulping pills at an even greater rate than when they had first met, Göring had waved his hands in the air, before bringing one pudgy palm down on the oak table with a crash that dislodged a heavy glass ornament onto the floor.

Helmuth Wenck had flown to the Air Fleet headquarters near Warmsee within hours of receiving his superior's orders. There had been no formalities. On his arrival he had been immediately ushered into the presence of the Luftwaffe chief.

"Well, Herr General," he said immediately and Wenck knew he was in trouble. The use of his rank, rather than his Christian name was a always a portent of official displeasure from Göring. "What is the status of this grand plan of yours to hit Eisenhower where it hurts, eh? Well, why have you not kept me informed?" Before Wenck could answer he continued imperiously. "I am assembling the largest fighter force ever seen by the Reich, 3,700 aircraft and pilots and the officer-in-charge of one aircraft, for one raid, has not the decency to inform his commanding officer what is happening. Well, don't just stand there. Tell me!"

Wenck kept his temper. He was on dangerous ground and he knew it. Calmly and succinctly he explained what had happened. How the only Junkers 390 was so badly damaged they had not been able to repair it. How they had managed to commandeer a Junkers 290 and how they had tried every means possible to increase its range in order to reach New York. Finally, he said, "Herr Reichsmarschall, we just cannot do it. I love my son and I just cannot send him on a one-way suicide trip to bomb New York. Think what the Allied press would say. They would claim Germany is reduced to sending its best pilots on suicide missions while they can bomb Germany every day with a reasonable chance of getting back." He paused, saw his words were having an effect and hurried on. "However, Sir, I have come up with another idea that might prove to be a possible substitute. Not as good, mind you, but still worthy of consideration."

Göring grimaced and nodded his head. He motioned Wenck to

be seated. "Go on, Helmuth, tell me what you have in mind." He suddenly looked weary.

"As you know, for the last four years the Allies have been using Iceland as a staging area for their convoys and to fly long-range patrols to harass our U-Boats and long-range maritime reconnaissance aircraft. What I have in mind is this." He paused and saw he had Göring's attention. "We use the 290 to bomb Reykjavik. I don't just want to bomb ships in the harbour, I want bombs to actually land on Icelandic territory and with luck kill Americans. The outcry will be so great the Allies will have to divert aircraft to the island."

Göring nodded his head.

"Then, if the raid is successful we do it again, but this time at night and force them to also divert night fighters to protect Iceland. We could also follow these raids with a propaganda campaign saying that we now have the capability to bomb New York."

Göring bought the idea.

As he flew home, Helmuth Wenck breathed a sigh of relief. They had garnered some more time, but at what a cost. His son would still have to undertake the raid and do so properly, because Göring was to send an observer for the proposed mission. Whether this was because he was suspicious or just wanted first-hand information, Wenck did not dare ask.

The next day Göring's emissary arrived at Kragero. Both Wencks took an instant dislike to the man. Captain Wilhelm Getman was the archetype German Aryan. In fact, he had even featured in *Signal* magazine. Peter Wenck was tall with fair hair and blue eyes. Yet Getman was taller, with hair the hue of pale corn and eyes the colour of a tropical sky.

If the Wencks had their reservations, the dark haired Swabisch positively disliked the man. The feeling was mutual.

Before Getman arrived, Peter Wenck had taken Swabisch aside and told him not to mention the B17 or their activity at Halden. Swabisch had laughed and jokingly enquired as to what would happen if he did.

A worried and harassed Wenck did not see the joke. He rounded on his friend and in an irritated voice said, "Then, my

142

friend, I will have you and that fucking snooper shot."

The vehemence in his voice and the expression on his face shocked Swabisch to the core. He felt utterly out of his depth and seeing the pressure his long time comrade was under only heightened the feeling. The arrival of Getman compounded his own anger, so he turned his frustration on the interloper.

Getman was a party member and proud of it. A fighter pilot with twenty-two victories, he had been badly wounded in the Crimea and had been sent home to recuperate. Appointed as an aide to the Reichsmarschall, he was now being sent to Norway to check up on the Wenck's Icelandic sortie.

Getman arrived a few hours after the 5th and 6th Panzer Armies of General Sepp Dietrich and General Hasso von Manteuffel, plus the 7th Army under General Erich Brandenberger, broke through the American lines on a seventy-kilometre front in an attempt to reach Antwerp and split the Allied armies.

Luckily for the pilots the 290 was almost ready. All that was needed was to fuel and arm the big Junkers and obtain the latest weather reports from the target area.

On the seventeenth they flew to Trondheim and waited for the decision to go ahead.

On the morning of the eighteenth, with the German offensive in full swing and the German Sixth Panzer Army having just crossed the River Ambleve, Wenck lifted the heavily-laden bomber off the runway and headed west out over the Norwegian sea and towards the North Atlantic.

Although not a bomber pilot and with almost nil experience flying multi-engined aircraft, Getman had insisted on sitting in the co-pilot's seat. His arrogance had enraged Peter Wenck. He glared at the staff officer trying to contain his temper, but he lost the attempt.

"Now you listen carefully, Captain. Very, very carefully." He lowered his voice until the words were a hiss forced through pursed lips. "I don't care where you come from, what your party number is and who you report to. If you come with me, and I'll be the one to decide that, you will do what I say. Verstanden?"

Getman nodded his head. He was not sure what the relationship was between the Wencks and Göring, but he quickly realised that the man glaring at him was not afraid of anybody. Peter Wenck's record, together with the Knight's Cross at his throat meant he was used to getting his own way. At the same time he realised that although he was an ace with twenty-two victories, he was only twenty-one years of age and simply a humble captain to boot. Though the man opposite was only a few years older, he was already a lieutenant-colonel and a famous one at that.

Wenck went on, his voice now clipped and imperious. "Right, now that we understand one another, here's what you will do. You will help Captain Swabisch with the preparations. You'll sit in the co-pilot's seat during the flight, but not during landing and take-off and not for the attack, understand? Good, you're dismissed."

Now, with the Lightnings boring in at 400 miles an hour Wenck forgot these words and Getman remained in the co-pilot's seat. The fighter pilot noted Wenck's calm expression and the measured way in which he informed the crew of his planned moves and urged them to be careful. He was much impressed.

They had nearly made their target. The Junkers had just passed the island of Vestmannaevyjar and they were on course to cross the Icelandic coast between Stockseyri and Hella before turning westward to approach Reykjavik from inland. Of course what Getman did not know was that Peter Wenck had never planned to bomb his mother's homeland. If he had really wanted to do so he would have crossed the coast further to the east and north to reduce the risk of interception and then flown overland to the target.

Peter Wenck did not have a death wish, but he nevertheless welcomed the appearance of the two American fighters. It was what he had been hoping for.

The tail gunner warned him how the approaching fighters were closing in. This explained their intended method of attack: line astern, one after the other.

"Good," muttered Wenck half to himself. He now knew his chances of survival had increased measurably. The American pilots were amateurs. Instead of splitting up and dividing the German bomber's defensive armament by attacking from different quarters, they were playing a follow-the-leader routine.

The Junkers was no easy meat. Its defensive armament was made up of half-a-dozen twenty-millimetre cannons and several heavy calibre machine-guns while the pilot was one of the most experienced, wily and cunning men in the Luftwaffe.

Wenck hoped the two fighters would continue with their classic up-wind approach and attack from the rear. He planned to lower his flap and throttle back, so the attacking fighters would overshoot the rapidly slowing bomber and would therefore be forced to break away. If they turned and climbed he would let them go and then break for some nearby clouds, but if they dived below him, he planned to follow their dive and attack them. It was a risky manoeuvre, for he was depending on his gunners with their heavy cannons forcing the Lightnings to break away early.

His plan almost failed. As the big Junkers suddenly slowed down and filled their windscreens and with the two upper turrets and tail gunner beginning some accurate and unnerving defensive fire, the second American pilot bravely hung onto his dive for a second longer and tried a quick deflection shot. He was right on target.

Four cannon shells and some two dozen fifty-calibre machine-gun bullets struck the German aircraft. Luckily, none of the former hit the cockpit area, but unfortunately seven of the latter did. One machine-gun bullet hit the edge of the armour-plated co-pilot's seat and split in two. One half buried itself into the instrument panel while the other angled upwards and took off most of Getman's head. A horrified Wenck was suddenly splattered with blood, bone and brain matter as the near-headless corpse slumped in its harness.

Worse was to follow. The radar operator yelled into the intercom, saying cannon shell had entered the rear compartment killing the wireless operator and smashing the radio.

Momentarily distracted, he lost sight of the Lightnings and when he caught sight of them again his chance for an attack was lost.

Cursing, he swung the Junkers away and headed for the nearest cloud. He knew he would reach it before the attacking fighters were able to latch onto him again, but there was a problem, the cloud was too small. In order to reach the safety of a larger snowy blanket five kilometres away he would first have to emerge from the smaller one into clear sky.

This would be much too risky. He had to act boldly.

As soon as the small cloud enveloped the fleeing bomber, he threw it into the sharpest skidding turn he could manage and emerged from his cover to face the Lightnings.

The move caught the Americans by surprise. At a closing speed of better than 600 miles an hour there was no time to think. Having prepared for the manoeuvre, the crew of the Junkers were at a distinct advantage and they utilised it to the fullest. Both Lightnings pulled up and over the German bomber and in that split second one of the gunners swung his turret around and sent a deadly stream of armour-piercing shells into the belly of the leading fork-tailed fighter. The end was swift. With one engine on fire and its pilot dead, it turned on its back and dived into the sea.

Taking advantage of the mayhem he had caused, Wenck swung the Junkers around once more and before the second American pilot could gather his wits the Junkers was safely in the confines of the large cloud bank.

When they emerged thirty minutes later, they were almost 200 kilometres away and there was no sign of the remaining American fighter.

The sunshine, though, was transient to say the least. They had barely time to catch their breath when the weather closed right in and enveloped the Junkers. Minutes later they were struggling through a massive rain storm that reduced visibility to almost nil and made Wenck call on every bit of his prodigious skill to keep the big aircraft from being inverted, or worse still, from being torn apart by the elements.

The task was not made any easier by conditions in the cockpit. There was a hole in one of the side windows through which an icy sleet raged and much of the instrument panel was inoperative and smoking.

Then there was Getman, or what was left of him. Most of the man's brains were liberally spread on the roof and cockpit surrounds. A horrified Swabisch, on entering the cockpit, took one look at the remains and promptly vomited, adding to the mess and the smell.

With his nerves on edge, Wenck swore at his friend. "For fuck's sake Leo, can't you control your stomach? No, no leave that mess," he yelled above the noise of the storm as Swabisch took off his scarf and attempted to wipe away some of the bile and foodstuffs dripping down the back of the co-pilot's seat. "Just get Getman out of here and help me pilot this fucking heap of shit."

The grizzly task was completed and then Swabisch used his scarf to plug the hole in the window. One of the crewmen unscrewed the cap from a thermos and with an unsteady hand poured the two pilots some Ersatzkaffee. Refreshed, Wenck's heart rate slowed somewhat and he relaxed slightly.

Gradually the storm petered out and by the time they were within sight of the Norwegian coast the rain had stopped and the cloud was beginning to thin out. They landed at Trondheim without fuss and taxied to one of the dispersals areas. As he switched off the engines Wenck looked at his wristwatch. They had been in the air for just over nine hours. God, no wonder I feel weary, he thought.

The ground crew arrived, their faces pinched and blotchy in the cold air. Grimly they helped the crew take out the bodies of the two dead airmen and laid them on stretchers. As they picked one up, the bloodied hand of the wireless operator fell onto the snow leaving a small red smear on the white crystals. One of the gunners placed it back on the stretcher and swore under his breath. There was no particular feeling for Getman among the crew. They hardly knew him and, anyway, his demeanour had not endeared him to them. The wireless operator was different. They had flown with him, shared their rations and laughed at his jokes and now, like so many countless numbers of their comrades, he was dead. At nineteen years of age, his face still covered with acne, he was just another casualty of the war.

For a moment Peter Wenck felt guilty. The youth's death was unnecessary, as he had died for a sham. The pilot tried to ease his conscience. It was Göring's fault, he reasoned. If he had not insisted on the raid then the youth would have been alive. Despite the logic he knew he was also to blame but, since there was nothing he could do about it he mentally shrugged his shoulders and cleared his mind of the fact.

It took the engineers and ground crew thirty-six hours to repair the cockpit and wireless cabin and as soon as the last screw was in place, Leo Swabisch took off and headed for Kragero. Wenck had preceded him by the length of a twelve hour sleep.

On arriving at Halden, Wenck reported to his father, who in turn had contacted the Reichsmarschall. Göring, distracted by the Ardennes offensive and still planning the Luftwaffe's role in it, hardly bothered to reply. A curt "bad luck" was all he telegraphed, although a member of his staff asked for a full report. Getman's death hardly raised an eyebrow.

On the Western Front, things were not going to plan for the German army. Von Manteuffel had failed to capture Bastogne as planned and was forced to surround the town in an attempt to bludgeon the stubborn American defenders into submission. This failure was to have a far-reaching effect on the German offensive for it forced them to waste much needed armour and artillery on the town and caused them to waste the one commodity they had little of: time. Some of their armoured spearheads still continued westwards and almost reached the Meuse river on the twenty-fourth. However, Christmas Day saw the Allies begin their counter-attack. Montgomery in the north and Patton in the south began to squeeze the pimple that was the bulge of the German offensive. Boxing Day saw Bastogne relieved. By New Year's Eve the Wehrmacht and SS troops were being pushed back everywhere.

Despite this, the Germans tried two last attacks.

As the last remaining hours of 1944 ticked away, General Hermann Balck's Army Group G launched Operation Nordwind, an attack designed to destroy the allied forces in Alsace. It failed in its objective. A few hours later the Luftwaffe mounted what was to be its last major offensive of the war: Operation Bodenplatte. This was the massive offensive that Göring hoped would smash the Allied aircraft on the ground and, in doing so, enable him to be, once again, pre-eminent in Hitler's court.

Though Göring had hoped to muster 3,000 fighter aircraft for the attack, the Luftwaffe had only managed to garner together just over one third that amount. Nevertheless, 1,000 fighters were a large force in anybody's language.

Grouped into ten major Jagdgeschwader, the heavily-armed fighters mounted a simultaneous attack on some sixteen Allied tactical airfields in north-eastern France and the low countries. Shortly before half-past-nine in the morning on New Year's Day, the Focke Wulfs and Messerschmitts, all armed with bombs and/or rockets, struck the snow covered Allied airfields.

Though not as successful as they had hoped, the German pilots still managed to destroy some 300 British and American fighters and bombers, mostly on the ground. Unfortunately, in turn, they lost almost the same number. While the Allies could afford such a loss, the Luftwaffe could not. The loss of planes was magnified because the Germans lost almost 250 trained pilots and these were irreplaceable. The Allies on the other hand lost few fliers.

Like the whole Ardennes offensive, Operation Bodenplatte was a tactical victory that became a strategic failure. Thus weakened, the German forces, through those two failed offensives, hastened the demise of the Third Reich.

With the new year just dawning, the Allies were now readying themselves for the final push. In the west, Eisenhower was carefully and methodically preparing to continue with his offensive, while in the east, the Russian steamroller was almost ready to move once again.

All three Allies were now ready to exert the maximum pressure on what was left of the Third Reich. Germany was now like a nut in a nutcracker just waiting for its enemies to exert pressure on either end to split the whole rotten edifice wide open for the world to see.

For Grauwitz, Schonewille and the Wencks, time was running out.

Chapter Fifteen
15 January 1945

The night was the colour of Indian ink. Thick clouds hid the moon and the stars to such an extent that even the horizon and sea were invisible.

A film of perspiration formed under his flying cap as he spoke to his father seated behind him.

"Can you see the bloody lights?"

His father answered in the negative. Another few seconds elapsed and Peter Wenck had just decided to use his radio again and call up the airfield when a string of lights appeared just off their port wing tip. He quickly turned, aligned the Messerschmitt 410 with the lights, lowered his undercarriage and flaps and eased the fighter onto the tarmac.

The moment he reached the end of the runway the lights were turned off and, except for the dull glow from his instrument panel, he was left in total darkness. Suddenly, a torch light was waved in front of them and began moving slowly away. Easing off the brakes, he followed the dim light, his eyes straining to make sure the twin-engined night fighter did not stray off the edge of the taxi strip. A structure loomed out of the blackness so he braked to a stop. The torch was switched off and again he was left in darkness. When the lights did not re-appear he cut his engines and swung back the hinged cockpit canopy.

Awkwardly he hoisted himself out onto the wing root and helped his father clamber from the rear seat. Moving down the wing Peter Wenck jumped to the ground and then reached back to help the older man reach terra firma.

Two figures approached, a Wehrmacht sergeant carrying a torch and a leutnant in the uniform of the Kriegsmarine. The sergeant stopped two or three metres away, while the naval officer walked right up to them and saluted. "Welcome to England," he said.

After the abortive mission to Iceland, Göring had left the Wencks alone. Helmuth Wenck still had a legitimate job to do and was forced to spend a great deal of time re-organising his depleted command. Although Hitler was refusing to evacuate Norway, thereby strengthening the Reich, there were still considerable reinforcements that could be leached away from that country. In order to make sure his son was not transferred back to some operational squadron, the general made sure he was busily engaged in flying transport missions to and from Norway.

In Germany, on one such transport flight, Peter was contacted by Schonewille who engaged him to fly some of Grauwitz's Jews to Stockholm.

Although somewhat dishevelled and gaunt, the thirty-odd Jewish men and women did not seem too worse for wear and their appearance did much to allay his fears about what he had been told by his father on the happenings within the concentration camps.

While all this was going on, work continued on the B17. The Junkers 290 was a different matter entirely. Now repaired, it was still a valuable commodity to both the Wencks and the Luftwaffe. The former wanted to retain it in case something happened to the Boeing while the latter badly needed aircraft with the size and range of the Junkers.

To make any requisition difficult, Helmuth Wenck had the German bomber disabled by removing one engine (ostensibly for a complete overhaul) and partially dismantling the instrument panel.

In between their legitimate jobs, both men continued to plan and plot. Their biggest hurdle was still the question of range, though since it was a one-way flight it was not an insurmountable problem. The Junkers had almost sufficient range, but the B17 in its standard configuration did not. Straight as the crow flies, the distance from Oslo to the Dominican Republic was just over 10,000 kilometres. The Junkers-standard range was a shade over 6,000 kilometres and with the extra tankage it now carried it could fly the distance. Unfortunately, they realised that to fly a German aircraft into the Caribbean and then land in a country that was at least nominally on the Allied side would be highly risky, if not impossible, even if they disguised it with spurious markings.

Therefore, the Boeing was their only logical choice for slipping undetected into the Dominican Republic.

It was Peter Wenck who stumbled onto a possible solution to the problem. Just returned from a transport flight to Lubeck, he was idly thumbing through a back issue of *Signal* when an article caught his attention. Half asleep and with his tired brain not fully comprehending what he was reading, the implication of the article at first made no direct impact on his conscious thought. Yet, even as his fingers turned the page something slipped through and registered.

Turning back the page he stared at a large photograph of a huge gun hidden in a cliff face, its barrel pointing menacingly out towards the sea. Now, fully alert, he turned back another page and began to read further.

The article was about the Channel Islands, the only part of the United Kingdom to have been captured by Germany. What's more, even though France had been liberated and the front-line was 500 kilometres away, the Channel Islands were still very much in German hands.

Peter Wenck had actually visited the islands. Back in 1940 and with the Battle of Britain at its height, his squadron had been sent to Jersey for forty-eight hours. The island and its neighbour, Guernsey, were being used as bases from which the Heinkels could bomb southern England.

The *Signal* article was several months old and gave a highly colourful and slanted picture of conditions on the Islands. Although he knew they had not been re-captured by the British, he did not know just what their true state was and whether they could be of any use to him and his fellow plotters. He immediately contacted his father and requested a meeting, first thing the next morning. Over breakfast they discussed this important breakthrough.

The elder Wenck knew no more about the Channel Islands than his son, but he also realised their political status and their strategic worth to their plans.

"Christ, Father," said his son excitedly. "Do you realise that if we can utilise them as a re-fuelling point we can cut about 1,900 kilometres from the maximum needed range of the Boeing?"

Placing a ruler on a map that showed southern Scandinavia, part of Britain and all of France, he drew a line across the map and turned it so it faced his parent. "See, if we can follow this route we have a 1,600-kilometre flight to either Jersey or Guernsey. By my calculations it's just over 8,000 kilometres from there to the Dominican Republic." He stabbed a finger at southern England.

"Now, because in any flight from the Channel Islands we will not have to skirt the northern part of England, we will actually save another 280 kilometres or so. Therefore, as I've just said, the total saving is about 1,900 kilometres." His father nodded his head enthusiastically. "All we have to do now is find out what the political situation is on the islands and whether there is still an airfield capable of being used as a staging post. I mean, we don't know whether the Allies have bombed them to rubble."

After further discussion it was decided to utilise Meunier once more in order to gain sufficient intelligence about the situation on the Channel Islands.

On 5 January, Peter Wenck again flew to Lübeck. Complaining about an engine overheating on the FW200 Condor transport he was piloting, he left the aircraft in the hands of some mechanics while he took a train to Hamburg. He had arranged to meet the diplomat at a barber shop on the outskirts of the city. Contact made, they headed for a small café where they sat in the corner, alone and undisturbed except for the discreet hovering of a waiter. In a low voice Wenck told Meunier about the Channel Islands and what they wanted him to find out. The diplomat was as enthusiastic as the young pilot.

"My boy, I think you have hit upon another solution to our problem. My information is a little more up-to-date than yours, but before we decide on any strategy I will determine what the latest status is with these islands so we can decide how to utilise them." He paused and then added mysteriously, "Also, I believe I have found another piece of the jigsaw: the whereabouts of our ultimate destination. Tell your father that with a little bit of luck I will also have this piece of information by the eighth, or at least by the tenth," he said winking and tapping the side of his nose theatrically.

Whatever the information was, it was not to be forthcoming by the tenth or even by the twelfth when both Wencks had their next meeting with Meunier. This time they met in an empty apartment belonging to a friend of Meunier who was on duty manning a flak battery on the outskirts of the city. Meunier opened the conversation with an apology, saying that he was still no closer to being able to tell them about their ultimate destination.

"I'm sorry, my friends," he said with a wry smile, " I have not yet been able to lock this vital piece of our plan into place. But, do not fret, I am fairly certain I can do so and quite soon. It's just ..." he paused for a moment searching for the right words and then gave up. "Let us just say it is much harder to lock in than I had at first expected," he said enigmatically. "Nevertheless, I have all the relevant information about our islands and the news is good. I am quite certain we can use them as a re-fuelling stop."

The diplomat opened a small leather briefcase and extracted a quarter folded map and three postcard-sized photographs. Opening the map he began to recount the recent history of the Channel Islands.

He explained that to Hitler and Goebbels the islands were a vital part of their propaganda machine as they were important psychologically. The Führer and his information minister felt it was important for Germany to be seen by the rest of the world as still having the strength to hold onto part of Great Britain, especially when the territory was so far behind the front-line.

In the three years preceding D-Day the Channel Islands had been turned into a veritable fortress with one of the smaller islands, Alderney, which was situated little more than a dozen kilometres from Cape de la Hague on the French coast, being particularly well-endowed with six huge batteries of heavy guns.

Although construction of any fortifications had finished shortly after the Allies had landed at Normandy the previous June (because of the impossibility of bringing in any major supplies), all the islands were still heavily protected. In fact, it could be argued that had these substantial fortifications, which equalled Hitler's much vaunted west wall on the French coast, been sited at Normandy instead, then the Allies would never have got ashore.

The islands' defence systems were mostly encased in thick ferro concrete and included fire control systems to direct huge 30.5-centimetre guns. These had originally been fitted to some old pre-World War One Russian battleships and had subsequently been sold to the Danes for their own coastal fortifications. These guns were installed on Guernsey and concealed in dummy cottages. With a range of sixty kilometres they were able to hit targets well within the coastal areas of France.

As well, these fortifications were backed up by a large concentration of troops. The principal towns on Guernsey and Jersey, St Peter Port and St Heller, were also home to several large minesweepers belonging to the Kriegsmarine. These ships were effectively permanently moored as any attempt to try and return to Germany via the North Sea and Baltic would end in their destruction.

Despite this concentration of power, the islands had been governed differently than that of any other territory captured by the Third Reich. The Gestapo were never represented on the islands and SS troops were few and far between, except on Alderney where there were almost 2,000 slaves under the control of the Todt labour organisation.

Most of the islands' control was vested in the Geheime Feldpolizei and the Feld Polizei. The former was the Secret Military Police and the latter the ordinary Military Police.

The fliers listened in silence as Meunier carefully detailed conditions on the islands. Finally, he judiciously re-folded the map and picked up the three black-and-white photographs. He placed them in his right hand and fanned them apart like a poker player would.

"Now, for the important cards in this little game." He placed them one by one on the table facing the two airmen. "There you are, king, queen and jack ... and I hope we hold the ace. Right ... now this is the king of the islands, Count von Schmettow," he said pointing to one photograph.

The man portrayed had the face of a classic aristocrat: high forehead, pointed nose with a teardrop end, short, clipped, thinning grey hair and a military bearing. Yet the visage was not stern and overbearing.

"Schmettow has been commander-in-chief since September 1940, a long time to hold such a post, although if my informants are correct this will change very soon. But, I'll get onto that in a minute," said Meunier. "As his name suggests he's an aristocrat of the old school, he's …"

Helmuth Wenck broke in. "Yes, I know him. Not well mind you, but I met him in the first war and I've run across him at a couple of functions back in the thirties. He's a relation of von Runstedt is he not?"

"Yes, a nephew," answered the diplomat nodding his head. "It is good you've had some dealings with him. Now, as I was saying. He was a colonel in the last lot. He served on both the eastern front and in the trenches in France where he was wounded, losing a lung."

Meunier went on to explain how the count had not introduced any repressive measures on the islands he controlled. He had been able to be a benign ruler only because the islands had not been under the auspices of the German administrative forces that controlled occupied France. His civil administration came under Feldkommandatur 515, which had its headquarters at Victoria College in Jersey.

The diplomat then pointed to a second photograph.

"Baron von und zu Aufess, chief of administration. He's not important, except that he has the ear of Schmettow," he said pointing to another photograph. "Now, here's the jack of the trio. What's more I believe he is shortly going to be elevated to the position of king," he said pointing at the last photograph.

The face under the battered Kriegsmarine peaked hat was beefy and jovial. He resembled Göring although the build was less severe. The shadow of the hat's peak hid the expression of the man's eyes, so it was not possible to gauge the true nature of the person's smile.

"Vice Admiral Hüffmeier. By all accounts he is now virtually in control there. I do not know him personally. Do you, Helmuth?" The general pursed his lips and shook his head. "Well, he is the person we have to liaise with and he's the one we have to court.

He's a fanatical National Socialist and, would you believe, he has even been using the islands as a base from which to run raids on the French Coast."

Meunier explained how Hüffmeier's position on the islands was crucial to their using them as a staging post.

The vice admiral had previously been in command of one of the prides of the German navy, the battle cruiser Scharnhorst. Known throughout the Kriegsmarine as the lucky ship, her career was finally ended by the fourteen-inch guns of the British battleship Duke of York on 26 December 1943. Although not in command at the time of her final voyage, Hüffmeier was reported to have been enraged by her sinking. He had subsequently been transferred to the Channel Islands in June 1944 as naval commander. His authority on the islands was considerably enhanced when in October 1944 they were put under the control of the navy. The man in charge of the region was Admiral Krancke, Flag Officer Commanding Naval Group West and, as such, Hüffmeier's immediate superior. Because of this he did not have to report to von Schmettow on operational matters, only on decisions affecting the islands' administration.

"Helmuth, you will of course understand why the navy was put in charge. Since the July attempt on his life, the Führer has not been very trustful of the army and has put most of his faith in the navy, plus of course the SS. Also, the Kriegsmarine has plenty of personnel and except for the U-Boats, not many ships left. Therefore, the Channel Islands with their strategic position out at the southern entrance to the English Channel are a logical choice for naval administration."

He paused for a moment and the two air force officers nodded their heads. Peter Wenck spoke up.

"Can we use the bugger? I mean will he help?"

"We only have to use Himmler's and Göring's letters and explain that we need him and the islands to stage a daring and important raid and he will be bound to help. The man's whole history suggests he will jump at the chance."

Meunier explained it was common knowledge that Hüffmeier was busily undermining von Schmettow and actively pressing for his recall to Germany so he could replace him as commander-in-chief.

After further discussion it was decided the Wencks would fly to Guernsey as soon as possible to speak to von Schmettow and the vice admiral and enlist their aid.

As they left, Helmuth Wenck informed Meunier that they would be meeting with Schonewille early the next morning.

Meanwhile, Obersturmbannführer Friedrich Schonewille was not looking forward to meeting his father and half brother. Although he had reached an accommodation with Peter, he was still wary of his father. This was compounded by the sense of injustice caused by his parents' divorce and the feeling of inferiority still lurking just beneath the surface of his psyche.

Allied to this was his mental state and general health. Existing in the SS was always difficult, but now leading almost a double life and feeling that he was being used by Heger and Grauwitz, who absolutely refused to tell him when they planned to activate their escape, his nerves were beginning to fray. There were also the constant visits to the concentration camps. The appalling misery of the inmates was beginning to wear him down.

He had always been able to keep his conscience subordinated to his ambition and prejudices. His cold blooded execution of the more liberal minded of his class had always been fed by this hatred and prejudice. Unfortunately, though he was now a military man this group was still personified by his father. Similarly, Schonewille had been able to suborn his better nature to undertake whatever job was expected of him in the course of his duty. Now, the constant misery that confronted him every time he entered the confines of the camps was beginning to sicken him.

On his recent trip he had visited Sachsenhausen and Ravensbrook. The latter was a camp primarily for women. Having finished his perusal of the figures Schonewille had been led to an office by the camp's deputy commandant and offered one of the camp's inmates for the night. The Jewess smiled winningly at him but, although she did not look at all like Sophia, her expression was similar to that often shown by his mistress when he came home.

158

The shock of this realisation was enough to make him very angry with the deputy commandant. He refused, shouting his disgust and anger that anyone would dare think he would besmirch his name by having relations with a Jew.

At his words, the woman's smile had been replaced by a look of helpless fear and this further enraged him. He had seen the same haunted look when Sophia became frightened.

As usual after leaving the camps he had gone to the nearest hotel to have a bath while his suit was sponged and pressed. Since Ravensbrook was in northern Germany it had not been too hard to gain permission to travel onto Hamburg. His mother's sister still lived there and he often went to visit the elderly woman. Family duty was very close to the heart of the SS hierarchy and it was not difficult for him to ask for twenty-four hours leave to see a close member of his family. Therefore, the trip to the two concentration camps, his visit to his aunt and his meeting with the remainder of his family all fitted in very neatly.

His brother had contacted him a few days previously and they had arranged to meet at one of the few good hotels still standing. Peter was waiting in the foyer as he stepped out of the lift at the appointed time. Ill at ease at the prospect of seeing his father, Friedrich nevertheless greeted his half brother warmly. The room was crowded and in the jostling throng nobody took any notice of them.

Peter indicated with his head that he wanted Schonewille to follow and together they stepped out into the street. The two walked for ten minutes until they reached a small café in the older section of the city near the docks. They sat in the corner with the flier facing the door. They ordered some sandwiches and to Schonewille's surprise the proprietor also placed two large mugs of real cocoa in front of them. At his raised eyebrows the other said matter-of-factly, "Good, eh? I deliver the odd delicacy or two here when I fly over from Norway and my old friend over there," he waved a hand in the direction of a man wiping a table, "gets hold of some rare treats from the Swedish ships that dock here. It's black market, of course, and costs the earth, but well worth it don't you think?"

Schonewille nodded his head and put his cold hands around the mug, taking a small sip and smacking his lips appreciatively.

"Friedrich, my boy. How are you?"

With his back to the door and deep in the appreciation of his drink he had not heard his father enter, even though the café was almost deserted and relatively quiet. He rose and, before he realised what he was doing, saluted the older man. Unselfconsciously Helmuth Wenck returned the salute and then extended his hand. His first-born took it and then they both sat down.

A few minutes were spent ordering some food for the air force general and another round of cocoa. Then there was a moment's silence. The conversation was nondescript at first: state of health, difficulty in getting to Hamburg and the problem of the air-raids. Then, it was down to business.

Sensing Schonewille's wariness Helmuth Wenck took the lead, explaining in low tones how they had managed to obtain an aircraft with sufficient range to fly them well away from the borders of the Reich and how plans for their ultimate destination were progressing smoothly.

Schonewille asked where that destination was and his father answered by saying that he was not yet sure. Schonewille's eyes narrowed and Helmuth Wenck, seeing the look, said with assurance, "That's right, Friedrich. We are not yet sure. We are working on something and in fact I hoped to have had the answer today. Unfortunately, this has proved not to be the case. We are also working on a vital re-fuelling stop and this detail too still has to be tied together."

Peter Wenck nodded in agreement and added, "Yes, and you had better believe me. We have this crazy scheme almost completed and as soon as we have locked it in we'll tell you. Now, how is your end going and when are your friends planning to break open the till?"

Schonewille shook his head ruefully, saying he did not know. He added that he was being kept in the dark and it annoyed him. His father and brother exchanged glances and in an effort to re-gain the initiative he re-assured them. "At any rate, you do not have to worry about it. They need my signature on any withdrawal. When I return to Berlin tomorrow I will seek out Herr Grauwitz and see what I can glean. It is no use my asking Heger, he just does as he's told and despite what he says, I don't believe he knows too much. That shit Grauwitz would not tell his mother what day it was."

Both Wencks had decided not to press Schonewille too hard on either the money or on what his duties were in the SS. However, Helmuth broke the agreement and said to the SS officer, "And what are you up to these days, Friedrich – that is, what have the good old SS got you doing other than looking after their books and booking flights for Jews on their way to Sweden?"

Schonewille's eyes narrowed once again and he said slowly and cautiously, "Why nothing, Father, what do you mean?"

"Oh, nothing important, Friedrich. I just thought that an officer with your record would be doing more than just doing the books or acting as a glorified travel clerk."

Schonewille just nodded his head and said lamely, "I just follow orders, Father. Like all of us."

There was no reason to pursue the conversation any further so Helmuth Wenck let the matter drop. After ten minutes of desultory conversation they paid their bill and left. Silently, they walked through the snow to the hotel where they parted company – the Wencks to the airport and Schonewille to a warm bed.

The next day they began to plan their trip to the Channel Islands.

Chapter Sixteen
16 January 1945

The small Austin Ten backfired, the sound magnified by the still blackness around them. Wedged in the back seat with his father, Peter Wenck turned and smiled at his parent's face scarcely twenty centimetres from his own. There was no returning smile.

Peter shifted his gaze and peered at his wristwatch. The luminous dial told him it was ten minutes after midnight. Barely half-an-hour had elapsed since they had landed and not more than a dozen words had been spoken between them and their guide.

It had been relatively easy to get to the Channel Islands. Helmuth Wenck had sent a coded message to Hüffmeier and von Schmettow informing them of their arrival on the night of the fifteenth and impressing on them the need for total secrecy. To reinforce his message he included a reference to the Reichsführer.

The Messerschmitt 410 Hornisse was one of a handful based in southern Norway for night defence and the Wencks had chosen it as their mount because not only was it fast and had a reasonable range, but it was equipped with an efficient radar. The last thing they wanted in any flight to the Channel Islands was to blunder into a bomber stream of British heavies on their way to unload their cargoes on the Reich. Not that the bombers would prove a hindrance. It was the accompanying deadly Mosquito night fighters with their sophisticated radar, heavy armament and good turn of speed that could cause a problem.

They had left Kragero shortly after eight in the evening, heading south-south-west over the North Sea. A direct route was out of the question. It would have quite literally taken them over London and south eastern England, a move which at that time was quite suicidal. The British defences were such that few German aircraft were able to penetrate the air space of the United Kingdom and survive. Therefore, they headed directly down the slot of the English Channel, travelling fast and low. The former equated to a maximum cruising speed of 500 kilometres per hour and the latter, a height varying between only 300 and 1,000 metres. The height was not good for fuel consumption but they had no choice.

Eighty kilometres north of Dieppe they turned thirty-eight degrees to starboard on a heading, which took them over the Cherbourg Peninsula and onto Guernsey. The airport was in the south of the island, six kilometres from the main town St Peter Port and relatively easy to find. The flight had taken just over three hours.

The Austin backfired again. This time the naval officer turned his eyes from the road and said out of the corner of his mouth, "I am sorry, Herr General, but we do not have much petrol left on the islands, and what there is, is of poor quality. Consequently, what few vehicles we have run a little roughly."

There were no lights visible as they negotiated the narrow roads. Even when they began to travel down the relatively wide promenades of the town itself, no lights or people were to be seen. During the whole trip they had passed through only one road block and the two soldiers manning the upright pole merely waved them on.

They passed the Gaumont Palace, the only picture theatre in St Peter Port. It was decorated with a large portrait of Hitler over the entrance. A few seconds later they stopped with a squeal of badly-worn brakes and were led inside a large stone building. There was no waiting, no formalities. They were simply ushered into a room containing two people. Both were instantly recognisable by the photographs the Wencks had been shown by Meunier. There was some saluting (mainly by Peter Wenck who was the junior officer present) and then von Schmnettow came over, extending his hand to Helmuth Wenck.

"Herr General Wenck, it is a pleasure to see you again. How long has it been? Seven, eight years?"

The air force general shook his head and said he did not know. At the same time he shifted his gaze to the other man who stood impassively in the corner of the room two or three metres away. "Vice Admiral Hüffmeier. I am pleased to meet you."

Hüffmeier's face broke into a shallow smile. In the dim light Helmuth Wenck could see that unlike von Schmettow the naval officer had not shaved and his burly features were darkened by a dozen hours growth.

"Tea, coffee?" asked von Schmettow. "The former is very good as befits this outpost of the British Empire and we still have some quantities left. The coffee on the other hand is the vilest ersatz concoction and I would not recommend it."

Helmuth Wenck and his son both requested the tea.

The island's commanding officer pressed a button and a uniformed lieutenant entered, took the order and left without a word.

Von Schmettow waved them to some chairs and came quickly to the point. "Well, gentlemen. What is this all about? You have the admiral and I very intrigued."

Helmuth Wenck chose his words carefully. He wanted to give the impression their mission had the highest possible clearance. Von Schmettow was a spent force and while it was obvious he was not a Nazi, he was equally a member of the old school and would not condone what the Wencks were planning. Hüffmeier, on the other hand, would probably have them arrested and shot as traitors.

"What I am about to say is top secret. It comes from the highest quarters. However, I must warn you of two things. One, I am limited in what I am allowed to tell you and two – you must not breathe a word of this to anybody. It must not be discussed. Do you understand?"

Von Schmettow looked a trifle bored, but the naval officer was quite patently intrigued. He nodded his head in enthusiasm. Helmuth Wenck went on. "My son Peter is a specialist on long-range missions. His success and bravery can be gauged by the decoration at his throat. You may have read about his exploits in Russia. What you will not have read, but may know about, is that he has actually piloted one of our secret long-range bombers to New York and back."

Both von Schmettow and Hüffmeier looked across at Peter Wenck approvingly.

"Well now, this is what I am allowed to tell you. We are planning a very special raid. A long-range mission, which will shake the Allies. As the Führer has said so often, all is not lost. We have new and even more wonderful V weapons with which to strike back and all we need is time. Our mission will give us that time." He paused for effect and went on. "All I can tell you is that we need these islands, or rather one of your aerodromes as a temporary base – a staging post, from which to re-fuel. We have a special aircraft being converted at the moment in readiness for the mission."

"What authorisation do you have?"

It was von Schmettow who spoke. Hüffmeier on the other hand was smiling broadly and rubbing his hands together.

Helmuth opened his briefcase and extracted the two envelopes. "I have two letters, gentlemen. They are open-ended, yet very specific. Their authors are Reichsmarschall Göring and the Reichsführer."

Helmuth Wenck offered the two envelopes. Von Schmettow shook his head and waved his hand. Hüffmeier on the other hand took the envelopes and asked which one was Himmler's. On being shown, he extracted the letter and scanned its contents. He did not bother to open the other. There was no doubt whose missive he regarded as the most important.

The vice admiral asked what it was that they required.

Peter Wenck spoke for the first time. "How much aviation gasoline do you have stored here?"

"Almost none, Colonel. We have no aircraft and we are lucky to receive one flight a month from the Fatherland," said Hüffmeier.

The airmen half expected this. The chronic shortage of petrol was slowly strangling Germany and it had been too much to hope there would be sufficient stocks on the islands to meet their needs. As usual, they had made a contingency plan.

Helmuth Wenck explained how they would contact them within a week to arrange the transfer of sufficient stocks of fuel to Guernsey. They were momentarily interrupted by the officer with the tea. There was a studied silence as the cups were passed round and the liquid poured.

When the man had left, von Schmettow asked some specific questions that the elder Wenck parried. Hüffmeier, on the other

165

hand, was duly impressed and obviously willing to help in any way possible. Finally, von Schmettow rose from his chair and again shook hands with the two fliers.

"Well, mein Herren, I must bid you adieu. I have to get some sleep since I have a busy day tomorrow. No doubt my comrade here will want to talk some more," he said with a slight touch of condescending irony.

They all rose and saluted, with the vice admiral extending his right arm in the Fascist salute. "Heil Hitler."

Von Schmettow half-raised his hand, but said nothing. The door closed behind him.

They began to ply Hüffmeier with questions. Was there a dump that could safely store large quantities of fuel? Were the containers clean and moisture-free? Were there sufficient pumps on hand and did they operate? Finally, how often did Allied aircraft fly over the island and did they ever attack?

The answers to the initial questions were all in the affirmative. To the remaining two Hüffmeier explained that Allied aircraft were infrequent and generally covered only the two principal towns and their ports. "We still have several naval craft which they keep an eye on," he said. He paused for a moment and then blurted out, "And well they might. I intend to use them for my own little raid," he said looking intensely at the Wencks.

Helmuth Wenck groaned inwardly. "I hope this will not endanger our mission," he said severely.

The other shook his head vigorously and denied the possibility.

The air force general did not believe him. He knew the ex-sailor was desperately trying to seek favour with his superiors and had already tried one raid on the coast. He had no doubt others were being planned.

The danger was that, in doing so, he might raise the wrath of the Americans who might mount an air-raid that could damage the airfields on Guernsey or Jersey and possibly hinder their escape plan.

He was tempted to pressure Hüffmeier into being more circumspect, but did not want the vice admiral asking awkward questions or referring the matter to his superiors. Therefore, he just used a veiled threat. "Remember mein Herren, this mission has the highest priority. I am to report to the Reichsführer in a few days about the status. Therefore, I want no problems, verstanden?"

Hüffmeier nodded his head and Helmuth Wenck let the matter drop.

If Hüffmeier's patriotic zeal was dampened by this affirmation, then it did not last for long. He invited the two fliers to visit one of the big gun emplacements.

Although Peter Wenck would have liked to, they both knew it would not be possible. It was already gone two o'clock in the morning and they still had a long flight back to Norway. Nevertheless, in order to keep in the vice admiral's good books they promised to do so when they returned.

The same Austin took them back to the airfield, backfiring and lurching along the narrow roads and lanes.

"I had an old horse that used to fart like that," said Helmuth with a chuckle as they reached their destination. For some reason, they both found that simple inanity very funny and to the amusement of their escort broke into almost uncontrollable laughter. They were still convulsed with mirth as they strapped themselves into the night fighter.

The cockpit drill brought them back to reality. They had barely enough fuel to get back to Kragero and would have to be very judicious in their use of the throttle. It would not be conducive to their health if they ran into enemy aircraft. Unfortunately, such proved to be the case. Their return route was a mirror image of the trip down, a slight dog-leg and then back up the slot of the English Channel. But, with Hull some 250 kilometres off the port wing they ran into a strong force of British bombers returning from a raid on Germany.

Helmuth Wenck, sitting in the rear monitoring the radar unit, informed his son there were a number of strong blips showing on the screen. They had both hoped that by flying very low the chances of encountering any enemy aircraft would be slight. The reality proved them wrong.

They ran into two British Halifaxes. Both were flying low for the simple reason that they could not maintain height. One was flying on two engines and the other on three. For a moment Peter Wenck was tempted to attack, but the uselessness of such a gesture and the need to conserve fuel negated any reason for heroics. It was as well that he did. A Mosquito also crossed their path and moved towards them, but as the Hornisse continued northwards, the British fighter moved back to protect its injured charges.

The fuel warning lights were shining brightly when Peter Wenck finally lowered his undercarriage and flaps and lined the aircraft up with Kragero's runway.

Chapter Seventeen
27 January 1945

The atmosphere in the Reichsbank had not changed. The Reich might be crumbling and its capital reduced to ever increasing piles of rubble, but the bankers and their clerks still came to work and still administered to the financial needs of the country and the millions of accounts ranging from those belonging to the mighty SS to the humblest minion of the state.

Schonewille sat in a heavy leather armchair waiting for Grauwitz. Since the meeting with his father and brother eleven days previously, he had been trying to gain a meeting with the SS legal officer, but to no avail.

Mindful of Germany's worsening situation and the need to find out Grauwitz's and Heger's timetable, Schonewille made repeated attempts to arrange a meeting with them. Heger he did meet, but with no results. Schonewille at first thought his old friend was just being obstructive, but eventually came to the conclusion that Heger was almost as much in the dark as he.

Finally, on the twenty-sixth, Heger informed him that Grauwitz would see him the following day at nine in the morning.

The room was cold, so he kept his overcoat on as he ruminated at the latest news on the military situation. Things were going from bad to worse.

The day before, Hitler had completely revamped his eastern armies, sacking generals and creating new commands. The Russians in the headlong push westwards had now cut off fifty-three German fighting divisions, twenty-six in the Courland peninsula and twenty-seven in East Prussia. The Führer had ordered the towns and cities of these areas to be turned into fortresses, particularly the famous old military town of Königsberg.

Up to now the German people had faced the growing threat from the east with stoicism and determination; but with the Red Army over the borders of the Reich and with ever growing numbers of refugees spilling across the country, pessimism and the first signs of panic began to appear among the usually docile German populace.

The Wehrmacht and its comrades in the SS front-line divisions were fighting as brilliantly and resolutely as ever, but faced with shortages of fuel and other materials and the numerically superior Red Army, they were constantly being pushed back.

Hitler hardly helped the situation by constantly interfering with the plans of his principal commanders. Finally, he formed a new command, Army Group Vistula, and placed this vital force under the leadership of none other than Heinrich Himmler.

Schonewille realised time was running out. In the west the army groups of Montgomery, Bradley and Devers were preparing to attack the west wall, Hitler's vaunted defensive positions on the German border, and in the air the Allied bombers were continuing to pound the cities and factories into rubble.

There came a sound of footsteps in the passageway. The door opened and Grauwitz strode in. Schonewille heaved himself to his feet and gave the Fascist salute. It was returned, but without enthusiasm.

Brigadeführer Emil Grauwitz looked tired. There were dark rings under his eyes and his body language was not as self-assured as when they had last met. He waved his arm, indicating that Schonewille should resume his seat. He himself sat behind the writing desk, which held centre stage in the small room.

"Well, Herr Obersturmbannführer, I understand you have been trying to see me. What can I do for you?" he said with an air of irritation.

Schonewille hesitated, but then decided that nothing would be gained by tackling the subject matter obliquely. Both knew why they were here. Nevertheless, he started cautiously and with a little guile.

"Herr Brigadeführer, I felt it was important for both of us that we should talk. I have done everything that you have asked. Funds from the camps have been placed into the special account and I have completed the necessary paperwork to cover our trail. I have managed to arrange a special aircraft to be on standby on forty-eight hours notice of any move you might wish to make and I have arranged the special flights of those Jews that you want to have flown to Sweden. What I want to know is, what now?" He paused for a moment, but as Grauwitz did not respond he went on. "I mean, when will we make a move?"

Grauwitz gave a thin smile and wearily rubbed his eyes with his forefinger and thumb. When he did speak it was with a measure of friendliness that Schonewille had not encountered from him before. "Schonewille, my friend. Let me just say this. The time is not yet upon us when we can make the moves that you mention. There is a lot more to this than meets the eye, as you would well realise. I will tell you what needs to be done when I feel everything is ready."

Schonewille tried not to let his irritation show, but it crept into his voice nevertheless. "With respect, Herr Brigadeführer, I need to know something. So far, I am the one taking the risks, and for what? At any rate, the profits from the camps are drying up. There is nothing to be gained from waiting much longer and I ..."

"Enough, Obersturmbannführer," snapped Grauwitz. His dark eyes blazed and his nostrils flared as he took a deep breath. "Now you listen and listen carefully. It is I who will decide what and when it will happen. Do you understand?" Schonewille sat stock still and silent and Grauwitz continued, his voice now low and menacing. "You will do as I say and when I say it. I am not a fool and I am aware you have been making plans of your own. Therefore, I warn you. Be careful. At the slightest hint of treachery I will have you up against a wall with a firing squad lined up in front, verstanden?"

For a moment Schonewille's brain froze. A tight band of nervous tension spread around his chest and he thought he would be sick. Yet, he focused on keeping his face impassive.

"I assure you, Herr Brigadeführer, that I have done nothing to endanger your plans," he countered. While strictly correct, it was part bluff. At the same time, he badly needed to know whether Grauwitz actually knew something or was just second-guessing. Unfortunately, unless he wanted to ask specific questions there was no way of checking. This he did not want to do since it might alert Grauwitz in some small way as to what was happening. So he tried another tack. He made his voice sound plaintive.

"All I wanted to know was when you thought our plan could be activated. After all, we do need each other."

Grauwitz gave another thin smile. "Don't be too sure, mein Herr. I don't need you. Oh yes, officially I do need your signature to get the money out of the account, but do not believe for one moment there are no other means available to me." He paused and waited for Schonewille to speak. When he did not Grauwitz went on. This time, his message having struck home, he was once more conciliatory. "Herr Obersturmbannführer, let me just say this, any move will come in weeks rather than months. The time is not yet right, but it is close."

Schonewille nodded his head in acquiescence. He felt drained and a little at a loss on what to say next. He need not have bothered. With an impatient nod of his head, Grauwitz dismissed him.

With the office door closed behind him and an empty corridor in front, he paused for a moment to catch his breath.

The man's warning worried him. Did Grauwitz know something about what he and his family were planning? He fingered his holster and the silencer in its pouch. One day I will kill you, he thought.

The cold hit him like a knife as he let himself out into the street. A flurry of snow hit his face as he hurried to his office. The white leant some colour to the grey of the buildings and hid some of the bomb damage. Everywhere there was devastation. The situation was rapidly becoming parlous. What he still needed to know was Grauwitz's timetable and, despite this morning's meeting, all he had learned was that it was weeks away. But, did it mean two weeks, three weeks, or six weeks?

In Norway, Schonewille's brother and father were slowly overcoming what was a major hindrance to the success of their plans. The problem was aviation fuel, or rather the lack of it.

Germany was now chronically short of petroleum products, whether it was just straight petrol or high octane aviation fuel. With extra tanks fitted in the bomb bay the Boeing B17 could now carry nearly 5,000 US gallons of fuel. As well as this huge amount

Helmuth and Peter Wenck wanted another 2,000 gallons stored on Guernsey. The problem was how to obtain it.

As commanding officer Helmuth Wenck could legally obtain some stocks, but as well as the load for the B17 there needed to be sufficient for the Junkers 290 so it could be used to transfer some of the stocks to the Channel Islands.

By nefarious means, the Wencks began on 17 January to have some of the Kragero stocks transferred to Halden. Every plane landing at either airport was, if possible, relieved of a few precious litres.

"Father, this is taking us forever. What we need is a short cut. Do you have any ideas?"

His parent shook his head. He could use the Göring and Himmler letters to obtain extra stocks, but this was fraught with risks. The problem was not that there were stocks available and all they had to do was obtain it, but rather that there were just no large caches of the precious liquid to be had. Most of the stocks were earmarked for the fighter forces, particularly those who were defending the Reich.

It eventually took eleven days before they had sufficient quantities available to transfer the necessary amount to the Channel Islands.

Consequently, on the night of 28 January, the Junkers 290 lifted off from Kragero with Peter Wenck at the controls and Captain Leo Swabisch in the co-pilot's seat. The other personnel were made up of a scratch crew of four, enough to man the key turrets and the radio. Swabisch also acted as navigator. This ensured none of the others knew their destination.

The trip south was made without incident as was the landing. From there on, however, everything went wrong.

Peter Wenck had planned to have the aircraft unloaded of its precious cargo immediately and be on his way as quickly as possible. At worst he wanted to be at least as far as the Skagerrak when dawn came. What he did not want was to have his precious Junkers parked on the island in daylight. Unfortunately, that is just what transpired.

Thinking it expedient, Helmuth Wenck had kept in radio contact

173

with Hüffmeier and had not contacted von Schmettow. However, when Peter Wenck landed he found to his disappointment that no arrangements had been made to have the extra fuel drained from the bomber's tanks and stored at the airfield. Somewhere along the way there had been a major breakdown in communication.

Realising good manners and appeal would get him nowhere, Peter Wenck used the full range of his rank, voice and imperious manner, as well as the prestige of his Knight's Cross, to put the fear of God in the hapless officer who had been sent out to greet him at the aerodrome.

The naval lieutenant who had just informed Peter Wenck how Vice Admiral Hüffmeier had been unavoidably detained and could not see him just yet cringed as Wenck raised his voice a dozen decibels.

"Leutnant, if you want to survive the war in this cushy backwater you will do two things. Firstly, I want you to round up as many men as you can to unload the fuel and have it stored out of harm's way, and you will do it quickly. Secondly, you will inform the vice admiral of my arrival. Now get your arse into gear and for your own sake, don't spill a drop of gasoline."

Shaken, the lieutenant went away to do as he was bid. Seething, Wenck waited. Behind him there came the tinkling sound of hot metal contracting as the engines cooled in the chilly night air.

Swabisch came over and silently handed him a thermos. He waved it away impatiently and his friend, recognising the signs, kept silent.

It took half-an-hour for some trained personnel to be rounded up, but it then transpired that the necessary hoses with the correct couplings had been locked away in a shed on the other side of the airfield. To compound this, nobody knew where the key was kept.

Enraged, Wenck was driven to the building and ordered one of the guards to shoot the lock out. It took four rounds before the mangled lock gave way and they could get inside. Then, on arriving back to the underground fuel tanks there was another hold up. The cap to the inlet and outlet pipes was also locked to deter pilfering. The problem was nobody knew the whereabouts of the key for the padlock either. Obviously shooting was out of the question.

The lieutenant kept a discreet distance while they waited for the Austin with a driver to travel to St Peter Port and fetch the necessary spare key.

This took almost an hour and by the time the fuel had been transferred dawn was at best two hours away. The airmen were left with an unpalatable realisation. If they took off now, first light would find them in the English Channel somewhere between Harwich and Rotterdam. The consequence of this would be simple. A horde of Spitfires or Tempests would be directed to them by the British radar and they would certainly be shot down.

Reluctantly, Wenck had the Junkers moved to the far end of the airfield and covered with camouflage netting. It was a poor attempt to hide an aircraft of the Junkers' size.

At seven in the morning he was called to the telephone where an apologetic Hüffmeier requested his presence at the island's headquarters.

Leaving Swabisch in charge he was driven to St Peter Port. Realising he had been amiss in his handling of Peter Wenck's needs, Hüffmeier was all charm. Peter Wenck let the matter lie and when the vice admiral suggested a visit to one of the huge gun batteries he accepted. Although he was curious, he could have done without the experience though, with nothing better to do, there was in reality no reason for him to refuse.

He was taken to the coast where he was given a guided tour of one of the guns of the Mirus Battery. The weapon was camouflaged by having the turret and cupola covered by a dummy cottage. Wenck thought it expedient not to tell Hüffmeier that while this would help it avoid detection from the sea, the long barrel of the 30.5 cm gun would be easily visible from the air.

To Wenck's horror Hüffmeier suggested the gun fire one round, "To wake up those decadent American soldiers sleeping with their French whores."

Wanting nothing to happen that might endanger the Junkers, he respectfully cautioned the naval commander not to do anything to compromise the special mission.

Back at Hüffmeier's St Peter Port headquarters, Wenck was

visiting the toilet when he heard the sound of an aero engine. Recognising it as a Merlin he rushed outside, but was unable to see any aircraft. Whatever it had been, it had travelled fast and low and was now not only out of earshot but also out of sight.

Worried, and with a growing nervousness, he hurried back to the airfield where Swabisch explained how a photo reconnaissance Spitfire had made one low-level pass across the aerodrome. Its speed had been so rapid that none of the anti-aircraft crews even made it to their weapons, let alone fired off a shell.

He knew that even if the British pilot had not spied the Junkers there were no doubt trained intelligence experts who, on examining the photographs, would quickly recognise what was under the camouflage netting on the edge of the airfield.

"Himmel, Leo, if the British are quick in examining those prints we will have some fighter bombers paying us a visit before nightfall and it won't be a friendly call."

In order to confuse any British attack, Wenck requested and received permission to transfer the Junkers to the aerodrome on Jersey, a flight of a few minutes conducted at a height of less than seventy-five metres. This they completed without a problem.

The remainder of the afternoon was spent in nail-biting anxiety, waiting for an attack. None came. Fifteen minutes after the sky had lost its last shade of colour, the camouflage netting was pulled back and the crew clambered back into the bowels of the giant bomber. In the muted light of the instruments, Swabisch's grin appeared to fill his entire face. "Stupid Engländer," he crowed. "Probably too busy drinking tea to examine those photographs."

Wenck paused for a moment and then cautioned, "Don't be too sure Leo. They're not lazy or stupid. Why should they risk pilots and planes to raid a heavily-armed airfield when there are other ways to bag a nice, fat, juicy target?"

Swabisch stopped grinning. He turned to his friend. "Oh shit," he swore then looked up at the night sky.

"Ja, meine Kameraden. If they have examined those prints I'd bet an English pound to a million reichsmarks there's a nice hungry Mosquito or two lurking out there."

"Well, what do we do, Peter?"

Wenck gave a snort of derision. "What can we do? We cannot sit here. We have to take a risk. If they haven't yet seen those prints, they will certainly do so tomorrow and then we will be in the same boat, only worse. So let's leave immediately."

Instrument check completed, Wenck taxied the short distance to the runway and carefully aligned the big bomber with a lone light out in the distance. The sky was clear and the natural light sufficient to see the edges of the runway. Therefore, he did not need any further lights to illuminate the strip.

Standing on the brakes, he ran up the four BMW engines until the Junkers trembled under the pulling strain of their combined 6,400 horsepower. It was a short airstrip and he needed every metre of ground. Less than a minute later, they were airborne. Wenck did not attempt to gain height but kept the Junkers low as he swung around and headed due north. Two minutes later with Sark and Guernsey already on his port wing tip, he called up the radio operator and told him to transmit a pre-arranged call-sign.

The man did as he was bid and immediately a ribbon of lights appeared on the southern portion of Guernsey lighting up its airfield for all to see.

"Donner!" exclaimed Leo, and then realising what Wenck had pre-arranged, turned to the pilot. "You cunning cunt, you bloody marvellous shit. Oh, Peter, once more I realise how shifty and cunning you are!"

Wenck grinned. He had arranged the subterfuge with Hüffmeier. He had reasoned that if there were any British fighters lurking in the vicinity they would be attracted to the light like moths, thereby leaving the Junkers to make its escape unmolested. However, such was not the case. As well as its FuG 200 Hohentwiel search radar on the nose, Wenck's Junkers, like all A5 variants of the bomber, was also equipped with the Fug 216 Neptun tail warning radar.

With Alderney only fourteen kilometres away, the radar operator informed Wenck in a high pitched voice that a bogey had appeared on his unit and it was closing fast.

"Shit," he cursed.

He edged the big bomber a little lower and ordered the gunners to keep a watch for the aircraft, at the same time asking the radar operator for more precise details of its likely direction of attack.

Although he thought his decoy had failed, such was not quite the case. There had been two British fighters patrolling in the general area. Only one had swung towards the Guernsey airfield leaving the second further out to sea as a guard in case any German aircraft managed to escape detection by the first fighter.

The British fighter was closing rapidly. The radar operator was not good at his job and was unable to give sufficient warning as to its proximity to the bomber. Luckily, the two gunners in the mid upper turrets spotted him before he opened fire, but the advantage was slight.

Hardly had the front turret gunner informed Wenck on the enemy fighter's position when there was a flash of tracer and a line of flaming elongated balls erupted from the black sky to Wenck's left. He cursed again, his pulse racing in a mixture of adrenalin and fear. He knew they were in mortal danger. The British had developed night fighting to a deadly art. Their aircraft were prodigiously armed, fast and crewed by highly-trained and aggressive pilots. As well, they were equipped with very accurate radar.

As he swung the Junkers round so it was heading almost directly towards the origin of the flame, Wenck saw the silhouette of the enemy aircraft momentarily etched against the horizon where the black of the sea met the dark grey of the moonlit sky.

Although he had never actually seen one, he recognised it immediately. A short rounded nose with long curving wings and thick engine nacelles thrusting well forward, so the large airscrews could clear the fuselage. It was a Beaufighter, a deadly two-man night and strike fighter equipped with a battery of four twenty-millimetre cannon and six Browning machine-guns.

The British fighter half-rolled and before the Junkers could turn and slip away under its wings it sent fifty cannon shells and 200 machine-gun bullets in its direction. Five of the shells and some two-dozen bullets struck the Junkers, one shell entering the rear of the cockpit and exploding. Most of the shell splinters were deflected by the armoured seats, but one fragment tore a five-centimetre gash high up on Wenck's left shoulder before burying itself in the cabin roof only inches from his head.

The shock and pain forced a deep groan from Wenck's lips, but he never lost control. He swung the Junkers around once more and headed directly for the coast of France at a height of only fifty metres. It was almost suicidal, but he had no choice. At that height it was hard to distinguish where the sea ended and the night sky began and one wrong manoeuvre would see them strike the sea.

The radar operator informed him he had picked up a second contact, but said he thought both fighters were not so purposeful in their course.

"Pray we might have lost them, Leo," the pilot said.

The gunners had been fighting back and their cannon had been accurate. Wenck ordered them to cease firing unless it was apparent the Beaufighters had found them again and were well within range. Now, any defensive fire from the bomber would only show the British where their enemy was. The Junkers crossed the coast and Wenck headed inland hoping the bomber's radar signature would be lost because of its proximity to the ground. With tall buildings, telephone poles, high tension electricity pylons and hills criss-crossing the area there was a good chance the clutter caused by these distortions would confuse or blind the Beaufighter's radar operators.

A few minutes later he turned a few degrees to starboard passing a few kilometres to the south of Valognes. Of their antagonists, there was no sign. Swabisch was leaning forward staring out through the Perspex, as if those few extra centimetres would give them extra warning of anything nasty up ahead.

They were low, dangerously low for such a large aircraft, but so far they had been lucky. They skirted a valley and swung around to avoid some lights. To their right, an anti-aircraft gun opened up on them, but the sleepy gunners were way off target.

Then they were back out over the sea, having crossed the Cherbourg Peninsula. Keeping as low as possible, he headed back up the English Channel. Swabisch suggested he take over so Wenck could have his wound attended. At first the pilot seemed not to hear the suggestion, but then he shook his head with an irritated gesture and continued at the controls.

They passed through the Straits of Dover without incident and for a moment Wenck allowed himself to relax. Then, the oil pressure on the starboard inner engine started to drop and the cylinder head temperature began to rise ominously. He throttled the engine back and set the trim to compensate for the extra pull of the two engines on the port wing and started praying for the engine not to catch fire. Although it never did, the temperature rose much too high and to be on the safe side, he switched it off. Almost six hours after leaving Jersey, they reached Norwegian air space. Only then did he allow Swabisch to take over the controls.

By now his shoulder was numb and to move his left arm caused a high degree of pain that enveloped his shoulder, neck and upper back. The entire left side of his flying jacket was stained with blood and the moment he relaxed he felt a trifle light-headed. All he wanted to do was have a hot bath and go to sleep. As always he was grateful that Swabisch was in the co-pilot's seat, and he handed over to his number two.

Swabisch piloted the 290 the rest of the way home and landed without incident.

Chapter Eighteen
30 January 1945

There were three men in the room. Two were wearing the blue uniform of the Royal Air Force, the third was in an ill-fitting and threadbare dark grey suit.

"Well, Flying Officer, what do the photographs show?" said the civilian in the suit.

He was in his late forties, with a thin, clipped moustache under a prominent nose over which a pair of grey-green eyes peered. The object of his question was one of the two RAF personnel sitting opposite, an officer in the photographics section. The man took out six photographs from an old manila envelope, all blown up to eighteen inches by twelve.

"Here they are, Sir. The airfields on Guernsey and Jersey," he said placing them on the table so they faced the other two men. "As you can see," he went on, waving his hand, palm upwards over the photographs, "these show both airfields free of any aircraft. They were taken one week ago. Now this one on the other hand shows quite clearly a large multi-engined plane parked under some camouflage netting on Guernsey airfield," he said, extracting another large photograph and placing it on top of the others. "It was taken by a PR Spitfire late yesterday morning."

The civilian picked up the photograph and then with his left hand idly spread the others apart. "So, we know a large German aircraft was on Guernsey yesterday."

"What was it doing there and was it the one that took off from Jersey?" The question was addressed to the second RAF officer, although the civilian did not look at the man.

Squadron Leader Roger Parker-Davis was in his mid-twenties. Under the wings over his left breast pocket was the purple and white striped ribbon of the DFC. A metal bar on the ribbon indicated he had been awarded this coveted medal twice. He was an ace fighter pilot and had flown one of the two Beaufighters that had unsuccessfully attempted to shoot down Peter Wenck only a few hours previously.

He spoke in an unhurried way. His accent was that of a native of Birmingham, although the intonation and accent was not strong. He knew the civilian was with one of the intelligence services and since he did not like spooks, he spoke more carefully than he would normally. "I cannot answer your first question, Sir, but I believe I know the answer to the second." The other man said nothing, so he went on. "I believe the pilot of the German aircraft moved his kite to Jersey when he realised it may have been photographed by the Spitty. He then took off the moment it was sufficiently dark and, as a decoy, had the landing lights on the Guernsey field turned on to fool us into thinking he was taking off from there. If I had not stationed my wingman as a second line of attack we would have missed the bugger entirely," he explained without rancour.

The intelligence officer nodded his head. There was silence for a moment and then he asked another question. "In what direction was he heading when your man intercepted him?"

"North, or as good as," the pilot answered. "He then turned almost due east and dropped even lower before crossing the coast of the Cherbourg peninsular at almost tree-top height. That's when we lost him."

The other nodded his head and sucked his lower lip, deep in thought.

"One final question, Squadron Leader. Do you think the aircraft was heading back to Germany?"

Parker-Davis shook his head. "No, I don't. When we lost him we headed into France and then turned back in an effort to locate him. There was nothing. However, my radar operator caught a small blip crossing the coast, but by the time we turned to check he had slipped away." He paused for a moment and then went on. "The aircraft was definitely a Junkers 290 and whoever was at the controls certainly knew his stuff. We should have got him, but he was too clever. A very experienced pilot, I would venture to say."

The intelligence officer nodded his head and dismissed them.

When the room was empty, he picked up the receiver of one of two phones on the desk and asked to be connected to a number in Whitehall. He drummed his fingers on the table and then idly picked up the photo that showed the shadow of Wenck's plane under the netting. Finally, the receiver on the other end of the line was picked up.

"George? Good. Well here is the gen. There is something definitely happening on the islands. Our pilot Parker-Davis said he doubted whether the Junkers was flying back to Germany. Therefore, it certainly was not a supply flight. At any rate, there is another bit of information. I've also received word that one of our radar units picked up an aircraft an hour-or-so later flying low up the Channel. Could have been our bird. If it was, then the Junkers was either making for Denmark or maybe even Norway ... What? No, I don't believe the Beaufighters shot him down."

The voice on the other end of the receiver continued on for a few minutes. The intelligence officer listened silently. Then he said with conviction, "No, George, I don't believe we should bomb the airfields. What for? Let's just keep a watch, a close watch. We both know Hüffmeier is a rabid Nazi and will try something funny. Therefore, let us just wait and see ... What? Yes, I do think it's the best course, all right? Fine, then I'll see you at two – cheerio."

"Well, Obersturmbannführer, what have you been up to, eh?"

Schonewille stared at the speaker for a moment before answering in a measured tone to hide his alarm. "What are you talking about, Hauptsturmführer Wünsche?"

The other grinned. He was a tall, good-looking captain with close cropped brown hair and good-natured brown eyes. A former officer with the 8th SS-Kavallerie-Division Florian Geyer, he had been badly wounded two months ago and had been transferred on temporary assignment to Schonewille's office while he fully recovered. "Oh, nothing really, Sir," I was just joking," he said, his smile vanishing as he read the expression in the other's eyes.

"The joke must have had some basis, Hauptsturmführer, so what was it?"

The other man shifted uncomfortably and explained how he had been instructed by another senior officer to make an inventory of any radio messages or wire messages made or received by Schonewille in the preceding three to four months.

"Whatever for?" he said, making his voice sound incredulous and faintly amused. At the same time, his mind was racing. Who would ask and why? The former was easy, Grauwitz had indicated he would keep a close watch on him. And the latter? He was not sure.

Lieber Gott, he thought. I'm glad all my radio messages have only been to Peter. Grauwitz knew of his brother. After all, he had been the pilot of the Jewish flights. Yet, he was not sure whether the legal officer actually knew Peter was his half brother. Even if he did, this in itself was no problem, but it could lead to their father, which would be disastrous for General Wenck since the bases in Norway had to be kept secret.

As an added precaution, Schonewille had always made certain any message that could have been interpreted as being even faintly suspicious had either been conveyed to Peter by letter or telephone, rather than by radio.

Wünsche identified who had instructed him to make the check: a major with the audit office of Schonewille's section. This on its own told him nothing and he knew that to question the officer would serve no useful purpose, so he let the matter lie, telling himself he would have to be doubly careful in the future.

Later, in the privacy of his own office, he stewed over what had happened. Obviously Grauwitz was checking up on him, but why? Did he know something or was he just being paranoid? The mere fact Grauwitz was making a random check meant he had no real information. If Grauwitz really knew what he was up to he would have had him arrested and shot by now.

The logic of this did much to comfort Schonewille. Still, it was unnerving and made his already frayed nerves even worse.

Unfortunately, when he got home Sophia's news made him feel physically ill. She greeted him affectionately, something she always did when she was frightened. Her agitation set Schonewille's nerves off.

On asking what was the matter, he received a strange reply.

"Oh, Friedrich, I'm not sure. Maybe I'm just being silly, but this woman came round and she behaved so strangely."

"Woman, what woman?" snapped Schonewille.

He took her by the arm and sat her on the sofa. She sat hunched over, nervously clasping her hands and rubbing her knuckles. She explained how the doorbell had rung shortly after five. On answering, she had been confronted by a woman who asked whether Schonewille was at home.

Sophia explained that he was probably still at his office, whereupon the woman had invited herself in. Flustered and unsure, Sophia did not know how to refuse politely. So she just said no.

"She became a little rude, Friedrich, and started to question me. Her manner annoyed me. I managed to calm down and told her to mind her manners. I explained I was your cousin and that I worked in the office of the Wirtschafts-und-Verwaltungshauptamt, like you. Then I explained that I was busy and if she had anything to say to you she could leave a message. She just shook her head and turned her back on me. Then she walked away."

Sophia paused and went on. "Did I handle it right, Friedrich?"

Schonewille shrugged his shoulders. "I don't know, Liebling. But, I need to know who she was. Please describe her."

She did so, accurately and without hesitation. He recognised the woman immediately, Frau Alice Heger. "What the hell does that shrewish bitch want?" he muttered. Ignoring his mistress's questioning look he went to the phone and dialled Heger's number. The banker answered.

"Klaus, Friedrich. I understand Alice came around to see me this afternoon. Why?"

Heger explained that he had wanted to send a message to him. He said that Grauwitz informed him how Schonewille had been trying to find out what was happening and he had therefore used his wife in an attempt to tell him things were moving ahead very rapidly.

"I do not know any more than you, Friedrich. However, Grauwitz let slip a few details. Apparently he is planning to move on or about the tenth or eleventh of February. More than this I do not know."

Schonewille asked a few more questions, which elicited no further useful information, so he said goodbye and hung up. He stood uncertainly by the phone. To put it mildly, he was completely nonplussed. It did not make sense. If Heger had wanted to speak to him why had he not rung or come over himself? Why send his wife?

Sophia was looking at him uncertainly. No need to worry her unnecessarily, he thought.

"Come on," he said. "Let's go to bed. I know the woman. She's the wife of a friend who works at the Reichsbank."

Some 700 kilometres away a doctor was replacing the bandages on Peter Wenck's shoulder. It had been two hours since he had first attended to the pilot who had then looked worse than he actually was.

Apart from loss of blood and a degree of exhaustion, Peter Wenck was not badly wounded. True, the wound was long and deep, needing ten stitches, but some rest and plenty of sleep would go a long way to return him to his normal robust self. He prescribed a mild sedative so the pilot could sleep, despite the dull pain enveloping the upper half of his body, and ordered him to take at least one week's complete rest.

On learning the news of his son's predicament, General Wenck's first instinct was to fly over, but a short telephone conversation with Peter eased his worries. It was better he stay away from Kragero.

From then on there was nothing left to do but wait. Now, of course, there was no need to immobilise the Junkers, the cannon shells from the Beaufighter had seen to that. While he did not want the aircraft made serviceable, he could neither afford to have it completely unserviceable, so he compromised. The damaged engine was completely overhauled in situ, although several key electrical components were left off. Similarly, the cockpit was not completely repaired, nor were all the bullet and shell holes erased. To a casual observer, the Junkers looked like it would take some time to fix, yet, in reality, it would take less than two hours to make the Junkers operational.

Grounded and with nothing left to do, Peter Wenck was left to his own devices. Also, with no squadron of his own to look after, he

186

did not need to catch up on the mountains of paperwork that were the lot of any commanding officer. In the past he had hated the toilet paper, as he had always referred to it, but now with time on his hands even the paperwork would have been a helpful diversion.

Similarly, there was nothing for Swabisch to do either, so he allowed his friend some leave, although he ordered him to report twice a day. On the first day of February his friend gratefully headed for the fleshpots of Oslo.

A few hours later Wenck was glad his friend was away. The reason was a junior lieutenant who was transferred to the base from Germany and assigned to the station commander. If Swabisch had seen her, no doubt he would have stayed.

Lieutenant Erna Hennell was something to behold. Even with her blonde hair pulled back in a regulation bun and her face devoid of make-up she was very attractive. The figure, under the severe uniform also held promise.

Peter had not been with a woman for over a year. A little fussy in what he wanted, either from or with the opposite sex he had, unlike most soldiers, not just taken what came along. With Erna, even his high standards seemed likely to be met and it was obvious right from the start that she was attracted to him.

She made inquiries to the station commander about him, but the man, warned by both Wencks to say nothing and thoroughly intimidated by the Knight's Cross at the pilot's throat, plus the authority implicit in Himmler's letter, gave away no information.

The man was also clearly ill-at-ease in her company. He had been lucky in that his wife and three children were with him in Norway. The proximity of his spouse meant any pretty woman working with him would clearly arouse his wife's ever-ready jealousy and trouble of this kind he did not want. His main aim was to finish the war in Norway, rather than do anything that might see him transferred back to Germany. Therefore, he also wanted nothing to do with the Wencks and whatever they were planning. The mere thought of Himmler's letter and what this implied made him deaf, dumb and blind.

Consequently, he gave Lieutenant Erna Hennell very little to do and virtually had her assigned to Peter Wenck. This suited the woman perfectly. She was very attracted to the tall handsome pilot with his imperious manner and sexy, slightly sardonic smile.

Since his left arm was in a sling to stop it dragging on his injured shoulder, writing had been an effort, so Peter had her help with what few bits of correspondence he needed to complete without allowing her to see anything linked to their escape plans.

Watching Erna work he felt a tightening at his groin and as he shifted in his seat to ease the strain on his crotch she looked up and caught his eyes. An experienced woman she recognised the look, and quickly dropped her eyes demurely. Inside, however, she smiled to herself. You are ripe for whatever I offer you, she thought.

That night he took her out to a local café for dinner. Back at the base he walked her to her quarters and then as she turned to say goodnight he took her chin with his free hand and lightly lifted her head. When she did not resist, he kissed her, at first gently and then with passion. She returned the kiss eagerly, but after a few seconds moved her head away. She caught her breath and said coquettishly, "Is this an order, Herr Colonel, or do I have a chance to volunteer?"

"The latter, Liebling. I always work best with volunteers," he answered with a grin.

"Then, Peter, let me give it some thought. Being a volunteer can get one into trouble and I would like to spend the night thinking about the risks," she said with a throaty giggle.

She leant forward and raised her head to be kissed again and then quickly slipped though the door and shut it behind her. She snibbed the lock and stood silently for a moment waiting. Only when his footsteps crunched away in the snow did she move. Trembling slightly, she went to her bed, removed her coat and lay down fully clothed. Her panties felt damp and she moved her left hand down to her groin. She rubbed herself two or three times and then, forcing herself to stand, she undressed and climbed naked back into bed. The bed was cold and with her ardour now thoroughly dampened she curled up and tried to go to sleep.

"I hope you are as good in bed as you are a hero," she muttered to herself.

Chapter Nineteen
3 February 1945

The morning was cold and overcast. It was a Saturday, although much like any other day for anyone in the services. The war took no holidays and in fact 3 February would be a fateful day for all those associated with the Reichsbank.

Peter Wenck awoke shortly after eight in the morning. His room had a boiler-fed column heater along one wall so it was quite warm. He had had a restless night. The combination of Erna's kisses and the pain from his shoulder had conspired to leave him sleepless for much of the night. Therefore, with nothing official to do, he stayed in bed.

Half-an-hour later there came a knock on the door. At his grunted " kommen Sie herein", the door opened and Erna Hennell stepped inside and bolted the door. Before Peter Wenck could say anything, she turned with a seductive smile and threw her overcoat onto the floor. Underneath, she was wearing a heavy polo neck ski sweater and a grey pleated skirt. She came over to the bed and stood looking down at him. The pilot looked up at her and smiled. Throwing the bedclothes back he said, "Come on, Erna, get into bed. It is cold out there."

She leant forward and kissed him lightly on the lips and then stood back. Lifting her hands she pulled the sweater over her head and tossed it next to the coat. She kicked her shoes off and then unbuttoned her skirt and let it fall. Her cotton panties followed.

Wenck drew in his breath. She was magnificent. Her skin was pale and shone with health. Her breasts were on the smallish side, but beautifully formed with large, pink and very pointed nipples. At her groin there was a bush of untrimmed reddish blonde hair.

She got into bed and Wenck caught his breath again as he attempted to move over, his shoulder giving him a warning not to be too energetic.

She raised herself on her left elbow and looked down at him, her face inches from his own. She smelt faintly of Lily of the Valley.

God knows where she had got that from, he thought.

"I'm afraid you are going to have to be careful, my hero, and let me take charge. But first, let us just lie for a minute."

She dropped her head onto his right shoulder and let her right hand slide down to his member, which was creating a sizeable mountain out of the bed covers. She began to caress it, running her thumb over its head until he began to move. She lifted herself slightly so the nipple of her left breast pressed against his face. Bringing his right arm around so that he could caress her back, he gently took the nipple in his mouth and rolled it between his teeth and tongue. She moaned and murmured an endearment. After a few minutes, she pushed the bedclothes right back and kneeling, looked down at him. Although the effort hurt, he moved his left hand to her vagina, gently caressing, feeling her wet and pliant.

"Lie back," she said with a throaty whisper, moving her leg and crouching over him. She gently guided his entry and then sat back with a smile and began to move, her body rising and falling to his thrusts. He held her waist with his left hand, the pain almost unfelt, while with his right he cupped her breasts and caressed her nipples.

Thus joined, they continued for five minutes or so until their shared urgency quickened the pace to a mutual climax, hers first and he following seconds later. She stayed upright for half a minute, her groin muscles flexing as the tremors coursed through her body and her breathing slowly returned to normal. Only then did she divest herself of his still half erect penis and lie next to him.

"Oh, Colonel," she sighed with a satisfied smile. "If I could, I would give you the Oak Leaves, Swords and Diamonds to your Knight's Cross."

Hundreds of miles away in Berlin, fate was taking a hand. As the lovers lay soporific and satisfied in each other's arms, a large force of American bombers crossed the Channel heading across the Zuider Zee and the Low Countries towards the German border.

The weather during that winter was bad, so much so that many German cities were spared the incessant air attacks that had marked the last half of 1944. Even Berlin had gained a respite from the attention of the Allied bombers. There had been no major raid since early December because heavy cloud had covered much of the city for most of the time.

Unfortunately, on this Saturday, the Allied weather forecasters had predicted clear skies in the morning, followed by intermittent cloud and rain. This window in the sky was just what the American Air Force chiefs wanted. They dispatched no fewer than 1,003 bombers escorted by almost 600 fighters to attack the Nazi capital.

Almost the entire force reached Berlin. For those few Berliners who had not obeyed the air-raid sirens and run for the shelters they were a magnificent sight. At 26,000 feet they appeared like silver arrows at the head of hundreds of long wispy vapour trails. The blue sky was clear except for the black sooty balls of the flak bursts, which soon appeared even more numerous than the marauding bombers as 1,200 anti-aircraft guns began to spew forth tracer, shell and high explosive.

Many of the bomb aimers in the B17s and B24s now in control of their respective aircraft used the Unter Den Linden and the Brandenburg Gate as aiming points from which to bomb their chosen targets, or just emptied their loads into the heart of the city.

It was to be the heaviest raid on Berlin so far with 2,250 tons of bombs landing on the city wreaking havoc. The force of the explosives destroyed what little of Berlin had been left standing by the earlier raids, reducing tall buildings to piles of rubble only a few metres high and choking the city into a maelstrom of fire, debris, dust and smoke.

Those few Berliners caught out in the open had no chance. They were killed by the force of the explosions, suffocated as the fires consumed all the oxygen, crushed under piles of bricks and concrete or burnt alive by the intense heat, their bodies literally melting on the pavement.

Some of those in the air-raid shelters and cellars faired little better. If they survived the horrors of the raids they found they were trapped, the entrances to their boltholes covered by thousands of tons of rubble.

Major buildings either hit or destroyed included some of the most important to the function of government for the Third Reich.

The Gestapo headquarters, the People's Court, Hitler's Chancellery and the Berlin headquarters of the Reichsbank.

Klaus Heger had joined the other 5,000 or so staff of the bank in the building's basement bunker, where they huddled in terror as the concussion from the bombs shook the concrete walls, filling the air with cement dust. Then the lights went out and women began to shriek in terror as they were left in the dark. Many people, both men and women, involuntarily urinated in their clothes in fear, or vomited as they attempted to breathe the fetid air.

Heger had remained relatively calm until the lights failed. Now he also joined the chorus and shrieked in pain, alternately calling his wife's name and that of God to help him. A naval officer who had been caught in the bank when the raid started flicked his lighter to find the origin of the noise and on identifying Heger punched him hard on the face, at the same time ordering him to, "Halt's Maul, Du verdammter Feigling!"

The banker lapsed into silence, but even as he struggled to re-gain his composure the basement reverberated with the crashing sounds of some direct hits on the building above them. The Reichsbank's president, Dr Walther Funk, seated on a bench only metres away from Heger, winced as he felt and heard the explosions. A banker even under these extreme conditions, he realised what they represented both to his bank and to the finances of the German government.

In all, twenty-one 1,000-pound, high-explosive American-made bombs hit the Reichsbank and its immediate surrounds. It was a credit to the builders of this solid and imposing structure that the whole building had not immediately collapsed into rubble. Nevertheless, to all intents and purposes, it was now virtually a shell.

To the staff emerging from what had almost been their tomb, it seemed as though their world had come to an end and they were in hell itself. It had started to rain, a slow drizzle, which helped lessen the fires without actually quenching the flames. The whole city was covered in a thick, black, acrid smoke stretching skywards to more than 20,000 feet.

Heger stared in shocked horror at the shattered, blackened

193

remains of his office. Much of the bank's roof had gone, some of the exterior walls were partially destroyed with the interior walls leaning on their neighbour or simply too badly damaged to hold up their section of the ceiling. There were no windows, few doors remained on their hinges and most of the bank records were spread amongst the rubble like confetti.

He picked his way through the broken glass and broken partitions to his desk. His filing cabinet had split open like an orange from the weight of a huge steel beam, which had dislodged itself from one corner of the ceiling. Half the cabinet's contents were lying on the floor or buried under plaster and other rubble.

Es ist zu ende – wir sind alle vetloren, he said to himself. His thoughts echoed his words. Everything was finished: Germany, their secret account and with it their escape plan.

Dismally, Funk and his senior staff picked their way through the rubble and tried to assess the damage. For the Reich, it was catastrophic. The printing presses used for printing German bank notes had been completely destroyed, as had much of the information vital to the running of an economy. Unless they had been stored in the vaults and strong rooms, most details of individual accounts, loans and major transactions had either disappeared or were so hopelessly mixed up that it would take months, even years to re-collate.

The only positive thing was the survival of the strong rooms and vaults, but Funk quickly realised another major raid would destroy even these hardy structures. Quite simply, it was imperative to have the nation's assets, the deposits, reserves of gold, other precious metals, diamonds, cash currency and bonds moved out of the capital and moved quickly.

The question was, by what means and to where?

Schonewille had been lounging half-dressed on a sofa reading through some documents when the raid started. He had been feeling very pleased with himself, because he had managed to clear up a problem that had been worrying him for months: namely, Sophia's identity papers. Originally he'd been able to gather together some convincing civilian papers, but with security checks becoming even more frequent he had decided to strengthen his mistress's identity.

For weeks he had been keeping a watchful eye on the staff records of various SS departments, searching for any members of the various SS female auxiliaries, or female officers in certain SS administrative departments who looked like Sophia and whose age and other statistics matched those of his lover.

Finally, he had a stroke of luck. He intercepted an official death notice, which informed the head of the personnel section, the personalamt, that SS Untersturmführer Käthe Haushofer had been killed in an air-raid. The second-lieutenant had been one of those on Schonewille's list. She had looked very similar to Sophia, was only two years younger, less than two centimetres shorter and, most importantly, as an officer with the personnel section was, like Schonewille, under the same overall command: the SS Economic and Administrative Main Office.

Schonewille simply destroyed the document and had a fresh set of identity papers made up under the pretext that Untersturmführer Käthe Haushofer's had been lost in an air-raid. A uniform was even easier to obtain. Although Sophia had at first refused to even contemplate wearing the uniform, it took little persuasion for Schonewille to convince her it would immeasurably strengthen her ability to pass through security and identity paper checks. He also hinted how the uniform would be helpful if they wanted to escape the Reich.

Any further questions by the Jewess were halted by the air-raid sirens, so they went to the cellar with two other residents.

When the all-clear sounded they emerged from its confines and immediately went outside. Already their suburb was covered in smoke and they could see the fires, which were engulfing the city. They were both horrified at the enormity of the flames and despite the light rain stood and watched the swirling black clouds turn the day into an eerie half light.

Finally, the acrid smoke became too much and they retreated inside their apartment, shutting the windows to keep out the pungent odour.

Schonewille was off duty, having been granted forty-eight hours leave, but he wondered whether he should report in. He attempted to phone his office, but was unable to get through, so he abandoned any thought of going into the city.

Shortly after four o'clock in the afternoon he received a phone call from Heger. His friend sounded pathetic. Scarcely watching what he was saying, he informed the SS colonel how their plan was now in disarray and that there was little chance of using their secret account.

"It's all finished, Friedrich, it's all finished," he repeated. "I cannot locate the account. All the records relating to it were in my office and that's a mess. We might be able to go through the central records if they have survived, but it will be difficult. I'm not sure what to do," he finished lamely.

Worried and angry, Schonewille tried to keep his temper in check. He half-succeeded, the effort causing his voice to choke. "Shut up, Klaus. Shut up, do you hear? Find out what the Brigadeführer thinks and report back to me, but not on the phone. Do you understand"?

He replaced the receiver and stood silent, shaking his head. If ever he had doubted the reality before, now he knew. The Reich would not last long, maybe a few weeks, at best two months. He had to get a message to his brother immediately informing him what had happened.

He still did not know what his father and brother had planned and the realisation that his life was dependent on so many people almost choked him.

They all have their own agendas, he thought. Grauwitz, his family, even that fool Heger, while he was the man in the middle with no escape route. A tide of helpless rage threatened to engulf him. With an effort he managed to control what was threatening his equilibrium for he realised there was nobody near who he could vent his rage on. Sophia was out of the question. He needed her and she had never done anything to hurt him.

Chapter Twenty
10 February 1945

The events of 3 February had completely changed the plans of the plotters. For a time there was no follow up, no new direction. To a degree, each of the parties now had to wait and see how events unfolded.

The bombing changed little for the Wencks. Norway was now a relative backwater in the wider conflict. For General Helmuth Wenck it was quite clear he had a command and orders to follow. For Peter Wenck it was also simple. Without a command of his own he was a relatively free agent so, as before, he was engaged to fly transport missions to and from Germany while under the guise of preparing for a secret mission.

For those in Germany, however, it was much more difficult. Schonewille's superior, Obergruppenführer Dr Oswald Pohl, the Head of the Economic and Administrative Department of the SS, made sure his role of concentration camp auditor continued. Although the amount of valuables that could be gleaned from those pathetic wrecks who remained was small, there was still sufficient to make certain Schonewille was gainfully employed.

Fret though he might, Heger was also too busy to worry over much. While Grauwitz remained his shadowy, elusive self, Heger was busy helping supervise the transfer of the Reich's reserves from the shattered remains of the Reichsbank.

As both Reich Minister of Economics and president of the Reichsbank, Dr Walther Funk was able to look at the disaster that had befallen his bank in two minds: that of a banker and that of a loyal servant of the Third Reich. Consequently, the decision he made as to the future of the bank's contents fitted in very neatly to the needs of Germany.

It fell on his second-in-command, Reichsbank Deputy President Emil Puhl, to implement the decision. The move was designed to fulfil two strategic aims. Create a safe haven for the bulk of the Reich's monetary reserves and provide the necessary finances to continue the war. Funk and his cohorts decided to evacuate the officials of the most important departments to Weimar and Erfurt to run the Reichsbank from there. A few middle managers would be promoted and would run the Berlin operations from some of the other smaller branches that had so far survived the bombing. One of these managers was Klaus Heger. The reserves were to be transferred as far from Berlin as possible. The site chosen was a potassium mine at Merkers just over 300 kilometres south-west of Berlin, well clear of any of the front-lines.

Normally the promotion would have pleased Heger, but now he could not have cared less. If the truth be known, he would have preferred being one of those transferred to Weimar or Erfurt and therefore away from the horrors of Berlin. Despite this, he dutifully did as he was bid and helped dispatch the Reichsbank's treasures from the battered capital.

On 9 February the first consignment left Berlin by train. The next day after work, Heger met with Schonewille.

"Over a thousand million reichsmarks, our entire paper currency reserves has been sent by train to the south," said Heger. "Would you believe it, Friedrich?" said the banker, shaking his head in disbelief. "There were more than a thousand sacks of paper money being tossed about like bags of wheat."

Schonewille nodded his head solemnly and asked, "Anything else? Is that all that's gone?"

Heger shook his head and explained how over four million American dollars had also been dispatched. Currency from other countries, including British Sterling and Swiss Francs, were to follow shortly.

The SS colonel questioned his friend further, asking if there was any way of extracting money from the Reichsbank in the future. Heger shrugged his shoulders. "I'm not sure, Friedrich. I now have much more authority than previously, and I certainly have the ability and the wherewithal to lay my hands on quite large quantities of reichsmarks, but certainly not large amounts of foreign currency, or for that matter any gold bullion. Deputy President Puhl informed me our reserves of bullion and foreign currency are also being shipped south, possibly in a few days."

Schonewille cursed softly. German paper money was useless. What they needed was foreign currency and bullion, things of use to them when they fled Germany's borders. His only asset was the diamonds he had received at Auschwitz and they were not readily convertible to foreign cash here in Germany. However, they were easily transported and for this he was grateful.

He asked about Grauwitz, but Heger shook his head, explaining how he'd had no word from the SS lawyer.

Returning home, Schonewille began to pack for yet another trip to those few camps remaining in northern Germany. As usual the visits would be utilised to mask his other activities. Once clear of Berlin, he planned to contact his brother and arrange a meeting in Hamburg.

His business completed, he reached Hamburg on 12 February, but was forced to travel onto Kiel for the rendezvous. They met in one of the city's more down-market hotels and sat in the corner of the foyer talking in undertones so they were not overheard.

Wenck gave his brother a new radio frequency and call-sign so he could be contacted in an emergency and suggested he should sit tight for a while. "Look, Friedrich, although I have never met him, I believe from what you've told me that Grauwitz is much too devious and hard-nosed to give up so easily. I bet he has a contingency plan up his sleeve. Not only is he a member of the SS but he's a lawyer to boot. That type always plays two ends against the middle."

Schonewille could not help smiling at his brother's reference to the devious nature of SS officers. Wenck, catching the smile, said half mockingly, "Present company excluded of course."

They grinned at one another and for a moment there was a bond between them. When they parted Schonewille hurried to catch a train south while Wenck went to a dilapidated office building near the docks to meet with Meunier. The reason he had not been able to travel to Hamburg for his rendezvous with Schonewille was because of Meunier who was in Kiel on official business and could not leave the city's environs.

The diplomat was all smiles. "My boy," he said breathing schnapps fumes over the pilot. "I have fitted the last pieces into the jigsaw."

He opened a battered leather satchel and extracted a small spiral pad from which he detached half-a-dozen pages that had already been torn from the metal rings. He then produced a number of maps and laid the paperwork on a card table covered in a green baize.

"Now, let's start from the beginning," said the diplomat with all the air of a tutor about to impart his wisdom on a recalcitrant pupil. "I have already suggested the Dominican Republic as the choice for a re-fuelling stop. While there are several countries in the Caribbean that could, on the surface, have fitted the bill, I finally picked the Dominican Republic for three reasons. One, although the country is nominally on the Allied side there are a great many Fascist sympathisers there who revere the National Socialist cause. And of course Trujillo, who runs the country, is a dictator like our own beloved Führer," he said with a sardonic smile.

"Two, we need an airfield on which the sight of a Boeing would not be too unusual and three," he paused for a moment before continuing. "We need someone who can be bribed to supply us with the necessary aviation gasoline and to keep his mouth shut."

Meunier unfolded one of the charts and spread it on the table. It was a large map of the West Indies and Central America, taking in the southern tip of Florida in the north, Venezuela and Columbia to the south, the Leeward and Windward Islands to the east and Mexico's Yucatan Peninsula to the west. In the middle was Cuba and the island of Hispaniola, which held the republics of Haiti and the Dominican Republic. He turned the chart around so it faced the pilot and stabbed a finger at the island.

"There, on the north coast you will see the town of Puerto Plata. Nice place, typical Caribbean port, white buildings, swaying palms, little cantinas, pretty girls … and an airfield."

Wenck looked up and grinned, but said nothing. Meunier went on. "The commandant of the airfield is Lieutenant-Colonel Ferdinand Savory of the El Cuerpo de Aviacion Militar," he said with a mock flourish of his hand, his Spanish accent perfect. "In case you did not guess, it's the Dominican Military Aviation Corps."

200

Meunier explained how he had met the colonel back in 1938 when he was helping Admiral Canaris set up an intelligence network. Before the war German agents had used the Dominican Republic as an important centre for their operations in the Caribbean. Their head was a man called Karl Hertel who operated under the guise of a sales representative for several imported German products.

Savory was a gambler and his penchant for spending money had brought him into the orbit of Hertel's circle of paid informers. Whatever his weakness, Savory was well-connected and possessed a shrewd brain. As a (then) captain with a good future and an active dislike for America because it constantly meddled in his country's internal affairs, he was to become a valuable ally.

Meunier explained how the Republic's dictator, Rafael Trujilo, had always sympathised with the Fascist cause until the promise of American military aid had made him throw in his lot with the Allies after Pearl Harbour. In the round-ups and arrests that followed, some agents and other members of the German legation capitulated, but not Karl Hertel.

"Hertel has been watched pretty closely, but he's still been of some use to us," said Meunier. "It took some doing, I can tell you, but through what is left of Canaris's network I was able to contact Hertel who in turn approached Savory, and we've come to an agreement. It's quite simple. I've arranged a coded signal. When we are ready to leave we transmit the signal and he'll make sure he is at the Plata base until we arrive. Then for 10,000 US dollars in cash he will have the Boeing re-fuelled."

At the mention of the money, Wenck grimaced. Meunier caught the facial expression and questioned its reason. The pilot explained about the bombing of the Reichsbank.

For a moment the elderly diplomat sat stunned. "Shit, I had not heard. Christ, they've kept that quiet," he muttered. "Well I'll tell you this, no money means no gasoline, wherever we stop."

Wenck held up both hands, palms outwards. "Don't worry, at least not yet. I have a feeling deep in my gut our secretive friend Brigadeführer Emil Grauwitz will still have a few tricks up his sleeve. I bet that scum has other ideas on how to lay his hands on some money. At the same time my brother might also come up with some cash through his own links with the Reichsbank."

Meunier shrugged with exasperation. There was no option but to continue, so they decided to go on with their plans. They turned to the question of fuel and the range problems with the Boeing. Wenck replied in some technical detail.

"Give or take a few kilometres the distance from the Channel Islands to the Dominican Republic is 8,270 kilometres," said Peter. "With the modifications we have completed so far on the B17 we have managed to extend her range to about 6,000-plus kilometres. We can put a couple more tanks in her which will probably add about 500 kilometres to that distance." He paused for a moment and asked if Meunier understood. The latter nodded his head. "Then there is the matter of performance. We can pare a great deal of weight from the bomber. In service trim the aircraft is well armoured and carries a dozen or so heavy machine-guns.

"I have no intention of flying unarmed, but since we will have a reduced crew there is no necessity to carry a full complement of weapons," continued Peter. "Father has already started to strip the aircraft. We have taken off the waist guns and all their ancillary equipment, plus the two cheek guns and a fifth weapon in the mid-upper position. Finally, we plan to remove the ball turret in the belly of the aircraft with its two weapons. That's a total of seven heavy calibre guns with all their mountings, ammunition and other equipment. The turret, which weighs a bloody lot, also creates drag so we will gain from this," he said pausing for a moment to see if his friend understood. Meunier nodded.

"Now, what this means in weight reduction we're not exactly sure, but I can tell you it's a few thousand kilos plus, of course, we won't have the weight of a full crew. The upshot is that we believe the aircraft will be able to fly 7,000 kilometres, maybe a little more, and that's still not enough."

Meunier pursed his lips and then surprisingly gave a little smile. He extracted another map. Placing it on the table, he turned it around so it faced the pilot. "I just might have the answer," he declared with a self-satisfied smirk. He stabbed a finger at the map. "Spanish Sahara," he declared, as though by mentioning the name he was immediately clearing the problem. "I've been a busy little diplomat and I've had some luck."

He first questioned Wenck on whether he remembered meeting a Spanish Air Force major in Berlin in 1941. "Major Andres Garcia Lacalle of the Ejercito del Air. He was part of a Spanish purchasing mission looking at the latest Heinkel He 111s. Apparently, you undertook to brief them on the new aircraft and gave some pretty fancy flying demonstrations."

Wenck shrugged his shoulders. He remembered meeting some Spanish pilots, but could not specifically recall Lacalle.

"Well no matter," said Meunier. "He remembers you and knows something of your subsequent career, courtesy of *Signal*. Quite a coincidence really. But, what is also of importance is that he is very pro-German."

Meunier explained how he had used some friends in the Spanish embassy to search out and contact a friendly Spanish Air Force officer who was based in Spanish Morocco and could lend assistance. The person they identified as a likely target was Lacalle. In the intervening four years the erstwhile major had risen in rank and was now a full colonel.

"Lacalle is based in Spanish Morocco, but his command and sphere of operations also includes the Spanish Sahara," he explained. "I have yet to finalise the details, but so far I have gained a promise of help from Major Lacalle. We will be able to land at one of two places. El Aiun on the northern coast of Spanish Sahara, or at a place called Ifni, or to be more precise, the town of Sidi Ifni. If you look here you will see that Ifni is a Spanish enclave within Morocco a couple of hundred kilometres north of the Spanish Saharan border."

Wenck became very excited. He looked at the map closely, mentally converting the scale to the distance from either of the two Spanish colonies to the Caribbean. "Donner, das ist gut, sehr gut. It is a saving of about 1,500 kilometres," he said enthusiastically.

"I'm glad you like the idea," Meunier replied. "It has other advantages as well. As I said, I had originally thought only of Spanish Morocco, but Ifni and El Aiun are infinitely better because not only are they well away from Spain and the British at Gibraltar, they are also very remote and therefore away from prying eyes."

Wenck was silent for a few minutes as he studied the map and tried to see if there were any holes in Meunier's plan. As far as he could ascertain there were none. He nodded his head in acknowledgment and then asked whether Meunier had any details of their final destination. The latter explained how originally there had been three possible destinations. The first two were Colombia and Costa Rica where there were still German agents operating.

"Unfortunately, they both have the same problem. Namely, how do we divest ourselves of the Boeing. If we simply leave it parked somewhere the Americans will eventually find it. By checking its serial number and tracing its origins they will find out how your bomber was last heard of over Germany. They will then put two and two together."

Wenck agreed with this rationale and suggested destroying the plane. Meunier replied how even burnt-out wrecks left serial numbers and a fire might create even more unwelcome interest.

"Your father and I have discussed at length on how you both had thought of ultimately getting to America. I also would not mind ending my days in the land of the free. Therefore, I have come up with something which is audacious, but could work. We fly to America, park the aircraft and leave her there."

"Ha ha ha," chortled the younger man. "Very funny. So we just park it at some airfield, unload the money and head into the nearest town?"

"Precisely!"

Wenck sat stunned for a moment. Meunier just looked at him beaming, then reached into his satchel and took out an American magazine. Flipping through the pages he finally found the one he was looking for and handed it to the pilot.

"Here you are, a good example of a popular American weekly magazine, courtesy of our Foreign Ministry, or to be more exact our embassy in Portugal. As you can see it is barely three weeks old ... there, on page sixteen."

It was a short article, obviously meant more for its propaganda value than its intrinsic news value. It contained a photograph and a short story about an airfield that was to be the final resting place of hundreds of useless and obsolete American aircraft. The gist of the article was how America already regarded the war as good as won and the authorities were beginning to earmark aircraft as surplus to their needs, with most being broken up.

One line caught Wenck's eye. It stated how even early models of the Boeing B17 were beginning to be withdrawn from service and transferred to this airfield that was situated north-west of Phoenix in Arizona.

It was so simple Wenck could not believe it. He shook his head and said, "You mean we just fly from Puerta Plata to Arizona, land our plane at this graveyard, unload it and drive away?"

Meunier just nodded his head.

Chapter Twenty-One
24 March 1945

Friedrich Schonewille peered down the railway track and wondered whether the train would be on time. It was a perfect spot for an ambush.

The track curved away slightly into a cutting that he knew from earlier reconnaissance stretched back about two kilometres. The furthest side of the cutting continued to almost where Schonewille was standing. This would make it easy to handle the troops on the train, for their own forces hidden on the top of the cutting could fire downwards with little fear of major retaliatory fire.

At the same time the soldiers to his right would be able to use their anti-tank guns to immobilise the heavy weapons on the train.

The Russian officer's German was poor. For the third time in as many minutes he asked whether the train would be on time. Schonewille was tired and apprehensive and his patience snapped. He rounded on the hapless lieutenant. "You know as much as I do, Lieutenant. Just wait like the rest of us and shut your mouth."

The man pursed his lips and flushed. He turned away, but not before the SS colonel had seen the hatred in the man's eyes.

Then, in the distance they heard a train whistle, mournful in the early morning air.

On the day Schonewille met with Peter Wenck, the bulk of the Reich's gold reserves were transported to the Kaiseroda Mine at Merkers.

Almost one hundred tonnes of gold bullion worth in excess of 200 million US dollars was boxed and loaded onto thirteen railway flat cars for the journey south. More trains followed until the operation was finally completed on 18 February.

By this stage, the value of the Reich's reserves stored in the mine was more than $310 million, with as many millions more in art treasures and other valuables. For the moment at least it was safe from predators and the dangers of war.

Meanwhile, as the winter receded, so the Russians began to stir and re-start their offensive westwards while on the other side of Germany the Americans, British and Canadians began their push to the Rhine. Although Germany was being squeezed on two sides, at its narrowest almost 500 kilometres still separated the two Allied forces. From the north to the south this area stretched from the Baltic to the Adriatic, a distance of 1,000 kilometres. It was still a huge area.

In this gap the German military machine and the industry that fed it with armaments still functioned, albeit under immense strain because of the Allied air offensive. For the millions of Europeans still enslaved and brutalised, their final liberation still seemed a long way off.

Poland had been liberated, as had nearly all of France and all of Belgium, but the Germans still controlled nearly all of their own country, plus half of Holland and all of Denmark and Norway in the north. In the south and east they still held sway over part of Hungary, nearly two thirds of Czechoslovakia, all of Austria as well as northern Italy and part of Yugoslavia.

On 2 March the first American units reached the Rhine, the last great defensive line left to the Wehrmacht in the west.

In the east the pressure on Berlin by General Zhukov was reduced as the Russian diverted his efforts to helping his comrade General Rokossovsky clear the German forces from Pomerania, thereby clearing his flanks before the final push to the German capital.

On 3 March the shadowy Grauwitz finally contacted Schonewille, ordering him to a rendezvous that evening. The meeting took place in an SS building near the navy headquarters overlooking the Landwehr Canal. An air-raid had just finished and although it had not been heavy, the city was again covered in smoke leaving the entire populace nervous and dispirited.

On entering the heavily guarded building he was greeted by an SS captain of about twenty-five who introduced himself as Hauptsturmführer Bremer, saying he was Brigadeführer Grauwitz's aide.

He recognised the captain as the same officer he had seen dining with Grauwitz when he'd had his first meeting with his brother the previous year. Bremer escorted Schonewille along a maze of passages and down into the cellar where a number of offices had been created.

The door of the office was left open and the captain stood watch outside. Grauwitz was obviously taking no chances on being overheard.

The SS Brigadeführer still looked tired. If anything he looked a trifle more haggard than he had at their last meeting and had obviously lost weight. Also, in the intervening few weeks a significant number of grey hairs had appeared at his receding hairline. To Schonewille he looked like a man under extreme pressure.

"Good evening, Obersturmbannführer, how are you?" he said pleasantly.

Schonewille was instantly on his guard, but he answered that he was well.

The lawyer gave his characteristic thin smile and then asked what he thought of the current military situation.

Schonewille hesitated, involuntarily shifting his gaze to the man in the doorway. Grauwitz saw the move and said off-handedly, "Ah don't worry about Lutz. Not only is he loyal to me, he is also a realist."

"Then, Gruppenführer, I think we have two months at best. The Americans and British are at the Rhine. It will hold them for two or three weeks at most. In the East ...well, who knows?" he shrugged his shoulders. Grauwitz nodded and Schonewille continued. "It all depends on how long we can hold them in Pomerania. The Russians won't advance on Berlin until they have cleared their flank, that's one rule of warfare we've taught them often enough."

Grauwitz nodded his head, then abruptly changed the topic. "How is your brother going? I understand he still has the big Junkers on standby."

It was more of a statement than a question. So Schonewille answered the former by saying his brother was well and the latter in the affirmative. At the same time, he mentally told himself to contact Peter and warn him of Grauwitz's knowledge. He's

208

obviously got somebody watching, he thought to himself.

The SS general then asked how quickly Peter Wenck was able to use the big Junkers if ordered. Schonewille lied. "I have not spoken to him for some weeks, Herr Gruppenführer, but I would imagine it would be at short notice."

Grauwitz looked pleased and so Schonewille quickly followed up with two questions of his own. "How soon before you plan to move, Sir, and have you devised a way of obtaining some money?"

"Direct as always, aren't you? Well, no matter, I have brought you here to explain all." He crossed to a wall where a large coloured map of central Europe hung. He pointed to Hungary. "As you are no doubt aware, Budapest fell to the Russians on 13 February. The last monetary reserves of the Hungarian government were moved to Prague by rail a few weeks previously. Now, my information is that we are planning to move some of this to Munich." He moved his finger across Czechoslovakia to southern Germany.

He then explained how a similar move was also being considered for some of the reserves at Merkers. Schonewille thought it was stupid and did not make sense. Why transfer money to a city that was being bombed by the Americans and British? So, he questioned the need to transfer such large amounts of money to Munich, to which Grauwitz gave a snort of derision.

"Some of our more fanatical National Socialists want to set up a National Redoubt, a fortress in the Alps, near the Führer's home at Berchtesgaden. They hope the Führer will flee Berlin and make his headquarters there." He paused to see if Schonewille wanted to ask any questions, but the latter sat mute. "Have you heard of Lieutenant-Colonel Friedrich Rauch of the Schutzpolizei?" The name meant nothing to Schonewille, who shook his head. Grauwitz returned to his desk. "No matter, but it is important you know where he fits in."

He explained that Rauch was adjutant to the chancellery secretary, Reich Minister Hans-Heinrich Lammers, one of the most powerful and influential businessman in the Reich who was now Hitler's personal Security Officer. It was Rauch who had dreamt up the idea of the National Redoubt and had convinced Lammers who, in turn, convinced economics minister and Reichsbank President Walther Funk.

"As well as the Prague and Merkers money there are other consignments being moved south. I intend, with your help, to waylay one of these consignments."

"Shit," said Schonewille involuntarily.

He was so surprised that for a moment his brain refused to function. He had thought the SS lawyer would simply withdraw some money from another branch of the Reichsbank. Finally, he asked how this was to be accomplished. Grauwitz gave a dry chuckle and asked whether Schonewille had ever seen an American western. Bemused, the accountant nodded his head.

"Well then, Obersturmbannführer, we just follow their example and hold up a train."

To say Schonewille was dumbfounded was a simplification. He sat stock still, his mind racing. He swore to himself. He was in too deep and knew too much, so there was no way for him to refuse being a party to such a harebrained scheme.

Grauwitz obviously took delight from the other's discomfort and laughed. Schonewille asked why he need be involved in the robbery. The other said soberly, "Several reasons, mein Freund. Firstly, obviously we cannot allow too many people to know what we are planning. We are not the only ones raiding the Reich's treasures and one never knows whom to trust and you, my friend, are already compromised. Secondly, you still have legitimate reasons to liaise with the Reichsbank, so together with Heger you can obtain certain information. Thirdly, you have front-line experience. Both Bremer and I are somewhat lacking in this department. And, finally, you are still our link with your brother and his aircraft."

Schonewille understood the rationale. Despite his doubts, he knew he would also have to be involved for his own reasons. The more he knew what was going on, the less chance there was of him being betrayed.

The conversation went on until the early hours of the morning.

It was obvious Grauwitz and Bremer had already made some fairly detailed plans, although there were still significant and, to

Schonewille, several worrying gaps.

Grauwitz and his aide would arrange for some troops to be stationed at either Pilsen in western Czechoslovakia or Regensburg in south eastern Germany. Both towns were on the main rail route from Prague to Munich. The problem was to obtain up-to-date and accurate information on when the trains bearing the money were on the move and to find a suitable spot where they could be successfully ambushed.

It was obvious Grauwitz would be able to obtain some information, but the more detailed timetable of the transfer of funds would have to come from Schonewille and Heger. This would be difficult, for what excuse could Schonewille invent to obtain such information? He doubted Heger could supply it since he was now effectively out of the mainstream of Germany's financial world.

"Herr Brigadeführer, there are three questions about Heger that must be answered. What if he cannot supply us with accurate information and how much can we afford to tell him? Also, if we are in the south, how is he to benefit?"

Grauwitz looked across at Bremer who half turned and smiled sardonically. "What do you think, Obersturmbannführer, can he be trusted?"

Schonewille answered truthfully and said he thought the banker could not be trusted and any further information imparted his way would have to be very sparing. Grauwitz's face went hard.

"Correct. You are correct. Quite frankly, he does not figure in our plans now. He and his wife will be a hindrance and there is no way they will be able to join up with us. If he causes us any trouble, I will see he is eliminated."

Schonewille gave his assent, although his heart went cold. Not that he cared anything for his old friend. It was just the knowledge that he also was expendable. His brother's Junkers and his brother's talent as a pilot were his only real safeguard. Certainly, he had front-line experience and some lines of communication with the Reichsbank, but both could be gained elsewhere. No doubt there were many other ruthless members of the SS who would be more than willing to take his place.

He eventually arrived home at just after two in the morning. The apartment was cold and quiet as he took off his boots and silently padded to a corner of the sitting room and turned on a small side lamp. In the corner near the fireplace was a metal coal and wood scuttle screwed to the wall. He carefully twisted both handles and pulled. The scuttle moved away revealing a hole in the wall thirty centimetres square. He put his hand in and extracted a leather pouch. Inside was a smaller pouch containing the Auschwitz diamonds and five passports tied together with string.

The passports were a perfect example of Schonewille's innate caution and Machiavellian nature. Since the failure of the Kursk offensive nearly two years ago, he had been carefully sorting through the mountains of personal papers left by the unfortunate inmates of the camps he visited looking for anything that could be of use to him if Germany lost the war. Of the five passports, four were Swiss and one was Greek.

He opened one and held it up to the light. As he had done many times in the past, he smiled appreciatively as he looked at the print of the woman contained inside. She could have passed for Sophia's twin, a little younger perhaps, but not enough to cause a problem.

He opened another. Again he smiled at the photograph of the passport's late owner. Except for the man's moustache, the likeness was nearly perfect.

Mentally he agreed, these were the two he needed.

At Kragero it was raining. Peter Wenck turned slightly and Erna Hennell reciprocated. A few minutes later they were making love, their bodies shuddering with the urgency of their pleasure. Later, in the quiet aftermath, Wenck lay still, ruminating at the events of the past few weeks, while the woman returned to sleep, her breathing steady and deep.

It had been a strange few weeks. Except for his meeting with Meunier and the odd transport flight, he had nothing much to do. His father at Halden had seen to the final changes to the Boeing and until he was contacted by his brother there was nothing to do but wait. So he had spent as much time as possible in Erna's company.

The woman was a delight. As with all soldiers, female

companionship was a rarity, especially when on duty and having spent most of his war in either Russia or Norway, sex was something to be prized. Now it was almost a surfeit. She had no inhibitions, enthusiastically enjoyed the act and was generous in giving in return.

Wenck wondered whether he was in love with her. Probably not, but given time, he probably could be. The fact troubled him for he doubted he could take her with him when he escaped. At the same time he found himself being careful in what he told her. Whether it was his own innate caution in dealing with human relationships – the emotional self-preservation felt by many fighting men in times of war, or something else, he was not sure.

However, like all women enamoured with a man, Erna wanted to delve deeper into the psyche of this dynamic male. She often asked probing questions and once he became extremely irritated at her blatant inquisitiveness. At his obvious displeasure she stopped probing, but later he caught her questioning one of the mechanics.

The man, a grizzled fifty-year-old veteran of the first war had refused to tell her anything, but Wenck had been disturbed at her obvious efforts to elicit information. He took her aside and spoke with some anger. "Erna, I do not know why you are asking so many questions, but ..."

"It is just that I love you, Peter," she broke in. "And I want to know what sort of mission you are planning. Everybody here knows you are about to do something very crazy."

The revelation of her declared love threw him somewhat and he hesitated. Nevertheless, he kept his distance although his first instinct was to take her in his arms. As a compromise, he softened the tone of his voice. "Liebling, what I have to do is highly confidential. Please, do not ask any more questions. It is not of your concern, versteh?"

She nodded her head but, before her face softened, he saw a gleam of annoyance flare in her eyes.

On 5 March he received a message from his brother informing him of his arrival some time in the next forty-eight hours. This pending arrival was not the only thing that surprised him. It was the blatant way in which Schonewille used an open radio channel, although the message was in code.

His brother, meanwhile, was having his own major problems. Following his meeting with Grauwitz and Bremer, he had made a scheduled visit to a number of camps including Bergen-Belsen. From there he had traveled back to Berlin and visited Heger at his new branch office of the Reichsbank. Their meeting was not a success. After transferring what meagre funds he had collected into a new account, he began to question Heger as to his lines of communication with Munich and whether he could supply him with any information about the transfer of funds from Merkers to Munich and/or from Prague to Munich.

Heger's long features had compressed themselves into an even thinner countenance. He gripped the corner of his desk so hard his knuckles went white.

He asked what Grauwitz wanted with the information, and even before Schonewille could answer, boldly stated how it was obvious the two SS officers were hatching another plan to obtain some more money.

"Where do I fit in, Friedrich?" he said in measured tones. Schonewille hesitated. It was not just the question that made him pause, but rather the uncharacteristic steel in his friend's demeanour and the tone of his voice. "I'm not sure what Grauwitz is planning," he lied.

Heger was not fooled. "Do not mess with me Friedrich. I am not being left here in this, this shambles." He waved his hand at the window through which a portion of a shattered and burnt out building could be seen. "Alice and I refuse to be abandoned while you make your escape. Others might fool themselves, but not I. The war is finished and while I could accept the British or Americans, I won't stay here with the Russians. One only has to look at the map to realise that it is they who will be here first."

Schonewille attempted to placate Heger, but when this had no obvious effect, he became a trifle testy. "Klaus, I repeat I do not know what is being planned. At any rate, there is nothing you can do and there is no way I can help unless Grauwitz decides to take me into his confidence."

Heger shook his head vehemently and suggested Schonewille force Grauwitz into helping. This prompted a sardonic laugh from the SS colonel who said he doubted Grauwitz could be made to do anything he did not want to, especially if he thought it against his interest.

Then Heger became threatening. "Friedrich, you will help us or I will make sure Grauwitz, or the authorities, know of your little secret."

A nervous spasm twitched across Schonewille's chest as he enquired what Heger was talking about.

Heger spoke confidently. "Your Jewish friend, or should I say mistress. Oh no, Friedrich, don't try to deny it. It is fortuitous that Alice convinced me to let her go and see you. You see she does not trust you and she thought she might be able to find out something. It was an interesting meeting and it certainly has strengthened our position. Alice can smell Jews and she is certain your lady friend is Jewish."

Schonewille blustered. The shock of Heger's words as much as his friend's hectoring tone causing his words to sound less than convincing.

"What are you talking about Klaus? I will not sit here and listen to this shit. You, you have no evidence of such a preposterous suggestion and I ..."

Heger cut him short. "If I am wrong, then let the authorities decide. In the meantime, I want you to contact Grauwitz and see what he can do to help."

For a moment Schonewille wanted to continue remonstrating with the banker, for he was now once more in control of himself. But then he realised further argument would be useless and under no circumstances could he let Sophia be investigated. Although her identity papers were good, any detailed investigation would soon unmask her and he doubted whether even before this happened the Jewess would not have incriminated herself. So, he acquiesced, saying he would contact Grauwitz to see what was being planned and make sure Heger and his wife were included.

As he left the bank, his anger began to unfold. You are going to regret trying to blackmail me, he thought. He went back to his own office and calmed himself down while he marshalled his thoughts. An hour later he emerged into the streets once more, knowing exactly what he had to do.

He was waiting in the shadows as Heger left his bank and headed towards the entrance of the nearest underground station. The evening throng of workers heading homeward made it easy for him to remain unnoticed in the background. When the train arrived, he entered the next carriage. Once the train was in motion he did not have to watch Heger for he knew just what station the man would alight onto.

When Heger stepped from the carriage, Schonewille hung back a little, for the crowd on the platform was less dense and he could not risk being seen. He waited until Heger had disappeared into one of the pedestrian tunnels before leaving the confines of the carriage.

In the distance, some air-raid sirens started their mournful wail, the sound soon picked up by their compatriots in the suburbs. The dark unlit streets emptied quickly, but Heger hurried on, obviously wanting to get home and utilise the safety of his apartment building's cellar, rather than face a crowded air-raid shelter. This decision sealed his fate.

As he followed the shadowy figure of the hurrying banker, Schonewille extracted his silencer and then withdrew his automatic from its leather holster. Quickly screwing the cylinder onto the barrel, he thrust the weapon into the right pocket of his leather coat and quickened his steps.

He could not have planned it better. As Heger caught the sound of his footsteps on the pavement, the moon slid behind a cloud so neither man was able to recognise the features of the other. This was a decided advantage to Schonewille for it enabled him to get closer.

The street was deserted with some of the buildings on either side bearing the ravages of war. Heger slowed down and half-turned as Schonewille reached him. The darkness hid the surprise on his face, but his words revealed his shock. "Friedrich! Gott im Himmel. What, what are you doing here?"

"I just want to talk, Klaus. We need to speak, so I thought it

216

would be better to talk at your home. In fact, it is fortuitous we have met. We can now walk together."

Heger hesitated. For a moment he seemed to relax after his shock and then the moon re-appeared from its hiding place and Heger saw Schonewille's face. It was hard and expressionless and, in an instant he read the intent of the figure now standing only two metres away. His hectoring and confident demeanour of a few short hours ago was certainly not evident now. In panic and horror he began to plead.

"No, no, Friedrich, don't, don't," he spluttered, too afraid to mouth the deadly words. Finally they came out. "Please, Friedrich, don't kill me. I would not have revealed your secret. For the love of God, please, please."

Schonewille scarcely heard him. He extracted the Walther from his coat pocket and lifted it menacingly, the silencer giving it an even greater air of deadly purpose. Heger became almost incoherent, moaning in fear. The SS officer motioned him towards one of the wrecked buildings and when Heger hesitated, lifted the automatic as though to aim. With a choking sound, Heger stumbled towards the rubble still entreating Schonewille to spare him.

Suddenly, in a last desperate effort at self preservation he twisted away and ducked into a doorway. Schonewille fired, but the bulled struck the charred remains of a wooden door. He followed and caught sight of Heger half-a-dozen metres away scrambling over a pile of fallen masonry. He moved to follow, but in his haste to chase the fleeing banker struck his left knee on a projecting length of wood, the pain causing him to slow his gait.

In desperation he took aim at the scrambling figure ahead of him and fired again. This time the bullet struck home, catching Heger in the thigh and pitching him onto a pile of plaster and wrecked furniture.

He jerked himself onto all fours as the SS officer reached him. Before his former friend could turn Schonewille aimed the Walther at the back of his head and pulled the trigger. The heavy nine-millimetre bullet struck the unfortunate banker at the nape of his neck before emerging just above his forehead. The exiting bullet shattered the skull and took with it half the man's brains.

For a moment Schonewille stood still, listening. Nothing stirred. In the distance there came the crump of bombs and the sound of anti-aircraft fire, but the war was ten kilometres away.

He bent down and turned the body on its back. Unbuttoning the overcoat, he began searching through the banker's pockets. To his disgust he realised that in those last terrified seconds Heger had wet himself. The sharp pungent smell of urine was strong in the night air.

He extracted the man's wallet and identity papers and again checked his pockets to make sure nothing remained. He then grabbed Heger's legs and with some difficulty dragged him over the rubble to a hole in the floor. Carefully, he skirted the sides and when the corpse was well positioned, pushed it with the toe of his right boot. The banker slid into the abyss and disappeared. Schonewille kicked some more rubble after the body and then made his way back to the entrance.

He paused for a moment and rubbed his knee before stooping to pick up the briefcase that Heger had abandoned in his desperate efforts to flee. He again stood quietly for a moment, listening, but the street was silent and empty.

Moments later, on turning a corner, he bumped into an elderly civilian who, on recognising the uniform, gave an apologetic squeak and hurried away into the darkness.

A ten minute walk saw Schonewille reach the erstwhile banker's apartment building. The Walther with its attachment was still in his overcoat pocket. Quietly he entered the main entrance and walked along the corridor. On reaching the front door of the Heger's flat he paused.

He extracted the Walther and let the weapon hang by his side half-hidden by the folds of his overcoat. With his left hand he extracted a set of keys that he had taken from the banker's briefcase. For a second he searched through the keyring until he came to one he thought would fit the front lock. Carefully, he inserted the key and turned the lock. It was the correct one. To his annoyance though, the bolt slid back with a loud click. He was inside the flat before Alice Heger appeared.

"Klaus, Oh I'm glad you are home, the air-raid sirens are ..." she said, but the remainder of the sentence hung unfinished as she stared in horror at the dusty figure in black. She turned in a futile move to escape into the small lounge room. The Walther coughed, the bullet striking her in the small of her back, propelling her forward until a sofa arrested her movement. The second bullet ended her life.

Schonewille jammed the weapon back into his pocket and, stepping over the slumped body, went into the kitchen. He spent several fruitless minutes opening cupboards searching, until finally he found what he sought: a box of candles. Extracting one, he returned to the lounge, spied a candle holder and inserted the candle. Placing them on a small table, he went back into the kitchen and went to the stove. To his relief, when he tuned one of the handles there came the hissing sound of gas. The bombing had disrupted all essential services so one could never be certain when either the gas or electricity was on or off. He turned the handle full on and repeated the act with the other three.

He turned and hurriedly left the kitchen, closing the door behind him. Crossing to the candle, he extracted a match and then sniffed several times. The gas had not yet had time to reach the room so he lit the wick. Satisfied that all was prepared, he let himself out of the apartment.

He strode away down the street before stepping into the same doorway in which he had hidden so many months before. Five minutes later, he was still standing silent and expectant when a loud explosion rent the air. From his hiding place he caught the flash of light.

He stepped clear of the doorway. A few hundred metres away he could see that the ground floor of the apartment block was already well alight. Schonewille breathed a deep sigh and quickly unscrewed the silencer from the Walther. Placing both in their holsters, he hurried away into the night.

By the time he arrived home he was emotionally and physically spent. Wearily he eased himself onto the sofa and with much difficulty took off his boots. In doing so he noticed a jagged rent in his left trouser leg, so he undid his belt and dropped the garment to the floor.

The knee was swollen and already badly discoloured while the cut, though not too deep, was dirty and oozing blood. He found a half-empty bottle of methylated spirits and, pouring some onto a face cloth, began to clean the wound.

It was then that Sophia found him. Without a word, she took the cloth from his hands and gently cleaned the wound. Despite the pain, he uttered no sound. The silence continued until the wound was clean and bandaged. Only then did she meet his gaze before averting her eyes and noticed the state of his trousers and the dust on his overcoat that he had carelessly dropped over a chair.

"What happened, Friedrich?" she enquired in a low voice. "Did you get caught in the bombing?"

He shook his head and stifled a yawn. "No Liebling, it was a problem of a different kind. Do not worry though, it has been solved."

There was no panic in her voice although her hand shook noticeably as she asked whether they were in danger. He shook his head as she asked another question. It was the first time she had directly made any reference to the future.

"Friedrich, what is going to happen? I read the newspapers and listen to the wireless and, despite what Goebbels says, I know Germany is finished. The Russians are not far away ..." Her voice trailed away.

"Listen, Liebling, and listen carefully. Heger and that bitch of a wife of his knew about you, they were trying to blackmail me ... no, no, no don't worry," he said quickly as a look of terror crossed her beautiful features. "The problem has been eradicated. They will not be able to tell a soul. At any rate, I am in the middle of a complicated plan that should see us escape from the Reich and if we are lucky, we will do so with enough money to start a new life."

For a moment he hesitated, wondering whether it was prudent to reveal much more. Yet, with what he was planning, he realised it would be necessary to tell her a few more details. He spoke of his brother and their father and how they were all part of an elaborate escape plan. Finally, he warned her to be ready to move at a moment's notice.

"From now on, you are to only use the documents belonging to

Käthe Haushofer. Your others are to be destroyed immediately."

Awkwardly he got to his feet, an incongruous sight in his shirt and socks. He went to a small wardrobe near the entrance, which was used to store coats and other wet weather gear. He extracted the woman's SS uniform.

"Here, Liebling. From now on this will be your uniform. Have it sponged and pressed." She took it without a word.

For Schonewille the night was almost sleepless. His brain, at times restless and at times conniving, refused to let him sleep. With the former he re-lived Heger's death and with the latter, tried to work out a way of obtaining the information needed by Grauwitz. Sophia, laying by his side for a change, was equally restless until finally she snuggled up to his body and placed her left arm over his chest. Thus, they eventually found some peace and slumber.

In the morning he once again journeyed to Heger's bank. The branch was not yet open for business but a clerk, on seeing the uniform, let him enter without hesitation. Schonewille summoned the branch's number two and explained he had urgent business with Herr Heger, and where was the bank manager?

The man shrugged his shoulders. "I'm sorry, Herr Obersturmbannführer, he is usually here very early, but he has not turned up as yet. I have tried to ring his home, but it appears the lines are down for I cannot get through." He shrugged his shoulders again.

Schonewille pretended annoyance. "No matter, we have some important business for the Reich to discuss, so I will wait in his office. See that I am not disturbed," he snapped.

The chief clerk was obviously happy to leave Schonewille to his own devices who, once he was alone, wasted no time in searching through his late friend's papers. There was a safe in the corner and extracting Heger's keys from his briefcase Schonewille quickly chose the correct one. He carefully opened the safe and found it to be stacked with files.

Not knowing what he was looking for, and doubting he would find anything of use anyway, he nevertheless began to peruse their contents. To his utter astonishment the second file contained a treasure trove of information. It was marked Top Secret and in bold, indelible pencil was the heading 'Foreign Currency/Bullion – Transfers'.

Inside were two documents. The first, dated two days previously, was from a Dr V Pfeiffer of the Munich branch of the Reichsbank. It referred to orders from the Reichsbank's deputy president, Emil Puhl, and gave details of a train leaving Berlin for Munich at 0730 hours on 9 March.

The second document was four days old. It was signed by Puhl and countersigned by Reich Minister Hans-Heinrich Lammers. Its contents were invaluable. It ordered Heger to gather all the remaining foreign currency held in his branch and have it ready for transportation to Munich. It listed various sums of foreign currency and requested Heger contact either Puhl or Dr Pfeiffer if his records showed these sums to be inaccurate.

Next to the list of foreign currency were a number of ticks. Somebody had obviously checked the sums and found them to be correct. He carefully copied the details of the documents and then replaced the file in the safe. Locking it, he extracted the safe's key from its ring and hid it at the back of a drawer. He then opened the office door and called the chief clerk over.

"Do you know where Herr Heger keeps the key to that safe?" The man looked surprised and shook his head. "No matter, I do." Schonewille opened the drawer and pretended to rummage around. On finding the key he turned to the man and handed it to him.

"I believe this could be the right one. I cannot wait any longer. Open the safe and you should find a file marked Foreign Currency, or something similar. It will be stamped Top Secret."

The man did as he was bid and extracted the file. Handing it to Schonewille he asked whether it was the one. The SS officer nodded his head and asked the clerk whether he had seen it before. The other was emphatic he had never laid eyes on it. Good, thought Schonewille. He handed the file back to the man.

"When Herr Heger arrives ask him to find out why the money must go to Munich. If he does not come, find out yourself, but do not mention my name. Also, make sure the orders contained therein are followed. I will be back this afternoon."

Schonewille returned shortly after five. Much had happened in his absence. The chief clerk was now the acting branch manager. He informed the SS colonel of some distressing news. Heger's apartment had apparently been the victim of a stray bomb and had been burnt to the ground. It was presumed the banker and his wife had perished inside.

Of more importance, however, were the man's next words. "I was not able to contact Dr Pfeiffer, but managed to speak to a friend of mine who has a reasonably senior position in the Munich branch. As to what you seek, all I can tell you is that several consignments of bullion and foreign currency from all over the Reich are being transported to Munich. My friend informed me there had been strict orders for all the consignments to be in Munich by the fifteenth."

The man paused and asked whether this was the information Schonewille sought. The other nodded and asked why all the foreign currency and bullion had to be in Munich by the fifteenth.

"I am not sure, Herr Obersturmbannführer, but I was told the consignments would then leave for another destination, probably on the sixteenth or seventeenth." The man again paused and then in a hesitant voice asked why Schonewille needed such information.

Schonewille tried not to appear too evasive and gave the man a vague concoction of half truths and lies. "Oh, I already have much of this information. As you can see I am attached to Amtsgruppe fünf and unfortunately I am trying to trace some documents relating to these shipments, which have been lost in the bombing. At any rate, there is no need for you to worry any further. You have done me a good service. When I speak to your superiors, I will see that your position becomes permanent."

The acting manager smiled in appreciation. Schonewille's explanation, though vague, was sufficient to ease any suspicions he might have had. Amtsgruppa fünf (or branch 5), was the auditing office of the Economic and Administrative Main Office of the SS. To the banker therefore, Schonewille's seniority and credentials were impeccable, so there was no need to seek further explanation.

The SS officer took his leave and immediately went to his office where he attempted to contact Grauwitz. The Brigadeführer was not available, so he spoke to Bremer instead.

He passed on the information he had gleaned and although it was not complete he knew it would give the plotters some further information as to when the Reichsbank's bullion and foreign currency would be moved south: some time after 16 March.

That evening he worked late to catch up on his own legitimate work. At the same time he prepared for his trip to Norway.

At his last meeting with Grauwitz, they had discussed the possible options for transferring the money from the train to an aircraft, which they both knew was the best way to escape from Germany. The general had still refused to reveal a destination, except to say that he had made arrangements to land in Spain, from where they would fly south to a destination somewhere in Africa.

What worried Schonewille was how the plans of his relations would fit in with those of Grauwitz. The more he ruminated, the more he realised that at some stage the stolen money would have to be separated from Grauwitz and Bremer. How, he was not sure. He desperately needed to talk to his brother again and luckily it was Grauwitz who provided the wherewithal.

In order to obtain the necessary troops to waylay the train Grauwitz explained how he would need some extra and powerful authority. "I need the Himmler letter back from your brother," he had demanded.

In return, Schonewille asked him to provide the necessary orders to fly to Kragero to obtain the missive. At this suggestion Grauwitz become quite agitated and ordered that under no condition was he to leave Germany. At Schonewille's questioning the reason, Grauwitz bristled with annoyance and snapped, "Just do as I order, verstanden?"

Perplexed, Schonewille shrugged his shoulders and acquiesced, though it was agreed he would have to travel to either Kiel or Hamburg and meet his brother there.

The subsequent trip north proved uneventful. For once there were no unnecessary delays and no re-routing to skirt damaged track.

He had no intention of staying in Germany. On leaving

Grauwitz's office, he immediately telegraphed his brother giving his approximate arrival in Norway. The mere fact that Grauwitz had wanted him to keep away from Peter Wenck made him suspicious. Therefore, he decided to disobey the SS general's instructions. There was also another reason. He wanted to obtain further details on the plans being concocted by his father and brother and believed his appearance in Norway might help elicit extra information.

At Kiel he was able, without difficulty, to hitch a lift to Norway with a transport flight bound for Oslo. Although his papers only authorised him to travel to Kiel or Hamburg, nobody asked any awkward questions. After all, a lieutenant-colonel in the SS was not somebody who acted against the interests of the Reich.

From Oslo he took a bus all the way to Kragero where he phoned his brother who sent a car.

They had scarcely finished greeting one another when Erna Hennell knocked and entered the room. The smile on her face vanished abruptly when she saw the black uniform. Then she looked at Schonewille and the colour drained from her face.

In a flash the SS officer knew how Grauwitz was obtaining his information. The woman excused herself and attempted to leave, but Schonewille was too quick for her. He moved to block her exit, at the same time kicking the door shut with his right boot. Ignoring Wenck's protests he grabbed Hennell's arm and pulled her to a chair.

"Setzen Sie sich," he said in a stentorian voice. The woman obeyed. Wenck again started to speak, but Schonewille cut him off. "Please, shut up for a moment, Peter!" Then, dragging a chair forward, he sat down in front of the woman and confronted her. He came directly to the point.

"Now, Untersturmführer … Hennell, is it not? Unless you are not using your correct name?" The woman nodded her head, her hands starting to tremble. Schonewille noted the nervousness with satisfaction. "Well, Untersturmführer. Who sent you here? Herr Brigadeführer Grauwitz?"

Again Erna Hennell nodded her head mutely. She stole a quick glance at the air force officer who was still standing dumbfounded at what was unfolding.

"Well?" snapped Schonewille.

The woman jerked her head back to meet his gaze. "Jawohl, Herr Obersturmbannführer. Das ist korrekt."

"Gut, then how and when do you contact him?"

"I use the SS office at Skien if I need to get a message back to the Reich ... I ... I only do so if I have something important to say," she stumbled under Schonewille's penetrating gaze.

"And what if you are to be contacted?"

"If it is an emergency I would be contacted by radio here, but if it is simple and not urgent it is sent to Skien and a courier will deliver it here to me personally."

He questioned her further while Wenck looked on in silence. The pilot did not fully comprehend everything, but he understood enough. Hennell did not look at him at first, and when she finally did so there was genuine pain in her eyes.

She revealed how she had received only one message and had only sent two back to Grauwitz. One to say she had arrived and another to reveal details of the Junkers 290 and its state of preparedness.

Finally, Schonewille stood up and took his brother's arm. He led him to an adjoining empty office.

"Well, Peter," he said speaking in a low voice. "Do you understand?"

"I understand part of it Friedrich, but fill in the rest."

"I know the woman, or rather I have seen her at my headquarters. She's an Offizier im Gerichtsdienst, an officer in the legal branch," he repeated. "She's with Amtsgruppe drei, the same section as Grauwitz." Wenck opened his eyes in understanding. "Quite simply, Peter, Erna Hennell was sent here to spy on you."

The air force colonel went ashen. He nodded his head. "Well brother, what do we do?"

"The best option would be to kill her," said Schonewille. "However, that could prove to be a problem if Grauwitz tries to contact her and, anyway, it might be difficult to arrange."

Wenck was shocked at the simple brutality of the words. He shook his head and said vehemently, "There will be no killing, of

Erna Hennell or anybody else. Do you understand? I will have her confined to these buildings, with strict instructions not to either receive, or send any messages from here." Schonewille nodded. It was, he agreed, the wisest course. Wenck went on. "Just so we understand one another, Friedrich. Erna means something to me. She will not be harmed. If you try to do so, our relationship is finished. Understand?"

It was not a question. Just a bald statement and the SS officer did not appreciate it one bit. His first instinct was to answer in anger, but he knew he had no power and it rankled. His brother did not need him. Peter and his father had the aircraft and undoubtedly a plan to escape. He had nothing. The realisation once more that he was the helpless intermediary between the two groups of plotters galled him. So, he took a deep breath and said in a low voice that he understood.

Peter Wenck touched him on his shoulder and said with relief, "Danke vielmals, Friedrich." The words and the gesture did much to assuage Schonewille's inner anger. "Please leave us alone for a moment or so. Go to my room, it's along the passageway, and freshen up. I will make all the arrangements here."

He turned and went back into his office. Erna Hennell was still sitting in the chair. She was pale and her hands were shaking. He sat down in front of her and gently took both in his own hands and said in a soft voice, "Well, Liebling, what have you got to say for yourself?"

The woman's whole body started to tremble and it was obvious she had been crying. She attempted to speak, but the words caught in her throat and tears brimmed in her eyes again.

The pilot's heart went out to her, yet he felt he dare not follow his instinct and take her in his arms. He needed to ascertain if she had passed on anything of note. It was vital to find out if she knew of his father and of what was going on at Halden. He doubted it, since he had never spoken of his father and had been quite deliberate in not giving her any information as to what and where he was going when he flew out on his frequent trips away from the Kragero base.

Finally, she took a deep shuddering breath and began to talk.

She explained how Grauwitz had ordered her to Norway with the express instruction of keeping an eye on him. Wenck questioned her carefully, choosing his words to make certain his probing did not reveal anything.

It was difficult to know for certain, but he finally came to the conclusion that she knew little, if anything. Certainly, she knew of the big Junkers and she explained how the base was full of rumours about a supposed secret mission that he was planning. However, she seemed truly perplexed as to why a senior SS officer in the legal section was taking such a strong interest.

"You see, Peter, I neither know nor care what it's all about. To leave Berlin was wonderful. There is no bombing here. The food is so much better and I have found you. Please believe me, Peter, the only reason I did not tell you was because it seemed so silly. I found out nothing that might incriminate you of anything and, anyway, after a few days I really did not try too hard."

She paused and then withdrew one hand from his clasp and attempted to touch him on the cheek. He did not draw away, but stiffened involuntarily. She quickly withdrew her hand and started to cry again, her voice hoarse.

"Peter, oh Peter please, believe me. I did not want to spy on you. I do not know what is going on and I really don't care. I love you, I love you," she repeated in a broken voice.

"All right, Liebling, we will talk again later. In the meantime you are confined to your quarters. I am giving orders that you are to neither give nor receive any messages. If you attempt to do so, well let us just say it will not be wise, verstanden?"

Dumbly she nodded her head and began to cry again.

For a moment, he hesitated, then he reached out and gently stroked her hair. She returned the gesture by rubbing her face against the cupped hand.

God help me, he thought. I love her and I know I am going to have to leave her here, because I dare not trust her.

He left her sitting with her head buried in her hands and went to his office where Schonewille was lounging on a leather sofa with one leg stretched in front, staring out of the window at a brilliantly blue sky. Without a word, he picked up the handset of one of his two telephones and called in the elderly Luftwaffe lieutenant in charge of the base's security. When the man arrived, he gave him strict instructions concerning Erna Hennell. He also ordered the officer to pass on the details to the base commander.

After the man had saluted and left, Wenck told his brother how he doubted whether Hennell had any knowledge of their father or what was happening.

"That is the key, Friedrich. If she does not know about Father, then Grauwitz will not have the slightest inkling of what we are up to. My belief is this: he is naturally suspicious, but has no real basis for any suspicion concerning us. He has just been covering his arse."

"I hope you are right, Peter, I hope you are right. At any rate, please answer me this. You have been having a relationship with this woman, nicht wahr?"

Wenck nodded his head and explained how he truly believed Erna loved him.

This turn of events suited Schonewille perfectly. He began to tell of his relationship with Sophia and even explained how he had rescued her from a detention centre. The words concentration camp were not used. To say his brother was amazed was an understatement. That the SS colonel was not only harbouring, but was also in love with a Jewess defied logic. It made him realise once again what a complicated man his elder brother was.

Peter Wenck thought he saw an opportunity of enquiring about the camps and of perhaps trying to find out what his brother's role was. Schonewille was dismissive. "Oh don't ask, Peter, they are not nice and, as for me. Well, I was there purely to handle some of their finances. I do not go to them too often, and I certainly do not like it."

His explanation was quite correct, although it was a considerable lessening of the full unpalatable truth. At any rate it eased Peter's suspicions about his brother.

"What I want, Peter, is to take Sophia with us. No, no, listen," he said holding up both hands as Wenck sat upright and attempted to interrupt.

"I have a perfect cover for her and can arrange for her to be in

Hamburg or Kiel in a few days. It would not be too difficult for you to pick her up. Her papers are perfect and she could then wait at Halden with Father."

Schonewille gave details as to her disguise and again requested that his brother help. Wenck shrugged his shoulders and gave a helpless gesture of compliance.

"Well, why not? It is just another twist to this crazy, crazy adventure. Shit, we must all be certifiable." Then, with a half smile, he said sardonically, "Is that all, Friedrich? I mean, you don't have a secret deal with the Führer and he is coming along as well?"

They both laughed uproariously. It was another bond between them. Schonewille relaxed a little and, looking at his brother's smiling face, decided that now was the opportunity to really find out what was being planned. He came directly to the point and asked what had been put in place. To his annoyance, he saw the shutters began to close on the pilot's eyes and the hesitation in his demeanour.

He felt dismayed and his voice for once did not mask his feelings. "Oh come now Peter. There is no need for secrets, not any more. I have just told you about Sophia. I trust you. So why don't you trust me?"

His brother paused and then nodded his head, albeit reluctantly.

Peter Wenck still did not want to give away all the information, but by the same token he did not want to let this be known, so he compromised. "I can let you know this. We have arranged for a secret re-fuelling stop and now have a destination. It is in America ... I know, I know it sounds crazy," he said as Schonewille's eyes widened. "But, believe me, it will work. I would like to tell you more, but there is another person involved and he has sworn us to secrecy. Therefore, this will have to do for the moment. All right?"

Schonewille acquiesced. It would have to do.

Wenck in return felt relieved. He had not given away the existence of the Boeing nor where the re-fuelling stops were. In fact, he had only very vaguely mentioned one. Their secrets were still safe.

Chapter Twenty-Two

Following the rendezvous with his brother, things moved rapidly. On returning to Berlin Schonewille met with Grauwitz again and handed over the Himmler letter. The SS legal officer seemed buoyant and said with bravura, "We are on the move, Obersturmbannführer. I have already put in train some moves that will allow us to waylay some of the Reichsbank's reserves and with this letter from the chicken farmer I can finish my plans without any undue questions being asked. I want you to travel to Regensburg and report to these barracks. Hauptsturmführer Bremer is already there." He handed over a piece of lined note paper.

Schonewille enquired as to the reasons, but Grauwitz cut him short.

"Not now, Colonel," he snapped. "Just follow my orders and find Lutz. I will reveal all in good time."

Schonewille clenched his teeth in frustration and saluted. Once out into the street he punched a gloved fist into a gloved palm in frustration and swore. A young captain in a flak regiment saw the gesture and heard the words. He grinned at the SS officer's display of anger and frustration. Schonewille glared at him and strode away.

At home he sat in his study and carefully went over his alternatives. That he had to follow orders and travel to Regensburg there was no doubt. Regensburg was scarcely more than a hundred kilometres north of Munich where some of the Reichsbank's reserves were headed. Therefore, it certainly was connected with the next stage of their plans.

He called to Sophia and told her to begin packing. He handed over an envelope that contained her orders. She extracted the two pieces of paper and scanned them quickly.

"As you can see, they are signed by me and countersigned by the second-in-command of Amtsgruppe fünf. Luckily, he is so busy he signs just about everything I put in front of him without reading the contents. So, as an SS officer and with these two signatures, nobody will doubt your authenticity or question why you are travelling to Kiel."

The Jewess nodded her head. She seemed surprisingly calm, he thought. He handed her another piece of paper.

"This is the name of an airfield just outside Kiel. You are to go there and ask for Major Wisch, nobody else, do you understand? When you introduce yourself he will contact my brother in Norway who will come and get you." He put his arms around her shoulders and said tenderly, though his voice was sombre, "Sophia, meine Frau. You have to leave tonight. There is a train to Hamburg leaving at eleven. You must be on it. I would have preferred that you go via Lübeck since it has not been bombed as heavily and there is less chance of a delay, but this is the first available train."

Although the word wife was a misnomer, it described perfectly how this strange and driven man felt about the woman. Then, as he felt her tremble, he dropped his voice even lower, telling her how everything would turn out right. She made no comment in return and for much of the next two hours, as she packed her small suitcase and prepared a quick meal, there was little conversation between them.

They journeyed into the city and he escorted her onto a train travelling north. It was crowded with all the usual flotsam of war. Troops, women, children and refugees, all fleeing the horrors of Berlin.

He put her in a compartment with three U-Boat officers and ordered them to look after her. His last sight of Sophia was when he looked back from the corridor. She appeared calm and held his gaze unwaveringly. Her parting smile, though small and a trifle wan, held a warmth that he had never seen before.

Back on the platform he crossed to another part of the station and sat down in an officers' waiting room to while away the hours until the train to Regensburg left for its trip south. The train was delayed and when it finally left Berlin the pace was slow and erratic. There were several unscheduled stops and they were shunted onto sidings on numerous occasions. It took nine hours to reach Leipzig, a distance of only 160 kilometres. Officially the train was supposed to have continued onto Regensburg, but without explanation the engine was un-coupled and the carriages left un-attended on a siding. Enraged, he climbed down from his carriage and went to the nearest signal box. The signalman knew nothing except to explain that most of the lines south of the city had been disrupted by Allied bombers who had struck two important marshalling yards.

He then went to the station master's office where a harassed official suggested he take a train to Prague. The line to the Czech capital was still open and it would take him further south and away from this bottleneck.

"Take my advice, Herr Obersturmbannführer. The line to Prague has been spared most of the bombing we've experienced over the past ten days. From there you should be able to head back across to Pilsen and then to Regensburg."

Schonewille shook his head.

"I know, I know," answered the official. "But, believe me, while it may seem a strange way to get to your destination it is the best way. So, why don't you use my office to clean yourself up a bit? There is a small washroom and you will feel much better. But make it quick. The train to Prague leaves in twenty-five minutes."

Schonewille was grateful for the offer and took the man's advice. The bath, though lukewarm, eased his bones and made him feel a little fresher.

Unfortunately, the rush was unnecessary for the train did not leave for almost two hours. The 200-odd kilometres to Prague took seven hours. Although there were only two unscheduled stops, the overloaded train barely travelled at more than forty-five kilometres per hour. More than half its passengers were soldiers being rushed to bolster General Schoerner's 17th Army fighting on the other side of the Elbe. Most did not appear too keen to reach the front.

The journey to Pilsen and then Regensburg, on the other hand, was trouble free, though the jolting, cramped carriage meant sleep was illusory. By the time he reached his destination, he was exhausted after twenty-seven hours of travelling and waiting in cold and dirty railway stations.

Grauwitz's order had been simple. Liaise with Bremer who was stationed at a barracks on the outskirts of the city.

Schonewille managed to cadge a lift from an air force truck being driven by a young Luftwaffe NCO who was terrified on being stopped by a senior SS officer in the dead of night and was only too happy to take him where he wanted to go. The barracks were certainly not purpose-built for the job, probably an old factory or warehouse, he thought. It was nearly dawn and the first hues of light were beginning to thin the black of the sky as he trudged to what looked like the main gate.

A sleepy private in a makeshift sentry post jerked himself upright at his appearance and, although he did not challenge him, looked warily as Schonewille walked past and headed to what was the only lighted window in the large stone edifice situated on the other side of a small paved courtyard. The window belonged to a large office that had been tacked onto the main structure and had at one time obviously been used as a dispatch centre.

Schonewille entered without knocking and was confronted by the soles of a pair of boots hiked up on a large wooden table. On the other end of the legs was the sprawled form of Captain Bremer, fast asleep in a large high-backed chair with his arms folded on his chest and his head lolling back.

The lieutenant-colonel surveyed the junior officer for a minute and then with a malicious smile used his right leg to push Bremer's outstretched legs off the table. Their weight almost jerked his body off the chair and for a moment it was touch-and-go whether or not the chair itself would tip over.

With an angry exclamation Bremer grabbed the edge of the table and steadied himself, at the same time focusing his eyes on the figure in the overcoat looking down at him. On recognising Schonewille he swore and demanded to know what the other was trying to do. It was the wrong tack.

"Stehen sie auf," he roared. As Grauwitz's aide hesitated, he repeated the order. "Stand up, do you hear Hauptsturmführer, stand up!" And then, added for good measure, "Where is your discipline, you slack bastard? Where is your salute?"

Years of obeying orders had their effect and Bremer stood up straight and saluted, though his eyes were defiant and angry. Schonewille returned the salute and with his free hand pulled a chair alongside. Sitting down he motioned Bremer to return to his own chair.

"Now, will you kindly tell me what is going on?"

Bremer took a deep breath and shifted in his chair before starting to speak. For the moment at least his arrogance had evaporated. He explained how Grauwitz was putting together a raiding force capable of stopping one of the Reichsbank's trains and that a contingent of troops was already garrisoned in the building behind. He jerked his thumb in the direction of a doorway at the back of the office.

"More are expected to arrive tomorrow. As usual they are late, as is everything and everyone these days."

Schonewille let the barb slip by. "Is this why your boss wanted the Himmler letter?"

Bremer nodded and reached inside his tunic and pulled out the envelope that Schonewille had handed to Grauwitz scarcely thirty-six hours before.

"When did you get that?" he said in astonishment.

"About six o'clock last night. Why?"

"From Herr Grauwitz?"

"Yes, of course," said Bremer with a smirk.

"Das ist unmöglich, shit. That is unbelievable."

He had spent twenty-seven uncomfortable hours in various train carriages while Grauwitz had either driven or flown south. "Why the hell did he not take me?" It was more of a statement than a question.

Bremer's smirk returned, but it vanished as he read the expression on Schonewille's face.

"Now you listen here, you shit and you had better listen and understand well. You and Herr Brigadeführer Grauwitz had better realise that I am not an Arschlecker. I am not somebody you can lead around by the nose."

He paused and saw Bremer regarding him with a trace of alarm, so he continued.

"Remember this. I have the aircraft, I have the pilot and I have

235

the means to get us out of this sinkhole we call Germany. Therefore, you had better give me due deference, otherwise you will end up with all the money you want and nowhere to spend it."

Bremer nodded his head and then in a flash of defiance said in return, "Herr Obersturmbannführer, I would watch what I say about, or to the Brigadeführer. He could have you shot."

Schonewille laughed in derision, though there was no mirth in the action. He had his anger under control and was thinking fast.

"Listen Bremer, and you can also repeat this to Grauwitz. Details of what has been happening have been left with a friend of mine. If I do not report to him every twenty-four hours, a sealed letter will be delivered to the Reichsführer. Then we will see who ends up in the cells of the Wilhelmstrasse headquarters before facing a firing squad, eh?"

It was all a lie, but by the look on Bremer's face this possibility had certainly not crossed his mind. His face was pale and he nodded his head several times in understanding.

Schonewille looked up at a clock on the wall. It read just past six and in the distance a cock was crowing.

"Since we understand one another, you'd better fill me in on what has transpired and what is about to happen. My diary tells me it's the ninth today and the first train is due to leave Munich in six or seven days. So we obviously don't have much time."

He asked about the troops garrisoned behind the door. Bremer smiled sardonically and said they were Russian.

"They're what?" exclaimed Schonewille in astonishment.

"Yes, they're Russians, but they're on our side, at least nominally," answered the SS captain.

He began to explain who they were and after hearing a few details Schonewille recalled reading something of their history. German propaganda had made much of Russians and other nationalities who had become part of the German armed forces.

In the latter part of 1942 a Russian Army of Liberation under its Russian name Russkaya Osvoboditelnaya Armiya, or ROA for short, was formed to help the Wehrmacht liberate the USSR from Stalin and the Communists. Red Army troops captured by German forces and other Russian dissidents were recruited to serve in its command.

The officer in charge of the ROA was Lieutenant General Andrey Vlasov who, as the commander of the 2nd Assault Army, had been captured by Dutch members of the Waffen SS a year earlier. Together with another anti-Communist army officer, Major General Malyshkin, the former chief-of-staff of the Russian 19th Army, Vlasov tried to put forward a united force that might fight with, rather than for, the German army.

The effectiveness of the ROA, or Vlasov Army, was hampered by two factors: the lack of support from the German High Command, especially Hitler; and the high number of desertions from its forces serving on the eastern front after the fall of Stalingrad. Subsequently, the ROA's forces were withdrawn and sent to the Balkans, Slovakia, Poland and France to fight the various resistance forces, a job they performed admirably.

By late 1944, the situation on the eastern front had deteriorated to such an extent that even the most rabid Nazi recognised the need to gain further allies and fighting forces. Consequently, with Himmler's blessing a new Russian force was set up.

Under the auspices of the Komitet Osvobozhdeniya Narodov – The Committee for the Liberation of the Peoples of Russia, or KONR for short – another fighting contingent was put together. The KONR Army was created amidst much pomp and ceremony in Prague in September 1944, a symbolic gesture since KONR was to be a Slavic army and Prague was a Slavic capital. Within a short time two divisions were created, the 600th and 650 Panzer Grenadiers made up of former Russian workers in Germany and former prisoners-of-war, numbering 50,000 in total.

It was members of this strange army who were being recruited by Grauwitz and Bremer.

"Can you trust them?" questioned Schonewille.

Bremer shrugged his shoulders and said in an off-hand way, "Oh yes. Mind you, if I was fighting on the Russian front I probably would want to watch my back, but by all accounts they have proved to be pretty effective as anti-partisan forces, particularly in Yugoslavia. At any rate, what we will use them for is pretty simple and should not involve any heavy fighting."

"And, unlike good German soldiers, they can be relied on to shoot other German soldiers if need be and I would imagine they will also be expendable when the time comes," broke in Schonewille.

Bremer hesitated and then with a crooked smile nodded his head in agreement.

Just like me, thought the other. He stared at Bremer who shifted uncomfortably under his gaze. Schonewille shut his eyes for a second so as not to let any part of his feelings show, for he knew if he was to escape from the Reich he would have to deal with Grauwitz and his aide.

He enquired as to the facilities at the barracks and was told there were few.

"But, do not worry, Herr Obersturmbannführer. This should be a temporary base of a few days at most. We will obviously need another base further south, that is when we find out exactly what is happening."

Too tired to talk let alone think any more, Schonewille lowered his tired body onto a camp bed in the corner of the room and tried to get some sleep. He dozed fitfully for three hours but realising that proper sleep was eluding him, got up and sponged himself at a basin in another room. The water was cold and the wash perfunctory, but he felt better for it.

Now it was vital he reach Munich and find out what was happening with the money trains. He questioned Bremer as to the availability of transport and petrol.

"We are a little short on what we need, Herr Obersturmbannführer," answered Bremer. The SS captain was now much more formal and correct in his dealings with Schonewille, obviously realising the lieutenant-colonel would not be pushed around. "We have two Kübelwagen and three trucks, two big three-tonne Opels and one very large four-and-a-half-ton Bussing-NAG. Obviously, we will need at least half-a-dozen more trucks to transport our troopers south."

Schonewille agreed and told him to try the local SS garrison. They would have the necessary clout to obtain the additional trucks. In the meantime he would take one of the Volkswagens and asked Bremer to choose a driver. "One who is reliable and who speaks reasonable German. I want to be able to make myself understood."

At 1100 hours Schonewille's Volkswagen headed south on the road to Landshut. The driver turned out to be a dour thick-set corporal of about thirty-five years of age called Ilya Chuikov. Bremer had recommended him since Chuikov was a veteran of both the ROA and the KONR and had served against Tito's partisans.

They passed through Landshut without stopping and continued on to Moosburg where they had a late lunch. On the move again they started to encounter heavy military traffic and with it came the Allied fighter bombers.

Twice they were forced to shelter under some trees as American Thunderbolts flew overhead. In order to keep off the main roads and so lessen the risk, they switched to some back roads, only to find others with the same idea. The increased traffic on the small Bavarian secondary roads caused traffic jams, thereby increasing the risk of Allied air activity, so Schonewille struck out across country and re-joined one of the main roads.

Through it all Chuikov said nothing accept yes or no, invariably in German although sometimes he slipped into his native nyet or da.

The two reached Munich shortly after nightfall having driven the last twenty kilometres-or-so in light rain. They drove to an SS barracks where Schonewille checked himself in and had a light meal followed by a bath and bed. He was exhausted. The Russian was left to his own devices.

The morning brought a heavy leaden sky and more rain. Chuikov was waiting with the Volkswagen and drove Schonewille to the Munich branch of the Reichsbank.

The SS lieutenant-colonel had a legitimate reason for visiting the bank, although it was more of a cover for his nefarious activities than an actual function of his SS command. With authorisation from his department, courtesy of a signature from his immediate superior, he opened another account, ostensibly for the proceeds of the concentration camps. He also spent time with the bank's second-in-command and ingratiated himself by remarking how efficiently the bank was being run and how this had been made known to him by none other than Dr Walther Funk.

Pleased to be so praised by a senior SS officer who was obviously a confidante of the bank's hierarchy, the banker spoke garrulously about his work and what was happening within the bank. By the time he left Schonewille had all the information he needed, plus an invitation for dinner the following evening with the banker's family.

The rest of the day was spent in the offices of the German State Railways assessing the likely alternative routes for any freight trains heading south-east for the mountains near Berchtesgaden.

By the thirteenth he was in possession of as much information as was available, so he set up the framework for the next part of their audacious plan.

He had arranged barracks for their troops in the town of Traunstein some forty kilometres west of Salzburg. On phoning Bremer he was informed that the necessary trucks had been requisitioned, as well as sufficient gasoline to move the Russian troops to Traunstein. The difficulty in obtaining petrol was of major concern to every German army or air force commander at this time, since the loss of the Romanian oil fields plus the constant attacks by Allied bombers on the synthetic oil plants was slowly drying up supplies.

On the evening of the fourteenth, Schonewille, Grauwitz and Bremer held a meeting at their new barracks in Traunstein. Schonewille's knowledge of what was happening to the Reichsbank's reserves and his thorough planning enabled him to hold court. It also cemented his new-found status within the group.

On his arrival at Traunstein, Grauwitz immediately held a private meeting with Bremer who filled him in on what had transpired between him and Schonewille. Grauwitz emerged from this private conference with a hard look on his face and his lips compressed into a thin line.

"Guten Tag Herr Obersturmbannführer," he said gravely. "What is this I hear from Herr Bremer?"

By this stage Schonewille was feeling even more obdurate and refused to be drawn. "What part of our conversation are you referring to, Herr Brigadeführer?" he answered in apparent innocence.

The SS general's voice dropped to a hiss. "Don't you play games with me. Verstanden?"

Schonewille smiled, a sardonic gesture, which for a moment seemed to throw the older man. The SS lieutenant-colonel immediately seized the advantage. "Oh I suppose you are referring to my refusal to be played for a fool. Well, what Bremer has told you is true and, let me add this little homily. We either work together in harmony and trust, or we fail together in acrimony and mistrust. The choice is yours." It was a statement not a question.

For a moment Grauwitz gave the impression he would choke. When he finally opened his mouth to speak Schonewille compounded his earlier action by cutting him off.

"Oh, and don't try to threaten me, it will be a waste of breath. As your aide no doubt mentioned, you can't touch me. There's a detailed missive in a safe place in Berlin that will be handed to the Reichsführer on my demise. Also, there are certain practicalities concerning this operation which, after I explain them, should reinforce your earlier assessment of how important I am to this operation." He paused and cocked his head at Grauwitz in a silent question.

The other raised his eyebrows in return, but refused to be drawn – a grudging admission of Schonewille's new found status. So, Schonewille continued.

"I have the connections to fly us out of the Reich. I well understand you also can lay your hands on an aircraft, though I doubt whether it will be as suitable as the one I have arranged. Nor will you be able to arrange for a pilot as accomplished as my brother. Then there is the question of our arrangements here. Neither you nor Bremer possess any legitimate reason to make business or social calls to the Munich Reichsbank and therefore cannot obtain the information that I already have in my possession. Let us accept the fact that I am a key component of your plans without whom the operation will probably fail and leave you deep in pig shit."

Grauwitz stood unmoving for almost thirty seconds. Finally his head moved up and down almost imperceptibly as he grudgingly accepted the words and fully understood what they represented. When he spoke it was without rancour, but with a trace of irony.

"I certainly underestimated you, Herr Obersturmbannführer. I had a feeling in my bones you would be devious, but not quite so Machiavellian. You should have been an Italian. But I hear you and understand what you say. Maybe I should have taken you a little more into my confidence, but old habits die hard." He took off his cap and ran his left hand through his dark hair. "So, Obersturmbannführer Schonewille ... comrade. What have you learned?"

Schonewille was not fooled. Grauwitz would eliminate him given half the chance. At present he needed him. But after the Reichsbank's valuables were safely stored in the Junkers, or maybe even before, he would become expendable.

Bremer was called in. By the expression on his face he had obviously been listening at the door and his manner was quite friendly, even mildly obsequious.

Schonewille spread out three large army ordinance maps covering southern Bavaria, the Tyrol and nearly all of Austria. He pinned them to a wall so their overlap corresponded and then turned to his conspirators.

"Now, meine Herren, this is what I have learned. The trains are still scheduled to leave Munich in two or three days, on the fifteenth or sixteenth as planned, although I have some doubts as to whether this will happen."

Grauwitz asked why.

Schonewille explained that there were three reasons. The first was the lateness of the trains from Czechoslovakia that carried the monetary reserves of the now defunct Admiral Horthy regime in Hungary. The second was the condition of the train tracks due to the constant predatory forays of Allied aircraft, while the third was the shortage of locomotives due to the same problem.

"The fact is we are under such severe pressure that no train ever runs on time, let alone uses its intended route. Our much vaunted punctuality has disappeared along with our chances of winning

242

this war."

He went on to detail the problems of trying to waylay one of the trains.

"All we know for certain is that the trains will leave from Munich, here." He prodded at the map and then moved a finger along a series of railway lines that he had marked in red pencil. "The difficulty is there are several routes south and east of Munich that the trains might take."

"Surely all one has to know is what their ultimate destination is and choose accordingly," interrupted Grauwitz.

"No, that's incorrect," answered Schonewille. "I do know the ultimate destination of the reserves and I am ninety-five percent certain I know the final railway route the trains will take. Unfortunately what I don't know is which railway route they will take to get to that final route."

Grauwitz shook his head, not understanding, so Schonewille tried to explain more clearly.

The information he had garnered was quite detailed. The reserves were to be transferred to the town of Bad Reichenhall some forty kilometres by road from Berchtesgaden, which was deep in the Alps near the border of Austria and Germany. The nearest towns to Bad Reichenhall were Anif and Salzburg, both situated to the north-east with Ruhpolding to the north-west. Of those three only Salzburg and Ruhpolding were fed by a railway line.

"My belief is this. The trains will go to Ruhpolding which, as you can see, is scarcely twenty kilometres south of here. I doubt they will go to Salzburg because it is too big, while the road from there to Bad Reichenhall is much further and much more difficult."

Grauwitz shook his head and remarked that if this was the case then surely it would be easy to waylay the train.

Schonewille disagreed. "Not so. We cannot have our troops hidden indefinitely near the point of ambush, and since we do not know from which direction the trains will come from we will not have adequate warning to move our men to the ambush site quickly enough. All we know for certain is that to get to Ruhpolding the train must first pass through Traunstein, which will not give us enough time to get our troops into position."

By use of the map he explained how there were seven main alternative railway lines for the trains to take to reach Traunstein. Although it was expected that the trains from Munich would take the most direct and quickest course, this might not be the case since Allied air activity could force them to make a detour and they might arrive at Ruhpolding by a circuitous route.

"There is another problem, Herr Gruppenführer. There is a good chance the trains will be armoured."

This news was greeted with stunned silence.

Throughout the war the Wehrmacht had been adept at using trains for offensive purposes, as well as for the transport of troops and munitions. With great ingenuity they had, over a period of several years, developed a large number of armoured trains. Although there were dozens of variations to the theme they all had one thing in common. The locomotives and freight cars were all protected with armour plating and were equipped with a wide range of light- to medium-calibre guns as well as specially trained shock troops.

In short, they were formidable weapons.

"I believe, however, these particular trains might not be too difficult a nut to crack," said Schonewille. "There is only a fifty-fifty chance the engine will be armoured with not more than two or three of the trucks similarly protected and fitted with heavy weapons. Nevertheless, each train will also pull at least two flat cars equipped with anti-aircraft weapons, probably multiple twenty-millimetre cannons."

Schonewille let the two SS officers worry amongst themselves for a few minutes before playing his hand. He could barely contain his smugness.

He explained how he had a possible solution. Sixty kilometres to the west was the town of Rosenheim. On its outskirts was an engineering works that was being used to repair and modify various types of armoured vehicles. "As soon as I learned about the armoured trains I made enquiries as to the availability of tanks or armoured cars. As you are no doubt aware, they are worth their weight in gold at the moment and, therefore, are not things left lying around."

Grauwitz allowed himself a small smile. He was beginning to appreciate just how useful the SS accountant had become. It also unnerved him, since he was having to rely even more on Schonewille's intelligence gathering abilities and obvious flair for improvisation.

"This engineering works was originally used for modifying and repairing farm machinery and has since been enlarged with the inclusion of a foundry and some equipment capable of cutting and fitting armour plate. With the help of the Himmler letter and/or your august presence, I am certain we can commandeer what we need."

He paused for a moment letting his words sink in. Grauwitz motioned for him to continue.

"Although I'm not sure what their inventory is, or what operational state it's in, I did see several self-propelled guns and a few armoured cars with large calibre weapons. With any luck we should be able to lay our hands on one or two."

The following day Grauwitz and Schonewille drove to Rosenheim leaving Bremer to see to the needs of their Russian troops and ready them for any immediate departure.

With their fuel stocks low, they first stopped at a fuel depot to arrange for extra quantities but Allied aircraft had been there first and what was left was barely enough to meet their needs. If it had not been for their combined rank and the persuasive quality of the Himmler letter they would not have been able to purloin even that, for the elderly captain in charge of the depot was none too keen to relinquish his remaining stocks, especially since they had been earmarked for General Woehler's Army Group South. Reluctantly he dispatched a tanker to their Traunstein barracks while they continued up the road to Rosenheim.

The former engineering works had been heavily camouflaged and had therefore escaped detection from the air. The main building was not large, covering about three quarters of a hectare, but the surrounding woods were filled with all manner of damaged military equipment, either awaiting repair or cannibalisation.

Due to the urgency of Germany's situation, the factory's engineers and workers were toiling non-stop in three shifts and yet were still unable to meet the demands of the hard-pressed Wehrmacht defenders. The appearance of Grauwitz and Schonewille did not help their situation, but it certainly eased the worries of the two SS officers.

They were escorted around the facility and told what equipment was ready for immediate dispatch and what would become available within the next week. Of the former, there was nothing suitable for their needs: three large self-propelled guns and two Panther tanks. The former were too big, too powerful and too slow, while the latter were too valuable and could cause problems. They chose instead an armoured car and a medium-sized self-propelled gun. Both mounted weapons of sufficient size and hitting power to take on the armoured train and were mobile enough to move quickly.

The armoured car was one of the most potent of its type developed by any combatant during the war. It was a Puma SdKfz 234/2, an eight-wheel, eleven tonne monster mounting a fifty-millimetre cannon. It was well-protected with armour and, despite its weight and size, could gallop along at eighty-four kilometres per hour.

The self-propelled gun was an example of the type of improvisation that had been dreamt up by the Germans. It was known as a Mader II and was the successful marriage of a German light tank hull with one of the most effective anti-tank weapons produced in the war, the Russian 76.2 calibre cannon which, amongst other things, was mounted on the feared T34 tank.

During the early stage of Operation Barbarossa, the German invasion of Russia, the advancing troops captured large quantities of Russian weapons. Among the few they regarded as useful was the 76.2 cannon, which they successfully married to a large number of tracked vehicles. These became known as Panzerjagers, or tank hunters. The Mader was one of these hybrids and saw the Russian weapon mounted atop the hull of an obsolete German Mark II light tank. It was a little crude, with the gunner and loader standing exposed on the rear of the superstructure and there was no

246

moveable turret. Nevertheless, the gun could be traversed thirty degrees left and right while the Christie suspension ensured the chassis was very manoeuvrable and could be quickly re-positioned.

Like the Puma, the Mader weighed in at eleven tonnes and, although not nearly as fleet-footed as the armoured car, was still capable of forty kilometres per hour.

It was agreed the two vehicles would become available no later than the morning of the next day, which was the sixteenth. If the trains left on schedule on that day this would give them little time to prepare but there was no option.

From Rosenheim they journeyed to Munich, which was in the throes of yet another air-raid. While Grauwitz went to the local SS headquarters, Schonewille went to the bank where he learned what he half expected, that the timetable for the dispatch of the special trains had been altered yet again. They were now scheduled to leave Munich at three-hour intervals on the nineteenth or twentieth, probably the latter.

In order to gain the best possible warning of the train's departure, Schonewille used the Himmler letter to arrange with his Reichsbank contact to ring him at Traunstein the moment they steamed from the Munich rail yards. Not wanting to go to the SS headquarters and use one of their radios while Grauwitz was close by, he decided to use a phone to contact either his brother or father. The bank manager placed his office at his disposal and, much to Schonewille's surprise, he was able to get through to Norway straight away.

The first question he asked his brother was whether the package had arrived safely. His brother assured him his package was safe and sound, and added for good measure, "You are a lucky dog. That is a very attractive package."

It was as though a weight had been lifted from Schonewille's shoulders. He had worried himself sick over the preceding days about the fate of his mistress and the news of her safe arrival made him smile with glee.

He told Peter to stand by to fly to a military airfield that was situated just north of Traunstein. He explained how he had made arrangements with the base's commander and would use the aerodrome's radio to contact him when it was time to make the hazardous flight south.

Light of heart, he went to the SS headquarters where a suspicious Grauwitz remarked on his levity.

"Oh, don't worry Herr Brigadeführer, everything is going to be fine. I have made arrangements for plenty of warning regarding the trains and my brother is ready to fly south the moment he receives my call."

Grauwitz's weary look vanished and he smiled, a rare occurrence that transformed his dour exterior.

Once back at Traunstein, Schonewille took Ilya Chuikov to reconnoitre the train track between the town and Ruhpolding.

Chapter Twenty-Three

As the Volkswagen drove through the beautiful southern Bavarian countryside with the Alps facing them, Schonewille wondered how much he could take the Russian into his confidence. In truth, if he was to survive the next few days he would have to make the tough Ukranian sergeant an ally, yet he did not know how he could do so. In the meantime he had to undertake a further reconnaissance of the railway line between Traunstein and Ruhpolding.

He had already picked a spot that he thought would be perfect for any ambush. The single line went through a low curving cutting at the end of which was a small valley. Traversing this valley and crossing the railway line was a dirt road, obviously not much travelled. At either end were dense woods and there was no house or dwelling within five kilometres.

Satisfied that he had found the right place from where to attack the armoured train, he ordered Chuikov to drive north. A few kilometres further up the road they came to a small town called Seigsdorf. Schonewille ordered Chuikov to stop and wait for him at a small inn. He then drove himself out of the town back from whence he had come.

Two kilometres out of the town he stopped the VW beside the road and alighted. He unlocked the boot and opened a long wooden box about two metres long. Inside were several standard issue German stick grenades.

He paused for a moment and looked around. The road was deserted and there was no sound of any approaching vehicle. He had chosen the spot carefully. To the south the road curved quite sharply, one side obscured by a five-metre bank and several thick bushes. On the other side was a deep ditch followed by a gentle slope and half-a-dozen large trees.

Extracting two of the grenades, he walked towards a telephone pole to the north of the corner. He took some cord from his pocket and quickly fashioned a noose at one end. He loosely looped the cord around the pole and fed one end through the noose. Then, fitting the handles of both grenades through the loop, he pulled it tight so the weapons were forced hard against the wooden pole. He wound the cord around several times and tied it securely before unscrewing the metal caps at the base of the grenades' wooden handles. This freed from each grenade a short string with a small porcelain bead at the end.

All that now remained for the devices to explode was to pull each string, which would pull a roughened steel pin through a sensitive chemical, causing it to ignite. This lit a five-second fuse which in turn fired the detonator that exploded each grenade. The bomb was tied low down on the pole so it was obscured by some tall grass and could not possibly be spotted by even someone walking along the side of the road.

Satisfied, he hurried to the car and drove back towards Segsdorf. However, he continued through for another three kilometres. Stopping once more, he repeated the procedure with two more grenades and then drove back to the inn.

The reasons for Schonewille's actions were quite simple, he was trying to ensure a measure of protection from Grauwitz and Bremer. He reasoned that when the time came he would have to escape from their command and do so with some of the Reichsbank treasure. He had no definitive plan, yet he now felt he could not afford to wait until he reached the airfield to divest himself of the other two SS officers. He was almost certain that once the train was successfully stopped and the money transferred to the waiting trucks, his usefulness would be over.

His comments to Grauwitz about the general needing him and his brother were only partly correct. There was no real reason why Grauwitz could not have him killed and force his brother to immediately fly the Junkers south-west to Spain and then on to Africa. Or, the SS brigadier general could even have his own pilot on hand at Traunstein.

Schonewille's suspicions about his fellow conspirators were not based on anything concrete, but rather his own devious logic and inherent suspicions. Several times he had surprised Grauwitz and Bremer deep in conversation, a conversation that stopped abruptly when he entered the room. Another time he had caught Bremer smiling sardonically at him behind his back and when he challenged the SS captain the other had apologised and said it was nothing of any consequence. Schonewille would have to kill Grauwitz before the SS officer had him killed first.

As he sat down at the table where the Russian was sitting, Chuikov looked at him expectantly, yet he did not speak.

Schonewille opened the conversation by asking if he had eaten. When the other shook his head he motioned for a man behind the bar to come and attend to their needs. He then ordered a cold beer, cold meat and fresh bread.

When they were alone once more, Schonewille tried the direct approach. "What would you say, Sergeant, if I told you the war was lost?"

Chuikov jerked his head back in surprise. He narrowed his eyes and stared hard at Schonewille, whose impassive demeanour gave nothing away. Finally he shrugged his shoulders and said in his heavily accented German, "I would say that if you have recognised this fact you are certainly wiser than most of your breed. But, I must ask, why you are telling me?"

Schonewille ignored the question and asked another of his own. "If you also recognise that the war is lost, what have you decided to do? Or perhaps I should ask, where have you decided to go?"

Chuikov gave a wry smile. It was not a pretty sight since his teeth were bad, and it did not lessen the devious look in the man's small green eyes. He again shrugged before speaking. "Oh, what can I do, Herr Obersturmbannführer? If I am taken by the Red Army, my former comrades will have me instantly shot. If I attempt to desert, your lot will have me shot. So, this leaves the Amis or the British. They might jail me, or they might hand me over to Stalin. At any rate, as you can see, my options are small and limited."

Schonewille readily agreed with him. The conversation was going better than he expected.

He told the Russian sergeant how he was part of a plot to take some money from the Reichsbank. That if the Russian helped him and guarded his back, he would have the option of obtaining a large sum of money with which to escape to Switzerland and freedom from prosecution, or he could join Schonewille who had devised his own route through which he could flee the Reich.

Chuikov took this revelation without any emotion crossing his craggy features, but he readily agreed and to prove his loyalty said something that confirmed Schonewille's suspicions. He explained that Bremer had ordered him to keep a close watch on him and to report what the SS lieutenant-colonel did and who he spoke to.

While Schonewille and Chuikov were talking, Peter Wenck was flying to Halden for a final meeting with his father. He found Meunier at the base, having taken a ferry over from Copenhagen the previous day. The diplomat explained how he had managed to reach Copenhagen where he had bribed some friendly officials to allow him entry to Norway. Meunier also revealed the final details of his arrangements with his Spanish and Dominican contacts and with a German agent based in Mexico. The latter was standing by at a border town near El Paso and would cross into America and head north for Arizona the moment the Boeing left Norway.

Meunier had also come up trumps in another way. He had brought with him half-a-dozen passports, all American and all genuine. "Believe me it was quite easy to lay my hands on them, although it cost me a lot of money. In fact all the Swiss francs I possessed," he said with a smirk. "I hope our little bank job will see me paid back with interest." He opened a small suitcase and unwrapped another parcel. He gave another self-satisfied smirk. "And this, my friends, is the piece de resistance. I have here all the necessary stamps, entry permits, personal papers, etcetera, etcetera, to make us all genuine, legal American citizens."

He waved his hands expansively and continued. "Believe me, I could have got more. You have no idea how much stuff like this is lying around in the Foreign Office. You would imagine some of von Ribbentrop's friends would be busily planning for their own furor, but no. They're all there doing their jobs like good little Germans." He smacked his lips in annoyance. "By Christ we are a stupid and pedantic race. Give us an order and we obey it to the letter and right to the end."

When all the final details had been discussed, Peter Wenck

turned to his father and enquired as to the whereabouts of the Jewess.

His father explained that Sophia largely kept to herself and said little about her past. He intended to talk to her again that evening in an effort to find out more about her background and how she had become involved with his son.

Chapter Twenty-Four
24 March 1945

0035 Hours

Peter Wenck was dozing in his office when his adjutant Leo Swabisch knocked and entered without waiting for an answer.

"Peter, it has come," he said, his voice hoarse and excited. "The call-sign you requested the radio room to watch for has come."

Wenck had been expecting the call. His conversation with his brother three hours earlier had been full of promise. There had been two false alarms in the past few days and throughout the entire time he and his crew had been on virtual standby. Now at last it was time to move.

He inquired whether there had been any additional message accompanying the call-sign, but Swabisch just shook his head. "Wonderful, so let us go. Get the crew … schnell!"

The captain hesitated. He wanted to speak but was unsure how to broach what was on his mind. Peter was more than his commanding officer; he was a friend and he trusted him implicitly, yet he was beginning to get irritated by Wenck's refusal to take him into his confidence. This did not only centre on the role of the Junkers and the Boeing stationed at Halden. There was also the question of the female SS officer, Erna Hennel. The woman intrigued him. He had seen Wenck in her company several times and it was patently obvious she was in love with the Luftwaffe officer, yet his friend appeared reserved and even somewhat reticent in her company. Despite this, Wenck scarcely stayed away and spent most of his free moments in her company.

Another thing annoyed Swabisch. Wenck had ordered him to keep away from her.

"Jesus, Peter, do you think I would steal her from you?" Wenck had refused to be drawn. He just rounded on Swabisch with a black look and told him to do as he was told.

All this left the adjutant totally confused.

"Well come on, Leo, jump to it. What are you waiting for? Get the fucking crew!"

"Peter, for Christ's sake, can't you tell me what the hell is going on?"

Wenck tried not to let his irritation show, but Swabisch felt it nevertheless. He shrugged his shoulders and turned away. Feeling guilty, Wenck put his hand on the man's left shoulder. "Look, Leo. You know the route we need to take. All I can tell you is this. We have to pick up a cargo, a very valuable cargo, plus a man who just so happens to be my brother. When we get back to Norway I promise you will be told everything. So for the moment, just do as you are told. Verstanden?"

Mollified, Swabisch went to rouse the crew while Wenck walked out to where the Junkers was parked, its engines ticking over.

As Peter looked up at the familiar silhouette of the bomber he felt a familiar tightness creep across his chest. It was a portent of battle, the warning sign of nervous tension that set the adrenalin pumping. The strain of the past few weeks had also taken its toll and he knew the flight south to pick up the Reichsbank's valuables would be no picnic.

Once he took off he was committed to two things, theft and desertion. As a loyal German officer, they were an anathema to everything he had been trained for and believed in, yet, he knew he had no choice. Not only was his father involved, somebody he both admired and loved, but he now understood fully that the regime for which he had fought so resolutely for nearly six years was rotten to the core. His conscience was clear.

As soon as he saw the crew enter the aircraft, he climbed into the cockpit and settled into his seat, giving himself a moment's calm and respite before Swabisch and the navigator joined him on the flight deck for any last minute instructions and to go through the pre-flight check.

He spread out his map and looked at the flight plan he had chosen. Ideally he would have liked to take the most direct route, almost due south through German-held territory. But this would be impractical. Even at night Germany was a huge shooting gallery with hordes of British night fighters roaming the skies, either

255

protecting their bombers or engaged on free-range search-and-destroy missions. Schonewille was aware that the Junkers 290 would provide a huge blip for any British radar operator or pilot and, well-armed though it was, the bomber would find it hard to protect itself against an aircraft as deadly as a Mosquito.

To counter this, he and his co-pilot had decided on a circuitous route to reach Traunstein. He knew the Russians possessed few night fighters and those were equipped to fly in the dark were not nearly as efficient as those of their British allies.

Their intended route was south-east through the Kattegat, to the east of Copenhagen and out over the Baltic Sea. They would cross the coast near Sassnitz, fly over the disputed territory of Pomerania and pass well east of Stettin. He then planned to bear almost due south passing east of Dresden and to continue almost until Budapest, before making another course change and heading south-west to Traunstein.

The distance was almost 1,400 kilometres and the trip would take just under six hours. They would arrive at dawn. He hoped the aerodrome's commander had taken his orders to heart and provided a parking area that would keep the Junkers hidden from any roving Allied fighter.

The cockpit check completed and with all four BMW radial engines warm and running sweetly, he released the brakes and swung the bomber away from the dispersals area.

0645 Hours

The sound of the train whistle in the early spring morning air was almost a relief. The last week had seen a number of false starts and mixed emotions, of which frustration was the most common as the plotters attempted to find out the whereabouts of the various trains carrying the reserves of the Reichsbank.

Late on the evening of the eighteenth, Schonewille's bank contact rang to inform him that the first train would leave at precisely 0700 hours the next morning. It would take the southern-most route via Peiss, Bruckmühl, Bad Aibling, Kolbermoor, Rosenheim and Übersee to reach Traunstein. The time of arrival was uncertain.

Grauwitz and Schonewille assembled the troops while Schonewille contacted his brother. But just as they were ready to move out they received a call from the bank to say there had been a heavy raid on the Munich marshalling yards and the train would now not leave before 1800 hours. The route was uncertain and, therefore, they were to wait for another call.

This call finally arrived at 2200 hours. This time he was told the train had indeed steamed out of the Munich yards, but had been re-routed along the most northerly track heading east to the town of Muhldorf.

"I am sorry, Herr Obersturmbannführer,' the voice on the other end apologised. "What route south it ultimately takes to reach Traunstein and the likely timetable it will adhere to, is very much in the lap of the gods. Unfortunately I have no real way of finding out until it actually happens. The Central Railway Office in Mühldorf is your best chance. Contact Reinhardt Lipechitz at the Mühldorf yards in a few hours, he will be the person most likely to know what the situation is."

Grauwitz greeted the news with a towering rage that showed how much on edge he was. Surprisingly Bremer, on the other hand, was quite calm and showed no emotion. For a moment Schonewille guessed the SS captain might have been relieved.

Maybe he is not too keen on this plan, he thought to himself. Whatever the man felt would be of no ultimate use to him so he went to Grauwitz's office where the radio was located and made contact with Peter Wenck.

When he returned Grauwitz had calmed down somewhat, although his anger was still clearly in evidence. Schonewille, on the other hand, tried not to let what was happening upset him. He knew he had to remain alert, not only to find out where the train was, but also to watch for any treachery on Grauwitz or Bremer's part.

"Well, Herr Schonewille," said the general, omitting to use his title. "What in hell's sake do we do now? It looks like your plan is falling apart."

Schonewille resisted losing his temper with difficulty and spoke calmly, his voice low and precise. "My plan? My plan, Grauwitz?" The loss of title was deliberate. "We are in this together ... Sir! It is early days yet. All we have to do is bide out time and be ready to move at a moment's notice. We will get what we want, you mark my words."

He could hear Grauwitz grind his teeth. The SS brigadier general was clearly not used to being addressed in this way by a junior officer. Yet he knew he was not in a position to do anything but take Schonewille's impertinence, and the realisation rankled.

Perversely Schonewille was quite enjoying the other's discomfort and the feeling surprised him. Over the past few years, the cautious accountant with the deferential nature had become a resourceful and ruthless individual. Membership of the SS and the rank that went with it had transformed the way in which he faced the world. To a degree he felt almost omnipotent, yet he was wise enough to know reality was not far away and the slightest slip would herald his demise. He tried for several hours to trace the train's whereabouts, but either nobody knew or they were not telling. Finally, just after three in the morning of the twentieth, he fell asleep fully-dressed on a sofa.

He was awakened by Chuikov who thrust a steaming hot mug of real coffee under his nose. He drank it greedily, burning his tongue. Cursing, he enquired as to its origins and was told Bremer had visited a local Allied prisoner-of-war camp. "Red Cross parcels," he muttered to himself.

For the next two hours he alternately worked the phone and the radio trying to find the whereabouts of the train, or any other of the Reichsbank specials, but to no avail. At first he was told all the trains from Mühldorf travelling south to Traunstein and Salzburg had been re-routed south-west to Rosenheim. Yet when he contacted the controller at Rosenheim he was told such a move was impossible for Allied aircraft had severed the rail line in two places both north and south of the town of Rott.

By now Schonewille was also becoming angry and dispirited.

All through the day there was no news. Exhausted he went to sleep early, leaving Bremer in charge of the phone and radio. Grauwitz had disappeared during the afternoon and his aide said he had no idea where he had gone. Although suspicious, Schonewille could do nothing, so he let the matter alone.

The morning of the twenty-first was quiet, there was no news. Just after noon Schonewille again tried to ring his Munich bank contact. The man had not been contactable for more than thirty-six hours and Schonewille was becoming suspicious. However, the man answered the phone and explained that the railway system in south-eastern Germany had been in turmoil after a series of heavy raids and was only now beginning to function properly again. He explained that all but the first Reichsbank special had been halted until the tracks were cleared and the various troop and ammunition trains, which had priority, were safely despatched and well on their way to their respective destinations. The banker then revealed how a second special had just this minute steamed out of the Munich rail yards and was now heading for Rosenheim via Haar and Zorneding.

Schonewille had barely digested this piece of news when Grauwitz strode into the room and threw down his attaché case. "Well, Herr Obersturmbannführer, where is our train, eh?" For a moment Schonewille was nonplussed. He stood uncertainly. "You don't know, is that it? Well I'll tell you, my clever friend. It fucking well passed through Traunstein two-and-a-half hours ago and I bet my left testicle it's being unloaded at Ruhpolding right now."

Schonewille was shocked and it showed. He had to regain the initiative so he told Grauwitz about the second train.

To his immense relief the SS general calmed down and they decided to contact the signal box at Rosenheim and ask the signalman to inform them when the train was passing through on its way to Traunstein.

They waited. Six hours passed before they heard from the signalman. The train had just steamed through. Except for an ammunition train five kilometres ahead, the line was clear.

Schonewille radioed Peter Wenck and asked him to get ready for the flight south.

They then contacted the signal box at Prien thirty kilometres down the line only to be told that the ammunition train had been de-railed and the special had been shunted onto a siding.

Schonewille went back to the radio to talk to his brother.

The hours passed and still no news. The morning of the twenty-second dawned. It rained. They contacted the signal box several times during the day asking for the status of the line. The answers were always the same. Crews were working non stop to clear the wreck and restore the line.

By this time Grauwitz's temper had returned with a vengeance. He had eaten something that obviously had not agreed with him, for he was suffering from a bad case of diarrhoea. Maliciously, Schonewille took great delight at his discomfiture.

Finally, late on the evening on the twenty-third, they were told the line was clear and the special was on the move again. It was time to set the trap. If there were no further major delays, the train would quickly reach Traunstein.

Schonewille had earlier radioed Peter Wenck and told him yet again to stand by. Now he was able to tell him to fly south.

As Peter Wenck eased back the control column and lifted the Junkers into the Norwegian sky, a convoy of twelve trucks, two Volkswagens, the Mader self-propelled gun and the Puma armoured car left the Traunstein barracks and headed south on the Ruhpolding road.

In order to give themselves as much leeway as possible, they left the Mader to make its own way to the rendezvous. With a top speed of forty kilometres per hour, it was a little slow and they wanted to travel at a steady sixty kilometres per hour. In the event, they need not have bothered. The train did not arrive for several hours after they had reached the ambush site and deployed the Russians.

Although Grauwitz did not interfere in the preparations for the ambush, leaving the task primarily to Schonewille with some help from Bremer, he did take a great deal of interest in what was being planned.

The general's bowel problems had still not abated and he was obviously in some discomfort, alternately clutching at his lower stomach or awkwardly scratching his backside. For the first time he was accompanied by someone other than Bremer, a thick-set corporal who had obviously been severely injured in the face quite recently since his lower jaw was twisted and there was a livid scar stretching from his right ear to the edge of his nose. Grauwitz introduced him as SS Sturmmann Kurt Kube, his praetorian guard.

The corporal saluted, but there was no change to his twisted features and he said nothing. He carried an MP40 machine pistol that hung low across his belly by a strap. There were two magazines attached, the second strapped to the first by tape. Numerous combat badges and an Iron Cross second class were pinned to his tunic. He was obviously a tough and seasoned soldier and his presence gave Schonewille a sense of disquiet.

Masking his feelings, he turned away and attended to the positioning of the Russian troops. A dozen or so men were hidden on the furthest side of the cutting where it continued almost to the railway crossing.

On the southern side where the cutting ended about a hundred metres short of the road, they positioned the Mader and the Puma twenty-five metres apart. Slightly back and to their right was a Pak 37 4.5cm anti-tank gun that had been requisitioned by Grauwitz the day before. The remaining soldiers were stationed in a semi-circle from the edge of the southern cutting or dispersed among bushes. The trucks were a hundred metres back hidden in some trees.

They waited, Schonewille with increasing nervousness, for as well as waiting for the train he had to keep a watchful eye on Grauwitz and his thug. Ilya Chuikov hovered near and even gave him a crooked smile when he looked in his direction, but he was still unsure of the man's loyalty.

The train's whistle caused a stir among the waiting troops.

Minutes passed. They could clearly hear the locomotive and see the distant puffs of grey-black smoke through the tree tops.

Then the train was in the cutting, the sound magnified in the enclosed space until it suddenly emerged, travelling at fifty kilometres per hour.

At its head was a quadruple two-centimetre anti-aircraft gun mounted on a flat car with lightly armoured sides about a metre high. Then there was a large wagon covered with sloping armour topped by a large slab-sided turret mounting a light field Howitzer.

Next was the locomotive and tender, both protected by armour plate although not to the degree of the wagon. Attached to the tender was another flat car, again with a quadruple anti-aircraft gun, followed by three carriages, their sides and roof also covered by armour plate. Bringing up the rear was a third anti-aircraft gun on a flat car.

The troops' first priority was to stop the locomotive. Originally, they had planned to de-rail the train, but Schonewille had reasoned that if this happened there was a risk the carriages carrying the money might roll over, thereby hindering the quick and easy transfer of their contents.

Both the Mader and the Puma fired, the deep sound of the Russian cannon coming a second after the crisp crack of the Puma's fifty-millimetre weapon. The locomotive was an easy target and both shells struck. The 76.2-millimetre gun was the most effective, its armour-piercing shell penetrating the armour plate and the locomotive's steel hide with relative ease. There came a massive explosion as the boiler erupted, sending steam and chunks of metal flying in all directions. The train immediately rolled to a stop with the first flat car coming to rest across the roadway.

The soldiers manning the Pak 37 were also quick off the mark, their shell carving through the thin armour of the flat car and striking the base of the anti-aircraft gun, totally destroying it and killing its crew. Its brother on the second flat car behind the tender was equally quick to respond and exacted a horrible revenge. A hail of cannon shells wiped out the Pak's gunners and immobilised the weapon.

The turret on the armoured wagon traversed and the barrel of the Howitzer depressed as its crew looked for a target. It managed to fire one round but missed the now moving Mader before the self-propelled gun and the Puma fired, almost in unison, both hitting the wagon. There was no answer from the Howitzer, but both fired twice more into the armoured hull to make certain.

Above the din of the heavy guns came the rattle of automatic weapons and the sharp steady crack of the two pairs of multiple anti-aircraft cannons as they fired a steady stream of cannon shells at the armoured car. Although they did not penetrate the Puma's armour they completely shredded the tyres on one side, immobilising it. Wounded, the Puma's turret swung round and fired twice, its shells striking the second flak car putting its multi-barrelled weapon out of action. At the same time a soldier on the furthest cutting leant over the edge with a Panzerfaust anti-tank weapon and pulled the trigger. The hollow charge shell hit the floor of the third flat car a metre from the base of its anti aircraft gun and exploded, lifting the whole weapon from its mounting and pitching it on its side. All but one of the crew were killed outright.

Automatic weapons continued their staccato beat for a few more seconds before gradually fading to a stop.

For a moment there was an eerie quiet. The steam from the wrecked locomotive escaped silently into the sky and not even the wounded uttered a sound.

The silence was broken by a loud clang as a door on one of the carriages was swung open and a broom handle with a white towel tied to the end was thrust out and waved vigorously.

"No shooting, no shooting," yelled Schonewille.

He ordered the Russian lieutenant and Bremer to check the carriages, for he had no intention of placing himself in any danger unless it was necessary.

The two officers walked forward, Bremer carrying a white handkerchief. He stood at the doorway and spoke to someone half-hidden inside. Eventually, the man carrying the broom appeared and stepped down onto the ground. A short conversation transpired before he turned around and yelled something to those inside.

Another man appeared in the doorway, followed by three more.

Doors on the other two carriages were flung open and another dozen or so figures emerged.

Schonewille strode forward, stopping when he reached the group.

The man with the broom handle turned his head and, on recognising the rank, said in an irate voice with no trace of fear, "Obersturmbannführer, what in God's name is going on? I demand to know who has authorised this outrage."

He was a tall man, wearing civilian clothes and obviously used

263

to dispensing orders and having them carried out. Schonewille ignored the question. "Are there any soldiers in these compartments?" he barked. "Well, come on, answer me," he said, his voice rising in irritation as the man stared at him.

"No, no soldiers. All who were in these carriages are standing here," he said his voice now a little uncertain.

Schonewille turned his back on the man and climbed into the first carriage. It had obviously once been an elegant sleeping car, although half the compartments had been cleared away and there was now a large open space filled with sofas and a large card table. At one end was a small cubicle that he took to be the toilet and on the opposite side was a large and very neat wash basin.

He climbed down from the carriage and walked to the next. Pulling himself up the short, steep ladder he climbed inside and found what he was looking for.

The Reichsbank's reserves were stacked haphazardly at one end and along both walls. Long wooden crates and square wooden boxes were surrounded by canvas sacks with the words 'Reichsbank Hauptkasse' stencilled on their sides.

He went to the third carriage and found more valuables. He bent down and broke the seal on one of the sacks. Loosening the cord he pulled it open and was confronted by a hoard of gold coins glistening in the carriage's light.

He squatted silently for a few moments, almost overcome with the emotion of what surrounded him, quickly picked up the sack and with an effort lifted it to the doorway. It was an even more difficult task getting it down the ladder, but he managed it. He called Bremer over.

"Hauptsturmführer Bremer, I am delighted to say it is here. All the money we need is here. Take these men to the woods and have them guarded. I'll get the trucks moved over here so we can start unloading."

Bremer opened his mouth to speak and then, catching the look on Schonewille's face, shut it quickly. With a muttered jawohl, he turned away and began to lead the bank officials away.

Schonewille hurried to where the trucks were parked and ordered their drivers to back them up to the three carriages. For the next ten minutes he supervised the transfer of the carriages' contents into the lorries. The first, which was being driven by Chuikov, received a carefully chosen cargo of boxes holding gold bars, plus various sacks of gold coins and foreign currency. Where possible, he chose sacks carrying Swiss francs or American dollars but, as some were unmarked and he did not have time to examine their contents, he just had them transferred to the back of his chosen vehicle.

When it was loaded, another took its place and he had his truck driven to the edge of the wood. If he could, he wanted to try and escape straight away, but the crackle of gunfire stopped his thoughts dead.

The sound came from the woods some hundred metres away precisely where the surviving troops and civilians from the train had been taken. He ordered Chuikov to wait for him and then began to walk in the direction of the gunshots. Then just as suddenly it stopped.

What the bloody hell am I doing? he thought. Now was the time to make good his escape. It was obvious what had just happened. Grauwitz and his cohorts had slaughtered the prisoners and there was an odds-on bet his turn would be next.

Just then Grauwitz emerged from the trees with Kube a metre or so behind. Schonewille was caught off-guard and knew if they attempted to try and kill him then and there, he would stand no chance for his weapon was in its holster.

To his relief, Grauwitz seemed to have other things on his mind. His eyes were closed and he looked to be in some pain. His bowels were heralding another attack. Suddenly Schonewille had an idea.

"Herr Brigadeführer. There is a toilet in the first carriage. Why don't you use it? There is also a wash basin and I believe some hot water."

Grauwitz turned his head and a smile flashed across his face. "Danke, danke, Friedrich," he said gratefully.

Motioning for Kube to follow he walked awkwardly to the carriage and climbed inside. For a moment Schonewille's thoughts were only of escape, but he knew Grauwitz would have him followed. He had to get rid of the SS brigadier. He turned and ran to the truck. Chuikov was standing by the tailgate watching.

"Do we leave now, Sir?" he said.

Schonewille shook his head. He had to trust the Ukrainian who, on the surface at least, seemed quite prepared to leave with him. He went to his Volkswagen and extracted two stick grenades from behind the seat. Sticking them in his belt, he ordered Chuikov to wait and then moved quickly towards the shattered locomotive. On reaching the front buffers, he turned and looked around. Nobody seemed to have taken any notice, so he slipped between the locomotive and the armoured truck and onto the far side of the train.

Walking as quietly as he could, he stopped by the tender and extracted his P38 and the silencer. Screwing the cylinder to the barrel he paused, listening. Then, taking a deep breath he climbed up the ladder to the doorway on the opposite side of the carriageway. Luckily it had been left open. Silent or loud, he thought to himself and quickly chose the latter. Silence is never absolute and the slightest sound would alert the SS corporal. So as he climbed the steps, he called out Grauwitz's name. Once in the passageway he paused and then called Grauwitz's name again. As he did so he moved inside, left side first, his right hand holding the automatic down low behind his right thigh.

Kube was standing half-way along the carriage leaning against one of the sleeping compartments. Although he did not look suspicious, he was alert and his right hand clutched the handle of the Schmeisser machine pistol. Not daring to get any closer, Schonewille lifted the Walther and fired twice. Even so, he was almost not quick enough and the SS trooper started to move away from the wall and lift his weapon when the first bullet struck him in the stomach. The second hit him in the chest. As he sank to the floor, Schonewille strode over to where he lay and shot him again for good measure.

All three shots were virtually silent, the automatic making only a dull cough every time Schonewille pulled the trigger.

Quickly stepping over the body, he reached the compartment housing the toilet.

He turned the handle with his left hand, found it unlocked and kicked it open.

Grauwitz was sitting on the bowl, his trousers around his legs and a look of surprise on his face. Schonewille allowed himself a moment's triumph. He smiled as a look of realisation and panic crossed the SS lawyer's face and then before he had time to move he shot Grauwitz in the chest. The impact of the bullet jerked the man's body backwards and his head hit the pipe running down the back of the wall with a hollow clang. Schonewille fired twice more at close range, the Walther jerking in his hand.

The man's body was still perched on the seat, a large pool of blood soaking the front of his tunic. Schonewille smiled again and then closed the cubicle door. His heart was pumping as he stopped to listen. He could hear voices outside, but nothing untoward.

Quickly he dragged Kube's body over to the toilet and laid it on the floor, hard up against the door. Crossing over to a notice board screwed to one wall, he extracted a drawing pin and knelt down besides the body. Pulling one grenade from his belt, he unscrewed the base cap and carefully jammed the bomb under the SS corporal's body so it could not be seen. Then, with the utmost care he pinned the string protruding from the handle to the bottom of the door.

It was a crude but effective booby trap. Anybody opening the door would prime the grenade and five seconds later it would explode.

Unscrewing his silencer, he put it back in its pouch and holstered the automatic. Picking up Kube's machine pistol he made sure the safety catch was off and climbed outside. Nobody took the slightest notice.

With an unhurried step, he made his way back to his lorry. Passing one of the Volkswagens, he opened the driver's door and jammed his second grenade between the seat and the sides of the vehicle. Unscrewing the base cap he shut the door and then, leaning over, he wound the priming string around the door handle. Hey presto and another booby trap had been set.

The other Volkswagen was too far away to bother with, so he continued walking towards where Chuikov was still standing.

Suddenly, Bremer appeared from behind another vehicle and

hurried towards him.

"Where is the brigadier?" he shouted

"He went to the first carriage to have a shit," said Schonewille.

Bremer frowned at Schonewille's impertinence and turned towards the carriage. Schonewille waited until he was inside before he ran to his truck.

"Now Ilya," he said clapping the Russian soldier on his shoulder. "Are you with me?"

The other nodded enthusiastically and climbed into the lorry's cabin. Schonewille clambered over the tailgate into the back of the vehicle and noted with satisfaction that Chuikov had placed a Mauser Mg 42 light machine-gun inside. He banged the back of the cabin and the lorry began to move off. They had scarcely moved a dozen metres when from the first carriage came a dull explosion.

In the rear of the truck Schonewille slapped his thigh with satisfaction.

"Fuck you, Grauwitz and you too, Bremer," he said out loud and chortled with glee. He looked out the back, but the wrecked train was already shielded by trees and was out of sight.

Chapter Twenty-Five

0750 Hours

As Bremer hurried to the carriage looking for Grauwitz, he cursed under his breath. He had found the execution of the civilians and troops who had manned the train extremely distasteful. He recognised the necessity, but nevertheless would have preferred to have had somebody like Schonewille oversee the killings.

At the same time he badly wanted to have Schonewille killed and he wondered why Grauwitz had waited so long. His distaste for Schonewille was by now almost overwhelming and over the past few days he had been having difficulty in trying to mask his feelings while in the SS officer's presence.

Maybe he is going to wait until we get to the airfield, after all, he thought.

As he climbed up the carriage ladder he called out Grauwitz's name, just as Schonewille had a few minutes prior. Annoyed by the lack of response, he pushed open the door leading to the main part of the carriage and called out again, a sharp edge to his voice.

"Teufel, zum Teufel," he swore as he caught sight of the corporal's body.

He moved forward and without a moment's hesitation pushed open the door of the toilet cubicle. Grauwitz's un-winking, sightless stare confronted him. In shock, he lowered his eyes and this saved his life. The movement of the opening door had not only pulled the string, priming the grenade, it had also jerked the bomb forward so it protruded slightly from under Kube's inert form.

He flung himself back and, twisting round, made for the entrance. He had only moved half-a-dozen metres when the grenade exploded, pitching him onto a pile of suitcases stacked near the entrance. Luckily for Bremer, Kube's body deflected and soaked up much of the explosive force and shrapnel. However, it ripped out a large section of the cubicle wall and sent a splinter the

269

size of a child's school ruler spinning across the carriage and into the back of the SS captain's left shoulder. Immobilised with shock and temporarily deafened by the blast, he lay unmoving for almost two minutes.

He was found by the Russian lieutenant and gingerly helped to a sitting position.

The Russian called out through the shattered train window for a first aid kit and when it arrived he ordered two soldiers to pinion Bremer's arms and hold him tight. Then, with a large pocket knife he cut open the back of the SS officer's tunic, laying bare the wound. Without any preamble, he clasped the splinter tightly and yanked. Fortunately, it was not buried deeply inside the flesh, although it ripped out a large section of Bremer's shoulder and caused its owner to shout out in pain and anger.

The Russian then liberally poured some disinfectant onto a wad of cotton wool and again, without any preamble, applied it to the bleeding wound. He cleaned it as best he could and then roughly applied a thick gauze bandage.

By this time Captain Lutz Bremer was re-gaining his faculties. Groaning with pain, he pushed himself to his feet and lurched over to the cubicle. Kube's remains were quite literally spread over the opposite wall and ceiling, but it was not the corporal he was concerned with. He wanted to make certain his former commanding officer was in fact dead, although he realised there was not the slightest chance of him having survived the explosion, even if Schonewille's bullets had not done their job properly.

He need not have bothered. The force of the blast had ripped off a large section of the door, sending it scything upwards like a large blade. An executioner's axe could not have done a better job, for it had neatly severed Grauwitz's head from his mangled body and carried it upwards, impaling it on a shattered piece of the ceiling.

By this time Bremer's rage had completely suborned his pain and he turned to the lieutenant who was standing impassively watching.

"Where is Obersturmbannführer Schonewille?" he asked his voice shrill.

The Russian turned down the sides of his mouth and shrugged

270

his shoulders. He did not know, although he had seen a truck drive away moments after the explosion.

Bremer pushed passed the three Russians and, still oblivious of the pain, climbed down the ladder. Once on the ground, he looked up at the two Russian privates and ordered them to douse the inside of the carriage with petrol and set it on fire. He did not want Grauwitz's body identified by the authorities when they found the train. If they did, it would ultimately lead to him and if he was unable to escape he did not want either the Gestapo or his fellow officers to be on his track.

He then paused for a moment thinking about his next move. He looked at his watch. The operation had taken just over an hour-and-a-quarter. They could not afford to hang around any longer.

"Lieutenant, order your men to drive the trucks to the airfield at Traunstein, just like we discussed last night. Leave your most senior NCO in charge. In the meantime, we must try and get to the Obersturmbannführer before he reaches the airfield. His lorry will be relatively slow and we still have the two VWs and one of the small trucks in which to catch him, but we must move quickly. Get half-a-dozen of your best men and some light machine-guns and follow me."

He hurried towards one of the VWs with two of the Russians in tow while the lieutenant quickly rounded up some extra men and guns and moved towards the small truck. A corporal and two soldiers loaded with weapons went to the nearest VW. The NCO opened the door and was already sitting in the driver's seat when Schonewille's second booby trap exploded killing all three and setting the wreck on fire.

A shocked Bremer quickly vacated his Volkswagen yet, when thirty seconds had passed and there was no further explosion, ordered his two companions to make a quick examination of the vehicle. When this showed nothing was amiss, he climbed back inside and headed off up the road followed by the Russians in the small truck.

With a start of almost fifteen minutes, Schonewille should have been at least a dozen kilometres ahead and almost to Seigsdorf. Such was not the case. They had been travelling for just under ten minutes at a steady forty-five to fifty-five kilometres per hour when the engine of the Opel gave a cough, cleared itself, coughed again and then died.

For the first time that day Schonewille felt truly frightened. As Chuikov lifted the bonnet and began to ferret inside the engine bay he began to pace up and down, alternately looking back down the road.

"For fuck's sake, Sergeant, what's the matter with the bloody thing?"

"Fuel blockage, Herr Obersturmbannführer."

"Can you fix it?"

"Of course, Sir, but I'm not sure how long it will take."

Schonewille breathed deeply. Every few minutes he enquired as to the Ukrainian's progress. After the third time Chuikov did not bother answering, just continued with his repairs to the engine's carburettor and fuel lines.

Then, down the road there came the unmistakable sound of engines revving hard.

"Shit, oh shit. I hear motors. How long now?"

Chuikov was tightening the last clamp on the fuel line. He had cut a finger and the petrol was causing it to sting. It also made working difficult.

"Almost ready ... a few more seconds ... there. Now let's try the pig."

Schonewille turned the ignition on. For a few agonising seconds the engine turned over and refused to fire. Then, as the petrol reached the carburettor it fired ... died, fired again and caught.

They both clambered into the cabin, Schonewille at the wheel.

"Now, Sergeant, listen carefully. A kilometre or so along the road I've prepared a little surprise. Originally it was designed just to sever the phone lines. Now it might just be a little more useful. When I stop, grab the forty-two from the back and find yourself some cover, but make sure you can see around the bend for at least fifty metres or so, verstanden?"

Chuikov was not quite sure what Schonewille had planned,

although he now knew enough about the SS lieutenant-colonel to recognise the man's devious foresight. He also remembered the time when he had been left at Seigsdorf's inn, alone.

The Opel was pulling well with no hint of another blockage. Yet he was in no doubt that if one of the pursuers was a VW it would catch him relatively quickly. They reached the bend where the telephone pole with the two grenades was located. He negotiated around it and drove on for fifty metres before pulling over onto the grass verge so the pursuers would not see the Opel as they came up the narrow road.

Chuikov alighted with alacrity and scurried around to the rear of the lorry. Reaching over the tailgate he grabbed the light machine-gun and, looping two belts of ammunition around his neck, walked a dozen paces to a ditch where he dropped to the ground and carefully sighted the weapon. Schonewille, meanwhile, was crouched low next to the telephone pole. It was with relief he spied the two grenades still in position.

The Volkswagen and the small truck hove into sight, travelling fast. Schonewille waited until they were almost at the bend, before pulling the two strings and then rolled backwards down the slope, clear of the pole.

He could not have timed it better. The grenades shattered the base of the telephone pole and it toppled across the road dragging down the telephone wires just as the driver of the Volkswagen turned into the bend. It landed scarcely half-a-dozen metres in front of the vehicle and such was its speed that the driver had no chance to stop in time. In panic he wrenched the wheel hard over and careered into the pole at an angle, the force of the impact causing the VW's front left-hand wheel to rear up over the obstruction before being torn off. The vehicle then turned over and landed upside down in the ditch.

At the same time Chuikov fired two long bursts at the following truck, killing the driver and severely wounding a second man in the cabin. It veered to its left and struck the bank, coming to a dead stop with its engine stalled. The Russian lieutenant in the back quite literally dived over the tailgate onto the road, followed by two of his men as another dozen or so bullets hit the truck.

As soon as the pole struck the ground, Schonewille leapt to his feet. Lifting his Schmeisser, he loosed off its entire magazine at the upturned Volkswagen spraying the bullets in a short arc. Satisfied its occupants were either dead or dying, he yelled to Chuikov to get into the back of the truck while he clambered into the driving seat. As the big Opel moved off down the road, the remaining Russians cautiously peered around the bend. A stream of bullets from Chuikov's machine-gun cured their curiosity and sent them scuttling for cover.

In a few seconds the Opel was safely around the next bend and out of sight. Scarcely a kilometre ahead was Seigsdorf, followed by the second telephone pole.

Back at the roadside the survivors were attempting to push the Volkswagen back onto its wheels. It was a useless exercise and would gain them nothing for the vehicle was a write-off, yet they did manage to drag Bremer from underneath the wreck. Miraculously, he had survived with nothing more than cuts and bruises, although the hole in his shoulder had started to bleed profusely again.

They helped him up to the roadway and attended to his various wounds. By this time Bremer was not thinking too clearly. His own safety now scarcely mattered. All he wanted was Schonewille's demise. The fallen telephone wires gave him an idea. The following convoy contained some field telephone equipment. When it arrived, he would tap into the line and contact the airfield.

Unfortunately for Bremer, by the time the other lorries arrived Schonewille had already blown the second telephone pole across the road, severing the telephone wires.

Chapter Twenty-Six

0900 Hours

The airfield at Traunstein was a hive of activity with fighter bombers and various types of transports landing and taking off since first light. That they were risking interception by Allied fighters in daylight showed how urgent the Wehrmacht High Command regarded the situation here in the south. On the airfield's eastern perimeter, the big Junkers was hidden in a grove of pine trees stretching back from one perimeter for several kilometres.

On his brief visit to the station commander's office soon after he landed, Peter Wenck had been informed that two nights previously, on the evening of the twenty-second and the twenty-third, the American General Patton had crossed the Rhine at Oppenheim and was now heading east with a strong mechanised force. On the previous evening and further to the north, the man in charge of the Allied 21st Army Group, Field Marshall Montgomery, had also successfully crossed the Rhine.

Consequently what few aircraft were available in northern Italy and western Czechoslovakia were being transferred to southern Germany to try and aid the ground troops and destroy the pontoon bridges that had been thrown across Germany's last defensive barrier in the west. At the same time and much closer to home, there was something else to worry about. Just after seven o'clock an FW 200 Condor transport bearing SS markings landed and taxied to a similar hiding place a few hundred metres away. Although several figures emerged, no one from the aerodrome's administration buildings ventured forth to meet them and nobody left the aircraft's immediate vicinity.

To a suspicious Peter Wenck standing beneath his bomber's nose, it seemed as though Grauwitz was hedging his bets and had another option in place to escape the Third Reich, in case there was a problem with the Junkers. Or the SS lawyer had no intention of using Peter Wenck and his aircraft.

He called to Leo Swabisch and told him to keep an eye on the Condor. "If anything, and I mean anything, remotely suspicious happens with that aircraft let me know immediately."

He went to the forward hatch and climbed back inside. Negotiating his way along the inside of the fuselage, he came to the mid-upper turret. The gunner was checking the ammunition feed at the foot of the turret.

"Hans, are you fond of the SS?"

The gunner looked closely at the pilot and then said with a faint smile, "Not particularly, Sir. They are always too arrogant for my liking. Why?"

"I'll let you into a little secret. A little way to your left is a Condor belonging to the SS. I want you to get back into your turret. If I start the engines and give you the order, I want you to use your cannon on that plane, understand?"

The gunner stared at the pilot to see if he was joking, then he nodded his head. Strange things were happening, but orders were orders.

A shout from Swabisch had Wenck hurrying to the cockpit. When he got to the flight deck he immediately looked towards the Condor, but except for some animation from the figures standing next to the plane, nothing seemed amiss.

The cause of Swabisch's excitement quickly became apparent. A large Opel lorry was cutting across the airfield, ignoring the perimeter access road. Wenck immediately knew it was Schonewille for there was nothing remotely suspicious about the approaching vehicle's speed.

By the time he had clambered down to the hatch and lowered himself onto the ground, Schonewille had swung the lorry around and was backing it up to the Junkers. In the back was the grinning face of a soldier toting a MG42 and for a moment Wenck became alarmed. However, once the engine was turned off and Schonewille clambered down from the cabin, he gave a sigh of relief.

A similar feeling engulfed Schonewille as he strode over to the pilot. For the past few kilometres his tired brain had been causing his nerves undue strain. What if he is not there? had been the constant thought. From Segesdorf, the lorry had behaved impeccably. They had only been stopped by one road-block and now his brother was here as planned. For the third time that morning Schonewille felt exultant.

"Mein Gott, Peter, it is good to see you," he said, patting the pilot on the shoulder.

It was a peculiarly intimate gesture for the SS officer and it touched Wenck. He saw how exhausted his brother was. Schonewille had been on the go for thirty-six tense hours and it showed. He was unshaven and his eyes were red-rimmed from lack of sleep and nervous tension. His usually impeccable uniform was creased and dirty and the sub-machine-gun that hung off his shoulder gave him a raffish business-like air.

"Have you got …?"

"Yes, I've got it all, money, bullion, coins," he interrupted, guessing the pilot's question. "But we must hurry. There are some people following me and, believe me, it would not be healthy for us to be caught."

"Herr Grauwitz, eh?"

Schonewille gave him a sidelong glance and said with an off-hand air, "Oh no, we don't have to worry about him. I've killed him, but some of his command are after me and if it was not for Chuikov here I might not have made it." He pointed to the Ukrainian who immediately straightened and saluted the flier.

Wenck was intrigued, but he realised any questions would have to wait. Loading the Junkers was the primary consideration. At the same time he told Schonewille about the Condor. The SS officer just nodded and remarked that its appearance did not surprise him in the slightest.

With the crew busily loading the crates and sacks, Schonewille went over to where Chuikov was standing impassively, smoking a particularly foul smelling cigarette. Originally he had meant to kill the Russian soldier, but now such a move would be difficult and anyway, he owed the corporal.

"Well, Corporal Chuikov, this is where we part company. I cannot take you with us, though I have a plan that might see you safely in Switzerland. Are you interested?"

The other nodded, so Schonewille took his briefcase over to the Opel. Extracting some paper, he leant on the vehicle's bonnet and began to write. Minutes later he took out several official rubber stamps and an ink pad from the briefcase. Choosing one he stamped the bottom of the missive and signed his name across it. It already contained the signature of Schonewille's commanding officer. The SS lieutenant-colonel had had the foresight to ask his general to sign several letters so he would not be disturbed every time Schonewille needed to obtain permission or clearance for some administrative matter.

Handing it over to Chuikov, he explained how the letter purported to be an order for Corporal Ilya Chuikov of the KONR, under secondment to Amtsgruppe A1V, to travel to the town of Bludenz in western Austria to fetch some important documents and return them to Munich.

"Corporal, there is an Amtsgruppe fünf office in Bludenz. Therefore, with these papers you should not be hindered in any way. Unfortunately, my friend, from there you will be on your own, though the Swiss border is not far away. I suggest you drive east to Salzburg and stay clear of southern Germany. From there, drive south and then strike west. You will probably have enough gasoline to reach Worgl, or thereabouts, before you'll need to re-fuel."

Chuikov thanked him and asked about money. Schonewille nodded and went to where the Reichsbank's contents were being loaded onto the plane. He found the bag he needed and carried it behind the truck so its contents could not be seen. He extracted a thick wad of Swiss francs in large denomination notes and handed them to the Russian. Then, almost as an afterthought, he reached into the sack and extracted another wad. Together they amounted to 60,000 francs.

The Ukrainian's face broke into a broad smile and he gave a crisp military salute and clicked his heels together. "Danke, danke vielmals, Herr Obersturmbannführer, das ist sehr gut."

Without any further ado, Chuikov started the truck's engine and drove away to the main gate. He passed through with ease and quickly disappeared. I bet he escapes thought Schonewille and, surprisingly, felt good about it.

A few minutes later and the loading had been completed. They all climbed back into the Junkers and Wenck, backed by Swabisch, started their pre-flight check. This completed, they started the engines and immediately saw a flurry of activity from the crew of the Condor.

Wenck ordered the gunners of both the upper fuselage turrets to watch the Condor and then contacted the control tower requesting permission to take off. They were told curtly to wait. They waited for two or three minutes and then Wenck repeated the request. Again take-off was denied.

Schonewille, who was standing on the flight deck between the two pilots, saw some trucks enter the main gate and head in their direction.

"Donner, Peter, those are the remaining trucks from our raiding party. We have to get away. Now!"

At the same moment they heard one of the Junkers turrets start turning and before anybody could say a word its twenty-millimetre cannon began to yammer away in short sharp bursts.

Wenck looked over to see that the turret behind the cockpit of the Condor had swung in their direction, but their own gunner Hans, forewarned by Wenck, had been quicker. The whole forward section of the Condor was lit up with the flash of striking cannon shells.

Without a moment's hesitation, Wenck released the brakes and gunned the engines, swinging the Junkers 290 out onto the perimeter strip. They reached the main runway just as a Junkers 52 transport landed and, scarcely had the ancient tri-motor taxied past than Wenck aligned his bomber in the middle of the long strip of concrete.

Over the radio came the angry voice of the air controller ordering them to get off the runway. Wenck ignored him.

"Keep a sharp look out for other aircraft," he yelled into the intercom as the plane picked up speed and the tail wheel lifted itself clear of the ground. Although he had not the slightest idea what was going on, Swabisch held his left hand over Wenck's right as the pilot carefully hauled back on throttles. At the same time he read off the airspeed.

"Now, now, Peter," he said as the pilot, feeling the wheels begin to stretch on their oleos, pulled back on the control column to lift the Junkers into the sky.

"Christ, I hope they don't use any anti-aircraft guns on us," he said out of the corner of his mouth.

"Fuck me dead. That's all I need. To be shot at by my own side when I don't even know what the fuck I'm supposed to be doing," said Swabisch looking accusingly at Wenck. The pilot ignored him.

There was no anti-aircraft fire and at 5,000 metres he gratefully reached the safety of some clouds. He immediately turned north-east over the Alps and headed for western Czechoslovakia. His plan was to follow the same route to Norway as he had on the way down, only this time he would fly as high as the loaded Junkers was able.

Whereas the initial flight had been cloaked in darkness and therefore relatively safe, they were now in broad daylight and the Allied air forces would be in the air. The Junkers had a service ceiling of only 7,000 metres, but Wenck managed to coax her up to just over 8,000 metres before he levelled out. Luckily, the Red Air Force seldom flew above 6,000 to 7,000 metres, so he hoped the Junkers would not be intercepted at this height. If the Americans, who always flew much higher, appeared, however, he knew their adventure was finished.

Although they were now well away from Traunstein, the control tower at the airfield still tried to raise them on the radio, ordering them to turn around and come back. Schonewille did not bother acknowledging their blandishments or threats.

There was a long flight ahead of them and both Wenck and Swabisch wondered whether any German fighters would be sent up to intercept them. Even though the air would be full of German aircraft, the Junkers 290 was sufficiently rare to be easily recognisable, especially since its main sphere of operations was maritime reconnaissance. It was seldom seen in the skies of central Europe and rarely appeared in daylight.

At any rate, it was not the Luftwaffe that caused them any

bother. Heavy cloud cover and intermittent rain squalls helped them hide throughout most of their journey and Wenck had almost believed they would reach Norway unmolested when the Red Air Force found them.

They had just crossed the coast near Kolberg when a flight of three Yak 9s appeared on their port wing tip. As usual, Wenck did not give the enemy fighters a chance to choose their method of attack and immediately went on the offensive. He swung the Junkers around and headed in their direction, giving the gunners in the front upper turret and the belly gondola a chance to fire first. Although they did not hit the Russians, it broke up their formation and by the time they had turned away and then back on a course from which they could intercept the Junkers, Wenck had gained another fifty kilometres and was now well out over the Baltic.

Now that they had been found, height was not worth much so he put the bomber's nose down to give him extra speed and pushed the throttles though their gates. The interchange was short and sharp. The Russians made two passes and succeeded in setting the port inner engine on fire. They paid for it with one of their number who tumbled away minus one wing. In truth the Yaks did not really frighten the German pilot. They were lightly armed and had insufficient range to challenge the bomber for long periods. Such proved to be the case. Now down to two and faced with a well-armed Junkers whose pilot showed aggression and skill, the Russian pilots turned away, leaving the Junkers to fly on unmolested with one engine on fire and trailing a long plume of smoke.

Swabisch activated the damaged engine's extinguisher and with relief they saw the foam douse the flames. Then Wenck had a brainwave. For some time he and Schonewille had been discussing what to do if the authorities had managed to track them and knew where they were heading.

Schonewille felt sure Bremer was dead, yet he did not know for certain. If by some chance the SS captain had survived there was no doubt he would try and interfere with them at Kragero since Grauwitz knew about the base and consequently his aide would also. Even if they flew straight to Halden as was their plan, it would not take the authorities, be they Luftwaffe or SS, very long to try to look for them at Halden if the Junkers could not be found at Kragero.

Now there was a possibility of gaining time.

Wenck began to utilise his radio. Giving his plane's approximate position he appealed for help saying he was on fire and under attack from several Russian fighters. He was in no doubt that radar would have picked up both the Junkers and the Yaks.

After thirty seconds of pleading, he informed all who wished to hear that they were going to crash into the sea. Halfway through his message he switched his radio off and dived the Junkers down to the grey waters of the Baltic.

He levelled off, scarcely seventy-five metres from the grey, heaving sea and headed for Halden.

Hopefully, their apparent demise at the hands of the Russians would give them enough time to transfer the treasure to the B17 and take off for the next leg of their flight.

Chapter Twenty-Seven
25 March 1945

Peter Wenck braked the starboard wheel and gunned the two port engines. The plane basically stayed in the same position, although it swung around on its own axis by forty-five degrees. When he was sure the rear turret with its limited traverse could bring its guns to bear and the dorsal turret could also be brought into contention, he let the engines idle and looked at his father.

"Well Father, do we do it? You know it's close to murder."

The older man shrugged his shoulders and said softly, "For Christ's sake let us not go into this again. What choice do we have? We need the petrol and they won't let us have it."

Nodding wearily, Peter Wenck extracted himself from his seat and made his way through the cramped and crowded fuselage to the radio compartment. Sophia was sitting at the wireless operator's station, her face impassive, although there was sweat on her forehead. He ignored her and looked out of the wireless operator's dorsal window just in front of where the extension of the main fin started back along the rear fuselage. There was usually a single machine-gun mounted in this position, although like many others it had been removed to save weight.

The line of sight was not perfect, but he could clearly see the half-dozen soldiers standing in front of the main building, watching. The seventh man was still standing next to the weapon pit.

He plugged in his intercom and asked if the two gunners were ready. The answer was in the affirmative, so he gave the order to fire.

Schonewille in the rear turret was the first to open fire, the two heavy-calibre Brownings sending several hundred rounds in the direction of the watching men.

His first burst was aimed at the man standing by the weapon pit. The unfortunate soldier was hit by half-a-dozen bullets and virtually cut in half. Even as his body hit the ground the two barrels traversed and swept the other men. They did not have a chance and it was over in seconds.

Swabisch in the dorsal turret never fired a round at the men. There was no need, the SS officer's withering arc of fire had been so deadly. Therefore, he swung his turret around and fired two short bursts at the fighter standing in the shade of the hangar. The bullets tore at the engine and undercarriage, causing it to collapse. Then the guns fell silent.

The previous leg of the journey to Halden had passed without incident. Anxious to keep radio silence, Peter Wenck did not herald his arrival or ask for clearance to land. He simply checked the wind direction by flying low and observing the direction of the wind sock and put the damaged Junkers down on his first try.

He taxied to where the Boeing was hidden, covered in camouflage netting and protected by a large blast pen in the lee of some trees.

Barely had the plane's engines been switched off than Helmuth Wenck's staff car was seen approaching from the main administrative building. Thirty seconds later it came to a wheel-locking halt next to the Junkers. The general himself was driving. His appearance was agitated to say the least, probably because the Junkers looked a little the worse for wear and its port engine was still smoking. The relief on his face when his son slid back one of the Perspex panels next to his seat and waved was clearly visible, even from this distance.

The affection the general had for his famous son was even more apparent when Peter Wenck finally stood on the tarmac. The first words his father uttered were, "Gott sei Dank! Du bist unverletzt?"

It was half question, half statement and the pilot answered with a wan smile. He was fine and not injured.

The remainder of the crew were now climbing out of the aircraft's various hatches and then Helmuth Wenck spied his other son. He had almost forgotten the possibility of Schonewille's presence and for a moment the SS uniform spoilt his pleasure. Then he smiled. "You too, Friedrich. This is wonderful." Almost as an afterthought he added, "The gold, the money. Did you get it?"

284

The pilot looked around before answering and noting the proximity of his crew simply answered with a movement of his head.

Peter Wenck was exhausted. In fact both brothers looked the worse for wear. Wenck, with a break of only three hours, had completed twelve hours in the air under very trying conditions. He also had only ten hours sleep in the preceding forty-eight hours. Schonewille had even less and had been living on his nerves. There were now dark rings under his eyes and his hand trembled when he removed his hat and ran his fingers through his cropped hair.

For Peter Wenck, this lack of rest was dangerous since he would have to take off again as soon as possible.

There were several hours left before darkness came and they could risk the dangerous flight down the slot of the English Channel to Guernsey. In the meantime, they could do nothing but wait and see if there were any pursuers and whether they would be traced to Halden.

The crew, with the exception of Leo Swabisch, were immediately told they could all have a forty-eight hour pass to Oslo. Subsequently, they should then report back for duty at Kragero. This would not only remove them from any further proximity to the Reichsbank's reserves, it would also keep them clear of the Wencks who were soon to disappear. Their disbursement into the fleshpots of Oslo would also further remove them from any potential questions by the authorities in the immediate sense, for by the time any of the crew returned to Kragero, the B17 and its cargo would be long gone.

The ground crew were ordered to cover the Junkers with camouflage netting and then Helmuth Wenck and his two sons climbed into the bomber and began to make an examination of the money that had been stolen from the train.

They emerged half-an-hour later shocked and a little bemused at the level of their wealth. Schonewille clutched at a piece of paper on which he had made a list of the plane's contents. Before leaving the plane the general left a three-man armed guard next to the two aircraft with strict instructions for nobody to go near them. They then retired to Helmuth Wenck's office. Another guard was placed

285

at the end of the corridor.

Schonewille asked whether he could see Sophia, but his father suggested they first sit and discuss their next moves.

Conrad Meunier joined them and from the moment they met it was clear the diplomat and the SS accountant would not get on. Meunier was part of Germany's old school. Despite his jovial nature he carried himself like a member of the class he represented. All Schonewille's latent inferiorities rose from the pit of his psyche and, although he managed to make sure they did not surface, it was clear to the two older men that he was not comfortable in the presence of the former Abwehr officer.

What's more, Meunier had been able to conduct a thorough search into Schonewille's background and what he discovered had filled him with distaste. He had not told his friends what he had learned, for on meeting the general's eldest son he quickly realised that if their plan was to succeed he would have to be careful what he revealed. Put simply, he neither liked nor trusted Friedrich Schonewille.

For Peter Wenck, however, there was a more immediate problem. His friend Leo Swabisch. He wanted his aide with him, yet he was not certain the Luftwaffe captain would join the plotters. His big fear was the outcome if Swabisch refused. Could he leave him at Halden? If so, what would happen to him when the authorities arrived. He would be implicated whether he liked it or not. More importantly, he knew about the Channel Islands and their secret cache of fuel.

The key was whether he could frighten Swabisch into believing that the authorities would regard him as being implicated even if he remained behind. Peter Wenck spoke to his father before the meeting got underway. The general agreed it would be better to sound out the pilot straight away so his decision could be discussed immediately.

As it turned out, no threats were necessary.

Swabisch readily agreed to join them after his commanding officer had revealed all. There was not the slightest hesitation. He simply said, "Peter, I have no relatives left alive except two aunts and I'm not close to either of them. As you know, my grandmother

286

was Dutch and I felt closer to her than everybody, except perhaps my dear mother. Therefore, I have no difficulty in abandoning my German ancestry." Then he added with a sly smile, "There is also something I want you to understand. I am not entirely blind and I had begun to suspect something out of the ordinary, something like this, although to be truthful I did not remotely consider anything about the money."

With this weight off his shoulders, Peter Wenck took his co-pilot to the office where the rest were gathered and Swabisch was fully enrolled into the select band of thieves.

It was a strange meeting. For the first time all the plotters were together and able to explain what had transpired and what they hoped was going to happen.

Schonewille was alternately annoyed and relieved at what was revealed. He had been extremely worried about the damage to the Junkers and it was with a certain amount of relief that he learned about Miss Nonalee Two. His protestations about having been kept in the dark was met with a sharp-edged rebuke from his father.

"Now, Friedrich, be reasonable. You have not told us everything about your life and from what I know of it there might be good reason. By the same token we were not sure what your relationship was with Grauwitz. Or, for that matter, if you fell out with Grauwitz and he put you through some rigorous questioning it was obviously better that you did not know what we were up to. So stop your bleating."

He glared at his son who remained silent. His point made, he became more conciliatory.

"At any rate, we know now what you have achieved and I suspect we are all in some awe of how you did it."

These words had the desired effect and a flush of pleasure crossed Schonewille's cheeks.

As the de-briefing and plotting continued, Helmuth Wenck looked at the group and realised what a disparate group they were. And, he noted, this was even without the Jewess being present.

There was Conrad Meunier, by far the oldest. Short and corpulent, with his brilliant brain, sardonic humour and love of the good life. His youngest son, Peter. Terrifyingly brave, a skilled pilot, a realist, though still with a touch of romanticism about him, a sound planner and able to instil loyalty in his men. Above all, he was a dutiful son. This was not something he could claim about his eldest offspring. There was a driven, harassed side to Friedrich and he knew a certain tension and reserve still existed between them. What could he say about the SS officer. Brave? Yes, he had demonstrated that. Cunning? Most certainly. Then there were his links with the camps. It worried him and he knew he would have to get to the bottom of it sooner or later. He had tried to question Sophia about what she knew, but the woman had remained resolute in her silence. There was Swabisch. Much like Peter, but a shade less in every category.

Finally, himself. What am I? he thought, as he gazed around the room. I'm an old soldier about to betray my oath. A man disgusted with the country of his birth. A man who longs to see his wife again and spend the remaining years of his life in peace and tranquillity.

"What are you dreaming about, Father?"

His youngest son's voice broke into his thoughts. Helmuth simply shrugged his shoulders and ignored the question.

The next item on the agenda was the Reichsbank's treasure. Schonewille took out his notes and they totted up the figures. If they had been shocked at the level of their haul when they had first seen it in the Junkers, they were now like gleeful children who had found a cache of sweets. The haul of valuables was extraordinary. As a senior accountant within the SS, Schonewille had a detailed knowledge of their value, but what was more important, he knew their value in the strongest currency in the world: the American dollar.

First the gold bullion. There had been fifty boxes bearing gold bullion on the armoured train and Schonewille had managed to transfer eight of them to his Opel truck. Each box measured just under a metre in length. It was 600 millimetres wide, 460 millimetres deep and weighed approximately fifty kilograms. Inside were four gold bars each weighing 12.5 kilograms and bearing the seal of the Reichsbank and a six-digit number. The official value of each gold bar was 15,000 in US dollars. Eight boxes equalled thirty-two bars, with a total value of $480,000. Since the price of gold was pegged Schonewille explained that on the black market each bar could be worth as much as $50,000, bringing the value of the thirty-two bars to $1.6 million.

There were also two large cases of gold coins of various nationalities and of various denominations. They were predominantly of Dutch, Hungarian and Romanian origin. Schonewille estimated the worth at approximately $200,000.

The rest of the money was in sacks. In German currency there was approximately four million in gold marks, with an estimated value of $1.5 million. Again, melted down, the intrinsic value of the gold on the black market amounted to very nearly $5 million.

There were 425,000 Swiss francs worth $100,000 and $250,000-worth of American dollars in large denomination notes. Finally, there were two small cases full of gemstones, mainly diamonds. Schonewille knew the latter largely consisted of diamonds prised out of rings belonging to the inmates of the concentration camps or those on their way to the gas chambers. Naturally he did not mention this fact.

In total, then, the official figure of their haul was $2.53 million with a black-market figure considerably higher. If one added the gold value of the German bullion and gold marks then the sum was well over $7 million and this did not include the value of the gems.

When the final figure was mentioned, a deep silence descended on the room. It was broken by Meunier who said with a chuckle, "Himmel, just think how many bottles of schnapps that will buy."

The laughter echoed around the walls.

"Now, now, enough of this levity, we still have much to do before we can think of spending it," broke in Helmuth Wenck. "Before we start transferring all our ill-gotten wealth into the Boeing there is still much that must be discussed, planned for and, above all, understood.

The next half-an-hour was spent in explanations from the relevant parties. Peter Wenck on technical details concerning the flight and the Boeing, Meunier on his arrangements with the Spanish major, the lieutenant-colonel in the Dominican Republic and the Mexican-based agent, while Helmuth Wenck explained how they would cover their tracks in Norway.

Peter Wenck's explanation was fairly straightforward. Meunier's on the other hand was a little more detailed since he also needed to put together the necessary paperwork and passports for all the escapees.

Helmuth Wenck gave another example of just how well their planning had progressed. In the preceding weeks he had twice visited a prisoner-of-war holding camp and requisitioned some US Army Air Force uniforms. These would be for himself, Peter and Leo Swabisch. Meunier and Schonewille would wear civilian clothes. These clothes were tried on to see how they fitted.

Among those wearing the American uniforms there was much jocularity until the general said soberly, "Just remember, Kameraden. If we are caught wearing these uniforms, under the Geneva Convention we can be shot as spies."

Helmuth Wenck also noted something else. Although he did not mention it,. Schonewille looked much less imposing and important wearing civilian clothes instead of his SS uniform.

They changed back into their respective uniforms. The American uniforms, civilian clothes and identity papers were packed in various soft bags and taken out to the Boeing.

For the next hour the plotters busied themselves with transferring the money from the Junkers to the Boeing. The boxes were hurriedly sprayed green and given spurious US Air Force serial numbers and even though the paint was still wet they were immediately stored in the American bomber. The contents of those bags that bore the stencil of either the Reichsbank or the Magyar National Bank of Hungary were transferred to plain sacks. The originals were burned.

Since the Boeing was so heavily loaded with fuel there was little room left in the bomb bay, with only six of the boxes stored in the aircraft's belly where the lethal cargoes usually hung. The remaining boxes, bags and sacks were stored in various parts of the aircraft, mainly in areas where ammunition or other heavy items were usually situated.

When all was completed, they assembled outside the bomber. One thing remained to be done: set out where each person would sit in the Boeing during the first two legs of the escape. The pilot was obvious and it was decided that for some of the trip Swabisch would be situated in the upper turret. Schonewille, who had some experience with machine-guns and was the shortest of the men, was the obvious choice for the rear turret. He was given a hurried verbal briefing on its operation with a promise of a more detailed tutoring once they were airborne. It would hardly make him an expert, but there was no other way. Swabisch, on the other hand had given himself plenty of time to learn how to extract the best out of the upper turret over the preceding weeks.

Once finished Helmuth Wenck took out a flask from his pocket and handed it to his youngest son. The pilot took a swig of the liquid and then passed it to Swabisch. One by one they took a mouthful and toasted the American bomber. Miss Nonalee Two was now wearing her rightful insignia with the white star on a blue circle adorning her wings and fuselage. To preserve her anonymity, however, the maiden on the nose had been painted over. In yet another attempt to change her identity and confuse any attempt at her being recognised, her serial number was now a fake.

The five men went back to the office for a final briefing. The general went from the room and came back with Sophia who greeted Schonewille with restrained warmth. The SS officer, on the other hand, looked at her with a beaming smile and Meunier, who had earlier met the Jewess, was quite taken aback. His obvious love for the woman was so apparent that the diplomat thought he might have to reassess some of his beliefs about the man. An SS officer he might be, but this certainly was no anti-Semite.

Although the light was fading it was decided they would not leave for another hour-and-a-half, so Peter Wenck went to another room to try and catch up on a little sleep.

His brother's reaction to his girlfriend had made him think about Erna Hennell. How he wished he could take her along. In the days leading to his flight to Traunstein he had spent a lot of time in her company. At first he had pretended it was because she needed to be watched, but after a few days he knew it was because he could not keep away from her.

They had started making love again and the memory of her eager body caused a stirring at his groin. He remembered their last time together. He had made love to her, urgently, a quick, thrusting consummation followed by half-an-hour's gentle contact in which he caressed her breasts and body, almost without pause. Then they had made love again, this time a long, slow journey to a lingering climax.

Yet, despite his feelings he knew it would be too risky to try and fetch her. He was still not certain whether she loved him enough to follow him into what was effectively a self-imposed banishment. Reluctantly he forced the thought from his mind. The result of this reverie was that he did not gain that precious sleep his body so desperately needed.

Chapter Twenty-Eight
24 March 1945

1900 HOURS

All four engines of the American bomber sounded healthy and Peter Wenck knew they would give all that was needed when it was required. Although the runway at Kragero was long, the B17 was very heavily loaded. She was just over her maximum weight limit and it would take a mighty effort to get her into the air in the available distance.

For the take-off, Swabisch was seated next to him as the aide was fully conversant with the Boeing and he needed all the help he could get.

Not wanting to risk any damage to the inside starboard tyre as they turned to get onto the main perimeter strip that led to the runway, he used the brakes only slightly so the wheel kept turning as he gunned one of the two port engines. Once in a straight line he released the brake fully and the Boeing trundled down the concrete strip. It was pitch black with only the minimum of lights showing the edges of the perimeter strip.

Once the bomber was aligned on the main strip of concrete he stopped and ran up each engine on its peak take-off power settings again; just to make certain.

Making sure she was on the precise compass heading, Swabisch set the directional gyro at zero.

"Flaps, coming down, twenty degrees ... and the cowl flaps trailed."

Both pilots kept a firm pressure on the brake pedals while the throttles were slowly advanced. Meunier, who had a strong curiosity and had asked to sit in the jump seat just behind the two airmen, watched in fascination as the rising manifold pressure was called out. Miss Nonalee Two was trembling like a bird of prey, testing the wind at its nest.

"Thirty-four inches, Skipper," said Swabisch. Wenck called the tower and the runway lights were turned on.

"Now," answered the pilot and they both released the brakes.

The Boeing started to move down the runway, gathering speed with every metre travelled. Manifold pressure was increased to just over forty inches and with all four engines bellowing the plane began to accelerate much more rapidly. Still, it was not until the plane's speed hit ninety-five miles an hour that the oleo struts on the undercarriage started to extend, indicating her nearness to flying speed.

"One-hundred-and-ten ... shit we're running out of runway," agonised Swabisch.

But it was fast enough. Peter Wenck eased back on the yoke and as he felt her rise called out, "Wheels up!"

Swabisch hit the undercarriage toggle switch. With speed building up and the drag from the wheels quickly dissipating the bomber lifted clear of the ground and began to climb into the night sky above southern Norway. The runway lights were switched off.

As the speed increased the flaps were moved back into the wing and the manifold pressure was reduced to thirty-five inches. Wenck lowered the engine revs and checked the engine temperatures. Despite the strain of the take-off, they read normal. Relieved, he gently swung the plane around and set his first course.

Behind him, Meunier gave a whistle of appreciation.

"Don't relax yet Conrad, the difficult parts are still to come."

The diplomat gave a chuckle. "That's it...frighten an old man to death."

2325 HOURS, 24 March 1945

Squadron Leader Roger Parker-Davis had just got into bed. It had been a quiet sort of day. The squadron had been placed on stand-down for forty-eight hours so his pilots could get some rest without actually going on leave and the mechanics could catch up with their servicing of the aircraft.

The squadron was due back on operations at 0700 hours the next morning, so he had spent much of the afternoon checking on the readiness of the aircraft before having a vigorous game of squash with one of his flight lieutenants, followed by a quiet dinner with his wife at an up-market restaurant in Weymouth.

Now, with his muscles pleasantly relaxed after their work-out and his nerves satiated by a glorious meal and half a bottle of Portuguese wine, he was just drifting off when the phone by his bed rang.

"Bugger." He let it ring. Finally he reached out and lifted the handset.

"Squadron Leader?"

The voice sounded official, so he sat up and transferred the phone to his good ear. "This is Parker-Davis. Who's speaking?"

The voice on the other end gave a name that the English pilot did not recognise. "Who?" he said a trifle irritably.

"Nankervis, Squadron Leader ... Now wake up!"

"Bugger!" The epithet was said under his breath. It was the intelligence officer who had come to the airfield during that abortive operation against the Junkers 290. "Sir ... I remember now. What can I do for you?"

The man ignored the question and asked one of his own. "How long will it take you to get some aircraft into the air?"

Parker-Davis became even more irritable. What's more he did not attempt to disguise it. "Sir, at present we are officially off operations. So, before I answer the question, will you please be so good as to tell me how many aircraft you need, why and how quickly."

A snort sounded down the line, followed by a pause. "Fine, fine. That seems reasonable. You remember our little affair with that strange German kite that landed at Guernsey? Yes? Good. Well, we believe he's making another flight."

"When?"

"Now, right this minute. He was picked up by radar at Great Yarmouth thirty minutes ago and tracked south. The Dover boys have also been tracking him for a while and up until now we were not sure what he was or where he's going to. But now we are almost certain. There's no IFF, so it must be one of theirs. The same as last time. He's appeared from the North Sea, very low and hugging the Belgian and French coasts. A few minutes ago he was opposite Dieppe."

"Well, Sir, I can get some aircraft into the air in about fifteen minutes, give or take a minute, though there is no way we could intercept him before he reaches the Channel Islands."

Nankervis agreed this would be impossible at this late stage, but suggested they could try and intercept the German aircraft when it left Guernsey.

"If he leaves tonight, Sir."

"Ha. Well then. If he decides to stay we'll send over something in daylight to see he stays there permanently, eh."

Parker-Davis made a non-committal noise and rang off, momentarily putting down the receiver before lifting it back to his ear and dialling his aide's extension. He washed his face hurriedly and, feeling less than enthusiastic about the turn of events, put on part of his uniform and his flying kit. By the time he reached the briefing room some of the squadron's flying personnel were already in attendance, though their appearance was dishevelled and their clothing a little awry. Outside, an aircraft engine burst into sound, shattering the stillness.

Exactly seventeen minutes later, Parker-Davis lifted his Beaufighter clear of the airfield and headed across the Dorset countryside south-west towards the Channel Islands. Following, were two more and back at the base a further three were being readied to follow the same route in approximately three hours.

By now, the English squadron commander was thoroughly bad-tempered and he blamed his unexpected flight entirely on the crew of the aircraft flying towards Guernsey. This time he was determined it would be successfully intercepted and shot down.

0040 HOURS, 25 March 1945

With St Peter Port disappearing under his port wing tip, Peter Wenck lined up the B17 with the runway on Guernsey. Their coded call-sign had been answered almost instantly by the main runway lights.

It had been an uneventful flight, though exhausting nevertheless. He had flown for all but the first hour and once entering the English Channel had hugged both the sea and the coast of Europe in order to reduce the chances of them being tracked by British radar.

How successful he had been he did not know, but they had not been intercepted by enemy aircraft and not so much as a solitary anti-aircraft shell had been launched in their direction. He spoke out of the corner of his mouth to the figure sitting next to him.

"Well, Father, if there are any Engländer lurking nearby, these lights will attract them like moths to a candle. I hope Friedrich and Leo are awake up there in their turrets."

The airstrip on Guernsey was not very long and he knew it would be difficult to stop before he ran out of runway. It meant he had to judge the distance very carefully to make certain the wheels touched down as early as possible. In order to give himself a chance if he overshot, he asked his father to set up for full power in case he had to pull up and go around again. By necessity this would be a last resort, for the longer he spent over the airfield with its blazing runway lights, the easier it would be for any enemy fighter in the vicinity to intercept and possibly shoot them down.

In the co-pilot's seat Helmuth Wenck made sure the booster pumps were on and that the manifold pressure, revs and fuel mixture were right. Although he had taken only one flight in the B17, he had spent many hours pouring over the flight manual and familiarising himself with the plane's controls.

"Twenty degrees of flaps. They're coming down," said the general.

"Gut, gut," answered the pilot almost absent-mindedly as he banked a little. "Teufel, there must be a hell of a wind," he said almost to himself. A bead of perspiration appeared at his forehead.

He'd had the Boeing lined-up nicely but she was beginning to drift away, although he still had time and distance to bring her down.

"Wheels down."

"Wheels down," repeated his father, and hit the toggle switch. "And locked."

With the wheels down the speed started to drop significantly, so he called for full flaps.

"Coming down," said his father. "There, full flaps."

Peter looked at the altimeter. It was a German instrument,

calibrated in metres. It read 150 metres. Nice, nice, he thought and continued to ease her down. The rest was easy, though the moment his main wheels touched the ground the lights were turned off, a risky move because the strong sea wind blowing across the airfield could force the bomber to drift off the darkened runway. As it turned out, there were no problems. The brakes pulled the big bomber up with plenty to spare and it was with considerable relief that he turned to his father.

"There you are, Papa," he chortled in the voice of a little boy. "As easy as riding a rocking horse."

He turned the aircraft and taxied back towards the buildings. Lightly locking the brakes on the port wheel he pivoted the Boeing so it faced away from the hangar and then switched off the engines. In the silence that followed, he took a deep breath and suddenly wished he could go to sleep. His eyes ached and his mouth was dry and tasted like rancid butter.

Even in the semi darkness his parent recognised the look. He had experienced it many times in the first war, but the young man beside him had flown many, many more hours without a real break. His weariness bordered on exhaustion.

Peter peered through the Perspex and saw several shadowy figures approaching. It was time to vacate the aircraft for he did not want anybody looking inside. They divested themselves of their harness belts and intercom wires and, with stiff legs, stumbled to the hatches. Once on the ground they stretched like bears after a long hibernation and took deep breaths of the cool, clean air.

A soldier holding a machine pistol moved cautiously towards them. Wenck senior smiled. He had warned the island's radio operator of the aircraft's origins when he had sent his last coded message just prior to their take-off, yet quite rightly the garrison's defenders were still suspicious.

In order to set the right tone he barked, "I'm a Luftwaffe officer as you can see, so put that dammed gun away and get your finger off the trigger." The last thing he wanted was to have some nervous soldier fire off a round in the proximity of the still heavily fuelled B17.

The soldier snapped to attention and immediately, as if on cue, several more figures came forward out of the gloom. With dismay, he recognised the burly figure of Vice Admiral Hüffmeier.

"Ach so, it is you, mein General," said the sailor. "Das is unmöglich," he said, looking up at the bomber and shaking his head.

Helmuth Wenck wanted to get the re-fuelling done straight away, so he asked the island's commander-in-chief to have the work done immediately.

Hüffmeier frowned. He clearly was not used to being ordered about, especially by an aristocratic flier, but he immediately complied and ordered his men to start re-fuelling the bomber.

Helmuth Wenck would have preferred dealing with Count von Schmettow, but the Wehrmacht officer had been re-called to Germany the previous month. Now in full control of the islands, Hüffmeier had carte blanche to do as he wanted and was making sure his soldiers and sailors harassed the enemy on the nearby coast as often as possible. Though he did not like the man, the air force general had a sneaking admiration for his daring and verve.

Peter Wenck, who had been examining the undercarriage and tyres of the Boeing, ambled up and Schonewille, who had so far stayed inside the fuselage, dropped down from the forward hatch and strode towards them. He was wearing his SS uniform and it had an immediate effect on the vice-admiral.

There came a hissing sound as he sucked in his breath. Schonewille extended his right hand and clicked his heals together. "Heil Hitler," he barked.

This was something Hüffmeier understood. He returned the salute with alacrity. Before they had left Norway, Schonewille had changed the insignias and some badging on his uniform so it no longer showed he was a member of the administrative wing of the SS. Instead of identifying him as an SS Fachführer, it identified him as a member of the SD, or Security Service and therefore a much more powerful individual.

"Obersturmbannführer Friedrich Dohndorf," he said, introducing himself.

It was a cunning move. In keeping his Christian name he ensured that anybody in his party would always identify him correctly. Yet, the different surname ensured his anonymity. Helmuth Wenck could not help smiling. The rest of his party were using their rightful names while his eldest son was still being secretive and crafty.

Vice-Admiral Hüffmeier turned back to Helmuth Wenck. "Will you be so good as to tell me what you are planning"?

The flier shook his head. "Reluctantly, I must refuse. I have orders from the Reichsführer that I must not divulge anything to anybody."

Hüffmeier looked disappointed. Then he tried a different tack. "I have kept everything secret so far and I must admit I am very curious. You know you can trust me."

Helmuth Wenck began to shake his head, but Schonewille stepped in. Even though his father out-ranked him he knew by purporting to being a member of the SD he had a power out of all proportion to his rank. He put an imperious tone to his voice to heighten the effect of his importance.

"I'm sure we can let Vice Admiral Hüffmeier know something. The Reichsführer was only telling the Führer the other day what a loyal and brilliant soldier the commander-in-chief is." Turning his face to the burly figure he said, "Let us go a little way from here and I will tell you a few details, but you must swear never to reveal the story to anyone, unless we win the war. There are many lives at stake."

Hüffmeier nodded his head vigorously and the two walked a few paces away. Schonewille spoke softly for two or three minutes and at the end Hüffmeier was heard to say quite loudly. "Mein Gott!"

Schonewille left the man and came back to where the two pilots stood. He gave a little grin and winked. Hüffmeier followed the SS man and extended his hand.

"Please, let me shake each of you by the hand gentlemen. It is a privilege to have been of service. In the name of the Führer, I salute you." He extended his arm and said very solemnly, "Heil Hitler."

Peter Wenck badly wanted to laugh, though more from relief than genuine levity, but he kept a straight face. Helmuth Wenck was dumbfounded. Whatever his son had told the naval officer certainly had the desired effect. There was now no curiosity let alone suspicion in the mind of the former captain of the Scharnhorst.

He wondered how Meunier, Swabisch and Sophia were feeling, hidden in the bomber. On the flight down they had only used fuel from the wing tanks. Therefore, there was no reason for any of the ground crews to enter the fuselage to check the internal tanks. Still, the re-fuelling was taking an age, or so it seemed. Helmuth and Peter Wenck went over to where Schonewille was standing alone, a dozen or so metres out in the clear near the nose of the aircraft.

"Obersturmbannführer Dohndorf ... a moment please," said the SS officer's father quite loudly, so anybody in earshot could hear. Then, when all three were standing close together, almost in a huddle, Helmuth Wenck enquired as to what he'd told the admiral. "Friedrich, I am quite curious. Whatever did you say to that Fascist fool over there?"

Schonewille looked around before giving a little laugh. "Oh, quite easy really. I gave him a little information about what would be the raid of the war."

"What raid?"

"Ah ha, well that's my secret," he said mysteriously with a smile.

"Shit, Brother, what the hell did you say to Hüffmeier? Stop playing the fool."

"Well I told him we were going to fly to Gibraltar."

"What the hell for?" broke in the pilot.

"Let me finish. If he's smart he will track us when we leave and he'll see we are flying almost due west. Therefore, I told him we were going to Gibraltar. I said there was going to be a high level meeting there today between Churchill, Stalin and Roosevelt. I explained that the Boeing was packed with explosives and unless our agents who were inside the plane could get close enough to shoot all three, we would taxi the aircraft near the hangar where they were meeting and detonate the explosives, thereby committing suicide. So, as you can see, it's shut him up."

"Wunderbar Friedrich, wunderbar!" exclaimed Peter in a low voice, and clapped him on the shoulder, while their father gently shook his head in wonderment.

It took almost an hour for the re-fuelling to be completed. A sergeant came up to Peter Wenck and saluted. "The tanks are full to the brim, Sir, and all valves have been checked as you ordered. Sir!"

At this point Hüffmeier came over. He was holding a piece of paper and frowning. He explained that his radar had picked up the tell-tale blips of enemy aircraft. He addressed the two Wencks.

"There is no doubt they are waiting for you. My men tell me that they arrived twenty minutes ago and have been patrolling in a crescent to the north-east of us. The moment you take-off I believe they will pounce."

"Thank you, Herr Vice-Admiral," said Peter Wenck. "But I believe they will not be of worry to us. All I ask is that your men do not turn on the runway lights until we are about a third of the way along the runway. Then, the moment we lift off I will give you a call and tell you to turn them off."

Hüffmeier raised an eyebrow and turned to his lieutenant, asking whether the man understood.

Minutes later, Peter Wenck was strapped into the pilot's seat with Leo Swabisch next to him. His father leant over. "Can we get away from the British?"

"Oh, I think so. They will be expecting us to head back up the Channel or over the Cherbourg peninsular like I did before, not to head west. But, just to make certain I will keep very low. I think, and I hope I'm right, they won't have a chance of finding us."

The plan worked without fault. A third of the way down the runway and just when it became difficult to see, the lights were switched on. Scarcely thirty-five seconds later, the Boeing became airborne and Peter Wenck called over the radio to Hüffmeier's lieutenant and the lights were instantly turned off.

He kept the Boeing low as he crossed the coast and then, banking gently, pointed her nose to the west and headed out of the English Channel towards the Atlantic.

For Parker-Davis and his men there was nothing. The moment he spotted the runway lights he banked sharply and stood the night fighter on one wing so he could view the whole panorama of the night sky stretching down to the sea, where the dim outline of Guernsey and the other Channel Island could be seen 8,000 feet below.

Calling to the radar operators to keep a sharp watch he peered into the darkness. Yet neither he nor the radar operators found anything. Then the lights vanished and, cursing, he banked once more and headed for Guernsey.

Nothing.

Five minutes, later he gave up.

"Maybe he did not take-off after all, Skipper," suggested his radar operator and navigator.

"No, Jimmy. I don't know why, but I bet my Aunt Fanny to a pound he's slipped the net … we've lost the bugger again."

Just to be sure he turned and flew to the eastern side of the Cherbourg Peninsular and then up the Channel at full emergency boost, but found nothing.

Already almost one hundred kilometres away, Peter Wenck was starting to breathe easier. Lizard Head and Land's End were about 150 kilometres from his starboard wing tip with the Isle de Ouessant a similar distance from his port wing tip and in front the Atlantic beckoned. He slowly began to ease the Boeing upwards into the inky sky. From now on, they were clear of their countrymen and the ills of Europe.

Chapter Twenty-Nine
25 March 1945

0310 Hours

As well as specific German gauges that had been added to help the Luftwaffe crews, Miss Nonalee Two still had all her original instrumentation. Since her crew were German and the flight manual was written in English with its imperial measurements, it was necessary for any Luftwaffe personnel to be completely familiar with what needed to be done and how to accurately read the original gauges and dials.

Consequently, as the Boeing continued its climb Peter Wenck kept a wary eye on the American altimeter. When it reached 10,000 feet he checked that its German equivalent read just over 3,000 metres and then switched on the booster pumps to ensure the engine-driven fuel pumps increased their pressure to keep the flow of petrol at the desired level.

The Boeing had been designed essentially as a high altitude aircraft and operated more efficiently above 20,000 feet or 6,500 metres. Below this altitude, its fuel consumption was much higher. However, since they did not carry a full load of oxygen they had to compromise and fly a little lower.

On reaching 16,000 feet he levelled off and checked all the instruments. The cylinder head temperatures of the four Wright Cyclones were all in the range of 202 to 210 degrees centigrade, which was excellent. The oil temperatures only varied one or two degrees either side of seventy-five degrees Centigrade, while the lowest oil pressure was only seventy pounds per square inch. Again, the last two sets of figures were very good. Satisfied with all the readings, he synchronised all four propellers, trimmed the aircraft and switched to Auto-Lean. For long-range cruising the recommended speed was only 155 miles an hour, or 240 kilometres per hour, so that was the airspeed he set, though he would have liked to have flown faster.

Shortly after, Helmuth Wenck, who had been stationed at the navigator's position in the nose of the Boeing, used the intercom to inform his son of the need for a course change. Peter Wenck complied and banked gently onto the new heading so the bomber was now flying approximately south-west over the Bay of Biscay.

Scarcely eight months previously this had been one of the most hard-fought-over pieces of sky and sea in the war. The Kriegsmarine had used Bordeaux as one of their principal U-Boat bases and, consequently, the British had concentrated much of their anti-submarine efforts on and over the Bay of Biscay in an effort to keep the U-Boats from escaping out into the Atlantic. But now, with all of France in Allied hands the German submarines were long gone and this stretch of water was now a backwater empty of aircraft and ships.

Three hours after leaving Guernsey they crossed the 44th Parallel and shortly thereafter changed course slightly so Miss Nonalee Two was flying almost parallel to the Spanish coast 180 kilometres away.

Dawn found them passing through broken cloud almost opposite the Portuguese city of Porto some 230 kilometres from their port wing tip.

It was at this stage that Peter Wenck finally handed over to Leo Swabisch and then made his way to a fold-down bed situated near what would have been one of the waist gunner's positions. Scarcely half-a-metre directly opposite, Sophia lay awake. At first the sound of the engines and the cold had kept her sleepless, but after half-an-hour-or-so and with the problems of Guernsey far behind, the steady beat of the engines had had a soporific effect and she began to drift off. The sound of the pilot's movements down the fuselage and the dawn's bright light chased the slumber away. Even though she was dreadfully tired and the lack of oxygen made her feel a trifle lightheaded and listless, she lifted herself onto one elbow and looked directly at Peter Wenck. She noticed with concern how exhausted he looked: the eyes sunken deep with dark rings etched above his cheek bones.

Wenck sat hunched on the edge of the bunk and pressed his forefinger and thumb between the bridge of his nose before wearily rubbing his eyes. He gave a deep sigh.

Raising his head he noticed her dark, liquid eyes staring at him. He smiled boyishly and asked how she was faring. Sophia said she felt a little lightheaded, so he knelt beside her and unhooked an oxygen mask from where it was hanging, placed it against her face and switched the cylinder on. Telling her to breathe deeply he gazed intently at the woman, noting her beauty and the returning colour to her cheeks as the oxygen enriched her lungs.

"Are you feeling any better?" he asked as he took the mask away.

"A little, Oberstleutnant," she said.

"Please call me Peter," he answered and received a wan smile together with a little nod.

She enquired how he felt and whether things were progressing smoothly. He answered both in the affirmative and then lay down on his bunk.

He was asleep in an instant, but she continued to watch him. Sophia already had a strong liking for the two Wencks, particularly the pilot and since the flying kit hid the bulk of his Luftwaffe uniform, in her mind he had almost ceased to be a member of Germany's armed forces.

As the threat of the SS receded, so she felt a waning of her need for Schonewille. His persona and his presence still had an effect, but it was lessening and doing so quickly.

Since her rescue from the holding centre almost twenty months previously, she had lived a sort of half-life, never daring to be herself. It was a sort of suspended state where she existed, but no more. Once, when she had dared open her soul and confront her life, she had likened it to living in a tunnel.

At one end were the terrors of the past and on the other, the vagaries of the future. The former she dared not recall and the latter, so uncertain as to necessitate a denial of hope. She was alone, of that she was certain. While her mother had not been Jewish, her gentile background had not saved her or her son. Sophia's father and her brother had been taken away months before the Gestapo came for the two women. Why they had been separated and not taken away together she had never found out. Her father's parents had also disappeared, while her mother's family had been killed in an air-raid. So there was nobody left.

Although she was German, she now had a deep revulsion for anything to do with Germany or its people. She desired, above all else, never to hear the German tongue again. Of her future with Schonewille she was not certain, her feelings a trifle confused.

As she watched over the sleeping pilot she felt sad. Here was a decent man, an intelligent and brave soldier with whom she would have been happy to have had a relationship, but now, despite the feelings of affection the moment he opened his mouth, he was dammed by the language that came forth.

She lay back, daring to dream of the future for the first time since the soldiers had come for her and her mother. As the engines continued their gentle drumming beat, she finally drifted into sleep.

The travellers continued southwards through broken cloud that gradually thinned out until, shortly after crossing the 35th Parallel, the sky became clear of any white and Miss Nonalee Two was alone in an azure sky.

They had been flying for almost eight hours when Helmuth Wenck left the navigator's position and went aft to where Meunier and Schonewille shared the wireless operator's cabin next to the bomb bay. It was a bit crowded, so Wenck senior asked his son to go and sit next to Swabisch while he and the diplomat had a discussion. Reluctant to leave, Schonewille at first argued that he wanted to stay. Helmuth Wenck lost his temper.

"For fuck's sake, Friedrich. Meunier needs to use the radio and then I need to wake Peter so we can make a decision about our destination. We have to contact Lacalle. Four of us won't fit in here. You are not needed, so stop procrastinating and move."

When Schonewille had left the compartment, the two older men exchanged glances. Meunier raised his eyes and eyebrows to which the general just shrugged.

Meunier turned on the radio and attempted to raise the Spanish Air Force officer, Major Andres Garcia Lacalle. Early the previous morning, while Schonewille was looting the Reichsbank's train and Peter Wenck was waiting nervously at Traunstein, the diplomat and Helmuth Wenck had received a radio message from Lacalle, which instructed them to fly to a military airfield near El Aiun. But, to complicate matters, there was still a chance that at the last minute they might have to change course and land at the Spanish enclave of Ifni. He had instructed them to contact him when they approached the 30th Parallel for a final confirmation of their destination.

After ten fruitless minutes at the radio, Meunier gave up. Helmuth Wenck ducked his head and passed though the bulkhead that led to what usually would have been the waist gunner's position. Both Peter and Sophia were still asleep. He gently shook the pilot by the shoulder.

Four hours sleep had replenished Peter Wenck's reserves of nervous energy somewhat, but he was still desperately tired and he yawned continuously. A few deep whiffs of oxygen had the desired effect and he joined the other two in the radio compartment.

Meunier explained how Lacalle could not be raised.

"At present we are some 470, 480 kilometres from El Aiun. If we are to head for Ifni, we had better change course immediately," said Helmuth Wenck.

"Mm," grunted Meunier. "Lacalle was quite specific. We were to fly to El Aiun in the Spanish Sahara unless he told us otherwise. I don't think it matters where we end up, both fit into our plans, so I think we should head for his first choice."

"And hope that's where he will be," added the elder Wenck.

He was about to continue when Peter broke in. "We don't have a choice, Father. He obviously had his reasons for wanting us to fly to El Aiun so it's what we'll have to do. We just stay on our present course."

There was just one other thing that needed to be done before they landed. All the German uniforms were gathered and stuffed into two sacks. These were weighted with two empty oxygen cylinders and jettisoned into the Atlantic. All three soldiers kept their decorations and medals, a risky move considering their presence would identify them as German soldiers, yet given what it had taken to win them it was an understandable whim, risk or no risk.

Soon after they had their first sign of land since leaving Guernsey. In the distance off their starboard wing tip were tiny smudges of land, two of the Canary Islands, first Lanzarote and then shortly afterwards, Fuerteventura. On hearing the news, Peter Wenck scrambled back to the cockpit, although he left Swabisch at the controls and sat in the co-pilot's seat. Schonewille went aft to the rear gunner's turret and his father manned the dorsal turret. They did not want to be surprised by any Spanish aircraft, so it was best to be prepared.

Their precautions proved to be unnecessary with no aircraft being sighted, so after half-an-hour they all began to relax a little though the gunners stayed at their posts.

Nine hours and thirty-eight minutes after they left St Peter Port, they sighted the African coast and began the descent to the area near El Aiun where they knew the airfield was situated.

Meunier still sat at the radio trying to make contact with Lacalle, but the instrument remained mute. They also had some difficulty in finding the aerodrome. When it was finally sighted Peter Wenck, who was back at the controls, lined the Boeing up for its final approach.

Although the runway was rather crude, a parched, packed dirt affair with few markings to differentiate the runway from the remainder of the airstrip, the landing was made without undue drama.

They taxied in a cloud of dust to where a group of men had gathered next to what was obviously the main administration building.

By no stretch of the imagination was this a prepossessing structure. To Peter Wenck the main building looked a little like Hollywood's idea of a desert fort garrisoned by the Foreign Legion. It was topped by what was an open air control tower covered by a faded white canvas awning. Next to this building was a large open hangar and two or three large tin sheds. Just inside the hangar was a Fiat CR 32 biplane fighter and two trucks of indeterminate age.

The aerodrome was set in a shallow depression surrounded on three sides by low barren hills almost devoid of vegetation. There was no sign of any other habitation though a clearly marked dirt road passed through a double-strand wire perimeter fence and headed west towards the coast.

Peter Wenck cut the engines and they waited in silence as the dust settled and the propellers stopped turning. It was decided only three of their party should make the initial approach to the group of men still grouped impassively near a doorway in the middle of the main structure.

Peter and his father dropped easily onto the ground from the forward hatch, but the rather corpulent Meunier needed a little help. The heat hit them like the blast from a freshly opened oven. Twenty-four hours previously they had been in a cool early spring climate. Now they were experiencing the type of heat never felt in Europe. Both fliers were dressed in American Air Force uniforms, while Meunier was wearing a grey shirt and a light-coloured jacket with matching trousers.

It was fifty metres to the assembled men and they walked forward unhurriedly trying to keep their wariness from being noticed. By the time they had walked the short distance separating the Boeing from their welcoming committee, all three were sweating profusely.

There were five men in two groups facing them. Two were obviously mechanics for they were wearing what could have been overalls, although the sleeves and the lower portion of the legs had been cut away. Of the other three, only one appeared to be in uniform although such a description would have caused a Wehrmacht officer to have an apoplectic fit.

The Germans stopped and when none of the Spaniards came forward Helmuth Wenck spoke softly to Meunier in English. "Speak to them, Conrad. Try out your Spanish. Ask them who is in charge."

"Por favor, quien es el jefe aqui?"

There was some movement, which mainly consisted of some shuffling of feet, so Meunier tried again. "Senors, please, who is in charge?"

The man with the uniform stepped forward and announced that he was in command.

"Your name?" snapped Meunier, deciding that politeness might

310

not be the way to go.

The Spaniard hesitated before answering. "Porque quiere saber?" he queried arrogantly, asking who wanted to know.

Meunier turned to the two pilots and gestured with his right hand. "General White and Colonel Bradley of the Eighth Air Force. They are here to meet with Major Andres Lacalle."

The Spaniard again hesitated and then gave a lackadaisical salute. He was clearly not impressed. The Germans returned the gesture saluting in the American way. It was also a much more precise gesture and had the desired effect, for the other man stiffened noticeably.

"Lieutenant Luis Murillo," he said, but there was still a note of truculence in his voice.

Meunier enquired whether the other spoke English. The answer was a shake of the head.

"This is getting us nowhere," said Meunier to his friends in English. General Wenck hesitated for a moment and then suggested Meunier ask where Major Lacalle was. The diplomat nodded and enquired as to the whereabouts of their contact.

Murillo shrugged his shoulders and said almost matter-of-factly, "Major Lacalle, quedo de venir ayer tarde, pero no ha llegado y no sabemos nada de el."

Meunier cursed softly and then translated without looking at the Wencks.

"He claims Major Lacalle was due at El Aiun late yesterday, but so far has not arrived and they've heard nothing from him."

When he finished translating the Spanish lieutenant added a few words accompanied by a rather sardonic smile. Again Meunier translated. "He's just added that the major is well known for saying one thing and doing another."

"Shit, what do we do now?" enquired Peter Wenck to his father when Meunier had repeated Murillo's answer.

Helmuth Wenck mouthed his own obscenity and moved closer to Meunier. Keeping his voice low he suggested Meunier try to obtain the necessary aviation gasoline without Major Lacalle's presence.

Meunier agreed and began talking in Spanish, his voice rising and falling and his hands making short, sharp gesticulations to emphasise his wishes and exert the necessary pressure. Unfortunately, it had no effect on the Spaniard. He merely listened with a look of growing annoyance and then shook his head.

"Why will you not do what we ask?" said Meunier, exasperated more by the man's attitude than by his refusal to be of assistance.

"Pero no me hah ordenado hacerle."

"He says he does not have the necessary orders," translated Meunier before suggesting to the Spaniards how illogical it would be for the Boeing's crew to have made up such a story in the hope of obtaining some gasoline. He explained that Major Lacalle was under orders from his superiors to deliver gasoline to the American general.

Once more the only response he elicited from Murillo was a shrug, followed by a shake of his head.

The argument continued. They tried bribery, offering him $20,000 to provide the petrol. The offer had a surprising effect on the Spanish lieutenant.

His face turned a vivid hue and he became extremely agitated his voice becoming low and menacing.

"What's the bastard saying now Conrad?" asked Helmuth Wenck.

"He says all Americans are the result of a union between a whore and a donkey and he does not want to soil his hands with Yankee money."

"For fuck's sake," exploded the general in exasperation. "The one Spaniard who I've ever met who won't be bribed and we have to bloody well come across him now. Well, tell him we're German. Maybe that will change his mind."

The diplomat again spoke in Spanish, adding a few words of German to his explanation. The effect of his words were even worse than before. Lieutenant Murillo rounded on one of his own men and spoke rapidly in Spanish, whereupon the man disappeared into the main building. Murillo's face had turned ugly. His voice dropped to a hoarse shout and he was so angry that his lips began to quiver with rage. Flecks of spittle appeared at his mouth. The Germans stared in amazement, which turned to alarm when the missing Spaniard returned carrying a heavy machine-gun over one shoulder.

Ignoring the group the man went over to a weapons pit and deftly mounted the weapon on an anti-aircraft mounting and cocked the weapon.

Meunier walked away, motioning the two pilots to follow. When they were a dozen or so metres away he spoke very quietly in German.

"I'm afraid Helmuth, Peter that we're in deep trouble. He hates Germans more than he loathes Americans. Apparently, his father was on the Republican side during the war and was killed by what he terms a Fascist bomb. It's also because of his father's Republican leanings that he's based out here, so he blames Fascists for his troubles. At any rate, what he feels does not matter. He's adamant he won't supply us with any gasoline and threatens to open fire on us unless we're off the base in five minutes."

Peter Wenck glanced back at the Spaniards. They had not moved, but Murillo and the man in the weapons pit were smiling.

"Come on Peter, we're wasting our time. We had better go."

They hurried back to the Boeing and stopped by the forward hatch. Schonewille dropped to the ground and enquired as to what was going on.

Meunier explained their predicament.

"Well, what's our choice, eh? Can we get to the Dominican Republic if we don't get that petrol?"

"Ha, ha. Not a fucking hope, Brother. That is unless we swim half the way."

The SS officer's answer was a shock. Not just because of what he said, but the matter-of-fact way he said it. "Well, Kameraden, we have only one choice. We kill the lot of them now and take the petrol. I've no intention of giving myself up to the Allies or losing a fortune because of some wogs who are as stupid as the rest of their benighted race."

The other three stared at Schonewille for a moment. It was the air force general who made the decision.

"He's right, lads. We have no alternative. We either fly away and try to land God knows where, or we stay here and wait for

Lacalle ... that is if he is still planning to come here. The problem is, neither of those alternatives is exactly rosy, so I agree with Friedrich. Let's get rid of the bastards."

They climbed back into the Boeing and quickly discussed how they were to accomplish the massacre. This time they included Swabisch who nodded his head without comment and climbed up inside the dorsal turret. With Schonewille sitting hunched in the rear turret Peter Wenck fired up the four engines and began to turn the B17 so the two turrets would have a clear line of fire.

"Well, Father, do we do it?"

His father's answer sealed the fate of the Spaniards, so he went aft to the wireless operator's window and gave the order to fire.

When the four fifty-calibre machine-guns fell silent, the pilot opened the rear hatch and jumped to the ground. The rush of air from the airscrews tore at his clothes and the dust stung his neck. Thankfully, his father cut the engines and Peter Wenck moved forward, an American forty-five-calibre Colt automatic clutched in his right hand.

The Spaniards were all dead. The man in the weapons pit was reduced to a mangled bloody mess with most of his entrails spread grotesquely on the ground. There were huge pools of blood soaking the parched, rocky ground and such was the violence of the heavy-calibre bullets that all of the dead had suffered massive wounds.

Feeling the gorge rise in his throat he turned away and hunched over, trying to breathe deeply and swallow at the same time. After a few seconds he won the battle and his stomach stopped heaving. He straightened up as Schonewille, clutching a Schmeisser machine pistol, ran up.

"Come on Peter, we'd better check there's nobody else inside the building," he urged, completely ignoring the bodies.

Weapons cocked, the two combed the administrative building, followed by the hangar and the smaller tin sheds. All were empty. Finally the entire party, except for the woman, gathered inside the administration building in what was most likely the office of the late Lieutenant Murillo.

"All empty?" asked the general

Schonewille nodded vigorously as Peter Wenck returned the Colt to its holster. The pilot wondered what would have happened if they had found another Spaniard and asked himself whether he would have had the stomach to kill the man if there had been no resistance. He doubted it.

Like all airmen, he had done his killing from afar and although while in Russia he had seen many dead soldiers and even a few civilians, the violence had never been as close or fresh as this.

"Fine, fine. Now the petrol," said Helmuth Wenck, punching a clenched fist into his left palm.

They located a petrol tanker in the hangar, but found it to be almost empty. Nearby, though, was a fuel dump containing several dozen drums that appeared to be in excellent condition.

"It looks as if these were meant for us," said Swabisch. "Although we had better hope it is of good quality. I don't imagine the Boeing's engines are used to running on anything but the best."

It took two hours to transfer the gasoline from the drums into the petrol tanker and then into the Boeing. At last, with all tanks overflowing, it was time to leave the Spanish base.

It was Helmuth Wenck who stopped them climbing back into the bomber.

"Wait, before we disappear we have one more job to do. Peter, you and Leo go to the front of the building and try to find every spent bullet whether it is buried in the wall or in the ground. I'll pick up the shell casings. Then, you go to the Fiat and set it on fire. With luck, the flames should hide what caused its demise since our bullets will have melted. In the meantime, the rest of us will collect all the bodies, wrap them in canvas and transfer them to our aircraft's bomb bay. I want no evidence left behind. This airfield is going to be left like the Marie Celeste."

Peter Wenck questioned the necessity. As far as he was concerned, the quicker they left the better. "Surely, Lacalle will guess it was us?"

"He might, certainly. But what can he do or say? He's hardly likely to admit he's been involved in a scheme to sell Spanish Air Force gasoline on the side, especially when that scheme has gone wrong and has caused the death of Spanish personnel and the destruction of property."

"Therefore, if the Spanish authorities do not know what happened, there is less chance of Lacalle being suspected of any mischief and little chance of him telling anyone."

There was no argument to this logic, so the two pilots went about their task while the others started their grizzly job of gathering and packing the bodies and digging up the bloody earth, rock and sand. Since the bomb bay was largely filled with the long-range petrol tanks it proved to be difficult to fit the bodies into the space that remained. They first had to move some of the bullion cases to other areas in the fuselage.

The job was made even harder since they had first to be dragged inside and then quite literally stuffed down into the bay itself.

Peter Wenck waited until all had been finalised and they were ready to depart before emptying a five-litre can of solvent into the Fiat's cockpit and putting two bullets into the petrol tank. The timing was important since the smoke might cause some unwelcome attention and he wanted to be well away before anyone arrived to investigate.

He threw a lighted rag into the cockpit. The seat readily caught and he had only just climbed into the Boeing when there came a loud whump as the main fuel tank went up.

He lowered himself wearily into the pilot's seat and began to go through the pre-flight check. Suddenly, he felt very tired and for a moment leaned back and closed his eyes. A concerned Swabisch mentioned that perhaps it would be better if he took off, a suggestion that was met by a less than polite refusal.

The runway was a trifle short and the Boeing only just managed to claw itself into the air before the ground deteriorated and the perimeter fence was upon them. The pilot immediately headed south for a few minutes before swinging west to avoid the town of El Aiun. The coast came up quickly and he waited for twenty minutes before ordering the co-pilot to open the bomb bay doors and dump their cargo. Each body had been wrapped in canvas and weighted down with something heavy.

The bodies dropped away into the sea 200 metres below. The pilot then called up his brother on the intercom and asked him to check the bomb bay to make certain it was empty. Once it was confirmed that their dreadful cargo had gone, he closed the bomb bay doors and began to climb to a much more equitable cruising height. The bullion was then returned to the bomb bay.

Chapter Thirty
25 March 1945

2030 Hours

An advancing storm was beginning to buffet the Boeing quite severely and Peter Wenck realised he would have to make a decision very quickly about whether to climb for height or stay at this altitude and carry on a running fight with mother nature.

The decision hinged purely on the question of oxygen. In an effort to save weight they had decided to only carry a small quantity, certainly not enough to cover the whole crew for any extended time. Already the occupants of Miss Nonalee Two were suffering from the effect of the reduced oxygen levels at 5,500 metres. Headaches and chest pains were common, though they were alleviated by the occasional whiffs of oxygen. However, for the pilots oxygen was more of a necessity and they took regular turns to breathe deeply from their face masks while they were flying.

Peter Wenck handed the controls back to Swabisch and went down to the navigator's compartment to talk to his father. Despite a nagging headache, he now felt much more alert. Shortly after their last take-off he had at last heeded the advice of his father not to exhaust himself any further and to get some rest. He allowed himself five hours unbroken sleep and it had certainly helped, although his reserves were still dangerously low because of the minimal amount of sleep he had gleaned over the preceding sixty hours.

His watch told him it was just after ten o'clock at night, yet he realised by taking into account the time difference the local time was probably around about half-past-eight. To a degree they were flying backwards since they had been in the air for six-and-a-half hours since leaving the West African coast.

At first the flight had been without incident. They had climbed slowly, the bomber heavy like a pregnant sow. Some 500 kilometres out into the Atlantic they had struck the first banks of cumulus clouds that gradually became more concentrated as they continued. By the time they reached 5,500 metres it was quite thick. Worse still, the white had begun to streak and billow with the ominous black of nimbus clouds, though most of the latter were some way below.

As the flight continued and night began to close in, the rain-bearing clouds became even thicker and the buffeting became severe. Schonewille, Sophia and Meunier all began to suffer with varying degrees from air sickness. The diplomat suffered the least with Schonewille the worst.

Helmuth Wenck was awake, staring out of the Perspex at the vague shapes created by the dark sky and the broken cloud formation when the pilot joined him. Water was beginning to stream back across the pointed Perspex cone and in the distance there came the odd flash of lightning.

"Shit, I think we'd better start getting above that lot and quickly," Peter told his father. "What's our current position?"

Helmuth Wenck dragged out one of the charts. It was the same one he had used for the last few hundred kilometres to the Spanish Sahara and showed the Canary Islands and a portion of the African coast on its right hand side.

He fiddled with a ruler for a few seconds and then, picking up a pencil, he extended a line that already stretched half-way across the map. When the line was almost off the page he made a cross and circled an area that would have covered several hundred square kilometres.

"Without taking another reading, I guess we're about here. We've travelled about 1,700 kilometres, so we're a quarter way there."

The pilot pursed his lips. God, it's going to be like the New York mission, never ending, he thought. He wished the Boeing could fly a little faster. They were at the plane's optimum cruising speed of barely 260 kilometres per hour. Everything was set for the most economical journey. The four Wrights were set at the leanest mixture allowed without damaging the engines and the revs were just marginally above 2,000 per minute.

Despite these conservative settings and with their huge amount of fuel, the precious liquid could still not be wasted.

"Look, if we climb above that fug out there it is going to be pretty difficult without oxygen. I suggest we set aside two-thirds of our supply to cover everyone, but it will have to be used sparingly. Whoever is flying will need to keep alert, so either Leo or I must have a constant dose, all right?"

His father offered no argument, so Peter Wenck returned to the cockpit. He told his co-pilot to go aft and try to get some sleep and asked him to inform the others about his plans to climb above the bad weather and that while they could use some oxygen, they could only do so sparingly.

Peter Wenck settled himself into the seat and put on his harness. Before tightening the straps he leant down and unclipped a steel thermos flask, unscrewed the lid and poured himself a cup of black, sweet tea. He loved the English drink. It was a legacy of his travelling days and the brew in the thermos was courtesy of the Red Cross, having been purloined from a cache of prisoner-of-war cartons.

Refreshed, he put the thermos away and pulled the yoke gently back, at the same time increasing the revs and checking two sets of gauges to his right, the manifold pressure gauges and the cylinder head temperature gauges. Miss Nonalee Two hauled her bulk upwards as the storm began to shake her even more. It was as if the elements realised the bomber was trying to escape and were not charitable in letting her do so.

Finally, at 6,300 metres the aircraft broke through into relatively calm air. Except for some wispy cirrostratus a thousand or so metres above them, the sky was clear. He levelled off 300 metres from the highest cloud peak and checked his instruments again.

Adjusting the oxygen regulator, he sucked deeply, allowing the gas to flow cool and clean through his mouth. As he flew he searched the sky, though he knew the chance of another aircraft being in this same patch was almost zero. Yet, he kept turning his head, methodically checking each corner of his vision. It was an old habit, an instinct that was by now second nature. It was the mark of a successful pilot, one who had survived the war in the air for a long time.

As his eyes became used to the better light at this greater altitude, he could see through the higher clouds the stars and the moon, the latter's glow shedding a dim light onto the earth's upper reaches and giving the carpet of clouds beneath his wings a dull yellow glow. It was an eerie sight and made him feel he was flying in another world.

He checked the Boeing's original altimeter: it read just over 21,000 feet. He did not bother checking the metric gauge. Then he noticed how the airspeed indicator showed the plane had gained another thirty miles per hour. They had obviously picked up the upper reaches of the north-east trades that blew almost continuously at these latitudes. This air stream would be a boon in two ways. Not only would they reach their destination quicker, but it would ease their fuel consumption.

On a whim he set the auto pilot and unclipped his harness. Passing through the flight deck to the catwalk, which ran through the bomb bay, he went to the rear of the plane. In the wireless operator's compartment Schonewille and Meunier lay tossing fitfully, but he did not stop. Crouching, he let himself through the next bulkhead and came to where the co-pilot and the Jewess were lying in their bunks.

Sophia was awake, her face ashen in the dim light.

"Are you not well?" he asked.

She swallowed a couple of times and licked her lips before answering in a weak voice that she felt awful. He unhooked a mask and, as he had done previously, told her to breathe deeply. He pressed the mask to her face for five minutes and then as her breathing became easier transferred it to his own face. He took a few deep breaths and smiled down at her. The look was cut short as the Boeing gave a slight lurch and then re-adjusted itself under the guidance of the automatic pilot. Despite the device having always worked perfectly, like most pilots he did not trust radical or new technology and the thought of the plane flying itself made him very nervous, so he wanted to get back to the cockpit immediately.

"Do you feel any better?" he asked.

She gave a small yes, and on an impulse he motioned her to follow. As they passed through the wireless compartment,

Schonewille opened his eyes and saw them. He made an effort to raise his head, but he was too giddy and gave up the attempt. Sophia ignored him and followed the pilot, something that was to have dire consequences later on.

Once on the flight deck, he helped her to the co-pilot's seat. By now she was breathless and lightheaded from the lack of oxygen and the exertion needed to travel the bomber's length. He fastened an oxygen mask to her face, at the same time showing her how to remove the mask if she needed. He then resumed the pilot's seat to her left.

After a quick check of the instruments, he dis-engaged the auto-pilot and took control, feeling the B17 alive under the palms of his hands. No matter how long he had been pilot and under what extreme conditions of fatigue and danger he had flown, the feeling of a plane in his hands still had the power to thrill him.

He turned and saw her staring at him and he returned the look with an infectious grin. In spite of herself, she returned the smile. He told her to put her hands on the co-pilot's control column and to hook her thumbs around the spokes of the half wheel. When she had complied he gingerly lifted his hands away from the controls.

Like he, she felt the plane alive in her hands and, as if by instinct, gently turned the wheel to the left and then to the right, feeling the Boeing answer her command. It was like riding a horse for the first time. Although the aircraft was only a machine, it still felt alive to her and she suddenly understood what every pilot at one time or another always knew. Aeroplanes might not be flesh and blood and they might not breathe, but they are alive and they have souls.

For the first time in years she felt happy and free, the twin sentiments of anybody who has escaped prison and death. The smile that she gave to the pilot was covered by the oxygen mask, but he sensed it nevertheless. He gave her a friendly pat on the shoulder and then took over the controls again.

"She's a lovely lady, with no vices. The Americans build wonderful aircraft," he said.

As Miss Nonalee Two continued westwards, the two sat in absolute silence and contentment gazing at the night sky and the twinkling stars.

0130 Hours, 26 March 1945

They had flown 3,600 kilometres, a little over halfway to the Dominican Republic. His watch read a little after four o'clock, but knowing that dawn was still a long way off he wound the timepiece back so that it read one-thirty. He guessed this was an approximate of the real time.

The woman had long since gone and he had flown unaccompanied for the past five hours. The storm had petered out over an hour before and, even though there was still plenty of cloud, he had reduced height to ease the strain on both the plane's occupants and the oxygen supply.

There came a scrabbling sound behind him and Swabisch's face appeared, unshaven and covered in sleep. His face was pale and his breathing heavy since, even though they were now back down to 5,500 metres, the air was still thin and the temperature cold.

"Bloody hell, you look like a sick ghost, Leo. I hope you feel better than you look?"

The other rubbed his eyes with a fist like a three-year old urchin and gave a rueful grin. He then yawned, a wide gaping gasp for air, which revealed just how bad his breath smelled. Peter slapped a hand over his nose.

"Jesus, Leo, your breath smells like an Eskimo's fanny," he grinned. "Here take some of this chewing gum."

"Thanks, Peter. Yes, it tastes pretty lousy as well. Feels like I've been drinking boar's piss. How's it going?"

"Not bad Leo, not bad. The Americans certainly know how to build good aircraft. The engines have not missed a beat and the gauges all read normal. You know, I am beginning to believe we might just make it after all."

Swabisch settled himself in the co-pilot's seat and took over the controls. Peter un-strapped himself and went forward under the flight deck floor to the navigator's compartment. His father was asleep, lying wrapped up in a thick Arctic sleeping bag between the navigator's chair and the starboard fuselage side. His legs hung forward near where the Norden bomb sight would have been. On

323

either side there was a fifty-calibre ammunition box for the front machine-gun.

Peter leaned over his father and had just decided to let him sleep when the general opened his eyes and then his mouth. "What's up, what's the matter?" he said, his voice thick with phlegm. "Ugh, bloody awful taste in my mouth. Well what's the matter?" he asked again, struggling to extract his arms and sit up.

"Been drinking boar's piss like Leo, have you, Father?"

Helmuth Wenck stared uncomprehendingly at his son, who did not bother to explain. "Ah, don't worry," he said shaking his head.

"Don't you worry about anything. Leo's in charge and the old girl is behaving herself like the thoroughbred she is. Go back to sleep."

His father lay back grumbling. "Why the fuck did you wake me then? Piss off and let me catch my beauty sleep. I want to look my best when I meet your mother again." But he was smiling as he said it.

His son squeezed his shoulder and went aft.

Both Meunier and Schonewille were awake and he stopped to check on their condition. His brother was still feeling rather queasy, so he unhooked an oxygen mast and held it to his face for a few minutes.

"Keep it here Friedrich, and take a whiff every few minutes. It will help you feel better."

He lay down on his bunk and then felt a urgent need to urinate, but at first he felt too weary to move. Eventually he got up and went to the rear of the bomber where the toilet was situated near the crew entry door. He struggled with his flying suit zip before he was able to complete the task.

Back in his bunk he looked over at the woman who stared back unblinkingly.

"It's all fine. We're doing fine," he said, and quickly fell asleep.

0815 Hours, 26 March 1945

It was a brilliant morning. The sun shone through the nose Perspex and the ceiling astrodome above the navigator's compartment. An occasional small fluffy white cloud swept by. Meunier and the two

324

Wencks sat crammed into the nose of the aircraft, the pilot sitting with his back braced up against one of the ammunition boxes. They were discussing their next moves.

"Our approximate position is fifty-seven degrees west by twenty-two degrees north," said Helmuth. "The tail wind has meant we have travelled about 300 kilometres further west than we would have in the same time. It's nice to have it up our sleeve."

The others nodded in agreement, but added nothing more to the conversation. Wenck senior looked up from his map. "Bloody talkative this morning, aren't we?" He transferred his gaze back to his map and continued talking. "Now where was I? We're over three-quarters of the way there, another 1,400 kilometres at most. We'll probably arrive there around about noon local time. Conrad, I want you to go back to the radio and see if you can pick anything up of interest."

They discussed what call-signs were needed to contact Colonel Ferdinand Savory. Meunier explained that, as arranged, he had contacted the air force colonel when they had left Norway and again when they had left the Spanish Sahara.

"I hope he's more reliable than your previous contact and the natives are a little more friendly," said the pilot wryly.

"And that we don't have to machine-gun half the inhabitants," added Helmuth Wenck.

Meunier shook his head and said soberly, "If there is any problem there, Helmuth, we're finished. The airfield at Puerto Plata is a full working base for the Dominican Air Force and also caters for private aircraft. Taking this into account, we had better pray Savory is prepared to keep his part of the bargain and sell us the gasoline. Otherwise we are well and truly at the end of our voyage."

"I tell you what though," remarked the pilot. "We won't have long to find out. With what we've gained by the tail wind, we're ahead of schedule. So, Meunier dear chap, you'd better get back to your little hole and try and work that radio and see if Colonel Savory is waiting for us."

Meunier sniffed and cleared his throat. He obviously wanted to speak, but then just shrugged his shoulders and left the two

Wencks alone.

"How's the fuel situation?" enquired the general

"It's holding up well, Father. We should be well within our estimates. In fact, we might even have a couple of hours to spare."

They joined Swabisch, but Peter Wenck did not bother to take over the controls. He just sat in his seat and, although outwardly relaxed, still searched the sky, his eyes and head never still for more than a moment. Half-an-hour passed in silence. He checked with Meunier on whether the diplomat had managed to raise his contact on the radio. The answer was still a terse no.

A probable cause appeared soon after. The sky ahead was turning darker. Not the grey and white of an average rain-bearing cloud formation, but the ugly black mushrooms of nimbus, their bowels full of water and their temper ugly. The closer they got, the more alarmed the three fliers became. All had piloted aircraft through conditions like these at one time or another, and not one would have chosen to pit their skills against such extremes of nature if they could have chosen another alternative.

"Teufel, Teufel," said Peter Wenck, and then added another stream of obscenities under his breath as a huge multi-pronged streak of lightning flashed in front of them. "We can't risk flying through this lot," he said turning to his father. "Let me take over Leo. Jesus, we'd better go up." The plane was already rocking from the force of the wind as he manipulated the throttle levers and pulled the aircraft's nose up.

At 6,500 metres they were still not above the clouds and in desperation he increased power. The plane was now much more responsive than she had been earlier. With most of her fuel load consumed and much lighter because of her reduced gun armament, she was still climbing rapidly.

"Get everyone onto oxygen," he yelled to Swabisch, who put a hand to his mask and flicked on the intercom switch.

While the Boeing continued to gain height, Swabisch kept re-adjusting the turbo superchargers to make sure they did not over-speed. They finally broke clear at 7,250 metres and Wenck levelled off and re-set the plane's trim.

As they continued westwards, Meunier kept trying to raise the airfield at Puerto Plata, but to no avail. Finally, with perhaps one hundred kilometres to go, Helmuth Wenck informed his son that they would be getting close to the island of Hispaniola and it was time to descend.

The cloud formation below was as thick as before, although there seemed less violence in its midst. Gingerly, he eased the bomber downwards. While there was no more lightning, there was intense rain and wind and Miss Nonalee Two began to sway and shake like an alcoholic trying to dry out.

They were down to 2,400 metres when Meunier eventually made contact with the airfield. The voice at the control tower was evidently waiting for them for once they gave the correct call-sign it immediately requested them to wait while Colonel Savory was fetched.

Scarcely a minute later Savory's impeccable Spanish filled Meunier's earphones. Unfortunately, his message was not at all reassuring. The diplomat listened in disbelief as the officer informed them that they could not land just yet and they might have to wait for some time. He relayed the message to the pilot.

"Shit, Conrad. For Christ's sake ask him what the hell he's playing at. What does 'some time' mean?"

Meunier spoke into the radio and was told by Savory that an American political legation that had been due at the capital Ciudad Trujillo had been forced to detour because of the storm and had landed at his base. "Apparently the storm came from the south and first hit the capital. Now it has also closed right in on the air base."

"They are waiting in the terminal building for the storm to lift, Senor, and I do not think it wise for them to see you land." Meunier passed on his explanation to the pilot.

Cursing, Peter called up his father and they discussed what to do. In the meantime Meunier elicited further information from Savory and then relayed the details to the Wencks.

"He says the storm will probably last at least another three hours and asks whether we have enough gasoline to last that long."

Peter Wenck replied that they had enough fuel left for a maximum of an hour-and-a-half in the air. "Tell him that despite who's at his base, we'll be landing in just over an hour and it will be up to him to make sure we're safe. Tell him to get the bastards drunk, provide them with women, whatever he can dream up, but he only has an hour in which to do it."

Peter Wenck kept the Boeing relatively low. He had no choice. They had enough oxygen left for just over an hour's use and he wanted to keep this for an emergency. At the same time, although the rain was still heavy, the wind had dropped so the buffeting was less severe.

An hour later to the minute, Savory came back on the radio. He informed them the Americans were currently being wined and dined to a full lunch in the mess, which had no window facing the main runway and, consequently, he had given instructions for them to be allowed to land.

"My apologies for the delay, Senors, and my apologies for my manners, but you will be directed to a discreet parking area at which you will have to stay until the Americanos have departed."

Meunier thanked the Spanish colonel and effusively winked at Schonewille, who listened as the diplomat translated the message to the pilot.

The SS officer was out of his depth. His last role of importance had been at El Aiun. Now his future depended on other people and he did not like it. His old inferiorities were coming back to haunt him. Nobody now asked him what he thought about the current situation let alone deferred to any wishes he might have. His father and brother quite patently did not need him and barely spoke to him.

In reality his feelings were a little silly, since he had been key in the decision to kill the Spanish Air Force personnel at El Aiun. But under his present state of mind this was already forgotten. What was worse, his mistress was distinctly cool towards him. A feeling of helpless rage began to well-up inside him and it was with difficulty that he hid his feelings from the diplomat. So, in answer to the wink, he just shrugged his shoulders, a gesture that Meunier reciprocated.

The only trouble faced by the travellers over the next few minutes was actually locating the airfield, but once they found the town the base was relatively easy to find.

The wind had died down and even though the rain, if anything, had increased in intensity, the landing was smooth and not unduly difficult.

The runway was a little short and the pilot needed to be judicious with his brakes. An open Model-T Ford was parked near the end of the concrete. Two bedraggled figures waved at them through the teeming rain indicating for them to follow. It was obvious they were being led as far from the main administration buildings as possible, since they took a wide circuitous route by way of a series of perimeter runways before reaching several hangars at the extreme left of the airfield's administration buildings that were situated approximately half-a-kilometre away.

There were two hangars spaced some eighty metres apart and the Ford drove between them, its occupants gesticulating for the Boeing to follow. The pilot hesitated for he did not want to park the bomber with its nose facing away from the runway. Then, making a quick calculation on the space between the two hangars and his aircraft's wing span, he eased the bomber forward, keeping the port wing tip as close as possible to one wall of the nearest structure. When they were sufficiently deeply inside the space, he locked the starboard wheel and gently swung the bomber around on its axis until it faced the way it had come.

Cutting the engines, he vacated his seat and made his way through the fuselage to the rear crew hatch. There he encountered his brother holding his Schmeisser machine pistol.

"Weg mit der Waffe, Du Dummpkopf," he snapped, not wanting the Dominicans to see the German weapon. He was not sure what the occupants in the Ford knew and as far as possible he wanted to give the impression they were Americans. His brother did not take kindly to be spoken to like that.

"Was unterstehst Du Dich so mit mir zu sprechen!"

Peter Wenck ignored the words, but to his relief saw him place the machine pistol behind some blankets.

After hours of thin air and canned oxygen, the smell of the tropical Dominican atmosphere was like a heady aroma when they opened the hatch. Even though the rain was coming down in sheets it was quite warm and the wind was now almost non existent.

One of the Ford's two occupants splashed his way towards the aircraft. Despite the rain he was in no hurry, probably because he was already wet through and any more water would not matter one iota.

Peter Wenck's caution about the Schmeisser was justified because the Dominican addressed him in English. He apologised on behalf of Colonel Savory, explaining that the Dominican Air Force officer was engaged with his hosts and he would see to their needs as soon as possible. Then, as he left he added, "Oh, I almost forget. Colonel Savory orders for you to remain inside the aircraft until he comes."

When they had left, the Germans held a council in the rear fuselage.

Schonewille, still smarting from being called a fool by his brother, was belligerent, demanding to know why they should remain inside the bomber. The pilot was about to tell him to shut up, but a warning look by his father dried the words in his throat.

All were on edge. In the preceding two days they had spent just over forty hours in the bomber. Given the tensions of their escape and the dangers of their flight it had been a mammoth journey. All wanted to get some proper rest. Their ears were still not used to the engines being shut down and, except for the rain beating on the aluminium, all was quiet.

"Why should we stay here?" again demanded the SS officer. "I suggest we go outside and reconnoitre."

It was more of a demand than a suggestion. General Wenck, though, agreed. "He is right, we should check out our surroundings," he said, noticing the effect his words were having on his first born. Schonewille nodded his head, a self-satisfied smirk on his face. It was like they were little boys once again.

"Friedrich and I will check both hangars. The rest of you stay here." He proceeded to take off his shirt and jacket. When he had stripped to his underpants, he turned to Schonewille. "It is up to you, Friedrich. If you want to live in soaking clothes, you can go out as you are."

The other nodded and also began to strip off. The general made it clear they would not take any weapons with them and then,

330

without any preamble, climbed down the ladder, followed by his son.

Those inside the aircraft watched them walk to the hangar on their right, the one opposite the crew entry door and the furthest away from the aircraft. It was difficult to see clearly because of the rain's intensity, but they saw them open a door and slip out of sight.

Chapter Thirty-One
26 March 1945

1500 Hours

"The paradise of God," said Meunier.

"I beg your pardon?" queried Peter Wenck.

They were sitting on two folding canvas chairs under the belly of the bomber, just behind where the leading edge of the wings joined the fuselage. The rain had stopped and brilliant hues of blue began to appear through gaps in the rapidly clearing cloud. In the distance a huge rainbow added a dimension of colour to the sky. The heat was already bordering on the oppressive, humid and energy-sapping.

"The paradise of God," repeated the diplomat. "Those were the words of Columbus who discovered the island of Hispaniola. He thought it was the most beautiful place on earth." He stopped for a moment and then when the pilot did not answer continued with his history lesson. "You know, this island had the first permanent Spanish settlement in the New World, Santo Domingo, or as it's called now, Ciudad Trujillo, in honour of this country's esteemed leader," he added with a trace of sarcasm.

"Seems a long way from the Reich," mused the pilot and then added, "I wonder what's happening. I wonder how far the Allies have advanced."

"Who gives a damn?" said Meunier.

The vehemence in his voice was so strong that Wenck turned to look at him. He questioned his companion about his attitude. Meunier searched his face for a moment, his countenance creased into a frown. He seemed to be deciding on something. Finally, he spoke, his words low, his intonation clipped and his eyes never leaving the pilot's face.

"Have you asked yourself why your father and I have been so determined to leave Germany and why we have so little thought about our comrades still fighting for their lives, eh?" He almost spat out the words, his tone now rising in anger.

The pilot shrugged. "Well, I suppose it was like me ... a way to escape and do so with some money ..."

Meunier broke in, his voice sarcastic, his words belittling. "Don't give me that shit. Your father has told me you've been worried about the war for some time, but with us, it is much more than that. Quite simply, your father and I do not want to be in Germany when the Allies and the rest of the world realise fully what we've done." Peter Wenck looked questioningly at the diplomat who continued after another moment's hesitation.

"We all know of the concentration camps. What we don't know, or what we have not let ourselves believe is what actually goes on inside them." He again paused and this time when he continued speaking his voice was low and full of emotion. "Peter, my dear friend. Over the past two months I have been gathering, or rather verifying information about the camps and what I have found out is so horrible that I believe the world will wreak a terrible vengeance on the German people. The camps have been used as extermination centres. If my information is correct, we have quite literally planned and carried out the systematic murder of millions of people."

The pilot stared at the man, unable to comprehend what he was saying. "Oh, come now. Surely you must be exaggerating. It is beyond reason. And how does one kill millions of people and how or where does one get rid of the bodies?"

Meunier sat still for a moment and to the pilot's horror began to weep, the tears welling up in his eyes and running down his pudgy cheeks onto his shirt.

"My dear boy, we are an efficient people. As I've said, if my information is accurate and I believe it is, we are gassing the prisoners. Then we are burning them in huge ovens. Men, women and children. It has been going on non-stop for at least three years."

Peter Wenck sat rigid, a wave of horror spreading over his body. His chest began to hurt with a pain so strong he thought for a moment he was having a heart attack, and his mouth went dry.

Again, he tried to suggest that Meunier's information was wrong. The diplomat shook his head vigorously. He explained how he had received information from several reliable sources. One, he said, had been a close friend, another diplomat, who like he had worked for Admiral Canaris. The man's son had been a committed Nazi and had joined the Waffen SS in 1939. On being wounded on the Russian front he had been sent to Dachau and while on leave had boasted to his father what was happening at the camps.

"My friend came to see me, he was so shocked. He had made some checks of his own. It was very difficult to verify, you see, even at the most senior levels of the Reich it is a secret. At any rate, he confirmed what Kurt his son had said. He told me he intended committing suicide. And that's just what he did. He asked his son to come home because his mother was ill and then quite simply shot him. He then shot his wife and finally, himself. He committed suicide.

"Your brother, I'm afraid to say, knows all about it. He was part of the system. Although he was not part of the killing, his job was to visit the camps and liaise with their Kommandanten and do the book-keeping. You know, add up all the money and valuables stolen from the inmates," he said in explanation as Wenck's brow furrowed, not understanding, or rather not wanting to understand.

"Unmöglich, unmöglich," he kept repeating.

Meunier went on to explain how Schonewille had rescued Sophia from one of the holding camps prior to being transported to Auschwitz and although the Jewess had been extremely reticent in talking about her experience, she had confirmed several points.

"Jesus. Well what's their relationship like then?" the pilot asked.

"Oh, I believe it's like any relationship when somebody rescues you from hell. I think she's grateful and I think ... no I'm sure, she's used what women have always used when confronted with a choice as stark. She's used her body to protect herself, though to be fair, he is obviously very much in love with her and has risked a lot to do what he has done. You should bear that in mind when you spend time with her. He is very jealous and if you mix this together with his obvious sense of inferiority to both you and your father, you get a dangerous mix of emotions." He looked warningly at the pilot.

Peter Wenck felt sick. He had been enjoying the peace and the rest from their travels. Now he felt a deep anger. The sharp pain in his chest had been replaced by a dull sickening ache.

The sound of feet came from behind. His father, dressed again in his US Air Force uniform, stood over them. His son blurted out, "Christ, Father. Conrad has just told me about the camps. Christ," he repeated shaking his head. "Das is unglaublich," he said.

"Unbelievable it may be, but it is true nevertheless. Believe me, nothing felt better than taking off my Luftwaffe uniform. Nothing in God's name will ever induce me to call myself a German again."

All three lapsed into silence. Despite the clearing weather, the airfield still appeared deserted. It was over an hour since the general and Schonewille had opened the door of the hangar and slipped inside. Except for a DC3 and three other small nondescript light aircraft, the building had been deserted.

They had explored some offices on the far side that were also empty of any humans before crossing the tarmac and entering the second hangar. This too contained a motley collection of aircraft augmented by two petrol tankers and an immaculate Cord sports coupé.

On returning to the Boeing, the Germans had waited until the rain stopped and then all had stepped outside to stretch their legs. A few minutes later, the Model-T Ford re-appeared and the same man who had greeted them on their arrival handed over a large basket crammed with food and two bottles of light red wine. To their questions on what was happening, he just shrugged his shoulders and told them to wait.

It was at this time that Helmuth Wenck remembered seeing three folding canvas chairs in one of the hangars and went to fetch them. They alternated between sitting outside in the gathering sunshine and keeping watch from the cockpit of the B17. One of the hangars had also contained a small wash room and toilet so, one at a time, they had used the sink and its hot water to have a rudimentary wash and, in the case of the men, a shave, their first since leaving Norway.

Peter Wenck had insisted on one pilot always staying in the cockpit in readiness for a quick take-off. He was determined that at no stage would they be caught unawares. The minutes ticked by.

"This afternoon siesta you mentioned, how long does it take?"

"Oh, usually it takes from three to five hours, give or take an hour-or-so," said Meunier with a wide grin. He seemed to have re-gained his sunny disposition, the tears of a few minutes ago banished in the general well-being of the sunny Dominican afternoon.

Time dragged on. Then the stillness was broken by the sound of an aircraft engine firing up, quickly followed by the sound of a second engine coming to life. Both were obviously of the same type. After a few seconds, the noise dropped in crescendo and the engines could be heard idling. The two Wencks ran to the farthest hangar and peeped around the front in the direction of the aerodrome's administration buildings. They could see a dozen white-uniformed figures standing about twenty-five metres from a large twin-engined passenger plane.

"Curtis, a C46 transport," said the pilot in a low voice, his aircraft recognition impeccable as always.

"It's probably the American legation Savory was talking about."

They watched in silence as the transport's door closed and the pilot once again revved up the engines and began taxiing away from the terminal towards the main runway. On reaching it the American pilot did not hesitate, turning the big transport onto the flight line and immediately accelerating away. Once airborne, the plane banked to its right, away from the hangars and the parked Boeing, and headed south in a shallow climb in the direction of the Dominican capital.

The two Germans hurried back towards their own aircraft. Swabisch got into the cockpit in readiness for a hurried take-off. Peter Wenck wanted to stay outside with his father and Meunier, but the Luftwaffe general pulled rank.

"No, Peter, I want you inside. Man the front Browning. Put Friedrich in the top turret since this means he will not be able to use it unless the engines are started and you or I give the order to shoot."

The two older men then dragged the two chairs clear of the plane and sat down. The general took the safety off his big Colt and stuck it in his trouser belt in the small of his back. It was uncomfortable, but he ignored the pressure on his spine.

They did not have long to wait. The sound of the Ford could be heard and seconds later it had stopped only a few metres from the seated Germans. Both rose as a tall immaculately-dressed officer stepped from the car and moved towards them.

"Colonel Savory, I presume?" said Helmuth Wenck in English. His European accent was not noticeable.

The other man nodded and also spoke in English, his accent also impeccable. "I trust your rank is accurate, for I know the uniform is a misnomer."

"Yes, Colonel, the rank is genuine and so is the authority it represents. And yes, I do not hold the rank of general in the US Air Force."

Savory smiled and gave a crisp salute. He was a handsome man. Dark-haired, a little above average height, with soft brown eyes and a small, neatly trimmed moustache. The general returned the salute and Savory turned to Meunier. "And now, my old friend, Conrad. How are you?"

"Fine, fine, thank you, Colonel. How is the family?"

"Thank you, they are well. The two girls are now thirteen and ten years old. The boy, my son, is almost nine." His voice showed the pride in his heir.

Wenck listened impatiently as the two chatted. In exasperation he finally broke into the conversation. "Colonel Savory, the gasoline. You have it as agreed?"

The Dominican nodded and then asked whether they had the $50,000 as promised. Both Germans smiled at each other, though there was no mirth in the gesture, rather a 'I told you so' weariness. Meunier had warned his friend that Savory would probably try to extract more money from them, although the scope of the increase surprised them.

"This is the most corrupt country in all the Americas, and as you know that is certainly saying something," said the diplomat. "Colonel. Our agreement was for $10,000," he said, a querulous edge to his voice.

"I know, I know," said Savory in a cajoling voice. "But I have had added expenses, a few extra payments." He did not use the word bribes.

Helmuth Wenck's voice went hard. "And pray, what happens if we won't pay this extra amount?"

"Why then, you will have to stay here until the Americans discover your presence. I'm sure they would like to get their aeroplane back."

"Now you listen, Savory, and you listen very carefully for there will be no argument and no negotiation. I am a man of my word and we have nothing to lose. If the gasoline is not here in five minutes we will take-off and then we will machine-gun this base until it's so full of holes the rats will think it's cheese. Understand?" Savory's eyes went dark and he nodded very slowly, never taking his eyes from the German's face. "And just to make sure there is no attempt at a double-cross, there is somebody up there in our plane's nose with a nice heavy-calibre machine-gun. You will stay here until the gasoline is delivered."

"Very well, General, I will comply. But, I stress I will need more money."

"We can give you another $10,000. That's $20,000 in total. Unless you have paid an unnecessary amount in bribes, it is a small fortune."

Savory's eyes lit up at the amount. The offer went some way to salvaging his pride in the face of the German general's threats and stubbornness. Still, he thought, I can always have a word in the ear of the Americans about these people.

Helmuth Wenck almost read his mind. "Oh, and one more thing, Colonel. I know you don't know of our destination and South America is a big place but, if anybody starts checking on our whereabouts, and we get to hear of it, believe me, we have the means of finding out. Instructions will be sent to our agents and your family will suffer. Do I make myself clear?"

The threat seemed to have a salutary effect on the Dominican colonel. He turned to the man in the car and spoke to him in rapid Spanish. The car drove away and returned almost immediately followed by two small tankers.

"Will you instruct my men on how to fill your aircraft?" asked Savory.

Helmuth Wenck shook his head. He did not want any of the Dominicans near the bomber, so he called for Swabisch to come outside and together they coupled the hoses to the fuel tanks while the Dominican Air Force personnel manned the valves on the trucks.

Before loading the fuel into the Boeing, Peter Wenck vacated his position in the nose and carefully questioned Colonel Savory on the origins of the fuel and its potency. To his relief, the Dominican's reply was as good as could be hoped. "Do not worry on that score, Senor. The fuel comes from the United States and in fact was used on the legation's transport aircraft this afternoon. It is top grade, I assure you."

He hoped the man was not lying, so to placate his suspicions, he made some simple checks on the aviation fuel. Before starting to fill the Boeing's tanks and, several times during the operation, he filled a glass jar with the petrol and held it to the light. In all four cases it was clear of condensation and contamination. However, there was no way to verify its octane rating.

These checks, combined with the poor capacity of the pumps and the need to fill both tankers again, meant the operation took almost an hour-and-a-half. This amount of fuel clearly worried Savory. To placate him Helmuth Wenck said he would compensate him with some extra money, over and above the promise of $20,000. At this offer he visibly brightened, although he was curious at the amount of petrol being pumped into the bomber.

"Senors, your aeroplane is a flying petrol tank. You must have a long way to go?"

It was a question, not a statement, and to further confuse the man the elder Wenck reinforced his earlier lie. "Yes, we are carrying a lot of fuel, but then Argentina is a long way from here, is it not?"

Savory nodded in agreement and nothing more was said.

With the re-fuelling finished, Savory was asked to wait while Helmuth Wenck, his son and the diplomat held a short council.

They had originally hoped to spend the night at Puerto Plata and leave in the morning. That way they would have arrived at their destination at nightfall when they could mask much of their

339

features. As well, they reasoned, it was less likely any senior American officers would be on duty.

Now they were not sure what to do. Savory's attempts at blackmail worried them and the presence of the American legation so near at hand was also cause for concern. Reluctantly they decided to vacate the Dominican base straight away. Peter Wenck consulted his watch and did a quick calculation.

It was almost half-past-five. If they left immediately they would reach their destination early the following morning. Although it was not as good as landing at dusk, it might just be the next best thing.

The pilot was somewhat rested, but his father was still worried. Another flight of between fifteen and sixteen hours would almost finish him. "I agree. We should leave now, but only on one condition. Once we have taken off and are clear of landfall, Leo will take over. Is that understood?"

The son looked at his father and gave a smile that contained little mirth. "Father, I am too old to be told what to do. Also, I am too good a pilot to be told what I can or cannot do in my aircraft. I will make the decisions." He raised his eyebrows in a gesture that was not a plea for agreement, rather a bald statement of fact. He then turned his back and strode towards the crew hatch. "Oh, and you had better pay the colonel," he said over his shoulder.

The general waited outside while Meunier followed the pilot back inside the fuselage. He went to one of the sacks that he knew contained foreign currency and extracted several wads of American dollars. Satisfied with the amount he went back outside.

Much to the Dominican's delight he handed over $30,000. "Thank you, Colonel. There is $30,000 in these bundles, almost all the American money we have. I trust you are satisfied?" The colonel nodded his head, a wide smile creasing his lips. The smile vanished though, at Meunier's parting words. "And please remember the general's warning. I know you have had Hertel neutralised, but we have other agents and other people on our payroll. Therefore, it would be in your best interest if it is never known about our stay here."

Savory said he understood. He stuffed the bank notes into his pockets until they bulged and, turning away, spoke rapidly in Spanish to his men. The two tankers moved off leaving only the Ford. Without a backward glance, he got inside and drove away.

As Meunier walked towards the crew entrance, one of Miss Nonalee Two's Wrights coughed into life. By the time he had closed the hatch two were running sweetly and the propeller on the third was beginning to turn. When all four were bellowing in unison, Swabisch and Peter Wenck completed their cockpit check and, with nothing amiss, the co-pilot released the brakes and his partner gunned the engines, easing the Boeing out of its hideaway and onto the apron in front of the hangars. Seconds later they were trundling down the same taxi-way negotiated by the Curtis Commando a short time before and, like the American pilot, Wenck did not hesitate when the Boeing reached the runway. He opened the throttles and the B17 gathered speed, leaving the long runway halfway down the tarmac.

Once the wheels had tucked themselves into their housing and the flaps had been retracted, he banked the aircraft to starboard as though he was flying east. He continued on this heading for ten minutes and when the land had fully disappeared turned in a wide arc to port so they were flying roughly north-east. Fifteen minutes later he swung to his left again and in another ten minutes turned slightly to his right, aligning the aircraft so it would pass between the eastern tip of Cuba and the southern tip of the island of Great Inagua.

Although the sun was already sinking low in the horizon, the sky was still a brilliant blue and only a few remnants of the recent storm clouds hung in the sky. Up ahead the clouds petered out completely.

For a moment, he forgot all about Meunier's ghastly revelations.

The view through the Perspex was simply breathtaking and in appreciation of its beauty he turned to Swabisch and gave him a friendly punch on his left shoulder. His old comrade understood what the pilot felt. They were climbing slowly and he checked both altimeters before adjusting the turbo boost on all four engines.

Miss Nonalee Two droned homeward.

Chapter Thirty-Two
26 March 1945

2200 Hours

The Boeing's original altimeter indicated they were flying at 10,000 feet, or 3,000 metres by the German instrument. The reduced height and slightly higher speed of just over 300 kilometres per hour was indicative of the shortened length of this, the final leg of their long journey.

The night sky was clear, the stars twinkling and the moon shining a broad benevolent smile down at them. A dozen or so kilometres off their starboard wing tip they could see a few dim lights. Peter Wenck sitting in the co-pilot's seat was still wide awake, living on adrenalin and nervous tension. He pointed to the lights and Swabisch asked what they were.

Wenck consulted his map and did a rapid calculation.

"Could be Key West, although one would think the Americans would not be so stupid as to have no blackout. I mean, during 1942 and early 1943 our U-Boats laid waste to these waters, so much so they called it the happy hunting ground."

The Straits of Florida were already behind them. Cuba was some 120 kilometres due south and Cape Sable on the tip of the Florida peninsular some 140 kilometres to the north-east. Miss Nonalee Two was now heading into the Gulf of Mexico.

Half-an-hour later and now deep into the Gulf it was time for Miss Nonalee Two to change course. Helmuth Wenck, awake at his position in the navigator's compartment, switched on his intercom and gave them a new heading. It was a minor change and would enable the bomber to fly in an uninterrupted straight line to their destination.

They crossed the coast into Texas about halfway between Galveston and Freeport. Heavy cloud obscured this momentous event, but to their relief it gradually dissipated so, by the time they were 200 kilometres inside the United States, the sky was clear once more. The further in from the coast they flew the more lights they saw.

"Mein Gott!"

Swabisch's exclamation made Wenck jump. He had been dozing, his tiredness finally catching up with him.

To their right the ground was a blaze of light signifying a large city. Wenck called up his father who also exclaimed in wonder. To the crew it was an amazing sight. For the past few years the only lights seen by German aircrew at night were burning cities, the glare of searchlights and the flashes of anti-aircraft fire.

Helmuth Wenck was busy searching a map covering part of Louisiana, all of southern Texas and most of northern Mexico. His son, whose map was not as large or detailed, was doing the same, asked him what town it was. The parent told him to wait a few moments and then finding the spot, said exultantly. "Austin. It's Austin, Texas."

They were on course and travelling well.

The entire group stared out of their respective windows and canopies at the vista of the city's lights. The scene was so foreign to what they had been used to that most were for a moment quite bereft of speech.

The scene had an effect on all of them, though in very different ways and for the first time brought home fully to each just how close they were to succeeding and that in this success their lives would be irrevocably changed.

As the B17 continued on its journey, they were left with their thoughts, expectations and doubts.

Of the six it was the SS officer who was the most worried. For most of his life Friedrich Schonewille had felt adrift from those of his social strata. It was not until he joined the Nazi party that he had fully felt a part of something. It had given him prestige, power and a strong sense of belonging. It had also given him the opportunity to exorcise those hatreds and inferiorities that had bedevilled him most of his life.

Now, devoid of all that which had given a status and anchor to his life he was becoming quite frightened and unsure of his future. To divest himself of his uniform, soon after leaving Guernsey, had

343

been a traumatic thing. It was like shedding a protective armour. The action at El Aiun had for a brief moment given him a sense of importance, of belonging, both to and with the group but, since then, he had felt insignificant and useless.

In part these feelings of lack of worth were compounded by the attitude of his mistress. Sophia continued to be distant and evasive to his questions and attempts at intimacy, reduced as they were because of the proximity of the other travellers.

As they stared at the lights Schonewille fully understood for the first time just how alien was the culture of the country they were about to embrace. Strangely, he had never given much thought to their ultimate destination. He had never travelled outside Germany, even though his English was quite passable and he spoke a little Italian. His primary thought in leaving the country of his birth had been to escape the wrath and vengeance of the Allied troops, for he was under no illusion of what would happen to him in a conquered Germany. Although he had not been a party to the actual wholesale killing at the camps he had known what was going on and had personally executed a dozen or so members of the German intelligentsia.

He looked across at Sophia crouched a metre or so away as she stared at the scene below. Out of the corner of her eye she saw Schonewille staring at her and without hesitation she stretched out a hand to him. The effect on the SS officer was, to her, quite astounding. He took her hand in both of his and in the dim light she could seen tears welling up in his eyes. She had never seen such a display of emotion from him in all their time together.

"Danke, liebchen," he said.

He bent forward and kissed her hand and for a moment she felt a degree of tenderness for the man who had risked so much to rescue her from almost certain death. Yet, in part, the tenderness was because she knew what she intended doing, how her main aim now was to be rid of him and as much of her past as she could possibly shed.

For Schonewille her gesture had a strong calming effect and for a short while at least enabled him to feel more positive about his future.

344

Meanwhile, Meunier, lolling back on his seat by the radio, also felt at peace. All was working according to plan. On leaving the Dominican Republic he had been able to make contact with his agent who had been waiting just outside the town of Prescott 120 kilometres north of Phoenix.

The diplomat was looking forward to his future life. His only regret was his wife and how she would not be able to join him. Yet, he knew that where he wanted to go female companionship would not be hard to find. He had no intention of staying in the United States. Mexico was not too far away and with money and his American passport he would be able to live like a king within its borders.

In the navigator's station Helmuth Wenck stared at the unfolding panorama of the American south-west, the area made so famous by the cowboy novels and films of his youth. He knew the area well and he wished it was already daylight so he could see the desert landscape. Yet even at night it was enough to see the lights of the towns and the occasional solitary light of some isolated ranch to visualise what was below.

He too doubted whether he would make the United States his home. To a degree it would depend on his wife, for his longing for the woman, now that he was free to join her, was extreme. Five years was a long time. He intended travelling to Halifax and contacting her from there. If she wanted him to travel to Iceland he would do so and risk recognition, for he was well-known in the small island community. His fervent hope was that she would join him in America and from there they would journey to Canada or, if this was not favoured then the northern reaches of the United States where the weather was more conducive to their way of life. His favourite place in the USA had always been Montana.

In the cockpit, both pilots had vastly different dreams.

True to his nature, Captain Leo Swabisch had never given too much thought as to his reasons for escaping. Peter Wenck's going was enough for him join the band. Of course, this had been strengthened by the thought of seeing America and doing so with enough money to live without a care in the world for the rest of his life. The thought of all those American women made his loins twitch whenever he thought about them, which was often. For a short time before the war he had been a skiing instructor in the Alps, albeit a very junior one and it had never ceased to amaze him how willing the American women were to make love with any instructor once they had spent a few days on the slopes. It was through these women that he had polished his schoolboy English, especially the words designed to ingratiate himself and then arouse the opposite sex.

Although he had not discussed his future at any length with his friend, he was hoping to be able to stay with Peter Wenck, at least for the short term.

The plane's commander looked at his watch. It read just after four in the morning: they had been in the air for ten-and-a-half hours. He made a mental calculation as to the correct local time and came up with somewhere between one and one-thirty in the morning.

Peter Wenck had always had very definitive ideas as to what he wanted to do once he reached America. His years both in the United States and England had given him a good command of English as well as a reasonable understanding of what drove these two cousins and what needed to be done to survive in the American culture. He too wanted to see his mother, but he had no intention of either travelling to or living in Iceland.

While still in Norway the two Wencks had held numerous discussions on their future once they had escaped the Reich and reached America. This they had continued during their brief sojourn in the Dominican Republic. To their consternation, this last discussion had only reinforced the realisation of how both wanted different things.

His father now only wanted a quiet life. To him the wealth in the bomber represented protection from being caught by the Allies and the ability to live a restful, stress-free life with his wife. He had originally hoped to have both sons with him, though he now acknowledged this would not happen. The revelation of Schonewille's link with the concentration camps so sickened him that all he wanted was for his first born to disappear from his life forever.

346

As for Peter, he knew his adventurous second born still had a lot of living to do and his share of the money would only increase his ability to sample more of life.

In truth, his father's thoughts were not strictly correct.

Peter Wenck's one abiding wish was to continue flying, possibly in control of a small airline. This would bring some problems since he would have to re-train and re-gain his flying licence under his new identity. He had hoped he might ultimately be able to return to using his real name even though he quickly realised how this might bring about a number of difficulties into his new life.

In the meantime, his thoughts kept returning to operating a small feeder line in Canada or Alaska. Maybe Leo Swabisch would join him?

Wenck's mind then turned to the Jewess. He felt very attracted to the woman, though intuitively he knew she would have nothing whatever to do with him, not because of her relationship with his brother, but because of his German nationality. This thought allowed his mind to stray and he recalled Meunier's demeanour on revealing the details of the camps. The subject was so horrific and still so new that he was still not able to face it squarely, so he quickly turned his mind to other things.

He drifted into sleep as Miss Nonalee Two droned on. They crossed into New Mexico and shortly after flew over the Pecos River and passed south of the small town of Stanton. Then it was over the Rio Grande and into the mountains north of Silver City.

Their destination was a large airfield in the Arizona desert, almost halfway on a line running north-west between the towns of Prescott and Boulder City. A few hours more and they would be landing for the last time.

Leo Swabisch checked the instruments, a continuous check on the pulse of the aircraft, yet in their dull glow he saw no reason to worry. Boeing's finest was behaving herself like the thoroughbred she was.

Chapter Thirty-Three
27 March 1945

0600 Hours

Dawn revealed the full vista of the American south-west. The desert stretching away across the horizon, a range of mountains rose to their north and finally a huge airfield, jam-packed with aircraft under their wings. Had they arrived?

Helmuth Wenck took another reading just to make certain: thirty-five degrees, twelve minutes north by 114 degrees, four minutes west. Yes, this was it.

A nervous excitement permeated through the aircraft feeding from person to person.

Meunier had no difficulty in raising the airfield's control tower but, to his consternation, they were not expected. A sleepy voice in a slow southern drawl at first did not seem at all interested in who they were or where they were from.

It was now time to put their plan into action. Helmuth Wenck switched his radio mike to send.

"Now you listen here, son," he said in his most authoritative tone. "This is General Hanson and if you are real nice you can call me Dutch Hanson like the rest of my boys ... do you read me?"

The Dutch pseudonym was an idea of Meunier's to cover his friend's accent. There was a stunned silence on the other end of the radio.

"Sir, yes Sir, I'm listening, Sir!"

"Good. Now, what's you name, son?"

"Corporal Ruthven Kent, Sir!"

"Right, son. I want you to have a Jeep ready at the end of the main runway to direct us to a spot as far from your administration buildings as possible. Do you understand?"

Kent said hesitantly that he understood, so Wenck enquired whether there was a truck waiting for them. The answer was in the negative, yet the corporal took the initiative and said he would check to make certain.

While the line was dead, Helmuth Wenck spoke to Meunier over the intercom and asked him for the third time in the past hour what had been arranged with their American contact. The diplomat's answer showed his irritation.

"I've told you before, Helmuth. I spoke to him shortly after we last took off. It was all arranged. He would meet us here with a large lorry shortly after dawn. He would be in an American Air Force uniform."

They continued circling and then the voice of the American corporal came back on the radio.

"Sir, General Hanson, Sir, there is a truck and a lieutenant waiting for you at the guardhouse. He arrived an hour or so back. What do you want him to do, Sir?"

Peter Wenck punched a fist into his palm in exultation and Helmuth Wenck breathed a deep sigh of relief. It was almost too easy. He dared hope.

"Tell the lieutenant to follow the Jeep and meet us at the end of the runway and then, like I said, direct us to a spot as far from your administration buildings as possible."

"Yes, Sir. Sir! The base commander is not on duty at the moment. Do you want me to have him sent for?"

Wenck said it was not necessary and explained how his aircraft was carrying a great deal of secret equipment and he did not want anybody from the base present when it was unloaded. He then requested clearance to land.

Peter Wenck motioned Swabisch to start on their landing drill.

Despite knowing the drill almost by heart, Wenck was determined nothing should go wrong with the landing for he was aware how any mistake could bring unwelcome attention to their aircraft.

Swabisch put the pilot's check-list on his lap as Peter Wenck called the tower and introduced himself. The pilot then asked for the airfield's altimeter setting and enquired whether there were any specific details he needed to know about landing at the base. The former was given crisply and efficiently and while Swabisch set about making sure all the switches controlling the automatic pilot were in the take-off position, the pilot listened as Corporal Kent informed him there was a stiff cross-wind cutting across the main runway.

"Booster Pumps ... on. Mixture controls ... auto rich ... and intercoolers, off," said the co-pilot in English, half to himself as much as to Wenck.

Although they had all found it hard, it had been agreed that from the moment they left the Dominican Republic all conversation should be in English, especially the aircrew conversation.

"Peter, you know, I'm beginning to like being an American," joked Swabisch with a mocking half smile.

"Fine, fine. But let's not get side-tracked. Please continue with the check-list."

With a wind blowing, he expected a fair degree of dust and sand from what was essentially a desert airfield, so Wenck asked his friend to activate the carburetor filters to the engines. "De-icer boots?"

"Off, as well as the propeller anti-icers."

"Check landing gear warning light."

"Checked ... and there, it's working."

Wenck noted the airspeed, 155 miles per hour, so it was safe to put the undercarriage down. Swabisch turned his head from side-to-side and confirmed both legs were fully extended and then confirmed the brakes were off. It would be disastrous if they landed with the brakes on. Such a mistake would mean at best two blown tyres and, at worst, two collapsed undercarriages.

"Tail wheel down." He then returned the undercarriage switch back to neutral and told the pilot the warning light was safely on green.

Together they checked the hydraulic pressure. All normal at 800 pounds, followed by the operation of the hydraulic pump.

"It's fine. Over 300 PSI."

"Cowl flap controls?"

"Neutral, Peter. Ah she is a lovely plane. Everything always seems to work perfectly."

Wenck grinned and banked Miss Nonalee Two a little so she was properly aligned with the runway. His friend was right. The

350

bomber was a jewel. She had never missed a beat or given them an ounce of trouble. He would miss her.

He increased engine revs to 2,200 and decreased the manifold pressure to twenty-three inches. A moment's hesitation and then he requested his co-pilot turn the turbo controls to full on and then re-adjust the manifold pressure.

With the airspeed just above 140 miles an hour, the Boeing's flaps were lowered halfway and he began his final approach.

"Do you think the wind is too high to use full flaps?" he checked, his tiredness making him cautious.

"No, but be careful," answered Swabisch.

The wind was coming from his left, so he lifted his starboard wing slightly to reduce the lift on his port wing. And then, just to make sure, he crabbed the plane slightly into the wind and eased her down. It was a copybook landing.

"Ten out of ten. That dude knows how to handle a babe," remarked Corporal Kent to his assistant in the control tower.

As they rolled down the end of the runway, Wenck began gently applying the aircraft's brakes. Swabisch made a quick check of the hydraulic pressure and opened the cowl flaps of the engines. The turbos were turned off as were the booster pumps.

"Raise flaps?"

"Yes, raise them and cut the inboard engines."

They spied the Jeep at the end of the runway and as the vehicle moved off he gunned the two outer engines and turned to follow. There was a fair amount of dust being blown up by the two airscrews, but the aircraft moved easily enough, even when the ground became rougher. There were rows and rows of aircraft stretched into the distance on either side, all silent and forlorn.

To think all are destined for the wrecker's torch, he thought and felt very sad. This was no way for his beloved aeroplane to end, it was something akin to murder. Yet, he knew there was no alternative and, in fact, was shortly to initiate something that would hasten Miss Nonalee Two's demise.

They taxied for almost five minutes until at last a figure in the back of the Jeep waved them to a spot at the end of a long line of dormant aircraft. Applying the brake to one wheel he swung the big bomber around and then gunned the engines for a second or so to bring her into line with the nearest aircraft. When he was in the right spot, he switched off the two remaining engines.

For a moment he sat still, scarcely believing it was all over. They had arrived and never again would he sit in the cockpit of this plane. It was like the aftermath of lovemaking: sadness that the climax was over and yet relief that his part of their plans had come to a successful conclusion.

Out of the corner of his eye he noticed his co-pilot looking questioningly at him and in answer, gave an apologetic smile.

"Sorry. I was just realising I won't be flying her ever again and, ah, never mind. You'd better switch everything off."

Swabisch nodded in understanding and moved to complete his tasks. He first turned off all electrical switches followed by the master and battery switches.

Wenck's last acts were to move the control column fully forward, place the rudder pedals in neutral, raise the floor lock and place the aileron lock in the control wheel. The bomber was now safe from any wind or unauthorised use.

He looked at a small, innocuous dun-coloured switch protected by a flip-top cover mounted on the instrument panel on his left next to the fluorescent light switches.

No, he thought. I'll leave it for a moment.

He moved to the back of the aircraft followed by his father. It had been decided that at first, everybody except the two Wencks and Meunier should stay in the plane. The latter was dressed in an imposing grey-green suit and his role was to impersonate a scientist.

A sergeant stepped out of the Jeep and saluted Helmuth Wenck.

"General Hanson, Sir. Your truck is here, Sir," he said unnecessarily as a huge M32 six-wheel drive-truck bearing US Air Force markings drove up and stopped near the tail gunner's position.

A man in the uniform of an air force first lieutenant climbed down from the cabin, walked over to the three Germans and saluted. "Sir, Lootenant Ray Kiefer – reporting as ordered!"

Wenck returned the salute and looked over the man's shoulders.

352

There was another man in the cabin of the truck sitting behind the steering wheel.

"Who's in there, Lieutenant?" he said raising a hand in the direction of the vehicle.

"Oh that, Sir, is Private Garcia, my driver."

Inwardly Helmuth Wenck frowned, yet he knew it would have appeared a little strange if Kiefer as a full lieutenant had arrived driving that monster by himself. He motioned to his son.

"Lieutenant, this is Colonel Peter Wyatt."

Kiefer saluted and Peter Wenck returned the gesture, but did not speak.

Wherever he comes from, he must at one time have been in one of the military services, reasoned Helmuth Wenck, and looked at the man closely.

Lieutenant Kiefer was tall, well-built and carried himself with confidence. He moved easily and his gaze was steady. His demeanour exuded confidence and yet there was something about him that annoyed the elder Wenck. Without thinking the matter over deeply he finally decided it was the man's moustache, a thin straight affair that somewhat spoilt his manly bearing and looks.

Helmuth Wenck turned away and spoke to the sergeant who was standing watching with obvious curiosity.

"Sergeant, I want you to take your vehicle to the end of this row of aircraft and keep watch. We are going to unload some top secret equipment from our plane and I do not want anybody from this base to be nearby when we do so, understand?"

The man acknowledged that he did, saluted and got back into his Jeep. The driver gunned the engine and moved to the end of the nearest row of aircraft about 300 metres away.

"Now, Kiefer, get your man from the truck and help us unload our plane." Then as an afterthought he added, "And I must congratulate you on your timing and planning."

Kiefer's face showed little emotion. He inclined his head in acknowledgment and walked over to his truck. A few words were said to the man in the cabin and Private Garcia emerged.

If Kiefer was an impressive figure, Garcia certainly was the antithesis of this. Short, swarthy, about thirty years of age with a countenance that probably even his mother had not liked. His uniform was clean enough, though it fitted him like an old potato sack. His teeth when he smiled (if that's what it could be called) were the colour of the desert under his feet.

Peter Wenck went to the crew hatch and in a quiet voice asked the others to disembark.

In order to keep up with appearances, Helmuth Wenck stood back and took no part in unloading the aircraft or the loading of the truck. He just stood by, watched and directed proceedings. After five minutes or so he gave up on Kiefer. The man showed little emotion yet Garcia was another matter entirely. He was sly, that much was obvious, though even more worrying was the realisation that he knew the boxes and sacks contained valuables. The greed on his face was patently clear and once, when he thought nobody was looking, he even tried to open one of the sacks. He was seen by Meunier who curtly told him to desist.

Once the truck was loaded, Helmuth Wenck instructed Meunier, Sophia and Schonewille to climb into the back of the truck while Kiefer and Garcia should get back into the cabin. He then took his son by the shoulder and they walked back to the crew entry hatch. Peter Wenck asked his father to hold the door.

"Hold it carefully, don't let it slam," he warned as he grabbed both edges of the hatchway and hauled himself inside. Once back in the cockpit, he leant over his seat and lifted the protective cap on the dun coloured switch and flicked it on. A small light mounted next to the switch and connected to a separate battery came to life. Satisfied that the system was now active, he made his way back down the fuselage and climbed outside. Carefully taking the hatch cover from his father he gingerly pushed it shut and turned the handle.

"There," he said. "It's now primed."

The switch on the instrument panel controlled two incendiary devices: one next to the huge overload tanks in the bomb bay and one situated next to the main starboard wing tank. Since the device was now primed, the incendiaries would be activated in ten days time. As an added precaution Peter Wenck had also had the device wired to the door handle on the crew hatch. Anybody attempting to enter the aircraft would set off the device.

Miss Nonalee Two still carried a great deal of fuel and the incendiary devices were designed to set off a conflagration that would reduce the B17 to a twisted mass.

Originally, it had been decided not to destroy the bomber, but after further discussion they had come to the conclusion it would be too risky just abandoning the aircraft. Apart from the German instruments, there were the extra fuel tanks and the absence of the ball turret. All these might conceivably cause questions. The last thing they wanted was for the Americans to begin an investigation into the origins of this bomber.

Hopefully, by the time Miss Nonalee Two caught fire they would all be long gone and if any questions were asked, their whereabouts and identity would be a complete mystery.

Peter Wenck got into the back of the truck while his father climbed into the cabin with Kiefer and Garcia. He told the latter to drive towards the sergeant in the Jeep. When they reached the smaller vehicle Helmuth Wenck alighted and motioned the sergeant over.

"Sergeant, my aircraft is to remain untouched, do you understand? The other nodded his head.

"Sir, is she being struck off?" Wenck hesitated and before he could speak the sergeant continued.

"I mean, if she is being struck off, Sir, where is her status card? As you know, Sir, we must have it otherwise, we cannot get the paperwork in order."

Wenck cursed inwardly. They had presumed some sort of paperwork would be necessary but unfortunately they had no means of finding out the exact details. He guessed the status card was some sort of record of the aircraft, something quite separate from her log book. Even if he possessed this card, he felt it would have been too risky to hand it over.

He put an extra measure of menace in his voice.

"Sergeant, I want you to listen carefully. My aircraft is very, very special. It has been used for some top secret tests and although we have removed nearly all the special equipment nobody must go inside her. I will have a special team of people come here in about three weeks to completely strip her. Then you can have her status card, but not before. Now do you understand what I've said?"

The man looked perplexed, yet said he understood. It was all too much for him, that was obvious. He now quite plainly wanted to get away from the general.

Wenck dismissed him and then climbed back into the big truck and they drove between the rows of aircraft, past the administration buildings towards the main gate.

They stopped at the boom and the private at the guardhouse took one look at the general's two stars and quickly saluted. He opened the boom gate with alacrity and then they were through and driving with increasing speed up a fairly wide tarmac road.

"Where do we go from here?" he asked Kiefer.

The man answered with a degree of arrogance, which once again set off warning bells in Helmuth Wenck's mind. "We have to get rid of this truck. I have a place fifty miles away where we have some other vehicles. Then we can decide what has to be done."

Wenck did not like the use of the term "we", but said and did nothing except nod his head.

Some thirty-five miles from the airfield they turned off onto a dirt road that gradually petered out until it was no more than a rough track, though several tyre marks were plainly evident. The track climbed up an escarpment and then meandered around some low, craggy hills. Garcia seemed to be a competent driver and although he crashed the gears a couple of times they made steady progress.

Twenty minutes later, they turned right up another track and about a mile further on came upon an old derelict cabin set amidst some ancient and rusting mining equipment.

The M32 came to a halt and Kiefer turned to Wenck. "Okay, General, here we are. Now get out!" The tone was harsh and Wenck did not bother to argue, for Kiefer was pointing an automatic at his left ear.

As he climbed down from the cabin Garcia alighted from the driver's side. He too carried an automatic in his right hand. At the same time a third man emerged from behind the shack carrying an M30 carbine.

356

Chapter Thirty-Four

To the four sitting awkwardly in the back of the truck, the trip had not been at all comfortable. Although the back was covered by canvas, it still let in dust and exhaust fumes and since the flap was also fastened shut to avoid passers-by or following vehicles see what was inside, the interior was also fairly dark and very stuffy.

While the other three attempted to make themselves comfortable, Schonewille examined his surroundings. As well as the boxes and sacks carrying the Reichsbank treasure there were a number of large crates plus a large tarpaulin lying half-folded near the front.

The front of the tray where it butted up to the cabin was solid and, consequently, there was no window through which they could see into the cabin.

As the truck continued on its journey, Schonewille kept peering through the gap in the canvas to see where they were going. When they stopped, he saw his father emerge and was just about to move to the rear of the truck when he spied Kiefer with a gun in his hand. At the same time he saw the man with the carbine emerge from the direction of the shack.

He understood immediately what was happening. He turned to his companions. "It's a trap," he hissed. "Whatever you do, don't let them know about me," he whispered.

With that he crawled under the tarpaulin and lay still as the third man pulled open the canvas.

"All right you, get out, make it quick ... and don't try anything!" His voice was agitated and his manner nervous.

While the three climbed out, blinking at the sunshine, he stepped back and then motioned them clear of the vehicle. At the same time, Garcia and Kiefer directed Helmuth Wenck towards them.

"Okay, Manuel, search them. We'll keep them covered. These Krauts will all be armed, not just those in uniform ... Hey wait a minute. I thought there were six ... Jesus where ..."

Kiefer swung round towards the truck just as Schonewille wrenched open a corner of the canvas hood and fired two shots from his Walther. Both bullets struck Kiefer in the body and he lurched backwards clutching his belly. Garcia, who had been lasciviously running his hands over Sophia's breasts, moved backwards and tried to jerk his automatic from his trouser belt where he had stuck it in order to free his hands.

As the Mexican turned to face the truck, Peter Wenck aimed a vicious kick that caught him from behind, the toe catching the inside of his thighs before striking his testicles. The man gave a hoarse, agonised grunt, fell to his knees and then, ignoring the pain, attempted to turn and raise his weapon towards the pilot.

By this time Peter Wenck had freed his Colt automatic from its holster and he pulled the trigger three times without taking proper aim. The first two shots missed, while the third bullet struck Garcia in the face next to his nose, its exit taking away half the back of his head.

In the meantime, Swabisch and Helmuth Wenck had succeeded in disarming the third man who had been knocked to the ground in the struggle. Kiefer was lying on the ground moaning, the front of his uniform soaked in blood.

Schonewille jumped from the back of the truck, his face flushed. The man's quick thinking had undoubtedly saved them, but before anybody could thank him, he strode up to Kiefer, raised his automatic and fired three times into the man's body. Kiefer stopped moaning. Sophia screamed and Helmuth Wenck yelled at him to stop.

Schonewille whirled round, his face hostile. "Do not order me around, Father," he said in German. "That Schweinehund deserved to die. Do you think they had any intention of letting us live? Well, do you?"

There was silence for a moment and then the SS officer moved forward to the third man who was by now sitting up, a look of abject fear on his face.

"Stehen Sie auf Sie Schwein," said Schonewille, jerking his gun upwards. The man did not understand, so Schonewille had to repeat his order in English before the man did as he was told.

He rose unsteadily staring at Schonewille in hapless terror.

"Now tell me what you were going to do with us." His heavily accented English leant a measure of menace to the interrogation.

The man began to stammer, claiming he wanted nothing to do with any killing, that the others had planned the whole thing.

Schonewille's face went blotchy with rage and his voice dropped to a low hiss. "Tell me, my friend. Where were your comrades planning to dispose of the bodies?"

For a moment the man misread the menace in Schonewille's voice. "In there, they planned to put you in there and blow the entrance." He pointed to the entrance of a mineshaft sunk into the wall of a cliff some fifty metres away.

"But I tell you … no, no," he screamed as Schonewille lifted the Walther and quite calmly sighted the barrel before firing twice. The man was dead before his body hit the rocky ground.

"Jesus, Friedrich, stop this at once! Now give me your gun," roared his father. He moved towards his son who took a step back and again raised the weapon.

"No, Father. You stay clear. From now on we will do things my way, I have had …"

Nobody knew what made Swabisch move forward. He was more than five metres away and never had a hope of bridging the gap before Schonewille shot him.

Peter Wenck yelled in horror as his friend sank to his knees, a comical look of surprise on his face. Ignoring his brother, he moved forward and, kneeling down, caught his friend just as he pitched forward. Gently turning him round he laid him on his back, but just as he completed the act the surprised look went out of Swabisch's eyes and he died.

For a moment there was a horrified silence, and then Peter Wenck raised his head, his face stone hard and his eyes the colour of winter sleet.

"You fucking turd, you fucking miserable lump of shit," his voice choked as he rose.

Schonewille's face was deadly white. Whether he had intended killing Swabisch or had acted without thinking would never be known. Now, confronted by the implacable wrath of his brother, he made as if to raise his weapon again when a shot rang out. Schonewille staggered backwards and dropped the Walther. They all turned in the direction of the shot.

Sophia was standing quite still, her left hand holding her right wrist and her right hand holding a small automatic. She lowered the gun as Schonewille coughed, a reddish froth on his lips. Slowly his legs buckled and he half fell, half lowered himself to the ground like an athlete exhausted after a long run.

The Jewess let the weapon fall from her hands and quickly moved to the stricken man. She knelt beside him and cradled his head in her lower body. Schonewille attempted to speak, the effort bringing about another paroxysm of coughing, bubbles of blood welling at the corner of his mouth.

The woman was now crying and tenderly she used the hem of her skirt to wipe the froth from his mouth.

Schonewille looked up, the hurt went from his eyes and he attempted to reach up and touch her hair.

"Liebchen," he said faintly and then died.

Helmuth Wenck also knelt next to his son, his face drained of all colour and the tears welling up in his eyes. His other son and Meunier stood shocked amidst all the carnage, absolutely bereft of words.

Peter Wenck walked away and sat down with his back against a piece of rusting machinery. He felt absolutely drained and too exhausted to think any further. The strain of the past few days had finally caught up in the shock of what he had just witnessed.

He started to shake, his whole body trembling as though from the ague. It was Meunier who came over and gently held his shoulders, trying with his touch and soothing words to ease the shock. It took almost five minutes for the shaking to cease and when at last his body had re-gained some sort of control over itself, he stood up and went to his father who was comforting Sophia. In turn the woman was crying and apologising to the general for what she had done.

All four then walked with unsteady feet away to where they could see the uninterrupted desert, blocking out the horror at their backs.

Peter Wenck sat down cross-legged like a Buddhist monk and was joined a few moments later by Sophia, although she kept her distance. Nobody spoke, they just stared off into the distance.

Chapter Thirty-Five

There were two vehicles parked behind the shack, roughly hidden by two dirty tarpaulins. One was a 1939 wooden bodied Chevrolet station wagon in immaculate condition and the second, a rather battered two-ton Ford truck circa 1935.

"Good," said Helmuth Wenck. "Now we won't have to rely on that behemoth," meaning the M32.

After they had watched the desert silently for nigh on ten minutes Helmuth Wenck reluctantly told everybody except the woman that they had better plan their next moves.

They left Sophia sitting with her back to the old mine as they went to reconnoitre, each man trying hard to avert their eyes from the dead lying by the air force lorry.

It was Meunier who first examined the two vehicles and who called for the Wencks to come and see.

"Now that we know there is alternative transport, I believe our first move should be to unload the lorry and then see what we can do to get rid of the bodies," he suggested.

The other two offered no argument, so he continued.

"Peter, go to the mine shaft and see how far into the hill it goes and, while you are at it, see whether it's wide enough to take the lorry."

The pilot moved off as his father added, "And be careful, it could be in bad condition."

While the diplomat and the general set about unloading the Reichsbank treasure, the pilot ventured into the shaft. At first there was sufficient light to see clearly, yet as he went deeper inside he had to pause so his eyes could become accustomed to the growing gloom. There had originally been two separate sets of tracks running into the shaft and about seventy metres in they converged into one. There were still half-a-dozen ore trucks standing on the rails at this junction, and from here the shaft rapidly became narrower and the roof lower.

He walked back towards the dim light of the entrance and then stopped, turned and began pacing out the width of the tunnel before looking up at the ceiling, estimating its height.

When he emerged into the sunlight he went to the front of the truck, scraped two lines parallel with the widest part of the vehicle and then paced out the width.

He thought for a moment and then yelled out to the two men.

"It should just fit. It'll be a tight squeeze and I'll have to be careful I don't bring down any of the props on either side of the tunnel."

"That's good, now come and help us unload. Jesus, some of this stuff is heavy."

When the job was completed, they discussed what to do. It was decided to place all the bodies in the back of the lorry and drive the vehicle as far down the tunnel as it could go.

"What then?" queried Meunier. "I mean we cannot leave it just like that. Somebody is sure to come here one day."

Helmuth Wenck nodded. "You're right. Let's search the other vehicles and the shack. I would expect those bastards had brought some explosives with them so they could seal the entrance."

It did not take them long to find what they were looking for. Inside the shack was a box, clearly marked explosives. Inside there were several dozen sticks of dynamite.

"I told you so," he said in a low voice to no one in particular.

They turned to the grizzly task of moving the bodies into the back of the truck. The three would-be assassins were loaded in first and placed near the front of the tray and covered with some canvas.

Then Leo Swabisch was placed inside. They were just about to pick up Schonewille when Sophia walked up. Her face was impassive and she motioned for them to stop. Without a word she unbuttoned his jacket and reached inside to one of the garment's breast pockets extracting a small package wrapped in a handkerchief held in position by two rubber bands. She then gently caressed his face and turned away.

Father and son picked up their son and brother and as gently as they were able placed him face-up next to the co-pilot.

Peter Wenck climbed inside the cabin and started the engine. He carefully aligned the vehicle with the entrance to the shaft and as slowly as he could entered the tunnel with his lights on. He almost made it to the junction of the rails. When one of the outside mirrors brushed one of the wooden props he stopped and turned off the engine, though he left the lights on. Since the cargo tray was wider than the cabin he was able to open the door sufficiently to be able to climb out, though it was a tight squeeze to negotiate the length of the lorry.

Once past he called for his father who came up carrying a dozen sticks of dynamite and a large coil of fuse. It was not wire, but simple, old fashioned fuse, the type one lit with a match.

They carefully wound the wicks of several sticks around a length of fuse and placed them at the foot of the tunnel wall near the rear of the truck. They repeated the exercise on the other side and joined the two long pieces of fuse to the main coil that they gradually unwound as they made their way back to the entrance.

Once outside they gathered more sticks of dynamite and returned to the tunnel. About ten metres from the entrance they placed the dynamite by each wall and ran a separate fuse wire outside to where the first one ended.

Peter Wenck looked at his father. "Sufficient, do you think?"

"I should bloody well hope so. At any rate, we've used all the sticks so it had better be enough."

The pilot held out his hand and Helmuth Wenck handed him his lighter. He knelt down and, picking up the length of fuse that was attached to the explosives next to the truck, applied the lighter's flame. He dropped it onto the ground and watched as the flame ate along its length and disappeared into the tunnel mouth.

He waited for thirty seconds and then lit the other fuse. Satisfied it too was alight, he clapped his father on the back and they ran past the shack to where the vehicles were parked, a hundred metres away.

They reached the truck and turned round expectantly. They did not have to wait long. There came a muffled roar followed by the deep rumble of an explosion. Just as a fountain of dust gushed from the entrance there was another, much sharper explosion, followed almost immediately by a third as the nearest dynamite went off.

The face of the hill trembled and a section of its side slid away covering what was left of the entrance.

They waited for the dust to clear and surveyed their handiwork. They had done their job extremely well. The tunnel had completely disappeared and to the unknowing it would be impossible to tell if there had ever been one. True, the face of the hill had a fresh scar on its flank, but with time it would give the impression of an old wound, or even fade entirely.

Sophia appeared almost silently besides them and remarked in a surprisingly firm voice, "A fitting tomb to at least four of them. Sadly your friend Leo I did not know enough about."

Peter Wenck turned and said harshly, "He was a fine man. Murder was not in his line. He even found it hard being a bomber pilot." She blanched at the severity of his words and he immediately regretted having spoken. "Please forgive me," he said.

She did not look at him, and though her voice was soft, its message was harsh, "My words for Leo may have been unfair, yet, as a German he, as well as you three, don't deserve any forgiveness. I know you might plead ignorance of what abominations have happened in Germany, but you were all part of the machine that perpetrated those crimes."

Her voice broke and she swung away. Peter Wenck started to remonstrate, but was stopped by his father who laid a hand on his arm.

"Don't, don't my son. Let her get it out of her system. She is right, of course. Collectively, we all share the guilt."

Sophia disappeared inside the shack and they followed. Kiefer and his band must have been in the place for some time for there were three makeshift beds at one end of the dilapidated structure each covered in a sleeping-bag. Their culinary habits had been confined to tins, a large supply of which were stacked on some boxes with the empties simply thrown in the corner.

There was a kerosene refrigerator standing in the other corner. To their delight there were several cold bottles of beer inside. As he handed them round, the pilot noticed a newspaper lying folded on top and picked it up. It was dated the day before, 26 March.

The front page was devoted to the war. In northern Germany,

Field Marshall Montgomery's crossing of the Rhine had been successful while further south the US Third Army had made still further crossings. From the River Sieg south as far as the town of Mannheim the American troops were cutting across Germany in a speeding swathe.

In the east there were reports of fierce battles around the town of Kuestrin barely sixty miles from Berlin.

It's only a matter of time, he thought to himself, shaking his head. For a while he had forgotten the war and what was happening in Germany for it all seemed so far away. What surprised him was how detached he had become from the events in Europe.

"Here, Father. Are you interested?"

The general made as if to reach for the paper and then changed his mind, shaking his head.

They sat in silence finishing their beer. Sophia went outside and Peter Wenck followed.

"Are you feeling well, Sophia?" he asked.

"Yes Peter." She hesitated and then continued. "Forgive my words a few minutes ago. I do not hate you, or your father, or even Conrad for that matter. It's just ... I mean, I cannot describe what it feels like to be here, to be free, not to be in danger any more."

She looked at him searchingly and although her face was clear her words and intonation were scathing. "You might not really have known what went on in the concentration camps, but you certainly knew what it was like to be a Jew or any other minority in Germany over the past ten years. Our persecution was there for all good thinking Germans to see ... and did you or your father do anything to halt it?"

The pilot was silent, for there was no answer and he knew it. She went on softly. "You are a brave and decent man, Peter. Your Knight's Cross and your demeanour is proof of that, yet as I said, you are still guilty of what went on under Hitler and his cronies."

Another pause and he shifted uncomfortably under her steady gaze. She looked beautiful and unattainable. "One last thing, Peter. I killed your brother to stop him killing you, for I'm certain he would have shot you like he did your friend. I feel no guilt about what I did, even though Friedrich saved my life and I did feel something for him. He was a tormented person and his link with the concentration camps meant he did not deserve to live. I hope you understand."

He understood completely and left her standing alone with her thoughts.

"Come on, Father, we had better divide the loot. I don't think we should stay here any longer."

His parent disagreed. He argued that Kiefer had chosen the spot for its remoteness and he would not have stayed if there was less than a remote possibility of someone coming. Nevertheless, he agreed it would be prudent of them to divide the money and valuables and stow them safely in the back of the vehicles as quickly as possible.

The division took much longer than they estimated.

At first they tried to divide it evenly, but this proved to be too difficult.

It was made harder by Sophia's attitude since at first she refused to take anything except some American dollars and some Swiss francs. She had the diamonds that had been given to Schonewille at Auschwitz and reasoned they would be worth a good sum, so any further share of the treasure was not necessary.

Perversely, she did not want any of the Reichsbank valuables because she felt they were tainted, yet she was quite prepared to take the diamonds that had quite obviously been stolen from some unfortunate inmate. After this was pointed out to her she agreed with the reasoning, although at first refused to change her mind.

Eventually, she told the Wencks she wanted to travel to Mexico with Meunier and it was up to them to give her as much money as they felt she would need to protect herself and survive.

After further discussion they divided the gold and boxes of gold coins sixty-forty with the Wencks taking the lion's share. The extra percentage given to Meunier was for Sophia if she decided she either wanted, or needed more. The gems were divided into thirds, one third again in the Wenck's favour.

Meunier elected to take the Chevrolet station wagon so they helped him load his portion into the back and covered it with several blankets and a sleeping-bag.

They decided it would be prudent if everyone remained armed, so Meunier took a couple of automatics. One he hid underneath his seat and the other he stuck in his trouser belt near his left hip. The old diplomat knew how to use the weapon and the Wencks knew he would not hesitate if necessary.

The remaining valuables were loaded into the back of the Ford and were covered with various other sundry boxes of materials filched from the cabin. The two airmen also took the M1 carbine and the remaining automatics.

"A word of caution, my friends," warned Meunier. "Don't try to pass any of the gold or coins until you are well settled and there is no chance of it being recognised as Reich treasure. I am going to Mexico where it is much easier to pass off valuables, for many do not trust banks or the tax man. In the United States it is much more difficult. So please be very circumspect." Both said they understood. "There should be no need for us to start hocking the heavy stuff for some time since all four of us have almost $60,000 in cash each."

The noon sun was now beating down fiercely on their heads, so they returned to the relative shade of the shack and waited for nightfall. They had decided to stay at the old mine until it was nearly dark to lessen the risk of anybody recognising the two vehicles. Once out of the immediate area the Wencks planned to buy a new vehicle and dump the Ford, while Meunier said he would get rid of the Chevrolet once he had successfully made it to Mexico. He knew of several back ways of crossing the border and did not foresee any problems.

Peter Wenck lay down on one of the bunks and immediately fell asleep. Sophia and his father took it in turns to stand guard. The sun was halfway to the horizon when they eventually drove off. As planned there was sufficient light for them to negotiate the tricky dirt tracks and they reached the highway just when the last portions of the sun were sinking below the rim of the earth. They alighted from their respective vehicles and said their goodbyes.

"You know where to contact me in Mexico, Helmuth," Conrad's voice was warm. "Please, when you are settled, let me know what you are doing, or better still bring Vigdis with you and stay in Mexico with me … and Peter my brave resourceful friend. Look after your father and look after yourself."

The pilot smiled and said he would. Then turning, he said to the Jewess, "I hope you find some peace Sophia."

She inclined her head in thanks and without a word got back inside the Chevrolet. Meunier gave a half wave and sat behind the wheel. The vehicle's engine was still running and without hesitation he moved off and turned south onto the highway.

A minute later the tail-lights had faded into the darkness. Peter Wenck turned to his father.

"Achtung, mein General," he mocked. Then in English he said, "Come on, let us leave. I want to see Mother."

The End

Author's Note

In January 1944 a Junkers JU 390 six-engine long-range bomber carrying search radar and a heavy gun armament joined a special squadron Fernäufklarungsgruppe 5, at Monte de Marsan in France. From there she undertook a flight across the Atlantic to within twelve miles of New York and returned safely to base. The crew actually saw New York from their cockpit.

This mission was designed to test the feasibility of the Germans bombing New York regularly from bases within France. In this it was a success. It meant that if the Germans had been able to put together the necessary resources and political will, they could have bombed New York before D-Day in June 1944. The political and strategic implications would have been enormous.

During the last weeks of the war there were many un-logged and un-documented aircraft flights that left Germany. Some of these flew to the Alps where Hitler was to have made his last stand. Others flew to Spain and North Africa. Many of these missing aircraft then flew on to South America: Argentina, Uruguay and Paraguay.

In the mid 1980s one such transport was found in the mountains of central Europe loaded with sensitive papers, money and the skeletons of her crew. The problem with all these flights was that in order to reach South America (the most favoured destination), they needed to land in Spain or other neutral areas to refuel. This meant records and witnesses.

There were also other destinations.

Up until the German surrender in May 1945, there were three areas still in German hands: part of Norway, part of central Europe and the Channel Islands, which are part of the United Kingdom. It is not generally known that this part of the UK was in German hands. The German commander on the Channel Islands was a rabid Nazi called Admiral Hüffmeier. Hüffmeier was so audacious that even though his command was now a virtual backwater, he conducted raids on the French coast (attacking American Army and Navy units), until Germany surrendered.

During the war the Germans operated a top secret squadron, which was equipped almost exclusively with captured Allied aircraft. This included British and American bombers. The squadron was called KG200 and it flew long-range missions deep into Russia, the Middle East and Africa. Many of these flights took place in the last months (and even weeks) of the war.

Much of its work has never been revealed and is still shrouded in mystery.

Miss Nonalee Two was a Boeing B17F-100-BO serial number 42-30336. She was part of the 385th Bomber Group, which took part in a raid into eastern Germany on 9 October 1943. On her way there she lost an engine and the pilot, First Lieutenant Glyndon D Bell, attempted to divert to neutral Sweden.

Unfortunately the crew became lost but Bell successfully landed the B17 in Denmark where the plane was captured by the Germans. She was repaired and flown for over a year by the Luftwaffe on various missions and ultimately joined KG200. Her last recorded trip was to Leipzig-Brandis airfield in December 1943. From there all records of her activities end. She simply disappeared.